G000152187

RETURN OF THE YGGDRASIL

M.K. NADALL

to Dad,

I think you might have liked the bit about the yabby

Disclaimer

This is a work of fiction – contrary to appearances it has not travelled back through a Peruvian time gate. Therefore, any resemblance to aliens or persons living or deceased (other than historical figures) is coincidental. The reference to “Walking on sunshine” in Chapter 76 is from the song of the same name by Katrina and the Waves, 1983. Likewise, the dialogue line that includes “… blue windows behind the stars” in Chapter 43 is from *Helpless* by Neil Young, 1970.

No frogs or ukuleles were harmed in the production of this book.

[December 2020 Edition]

ISBN: 978-0-6450368-1-7 (ebook)
ISBN: 978-0-6450368-0-0 (paperback)

CAST OF HUMANS:

Both major and a smattering of minor. Spoiler alert.

Kat Adamson
Model. The face (and body) of local swimwear and cosmetic labels. Tragically killed.

Tayla Brooke
Star of local TV dramas *Denim and Dust* and *Dolphin Bay*. Tragically killed.

'Bear' Browning
Former IT entrepreneur turned "yggdrasil-compliant" farming exponent. Likes to whittle.

Matt Davis
Australian comedian. Cast member of *CCE* when invaded by aliens.

Vito De Lucia
Celebrity Chef on alien-invaded reality TV show. Makes fortune with yggdrasil-compliant food choice app *Vito's Veto*.

Ash Edmondson
Forestry student and lab technician. Coffee, electronic dance music and stationery store aficionado.

Ebony Hamilton
Runs popular *Mom Love New York* blog. Mother of Anne-Maree.

Anne-Maree Hamilton
Befriends an alien in Central Park aged five. Daughter of Ebony.

Jess Kelly
Platypus wrangling research student. Likes: cricket. Dislikes: artificial bentwood café chairs.

Allan La Fontaine
French philosopher. Seconded to Human-Yggdrasil Congress. Dislikes: cricket.

Niels Larsson
Swedish forestry academic, research interest: tree communication. Saab driver.

Kevin Leahy
New Yorker. Runs *Aliens and Monsters* website. Expert eliminator of virtual zombies.

Paul McKay
Good-looking celebrity vet. 'Go-to' man for home chicken production in the post-yggdrasil world. Still unmarried.

Lenny Madden
Celebrity ex-cricketer. Present on *CCE* when invaded by aliens. Survives.

Graeme O'Brien
Radio shock jock. First eliminated *CCE* contestant.

Cameron 'no puppies in the fallout shelter' Peters
Head of the National Shadowy Science Agency. Semi-nemesis of Niels.

Maggie Reynolds
Producer of *CCE*. Retired wealthily with cats.

Crystal Roche
Conservationist and yggdrasil-compliant farm volunteer. Plays the Ocarina.

Mike Ross
Veteran Canadian environmentalist. Seconded to Human-Yggdrasil Congress.

Kalinda Ryan.
Classically trained pop singer and surviving *CCE* contestant.

Mariam Turner
Controversial media commentator. Silent on the question of tattoos.

Tyson K Whitney
DJ, entrepreneur, and pioneer of yggdrasil-friendly electronic dance music.

The askr Yggdrasil

Eir Nyssa. Resides in Central Park, New York. Special companion of Anne-Maree.

Mir Arauca. Ambassador. Elderly alien companion of the Kelly family in north Queensland.

Sif Acer. Ambassador. First appears on *CCE*. Issues *Cairns Declaration.*

Sri Achras. Ambassador. After troubled start, works with 'Bear' Browning to develop yggdrasil-compliant farming in California.

Tau Ulmus. Ambassador. Befriends Tyson K Whitney in Washington DC. Instrumental in developing YDM (Yggdrasil Dance Music).

Tek Alnus. Political representative. Announces the yggdrasil arrival with the killing of Kat and Tayla on *Celebrity Council Elimination.*

Anekantavada

A doctrine of many-sidedness: That truth and reality are complex with multiple aspects.

PROLOGUE: If a Tree Falls in the Forest

With the benefit and smugness of hindsight, it might be said the strange events of this narrative had their origin, like so many adventures of the mid-2020s, on Amazon with a phone in hand. Or rather, the *Amazon, that long watery thing and its surrounding, ever diminishing forest. Hang on to your phones, people – you're going to need them.*

The elderly outboard motor added its limping chatter to the end-of-rainy-season forest sounds. Angelo paused and checked another net, adding two catfish and a much prized twenty-pound Tambaqui to his collection. Again, there was a dead electric eel to be carefully removed. Sadly, for fans of feisty freshwater fish, even this deep into the west Amazon basin, the legendary Arapaima had been uncommon since Angelo's grandfather had been a youngster.

Resetting the net with its improvised coke bottle floats, the lone fisherman aimed the irregularly crafted timber vessel further upstream. Time passed – the motor almost blending with the monkey and parrot calls. As the canoe edged deeper into the ill-defined boundaries between Ecuador and Colombia; between rainforest reserve and not-quite reserve (but still very foresty), the engine sounded increasingly strident. The last of the nets held no fish and Angelo steered towards the bank.

He didn't make it – the motor cut out.

The silence shocked Angelo and then, impossibly, his phone pinged. He snatched it up. The most-worldly member of his village, the fisher was the sole phone owner. Sure, it wasn't much use when visiting home, as now, but the children never tired of selfies. Confused, he stared at the mud-smeared screen. *What is a Bluetooth toaster, and how am I paired to one*? He took up the paddle.

The fisherman reached the riverbank and peered at the electric rays lurking in the shallows. But a little tentative poking showed they were dead, although still potentially dangerous. He stepped past the deceased fish, nostrils flaring at the pungent odours in the air – odours beyond even those expected when tropical forest meets rotting fish. Angelo moved warily inland and encountered a clearing formed by the felling of a large Ceibo tree. Its buttress roots clawed the air, instead of thoughtfully anchoring the heavens to the earth, as in his grandfather's stories.

There was no need for philosophical speculations on falling trees and the nature of sound. Angelo's limited education had never raised the question:

"If a tree falls in the forest and no one's about, does it still make a sound?"

The tree had not "fallen" to natural causes. The ranchers, soy farmers, or oil explorers likely responsible had sent a message. In distant parts of the world, this kind of thing might go viral, cause widespread outrage, and even result in the writing of folk-rock anthems.

Not here.

The cutting of the largest tree in the locality, the keystone tree: The Mother Tree, signalled the start of another clearing program. It was a message to the local indigenous people. But, viewed from Landsat satellite, just another incremental erosion of the once-mighty Amazon.

The worse-than-rotting-fish-by-the-riverbank-smell was caused by the carnage in the ragged camp set up around the felled giant.

Among the bodies, there was a smattering of fellow indigenous people. They'd been dead for days. The rainforest fauna and fungi had ignored the downed chainsaws, rifles and other tools and set upon the bodies in a frenzy of recycling, such to make a gardener's compost heap green with envy.

As Angelo glanced fearfully around, from the deepest shadows, strutted man-sized apparitions. The plant-creatures bore the spikes of young Ceibo trees, and their gait resembled upright insects. Eyestalks twitched, feelers thrashed, and on too-many legs they advanced. The philosophical, biological and cultural questions were many, varied and whirred moth-like in Angelo's thoughts as the intruders disrupted his body's electrical pathways. Rain began to fall with full tropical vigour, and the creatures were lost to sight as the fisherman slumped to the ground. Body twitching, his eyes rolled back in his head, Angelo's consciousness reeled through ayahuasca-brew visions. In his last coherent thought, grandfather instructed: Time again to gather the arrow frogs.

In these difficult times of alternative facts and inconvenient truths, it's important to note: Angelo survived and frogs were gathered, and months later, in another tropical forest far, far away, the leaf creatures reappeared. This time there were witnesses. Deliberately so.

Chapter 1 Ratings Spike

"C'mon Jess, you're missing it."

"Yeah," she paused significantly. "I think I'd rather finish the dishes. Anyone want to *help*?"

She heard apologetic mumblings from the shared lounge behind her. *Apparently not.* Jess Kelly, platypus researcher, perhaps soon to be ex-platypus researcher, reached for another dirty cup. Home was Cairns' James Cook University campus accommodation. Her research project had been in tatters for months. Cleaning was an excellent distraction.

Housemate, Lindsay was trying to persuade Jess and fellow student, Rob, to watch *Celebrity Council Elimination* with him.

"So, what channel's this bullshit on?" said Rob, not looking up from his phone.

"Channel Five," explained Lindsay.

"You sure? Didn't they go broke?"

"No, but if they make another *Guess My Star Sign*, they'll be heading that way," said the coral researcher.

Then why do you watch it? thought Jess. She sniffed suspiciously, "Nice! Who left prawn tails in this cup?"

Another burst of mumblings issued from the lounge at this dastardly breach of share-house etiquette. Mumblings of the: *one of the others who's not here now,* variety.

"Right," said Jess, quitting the kitchen. "So, the gorgeous Indian-looking woman's the pop-singer? I don't recognise most of the others."

"These shows … you don't need to: got your bogan sportsman, your outspoken refugee advocate, a sprinkling of models. Oh," said Rob, "I've seen that travel show-vet before, and maybe her …"

"Tayla's hot," said Lindsay to Rob. "She's always doing yoga poses. She's super flexible. And you know, they're filming it about half an hour's drive from here. My sister had her reception there, actually."

Jess had a vague, prior awareness of *CCE*; its forum of models, sports stars, and media personalities; it's unlikely premise of celebrity wisdom solving the nation's problems. "Is it so bad, that it's good?"

"Nah, it's just bad," Rob assured her.

But the pair *were* of that group that considered an unhealthy BMI or even being "super bendy" didn't readily qualify an individual to allocate medical resources.

The students' TV showed the seven remaining celebrities sitting at an outside dining table, surrounded by exuberant tropical foliage …

*

"It's turquoise, my birthstone," said Tayla the actor, stroking her nose stud. "And it's just *so* important to match your birthstone to your *real* star sign. Especially when, you like, don't identify with your birth star sign."

Matt ignored this inanity. A parrot flew overhead, and the floppy-haired comedian asked, "Is there any milk left – other than long-life stuff?"

"Just soy mate, what do you reckon this is, 'The land of milk and honey?'" snorted Lenny, the show's requisite celebrity sportsman.

"The colour really suits you, Tayla," said Kat, the model, ignoring Lenny as usual. "That *milk and honey* saying is just so wrong. I mean, who wants to live in a land built on the slavery of cows and bees."

Matt sensed yet another food politics squabble brewing. These had been less intense since the radio shock jock's elimination, but he didn't care for them. *Why are we always bickering over almond milk and soy burgers or discussing astrology?*

"How do you *tell* if someone's a vegan?" said Lenny, toying with the machete the celebrities used to de-husk coconuts.

"Ah, could that be, 'just wait five minutes, they're sure to mention it!'" said Matt affably. He grinned at Len. In the control booth, just visible through the trees, he guessed the producer would be displeased with his attempt at peace keeping. *Stuff it.* "Now, now, big fella, remember I'm here to make the jokes, spread fun and mirth." He waggled his finger in Lenny's direction.

"India," Kalinda suggested in her quiet, often serious way, "has more vegetarians than anywhere else, and most of them drink milk and eat yoghurt and cheese, even though cows *are* sacred to Hindus."

"Ah yes, the celebrated Palak Paneer," said Vito, the celebrity chef, straight to the camera and preening his waistcoat.

"My favourite," growled Lenny to Matt's amusement. He knew the cricketer *had* developed a liking for Indian food on tour, *and* that big Len much preferred tandoori oven *meats.*

Matt could tell Kat was unpleased with Kalinda's intervention. The model's shapely nose edged higher. She peered over it. *Political correctness dilemma*, thought Matt.

Then the model gave Kalinda a patronising smile and diced another sweet potato. Matt sighed as she and Tayla launched into a new discussion, enthusing over vegan chocolate, yoghurt and 'meats'.

"Plant-based meats are *so* convincing now, Tayla, that carnivores can't even tell the difference."

"Absolutely, they're to die for."

*

Matt turned to the loud rustle from deep in the bushes. They shook and parted. He would never forget what happened next.

No one would.

It would become the ultimate: *Do you remember when*? moment. One of those generational spotlights: the moon landing, Princess Diana's death, the Twin Towers, the Cubs winning the World Series. More surprising than the much-anticipated zombie apocalypse; less predictable than a feisty exchange of nuclear weapons.

In a way – an odd and tragic way – the moment marked the career-high point of Kat and Tayla. Mere hours before, they'd been fretting over their screen time and the next elimination episode. And there'd been all that unpleasantness about the butterfly effect and Hitler.

"Enough. Halt. Desist!" came the strange cry.

Like an anime nightmare, the creature crept from the shrubbery behind the dining table. With predatory mantis grace, it advanced on the bewildered contestants.

A static rasp and then, incomprehensibly, in the voice of the phone-app *Siri*, it said, "Decease the vegetarians!"

The comedian flinched as Kat shrieked. Tayla stood, clutching half a mango, then staggered. Matt tried to catch her as she fell. Both young women collapsed.

Deceased.

In a daze, Matt heard Len swear as the creature stalked towards the nearest camera. It asserted in fractured English how it was most annoying that the two young people were always twittering on about their dietary habits … that it was deplorable that those endlessly discussed habits chiefly involved the slaughter of innocent plant life and worst of all: The deceased celebrities regarded their awful choices as morally superior.

Blood pounded in Matt's ears as he attempted to process this declaration – struggling with both the philosophical implications and the syntax. This time, Mariam screamed. Two more of the green segmented things strode from the bushes.

The former cricket hard-man not noted for the sophistication of his processing – in sport or life – reacted first.

"No, Lenny!" cried Matt. Too late.

The cricketer seized the machete and buried it in the upper body of the nearer creature. It oozed a little and casually directed multiple eyestalks at its attacker.

Matt held his breath.

But even in those early moments, he sensed *this* individual's glance lacked the deadly intensity of a chip-focused seagull.

He remembered to breathe and watched the *worse-trip-ever* blend of banana palm and upright lobster remove the machete with fussy movements of its claws. Another static burst (part dial-up modem, part off-station radio) and the impossible creature said: "Abrupt comrade actions remorse. Please to continue televisual experience."

This remarkable televisual experience was occurring at the Cassowary Lodge, in thirty acres of remnant rainforest near Cairns (as the world was soon to discover: the largest town in exotic, far away, far-north Queensland, Australia).

Vegetation hid the tasteful low impact buildings, including the reality TV show's production base, maintaining the illusion of isolated jungle splendour. Illusory hardship was fine. However, the closest camera-crew member didn't care for the change in circumstances. He locked off his camera, turned his rotund person and set off at a rapid waddle towards the lodge.

Matt gasped as the alien returned the machete to Lenny. The cricketer sheepishly replaced it on the rough-hewn table. Before Matt had time to react, he was hit by a fine spray of alien fluids. In a squelchy green blur, the creature launched a tendril and tripped the fleeing cameraman.

*

Celebrity Council Elimination was to experience the greatest ratings spike in the recorded history of such spikes. More viral than a COVID-19-Ebola team-up. News readers, poor things, were to exhaust themselves in search of ever-greater hyperbole.

Among the viewers were Jess and her housemates. Those ratings figures were rapidly eclipsed by the *me2Screen* and *YouTube* hits. Surpassing examples of water bottle tossing excellence, kittens playing with soap bubble machines and even the long-ago but momentous occasion of a certain non-conventionally attractive singer appearing in a British amateur singing contest.

For the moment, such ratings gold lay in the uncertain future. Matt edged protectively closer to Kalinda. Despite the circumstances, he smiled – delighted as she clutched his hand. Albeit anxiously, and all too briefly. Oblivious to the cameras for once, the celebrity group huddled at the mercy of the aliens' intentions. With a waving of antennae and focusing of bits of anatomy best described as eyestalks, the intruders prepared to make their intentions clear.

Chapter 2 The Cairns Declaration

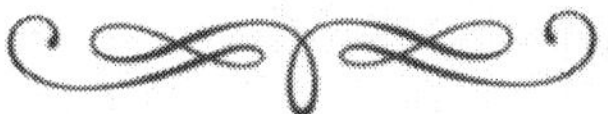

"Please, let him go," said Matt, voice hollow with fear.

The alien dragged the struggling cameraman closer. It raised its fearful leaf-wings, it flourished its antennae, focused its many eyes upon him and said, rather unexpectedly, "Please to resume duties."

The shadows had lengthened in the short tropical twilight, the day's heat began to slip away, and the sly, unsporting insects of the evening sharpened their fangs and waited. The world held its breath. Like the worst call-centre helpline ever, and with the familiar voice of Siri, the creature said, "Declaration of right: Underutilised solar energy."

The set was so quiet Matt heard the thing rustle as it adjusted the thin green structures (that came to be called wing-leaves). It directed its many eyestalks at both the camera and the cast and continued to speak:

"Light-foragers of planet be sentient."

Matt dragged his eyes from Tayla's body slumped against the table leg. He dropped the fork he found unexpectedly in his hand and directed a confused look at the vet. Paul mouthed, "Plants, plants are smart."

"Cease, slay-consume them."

Matt flinched as the killer of the two women abruptly folded its leaf-wings shut. Its eyestalks turned towards its companion and its feelers rippled. The companion edged closer to the camera and said: "Especially trees."

Matt Davis' gape resembled the proverbial stunned mullet. A small non-cowering part of his brain considered the edicts. *Hmm, well I don't think forestry is like non-consensual love, but I'm sure we can do better in that space.* He watched the leaf-creature hesitate, preening its many appendages, as if unsure what to say or do next.

Trees, Matt thought, *this all started with trees.* His subconscious selected a childhood memory: His father, laughing … Mum had discovered the council intended removing an old stately tree from their affluent suburb's street.

"You can't just cut down trees!" she'd exclaimed, shrill and indignant.

Eleven or twelve-year-old Matt said joking, "Yeah, you *can* actually Mum. The local hardware store's business plan is pretty much predicated on it."

Dad had laughed and complimented him on 'predicate'.

He very much changed his tune in later years when Matt declared his *professional* comic intentions.

The murderous member of the leafy trio advanced and Matt edged closer to Kalinda, their thighs touching as the creature alternatively flared open, then closed its "wings". It thrashed its feelers at its companion, then stalked away to the rainforest edge.

Matt took a relieved breath and the nearer alien turned from the camera and said to the celebrities, "Advise humans enhance like corals."

Kalinda's eyebrows knitted with concern, "What!" she whispered.

Matt shrugged, "It wants us to like corals more."

It was hardly the most crucial part of what became known as The Cairns Declaration. But the message seemed consistent with the city's status as the gateway to the Great Barrier Reef. As the business community could attest visitors were welcome in a wide variety of shapes and colours – provided they possessed a clean bill of health, a disposable income and a ticket home. It was a question of intentions: tourism, invasion, settlement, or colonisation?

And as the indigenous peoples of the area could attest, the English word 'colonise' is an irregular verb, the bane of all language learning:

I *colonise,*
You *invade,*
We *civilise,*
You all *go away, please.*

It soon became obvious the visitors were staying. It was a clear case of an irregular verb situation.

Chapter 3 "Keep Filming!"

At a safe but confused distance from these events, Jess Kelly favoured her housemate with an incredulous glance.

"Lindsay! What on Earth's going on? Isn't this a set up for Graeme what's-his-name, radio bigot, to yell at flaky hippy types and that opinionated Muslim lady, Mariam somebody." She waved at the screen. "What're *aliens* doing on it!"

"They think it's real, maybe …"

"The *celebs* think the aliens are real?"

"The aliens think TV show real," interjected Leong who'd now joined the others.

Nice to see you out of your room, Leong, thought Jess. "*You* think the aliens are real?" she dispensed with blinking.

"Hey, at least *they* care about the coral issue," said Lindsay.

"Seriously …"

*

A mere fifty metres from these momentous events, Maggie Reynolds exited the producer's chair for the control centre's fern hung balcony in order to better observe the unfolding drama. It relieved Maggie to see the camera operator released unharmed. Even more so to see him resume his duties.

"Camera-two," she barked, "enough of the bodies already! Let's keep Kat and Tayla out of shot now, shall we?"

As the producer stared at the trio of actual extra-terrestrials – one of which extracted a machete from itself and returned it to a faded sports-star – the previous year's rejected projects seemed mundane.

"Close-up on the thing that's talking," Maggie ordered as the tall, segmented alien delivered its position statement. This was turning out more surprising than the rejected *Surprise Celebrity Nanny*. And cheaper.

"Can we get that mic closer?" she snapped. "How the hell's it talking? It sounds like my damn phone!"

Maggie shook her head. *Could this be happening on a tawdry TV show*? The producer wasn't alone. The viewing audience was asking the same thing. Within days, the entire world would be asking.

And watching.

"Right! Now cut to spider cam. You listening, Jaspa!" Maggie sensed her crew – while skilled at capturing celebrity dramas – were all at sea when it came to filming live-to-air alien invasions. You just couldn't get the staff.

"Jesus! Maggie is this you?" swore one of the crew.

She snorted. "I'm good, but I'm not that good. They're aliens – real aliens. Now, close up on that professionally offended cow Mariam – she looks terrified. And it's getting dark. Bring up those lights. Step-up people!"

Maggie monitored the scene in the clearing and reflected the country would have to get by without the wisdom of the two dead stars. She shrugged, *no more beaded-hair-tossing and mid-riff revealing. No more of the inanities that had so riled O'Brien the shock jock.* Unfortunately, he'd been eliminated the previous week.

She refocused her attention. The remaining celebrities looked struck dumb – not great telly. The camera-two feed showed many of them staring blankly at the out-of-shot bodies.

"Close-up of Matt – at least he's looking at the thing talking." The producer sensed unrest behind her. She didn't bother turning, "Harden up, princesses – when I was a kid, we played with matches in the street and snorted peanuts." *Christ knows how – but my Reality TV 'Survivor' type program is actually a reality TV survivor program.*

"This is *way* beyond my pay scale," declared one of the afternoon shift's audio techs. He stopped cowering behind his bamboo KeepCup, tore off his headset, straightened his bowtie and headed for the control room exit. Around her the crew were on their feet, aghast and fearful.

"Hey Bob, leave your ciggies here, at least, you pussy," ordered Maggie. "Come on you lot, keep filming. Keep filming. This is history. We have a *duty* to record it." She reflected such instructions would be scarcely needed if Channel Five had cared to green-light one of her other proposals: *Mum, Who's my Daddy?* Or even *Bad Possums* (tag line: Don't be fooled by their big eyes and fluffiness!)

The alien being concluded its declaration. There was an awkward silence then it said, "Statement repeats. Hasty comrade action regret. Important televisual persons please to continue essential functions."

There was another awkward silence. *Jesus, this won't do*, "We'll take out the pauses in the edit," Maggie announced. "Call a commercial break."

*

Around the dinner table, the celebrities realised the crew had signalled a break. Only minutes before, Tayla had been discussing the significance of her nose stud. Now Matt could see her lying dead but unmarked against a chair. Paul checked Kat's pulse and shook his head.

Matt flinched at the crunch of gravel in the growing darkness, and the producer appeared from beyond the camera lights. *Small pixie haircut, surely over sixty*. She was a force of nature, almost as scary as the aliens. He hadn't seen her for months, not since his interview. There'd been no evident improvement.

"Listen up everyone," Maggie peered critically at the aliens, *yeah, you've got expertise in bloodless death and co-opting human technology. But...*

"It's obvious you three know squat about cutting-edge TV production!" The sky was becoming suitably ominous as she stood, hands-on-hips, and said, "We're all here for the influence and the fame. So, if you don't want altogether negative brand recognition, you'd better listen to me."

Even in those grim early minutes, Maggie sensed a monumental misunderstanding had brought the aliens to her show and being tepidly scrupulous concerning the truth – where personal finances were involved – a misunderstanding to be turned to advantage.

Arms now crossed; the producer listened as the vegetal creature explained that a lethal electromagnetic shield had been placed around the site.

"Maintain security as important personages learn and broadcast new paradigm!" it concluded.

Okay, thought Maggie, *that's taking celebrity TV isolation to the next level.*

And it meshed with her purposes perfectly – she had the ultimate exclusive. "But" she said in her clipped tone, "we're gonna need to remove the deceased contestants. And ..."

Maggie continued negotiating with the leaf-creatures, as around her the cast and crew watched, stunned. Nothing moved except the night bugs wantonly diving at the camera lights.

At last, to the comedian's relief, the celebrity vet stirred into action. Matt could recall the "bios" of his co-contestants'. And he'd added his own mental notes:

Paul McKay. The brightest star in Channel-Five's firmament. Host of *Outback Vet* and the travel show *Made in Oz*; Paul was equally photogenic and personable, wrestling pythons or wrangling latte. Born in Broome – the product of an adventurous English doctor and local nurse, he'd launched his media career with a pet talk-back segment on local radio. His handsome features were assembled from every ethnic group to grace the town's history. If you were a camel in need of a chestnut, well-muscled arm inserted in your nether regions, he was your man.

"Ah, this is wrong," said Paul. "There's been a misunderstanding. This is a reality TV show—"

"Affirmative, reality *Celebrity Council Elimination.*"

"Yes, but—"

"No buts, Paul!" insisted Maggie. "Please help the crew move Kat and Tayla respectfully to the production centre."

The vet moved reluctantly away to help the crew.

Head in hands, Matt heard, "You'll be the most-watched, most famous celebs *ever*. And if you didn't want that, then clearly, you've chosen the wrong professions. Others have agreed to televised body fat removal for such a chance."

Matt lifted his head. The show's host, Holly stood next to the producer, ashen faced. Maggie was facing the cast, hands on her hips again, she said, "Look around … you're humanity's representatives – God help us. Now we've put all that unpleasantness over vegetarianism to one side, let's get on with it, shall we?" She turned to the crew, "By the way: Bob's dead. You'll be doing a shitload of overtime – we're going to make great telly."

Negotiations completed, she stalked back to the lodge control centre.

Opposite Matt, big Len found his voice, if in a baffled tone, even by his lofty standards, "What the hell's happening? This is real, right?"

Across the country, bewildered viewers were asking the same pair of questions.

Chapter 4 Ahimsa

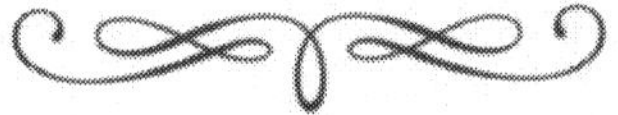

Quite the awkward silence, mused Matt as the vet Paul returned to the 'unexpectedly murdered-contestants-silence'. He and his remaining five companions were reluctant to make eye contact with each other; the intruders and their dinner – especially the non-meaty items. The faux pas of double-dipping the capsicum dip paled in comparison with the possibility that dipping might lead to one's body being carted off set.

Matt considered his options, hoping Paul might take charge in his usual confident way. Was it rude or weird to look at *them*? Or ruder not to? He was getting into 'character', recalling a recent stand-up performance … "This is how I look talking to breastfeeding people who I'm not related to …"

Matt relaxed his grip on an innocent fork. He looked the nearer alien in the eyestalks, hoped for a breezy light-hearted tone and said, "I guess we were expecting a surprise intruder sometime, but maybe not this surprising." He pushed the photogenic floppy hair back again. He selected a smile from his repertoire.

"And can I say – I reckon we can do better in the forest protection and appreciation space."

The alien rippled antennae but remained mute, as did Matt's co-contestants.

Bit of help, please guys. He tried for a tone of polite curiosity, "You've certainly raised some questions, my leafy proponents. Can I ask where you're from?"

The spokes-creature had lurked unseen among ferns and palms for over a week. It'd overheard much concerning stars and star signs. Not, however, terribly many references to standard galactic coordinates.

"Home world locates nominal Scorpio constellation."

"What does that mean?" asked Kalinda quietly.

"Negative meaning. Arbitrary collection viewed stars. Myth pattern mapped randomness."

"Hmm, we may be at cross-purposes. *And* I don't reckon it believes in astrology," interpreted Paul McKay.

"Why's everything about bloody astrology!" muttered Lenny.

"Indeed, yeah, but we might leave that to one side for the moment," said Matt. He looked the vegetal creature in several eyes, "I can't speak for the Earth you understand. I don't rule it or anything. Fun as that might be. But I don't see a problem sharing sunshine with you three. Are there just three of you?" he asked, puppy-dog eyes at their most innocent.

"Numerals as forest trees," came the phone-app response.

"Oh," said Matt, delving into the reserve tank of positivity. "And where are these other … comrades?"

"Information response negative."

"Okay," said the comedian, re-tightening his grip on the surprised fork. "Can you tell us how you can talk? Or not …"

"Absorb human broadcast transmissions. Articulate by assimilation phone application," replied the alien.

"When you say assimilate—"

"I'm sorry, but to clarify: you don't want us to eat plants, only animals?" said Kalinda, considering this the more crucial query.

Watching at home, you may have disagreed. The relationship between humans and phones had, in recent years, achieved more importance than that of humans and food. Just as for the child-rearer: "Where's my phone charger?" Had long replaced the quainter: "Good morning, mine-parent."

"Consumption-integration every life form distasteful," came the reply.

"Are you saying you don't want us to eat *anything*?" replied Kalinda incredulously.

It was so quiet you could hear a fork drop. Matt hovered nearby. *Kal, this's no time to get all unaccustomedly direct.* He attempted to project a relaxed 'let's not get anyone else killed unnecessarily' vibe.

"Relative indifference pertains to heterotrophs slay-consume heterotrophs. Outrage pertains heterotrophs slay photosynthetics, light-gathers, vegetal life," explained the alien to the bewildered celebrities.

Matt waited for this to sink in. It didn't. He peered at Paul. The vet said, "It's saying that they don't approve of humans and animals eating other animals. It's … err, unpleasant to them but tolerable. However, they won't let us eat plants."

The thing hissed static then: "Light-gathering lifestyle, only moral lifestyle."

"But eat or *kill* though?" said celebrity chef Vito De Lucia, the most flamboyant of the remaining contestants, speaking up for the first time.

"Yes Vito," said Kalinda. "There are people in India called Jains and they avoid killing any living thing. So, they don't eat any animals, and they don't kill any plants. So they wouldn't eat a carrot because you dig it up and eat it and the plant dies. I think they might only eat things such as fruits and nuts, because the tree, the plant lives on – it's not harmed."

"Bloody hell," said Lenny. He peeked at the spokes-alien, then said to Kalinda, "Are you making this up?"

"*Fruitarians*!" Declared the chef. "In western countries, people who follow this diet are called fruitarians – an extreme variation on veganism." He shook his head, "Not the most interesting cuisine," he added, addressing the camera and beginning to regain his usual persona.

"Great," said Matt, attempting a positive sort of nod. "So, what's your, err, opinion on what Kalinda and Vito said: People eating fruits and nuts from trees? Can you check information on the internet with your *assimilated* phones? Use *Avogadro* or *Google* or something?"

"Comrades ability interrogate informational human network, also selves knowledge database. Please to continue."

The communicative leaf creature lapsed into silence. Its companions had crept to the forest edge, treelike in the dark. And so, the celebrities waited in further confused and nervous silence for additional alien commentary.

"Geez, why is everything about bloody vegetarians?" asked Lenny to the table.

Lost in their thoughts and fears, his fellows, rather than the table itself, could only agree. Wooden tables, as was to become apparent in times to come, do have opinions when still part of living trees. (However, severing them from their necessary roots and leaves and drying them to a state of sturdy but inanimate wood rather limits expression of their sentiments).

The three creatures stood immobile. The fading tropical light glowed dully on their carapaces. The light had come an awfully long way, so additionally, it glowed on fearful celebrities and unfinished food. Without aliens, it wouldn't have been riveting telly. The crew continued to record this non-activity.

"Looks like they're still … researching then," said Matt doubtfully to the others.

In the control centre, the producer soon lost patience. "Oh, for God's sake," she said. "The world didn't get this way by sentient beings having considered opinions." Maggie issued instructions to her nervous crew; they replayed the lethal surprise intrusion; non-assimilated cell phones were used: calls were made, and messages sent. Tens of thousands more viewers tuned in. And still nothing happened on set.

Matt's thoughts drifted to recent events. Likewise, Channel Five and the narrator deemed it an appropriate time to reprise the highlights of the previous week.

The major controversy – now eerily prescient – started with the eliminated radio personality Graeme O'Brien, when he growled, "You can't call tofu burger *meat*. You try calling sparkling wine champagne in this country, and some beret-wearing cheese weasel will …" O'Brien stalled as a spectacular Birdwing butterfly fluttered past, causing a brief halt to hostilities.

Then the camera operator (with a talent for panning from the contours of tropical fruit to those of Tayla's breasts, and with an instinct for conflict) had zoomed in as she pronounced, "It's just so important to install solar panels and avoid the butterfly effect." She tossed her lovely, beaded hair in affirmation.

"Yeah, that's so true – like how more butterflies here can affect the Amazon greenhouse," agreed Kat.

Tayla nodded. Mariam rolled her eyes.

By a coincidence of the type that may plague a work of fiction from time to time, Matt glanced across the table at Mariam, recalling these events. She'd withdrawn into her scarf. *I've never seen her quiet for this long.*

He recalled her biography and his initial take on it:

TV presenter and social commentator. CCE was Mariam's first venture into commercial television. In the predictable world of reality TV casting the Anglo-Australian hijab-wearing, Muslim-convert, refugee advocate was sure to push Graeme O'Brien's buttons. For Matt, she brought back the horror of his early uni days. How innocent he'd been, breezing up to a "getting to know you BBQs" in search of cider and a free sausage to be trapped by earnest student politicians.

In the present, a moth flew unconcernedly past the alien. Thus prompted, Matt recalled O'Brien's disparaging comment …

"*Actually*, the butterfly effect is when they fly near a concentrated solar thermal (CST) tower – total spontaneous combustion. Quite a sight."

Tayla gave one of her sympathetic good-will-to-all-living-things (even 'Fossil Pig', as Kat had called the shock jock) smiles. She returned her focus to mango preparation. Kat displayed her perfect teeth as her smile ratcheted up – failing, as so often, to reach her eyes.

She said, "Since Steve [local sport identity] and I converted the old dairy to bushland and native gardens we have so many more beautiful butterflies. And I have my studio. To get away from it all and paint. So, blessed."

"Ah ... painting, vegetarianism, the love of nature. Now, who does that remind me of?" Graeme mused aloud. "Got it," he chortled, slapping his thigh. "Bloke named Hitler – heard of him?"

"Cheap shot Graeme," pronounced Mariam.

In the production centre the crew were primed for conflict. True to form, O'Brien didn't disappoint. He sought to drive a wedge between the three women, saying to Mariam, "So, Ms Turner, are Muslims *allowed* to be vegetarians?"

In an even tone, Mariam said, "There's nothing against being vegetarian in Islam. I have friends who are." She attempted a superior smile.

"Oh really," said Kat, "because there's that whole 'God made the world and the animals for *man* to use and rule' vibe. As with Christians."

Graeme nodded in rare agreement. "And Muslims are obliged to sacrifice animals at certain festivals – are they not? How do vegetarians feel about Muslim animal sacrifice?"

Tayla put her hand to her mouth in horror.

In the control room Maggie had been thrilled. In an industry where a shaky camera shot of a celebrity racing to the bathroom in tears was considered innovation, raising Hitler, Islam and animal sacrifice in the same conversation, was indeed, cutting-edge, contemporary TV.

*

Matt's week had been a difficult one since then, and those events no longer made it into his top three.

The mute "processing" pause continued.

Nothing but the night-shift moths dared move.

Matt didn't much care for the way Lenny was staring at the machete, "Err, so we're thinking meat's no problem and fruit and ... what berries and stuff might be okay?"

"Ah, meat and fruit cuisine: pork and apple, turkey and cranberry, prawn and avocado – there are possibilities," said Vito grandly. His flounce was returning.

"Happy to give up lettuce, mate, if I can still have a sausage with tomato sauce," declared Lenny, also recovering something of his usual persona.

"Len," explained Kalinda, pushing back her long hair and glancing at the alien trio. "Tomatoes are fruits; they get picked off a plant. The plant isn't dug up – not like potatoes or carrots."

Matt grinned at her, "If you don't eat it with ice cream – it ain't a fruit."

"I suspect the confusion comes from chefs and supermarkets defining veggies in one way and scientists in another," said Paul. "When I was a kid tomatoes were a veggie. Now they seem to bat for the other team. Anyway, what appears important to *them* – he indicated with a nod – is whether the plant gets destroyed."

"Classic Dr Paul," said Maggie approvingly in the production centre.

"Ah, but harmed or totally eaten, though?" said Matt. "Like if I was a lobster in a tank, and every few months the chef plunges his arm in, tears my claws off and serves 'em up to a party of up-and-coming climate change deniers – sure I can regrow 'em, sure I'd be alive – but pretty damn obstreperous."

"And mostly 'armless," noted big Len, clearly moving on from the machete incident.

"Yes, thanks for that Len. My point is, that's how I treat my kitchen basil, just tearing off a few leaves here and there."

"So, you cook Mathew?" asked Vito with interest.

"Well, no. Just pot noodles with basil, but you see my point."

As Matt knew, Vito's Channel Five show, *I am a Chef, you are a Cook* featured a wide range of food genres and predictably scripted confrontations between minor celebrities who thought they could cook, and chefs who thought they were minor celebrities. As Vito launched into a faintly condescending exploration of the attributes of vegetables and their potential stresses, Matt bent towards Kalinda and whispered, "You okay?"

The pop star slumped, "Matt, this changes everything. Not just food and phones, but everything."

With a burst of white noise, the chattier alien re-joined the conversation: "Planet encloses complexity unexpected. Primary principle emphasizes *Ahimsa* of photosynthetics – the light foragers."

*

Watching at her uni residence, Jess plucked her phone from the worn couch's broad arm. Across the country, *CCE* viewers did likewise. (You probably would have done so yourself). Jess' fingers danced. She glanced around, "Ahimsa's a term from Jainism – it's an ancient religion in India."

"Your Google-fu is strong," said Rob. "But what's it *mean,* Jess?"

"It's the principle of non-violence or non-injury," she read. "It's often applied to what's eaten, but Jains apply it more generally."

"Is she – Kalinda, a Jain?" Lindsay asked.

Jess shrugged.

"No," said Leong, confident in his Kalinda expertise.

Rob glanced at Leong and explained to Jess, "She's adopted – won a *music as a competition* show a couple of years ago. She was in one of those fundamentalist churches. Got the religious vote, the—"

"The 'Jesus rose up and gave the Israelites handguns variety?'" said Lindsay warily.

"Don't know mate – probably just the happy clappy variety."

"She talented and pretty," said Leong.

*

On the *CCE* set the subject of this discussion asked the necessary follow up question, the usual quiet sparkle in her eyes subdued: "Sorry, I didn't understand you. Is it okay for humans to eat fruits of plants?"

"Affirmative provided evident respect. Suggest consumer rear-grow tithe proportional."

"Gotcha, it's a fruit tax," said Matt, getting the hang of the alien's speech manner.

"And consumption of vegetables?" said Vito, straightening his waistcoat.

Again, the celebrities heard the static bark …

Essentially, (to paraphrase for readers who may have missed this episode of TV history) the spokes-creature-in-chief said it didn't intend to compile a detailed list of what humanity could and couldn't eat. It claimed people would try to find tricky ways around that. The guiding principle, it suggested, was minimising harm to plants … treat them like animal life forms … no … treat them like you treat each other. Well, maybe not that. It paused and announced the equivalent of:

"Just treat them well!"

Matt's skin tingled as it waved its antennae and said, "Attempt accord with humans." Then, directing its many eyestalks at its companions, it added, "Humans survival ambivalence."

With predatory grace, the alien trio strode into the rainforest, and the awkward silence of the evening meal resumed. Matt attempted a brave smile, "It seems I've mislaid my appetite." The celebrities nibbled at fruit and bits and pieces of critters that had formerly used their bits and pieces to walk, swim or flap. Still, nobody risked reaching for the capsicum dip.

Chapter 5 Inside and Outside the Perimeter

The worldly reader may well be aware that a surprise "intruder" is a reliable mechanism of the reality TV genre. The unsponsored, unscripted intrusion of the leafy, lethal aliens during the second week of *CCE* had saved Channel Five from economic doom and guaranteed the surviving contestants' celebrity status for life (however long that might prove to be).

In the tense quiet of the first night following the "intrusion" Matt and the others heard the distant sound of vehicles arriving. With the dawn, the first tinnitus-murmur of drones begun.

Now mere days later, interest in the events of *Celebrity Council Elimination* was so high the site could be identified from the air. Ironically, the reason for this was the continued failure of attempts to observe the site from the air. For ringing the compound were the crumpled remains of many drones, hundreds of remote-controlled flying toys of every kind and two downed helicopters. All manner of dead flying creatures further circled it, including, sadly, specimens of the Cairns Birdwing – Australia's largest butterfly.

"There're more dead birds and insects at the far end," said Matt. The celebrities were standing on the tennis court watching the drones.

"I reckon the barrier's three hundred metres that way," pointed Paul McKay.

As Matt wiped sweat from his eyes Mariam took several brisk steps, "I have to get out of here. I have kids at home."

Paul caught her in a stride, "I know but—"

"They killed the audio guy," said Matt.

Len Madden crossed his arms, "Maybe that's what they *want* us to think."

"Don't be a dick," advised the comedian. Footsteps thudded on the dirt path; a crew member ran past the court and onto the bitumen road without slowing.

"Careful, Paul!" yelled Matt as the vet ran to the gate and set off around the fence after the woman.

*

Rather than watch events unfold from home, with uncertainty hanging in the air like a student debt, Jess Kelly, with time on her hands and an enquiring mind, joined the crowd with a friend from her rock-climbing club.

"Apparently there were fans here outside the lodge compound *before* the aliens came out. Can you believe that?" she grinned. Generally, given a choice between reality TV or cleaning the kitchen – even a kitchen in shared accommodation, including non-domesticated boys – she'd reach for that crusty sponge.

Politics, sport, even shark attacks had been pushed off the front pages of newspapers. Jess noted a new paradigm; the usual political divisions broken and irrelevant. She stared at the diversity of homemade signs: "Welcome: Save the Earth"; "Aliens go Home"; "The End is Nigh"; "Bring Back Elvis ..." being wafted by warring parties. The proponents of both the pro-alien Forest Collective and the anti-alien Vegan Rights groups were indistinguishable with their bandanas, beads and hand-spun sandals (which was most unsettling for all concerned).

"Hell," she said (without evident irony) to her companion, "Let's avoid that lot." Protestors of a religious bent were out in force: pitchfork waving brigades claiming the aliens were agents of the devil; while others welcomed the extra-terrestrial arrival as a sign, the end of days was at hand. Arguments abounded ... was this the *proper* apocalypse?

Jess encouraged her nervous friend closer to the barrier, threading through the crowd. "How weird is this? A protest, well, several protests, crossed with a drone convention." For mingling with the crowd of passionate placard wavers were hundreds of people. Or as Jess now concluded, "They're mostly men."

Despite the excitement that pizza or drug delivery by drone brings, it's the surveillance possibilities that form the reality of usage. For drones grant a bird's-eye view of things to those of us who'd willingly exchange opposable thumbs for wings.

In a departure from aerial filming of wiener dog racing at the town agricultural show, it seemed to Jess every local with an old Phantom drone was attempting to film the *Celebrity Council Elimination* compound. A simple alternative was to view the compound's activities on free-to-air television. But if years of DIY telly have taught us anything: it's that some fellow with a GoPro gaffer-taped to a cheap radio-controlled toy helicopter and a can-do attitude can be a home-tech hero.

What the buzzing and whirring flying devices recorded before they crossed the alien exclusion barrier was a series of pipes projecting ten metres inside the lethal forbidden zone. Around these clustered soldiers, small nervous animals in cages and a plethora of machines of the beeping-and-green-wavy-line-generating variety.

The press contingent circled the barricade. They interviewed the placard-waving crazy people; crossed live to their various home studios and discussed both alien invasion ramifications and expense accounts with their colleagues. A local reporter Jess knew from *her own* recent platypus-related brush with fame and mystery recognised her.

"Hey Jess, Cairns has sure been in the news. Good for our profile, eh?"

"Hi, yeah … I thought they must have faked the aliens, but now that I see it: how could a TV show fake this," she gestured, "this bird and drone killing barrier?"

The crowd roared, then fell silent as the lone crew member emerged from the forest and ran towards the inner ring of commandos.

Jess gasped as the woman clutched at her chest, staggered a few steps and collapsed. The crowd exploded again with horror and excitement, holding hundreds of phones high and pointing. Jess now heard first-hand theories of alien electrical control; rumours of failed military incursions by air, land, and sea; of secret international advisors.

"But is she dead?" Jess asked.

The reporter shrugged, "Reckon so, unless it's part of the show. This security is costing a fortune, if it's a hoax, the government will destroy Channel Five."

With the help of obliging drone enthusiasts, the media reported on the military's attempts to probe the electromagnetic anomaly. Despite the vegetal-beings' proclamations – and in line with corporate apology strategies – various entities had attempted to apologise for the phenomenon: NASA, the CSIRO, Tesla and the Western Australia Secession Party – to name but a few.

Probing continued. At the edge of the perimeter, Corporal Vinnie Rocca of the Second Commando Regiment loaded another recalcitrant rabbit into a pipe. Nearby, a colleague prepared to launch an aerial bombardment of caged rats. Often in the history of human endeavour, progress has followed testing on such reluctant rodents. What had begun with very-long-stick-taped-mice had advanced in complexity to the current trial. Experimental bunny RT2512 bristled with both probes and indignation as Vinnie pushed it into position behind its neighbour (RT2507). Laboratory animals have ample time to ponder the motives and experimental design of their researchers (not to mention unrestricted access to charts and data). And while "Flopsy" and "Whitey" may have had trouble articulating "Trial Five, rabbit subjects, multiple simultaneous entry points simultaneous with deployment of Boeing electromagnetic probe weapon" they smelt the unease of those who had gone before.

*

The detonation of the electromagnetic probe, or "pinch", as the heroic bunnies crossed the invisible barrier was spectacular. In the Cassowary Lodge, the celebrities turned towards the explosion.

"Do you reckon they're trying to get us out?" Matt asked tensely.

"More likely they're trying to get in – for the aliens," suggested Mariam. "We're not that important."

"Speak for yourself," muttered the cricketer. Followed by a relieved, "There you are, mate," as Paul returned, sweaty and sombre.

"I tried to stop her, but she collapsed at the barrier. There must be thousands of people out there." Paul scratched his head, "There'd be less interest *here* if aliens were all over the shop."

"So, we've got them to ourselves," said Matt grimly. "We're *really* expected to stay here and negotiate with them."

"Hey look!" Kalinda pointed, "Little parachutes are coming down."

Matt waited and retrieved one as it landed in a nearby shrub.

"It's a, it's a dead rat in a cage," he stammered. They're shooting rats at us. *Get me out of here.* "There you go," he said, handing it to Paul.

The annoying whine of the drones ceased. A leaf-creature stood immobile and tree-like by the forest edge. It casually dismembered a crashed contraption.

"Wish I had a dog," growled Lenny, nodding at the interloper. "I'd train him to piss on it!"

*

"Ouch!" Jess shielded her head as flying toys rained from the sky. She couldn't get cell phone reception – even at full stretch standing on one leg. Nearby, the exciting monitoring machinery with the chunky toggles and all the green wavy lines stopped working. The attempt to destroy the alien barrier with the "pinch" while simultaneously monitoring the barrier and the experimental animals had resulted in the curiously circular destruction of the monitoring equipment.

Corporal Rocca and his co-handlers didn't need the EEG, heart rate and blood glucose data. Retrieving RT2512 and RT2507 by their tethers, it was obvious their bunny life force had departed this world.

Later, after the clean-up, the Corporal and his unit began the necessarily low-tech final trials.

"Unload the geraniums" was not the kind of command Vinnie had expected to make when he joined the Special Forces. His team worked swiftly and arranged the transit of the wheeled and potted house plants back and forth over the alien perimeter. The army's senior vegetation consultant declared the geraniums as cheerful and indestructible as ever.

That evening at a press conference, senior reassurers from the government's elite Occupational Health and Reassurance Department reassured everybody that everything was under control. Additionally, they declared martial law within a reassuring ten kilometres of the *Celebrity Council Elimination* compound.

Chapter 6 “Have you not heard?”

At a great distance from the excitement of these events, a largely oblivious lone forestry professor dismounted his bike and manoeuvred around a palm in a large blue pot (one that had not hitherto any business in that location) in order to enter Corvallis, Oregon’s finest coffee establishment. Niels Larsson mused: *That palm won’t enjoy the coming cooler nights*. ‘The Retro Bean’ buzzed with earnest chatter: as before football finals or perhaps a celebrity court-case verdict. Niels nodded at a few fellow cyclists.

He knew the approaching waiter, of course.

“Hi Professor, the usual?” she smiled.

This, he considered, was a little presumptuous. Sure, he’d taken his usual seat in the booth lined with the 1950s children’s books, toys, and board games. Still, he didn’t consider he was *that* predictable. After last night’s relationship-ending-events, this was a sore spot.

“Hello, Ashley. Perhaps I am choosing a cup of tea and a banana muffin today,” he raised an eyebrow. “Or maybe the blueberry…”

“Oh, sorry,” said Ash, taken aback. “Take your time, no need to commit.”

“No, not really. A latte please,” Niels smiled. “But I will try the banana,” he confirmed, thus asserting his unpredictability in matters of muffin choice. Fate and circumstance now lurked along with the crumbs of the previous diner.

*

Commitment. Niels shuddered. Like one of his recurring, and mildly embarrassing, 'talking to trees' dreams, the scene replayed:

"… should we do presents now? Or we can watch the footage of that Aussie TV show with the aliens."

"Err … I'm not much liking the reality TV."

"Okay honey, well, I got you this," she enthused, producing the emoji-paper clad anniversary present.

Ah, not the pear-handled whittling knife then, thought Niels, unwrapping the soft package.

"You *can* rip the paper."

Niels smiled grimly. *At least it's not that Soypunk graphic novel.* He turned the T-shirt over with a flourish and winced at the tasteless Botany-themed text.

"Don't you love it!" she whooped. Yes, unfortunately, she was a whooper. Niels credited her with the inspiration for his five-point whooping level system (WPL1: low level spasmodic failing to gather support whooping, through to WPL5: mass sustained whooping at volume). His time in the States hadn't accustomed the Stockholm native to the locals' tendency to whoop and clap at minor provocations.

"It's so hygge."

Involuntarily, Niels rolled his eyes. The evening deteriorated as he produced her present.

"Aww, a necklace. Is it glass hon?"

"Amber – you know, the fossil tree sap …"

It soon went into terminal decline …

"You're more committed to your car than you are to me. You're all scared of commitment."

Niels sighed, *okay, let us not generalise from the specific to the universal.* Clearly skiing and rock climbing weren't enough for the basis of an ongoing relationship.

She left the necklace behind.

*

His order arrived. "Ashley, are you knowing why pot plants are shifted outside – there's a palm blocking the bike rack."

"Have you not heard? People don't trust them now," she said to his considerable surprise. Ash took a seat at his table and drew out her phone. In the coming years, this is how the man who came to be forever associated with the vegetal aliens, recalled first hearing of them.

Chapter 7 Death of the Platypuses

Watching *CCE* news, commentary, and the show itself these last few days had given Jess a fresh focus. Despite little prior interest in the decades long cult of celebrity; reality TV with real extra-terrestrials was a different matter. Most of the seven housemates were present, the flat-screen was on – the pizza boxes were piling up.

"Why has no one referenced that 'Like corals more' statement from their initial declaration?" demanded Lindsay of the screen.

Rob raised his eyebrows, "Other priorities, mate."

Lindsay. Intense Lindsay. Jess sympathised with his coral bleaching woes. But sharing both a Uni office and residential accommodation was too much sometimes.

The demise of Jess' study population, the first such reported, had itself been newsworthy until recently. Those weeks following the first unexplained deaths had devastated the close-knit platypus community. Mortality rates were extreme in the Daintree World Heritage area, curtailing her master's degree research. (*Saltwater Crocodile Predation As A Range Limiting Factor In Northern Platypus Populations* was her study title and living platypus populations an obvious requirement.)

Death rates varied elsewhere: lower in agricultural areas and dismally high in other wilderness zones. Captive zoo specimens remained unaffected by the calamity. (Or by the extra attention as they paddled busily around their tanks thinking: "Geez, we're popular! Did those *unbearable* koalas finally die out?") News organisations replaced their usual end-of-bulletin heart-warming animal story with sombre reports of the mysterious demise. Reporters filed interviews with puzzled scientists and stared empathically at platypus* denuded streams. Jess had been among them. As had the reporter she'd talked to at the perimeter. Naturally, the story ran out of steam: then Flooper, the three-legged fire-alerting rabbit, and his ilk made their return.

"How come aliens are always green?" said a housemate derisively.

"They use sunlight, they must be green," explained Leong.

"Just look how nervous they are. That political woman looks scared, and the bogan cricketer," said Lindsay. "And the way the eyes on that thing move … it has to be real!"

"He's got a point," agreed another housemate. "See how before the alien didn't answer Dr Paul about what they call themselves. That seems real too."

After visiting the *CCE* site, Jess felt more invested in the doings there. On-screen, the evening's episode ended, and she shifted on the broad arm of the couch. It was striped and nearly thirty years old, as was Jess – though more freckled than striped.

"What do you think, Jess? You're a veggo, you worried? That why you went down there?" asked Rob.

"Mainly curiosity about the barrier."

"*And*?" said Lindsay.

"Well, it's not my field, but from what I could gather it's not tech anyone's heard of."

"Unreal," said Rob. "The other thing is … most of them aren't capable of acting." He shrugged, "It's gonna be embarrassing if I'm wrong, but I'm making the early call – I say it's real."

---

* For much of the population, the correct plural is a mystery. This was the bugbear of Jess' career. No sooner had her research topic come up, than someone would say: "I love platypi …"

Outdoor education students were repeat offenders. (An additional mystery: Why so many of them? And why so many named Brad?)

In her well-rehearsed reply, Jess would say: "You can't just stick a Latin ending on a Greek word. It's like putting meat sauce on vegan pizza."

A *CCE* advertisement ran. The cunning 'piss-taking'-Frankenbite-advertising that suggested actual politicians would consider whatever edicts *The Celebrity Council* put forth. The TV showed footage of the aliens' emergence, then part of the 'Hitler conversation'. Jess and the group listened as the evening news confirmed the deaths of military personnel who'd tried to enter the compound. They saw more footage of drones crashing – the frozen bomb-disposal robot and black-armoured warriors dropping like marionettes. Such images were also much viewed on phones and laptops. This, despite the government's attempt to suppress it 'in the public interest'. The public was very much interested.

While Jess watched the evening news end, and a panel of experts began their nightly speculations, an inkling of an idea flared. In these last platypus-bereft weeks, Jess had developed the unconscious habit of reviewing the mystery. Unsought overtime added to conscious deliberations and her testing of tissue, sediment, and water samples. She'd analysed and re-analysed the environmental probe data. Jess looked again at the strange pics on her phone: the deep textured impression in the riverbank sand, the weird tracks, the sodden little carcasses.

The TV opinions continued: the emphasis switching from the biological, cultural and philosophic to the mysterious electromagnetic shield. The flare of idea flickered, caught and spread.

"Platypuses hunt using electro-reception—"

"We know Jess, you mention weird platypus facts on a daily basis," smiled Rob. "Swim with eyes closed, detect discarded batteries, blah, blah …"

"Sorry, thinking aloud." Jess shivered as insight dawned:

The aliens manipulate electrical activity
Platypuses are highly sensitive to electrical signals
The invaders consider themselves guardians of the forests
Platypuses died in greater numbers in forested wilderness areas.

The young scientist buzzed with insightful certainty: The aliens had arrived months ago and were hidden in forested wilderness areas. A quick check confirmed no extra-terrestrial hotline. She rang the terrorist hotline.

Chapter 8 The Elimination

"Hey all," said Jess, returning home. "Wow, everyone's here. I'm gonna have a quick shower and change."

"How'd the field trip go?" asked Lindsay, turning from the TV – of the housemates, he was her only fellow science student.

"Okay. I retrieved the sensors from the second site – doesn't look like they're working," she shrugged and wriggled out of her backpack.

"No platypuses?"

She shook her head, "Not a one, back soon."

"She's a bit upset," said a housemate, not looking up from the Celebrity Council's activities. Shortly they heard the water cut out and Jess re-entered the lounge damp-haired and leaned against the back of the worn couch.

"So, what've I missed?"

"Hi Jess, well they had *the talk* about their tattoos," said Rob.

"Why?"

"It's what they do on these shows," laughed another housemate. "Mariam was so pissed that Lenny Madden asked if she had any ink."

"Yeah, Jess," teased Rob. "Get with the genre girl – you gotta have kerosene flares, lots of bamboo, masks someone's mum brought back from Fiji – and the tattoo talk." He rolled his eyes and opened a beer. "You gotta commit, root for a favourite character – ditch that unfashionable omniscient point of view."

Jess waved at the TV. "What *are* they doing now?"

"It's just finishing. The aliens let a guest through the barrier – she's been teaching the celebs tree meditation. Something about: 'Since the aliens can communicate with trees – we should learn to do the same,'" Rob smiled, "One alien watched them. We think they're gonna have the elimination vote next." He swigged the beer.

On screen, the celebrities were filing out of the fern-framed meditation clearing. Poignantly Kat's diatom-infused meditation mat remained in the women's sleeping hut.

*

On set Matt said, "How'd you find that, Kalinda?"

"Maybe it's kind of uncool Matt, but I've never meditated before." She paused and dropped her voice, "my parents are ultra conservative – they think meditation, yoga ... incense is half-way to devil worship." She flicked back her hair and smiled, "I've only just started drinking herbal teas."

Matt laughed, "Reckon my Dad would prefer a spot of devil worship to seeing his kid attempt tree meditation on national telly."

"Could you do it Matt – did you feel anything?"

"God no! We should ask Doc Paul – he was right into it." They were almost alone in the clearing. "Holly, Holly," called Matt scurrying after the show's host as she left. As usual Holly was resplendent in a floral print dress and a pink hibiscus (nothing says, 'Here I am in the tropics' more than ear-worn hibiscus – with the possible exception of malaria). She had a large personality. Matt feared a resume featuring theatre restaurants. "Err Holly, will there still be an elimination episode?"

"Yes Matt, our surprise intruders insist the show continues as usual. The voting closes soon." Hearing this exchange, the celebrities circled back. Holly informed them that despite recent contestant-reducing events, there would still be an end-of-week elimination (the aliens would lift the barrier again).

Rarely had such a reality TV declaration been met with comparable enthusiasm.

"What have I gotta do to get eliminated," muttered Len.

Maggie overheard the miked-up sportsman in the control centre. She scoffed, "Just be yourself, dear." Followed by, "Get that overhead cam into place one of *them* is approaching."

"Additional sky-mouse, deceased," said the vegetal creature; it proffered the small cage to Matt. The comedian passed it on. Dr Paul forced his features into a relaxed 'TV-as-normal' arrangement.

"Err thanks. Beyond help, I reckon," said the vet.

Later the crew gathered, as did the dusk and mosquitos. The kerosene torches were lit and in flickering light Holly read aloud the results of the viewers' poll. Matt thought Paul McKay hid his surprise well as the celebrities hugged him in turn.

"You lucky bastard," said Lenny gruffly, releasing the vet.

Matt gave a last wave as Holly escorted Paul off set and towards the perimeter and his new life*. Mariam's eyes were wet.

Matt turned to the static burst. He was getting better at telling the aliens apart – this was the murderous one.

"Important personages weekly edict."

Lenny crossed his beefy arms, "What! Are we still doing that bullshit—"

"Shh," hissed Mariam.

Matt stepped back, closer to Kalinda as it waved its eyestalks at them and said, "Proclamation required – display of intention." It did its white noise trick again, "Your minions will obey."

Matt rearranged the floppy hair. *I have minions*? *Cool*. The non-lethal leaf-creature on his left rustled, adjusting itself and said, "Display of ahimsa intent," it rippled its short antennae and added, "Welcome."

---

*Returning home, after feeding and polishing Schnapps (*Outback Vet's* freshwater crocodile mascot and quasi co-host) Paul McKay found he had won the ultimate career expansion pack: graduating from 'Outback Vet' to 'Extra-terrestrial Vet.' The care of stricken camels was put on hold as he was interviewed in secret by security experts and in public on every species of media.

Opposite Matt, Vito too crossed his arms over his waistcoated chest and mouthed, "*What are we going to do*?"

"Carrots," announced the comedian into the tense silence. He breathed deeply and gestured to the camera operator. He wagged a finger fiercely at the lens and said, "Don't eat carrots people!"

He closed his eyes. He held his breath.

"Statement of extreme limitation," said the lethal alien. Its various appendages thrashed. Matt retreated further as its companion waved its eyestalks about. Inexplicably, he found himself counting them: *five, six, seven, if you stopped jiggling, I might be able to count 'em.*

The alien rippled its small feathery antenna: "Conciliate. Allow patience." Its companion stalked away.

Vito nodded, crossed the ragged circle, and put his arm around Matt.

*

"It's just wrong in so many ways," said Lindsay as the station cut to an ad break.

"Well, yeah,"

"I mean Paul was the most popular celeb," (You're probably aware he'd also been voted: "Celebrity I'd most like my daughter to marry," by *Mum Magazine* three years in a row.) "*And*," Lindsay's voice quivered, "They still haven't addressed the issues around coral conservation."

Rob rolled his eyes. "Geez, Jess. So, it's true what your reporter mate heard down at the CCE barrier – about the fix."

"Yes," she finished drying her hair. "Somehow that makes it more real."

We would be unwise to believe every rumour that circulates outside an alien incursion site. Yet it was so. At the end of CCE *week two, Dr Paul was eliminated. As the most educated member of* Celebrity Council *in matters biological; the nation's security analysts had interfered with the voting and arranged his removal.*

Chapter 9 The Aerial View

"This is your pilot. Strap yourself in. Put on the headphones. If your security clearance doesn't cover secret aerial searches for extra-terrestrials, get the hell out of my helicopter." Of course, the pilot didn't say most of this. He merely grumped and glared at Jess – the only civilian on the flight.

She was strapped in and head-phoned following an expedition a few days before to retrieve environmental sensors from her study site. That little troupe had included an affable military scientist. The Major now strapped in beside her. Analysis had shown the probe's environmental data capture had ceased two days before the discovery of the lifeless platypuses. Not exactly a smoking gun – more a leaking water pistol. Still, that and her phone pics of mysterious riverbank impressions were enough to get her invited to join the aerial search in the army Black Hawk helicopter.

Her initial, *Wow! This is a different POV* moment had passed.

Three hours exposure to the aircraft's swirly vortex of sound later, Jess was feeling anxious and bored. The relentless auditory buffeting contributed to her anxiety but paled compared to the growing sense of failure and futility. Even flying low, the rainforest canopy was impenetrable. Forays down the spectacular Mossman Gorge, other meandering Daintree rivers and the few roads, revealed no aliens huddled conveniently in view.

Her speculation on platypus deaths and an undetected alien presence had been deemed worth a few hours of flight time by the

Major's superiors. Looking down, she mused, "*It would've taken one of those trees to make all the forms I signed to join this trip*.

"Oh" exclaimed Jess with a spontaneous squeak of excitement and intuition.

"Do you have visual?" barked the co-pilot turning his head.

"What do you see, Miss Kelly," said the Major with a mere hint of eyebrow-raising.

"No, it's not that. We should try Wollemi National Park." Jess observed the eyebrows elevate further as the frontalis muscles (as those in the trade call them) went to work. "If these, err, beings are interested in trees, especially rare, ancient trees, then they'll be protecting the Wollemi Pines."

Her co-scientist's features took on the expression of a child with only three jigsaw puzzle pieces to complete – one of them an edge bit.

"There's a secret canyon with twenty or thirty trees, and that's all – it's a tiny area, the aliens will be easy to spot. They'd have to be standing in the river for us to see them here," said Jess.

Australians love their sports and games: horse racing, swimming, tennis, cricket, incomprehensible self-invented football codes. Hide and seek, however, doesn't appear to be a strong suit. In 1967 they inexplicably lost a Prime Minister and failed, until 1994, to notice forty-metre trees – remnants from the days of dinosaurs – hiding just one hundred and fifty kilometres from the nation's largest city*. Discovery of the Wollemi Pine, *The Pinosaur* spread around the world. And not just confined to 'science news' of the 'New species of Antarctic moss discovered!' (looks like all other mosses), variety. Like a hip-hop artist going pop, it was a crossover hit.

---

*Following the initial discovery, two smaller groves were found nearby. In total, there are fewer than a hundred large Wollemi Pines in the wild: Vulnerable to fire, Phytophthora fungus, and every tree and moviegoers dread – the back-country axe murderer. Within five years of the discovery, a clever combination of conservation and commerce had led to the sale of thousands of cultivated trees. Some, seasonally adorned with tinsel, baubles, elementary school macaroni art and a star on top had become part of the family.

*

Jess felt the fabric tighten as she was blindfolded.

It was three days later, in another helicopter: this one owned by the State Park Service.

Also present was a laconic ranger. He sported a beard you could hide baby possums in, but he didn't have the look of a platypus-scientist-kidnapper about him.

"There you go," he said. "Just routine – as you know we keep the pines' location secret." As military secrecy trumps botanical treasure secrecy, the army pilots following Jess' aircraft weren't blindfolded (despite the usual boasts about being able to 'fly this thing with my eyes shut').

The Major's superiors had been partial to Jess' new search location but less so to actually taking her along.

"She can't abseil, can she?"

But she could.

Blindfold removed, she climbed on the helicopter's skids and dropped beside the others. *Ouch*, her hair whipped about under the fearsome downdraft, lashing her cheeks. She grinned at the ranger. *You look like something from one of dad's 70s record covers.* The barely hirsute commandos from the other chopper led the way over the canyon ledge.

Dangling from multi-coloured ropes, Jess was inclined to focus on not dying rather than enjoying the scenery. Safe on the canyon floor, she brushed herself down. "The contrast down here's amazing," she said. "It's so much cooler and greener."

"Yep." The ranger produced a laptop from his supplies and advanced on the closest of the sensors scattered throughout the canyon. With a look of consternation at the laptop and a significant glance at Jess, he said, "Yeah, the data's corrupted – nothing for more than a month."

They moved into the Wollemi grove. *It's like a pic from a kids' book*, thought Jess. The narrow sandstone canyon framed a scene where trolls, witches, or a band of hobbits might lurk between the astonishing trees.

Then, like finding Mormons on the wrong side of your front door, the little party halted, confused as much as astonished. The discovered object was alien in every sense of the word. It had no straight lines but blurred the lines between the manufactured and the grown. Caravan-sized, it was extravagantly textured like one of those fruits encountered on holiday in Vietnam and never seen again. Jess looked around warily. But whom or whatever normally supervises the laws of physics was elsewhere, probably keeping all the Bluetooth devices back in Sydney paired.

"Where are they," mouthed the ranger. The pod hovered, making a cheerful humming sound.

Oh, thought Jess. She pointed, *maybe in there.*

By mutual silent consent, they withdrew, recording the object.

Returned to the Defence Science and Technology Group's Sydney base at Eveleigh, Jess was rewarded with a few extra forms of the secrecy-keeping-variety. But within weeks they'd be redundant, as a group of commonplace tourists filmed a group of alien visitors enjoying the Mossman Gorge.

Chapter 10 The Beach and the Pond

“We’re on in five minutes people,” came the crew member’s impatient tree-muffled-voice. Matt placed a cunning finger over his mic and signalled the celebrities still deeper into the forest.

“Are we *going* to tell them?” said Kalinda.

“What’ll they do to us when they realize they’ve been deceived?”

“Not by us, Vito – it was just advertising,” said Matt.

“But *we* were in it, Mathew.” The chef had been unshaven and unwaistcoated for days.

“So better to tell ’em sooner, you reckon?” Len scratched his head.

Matt said, “Depends. Do you want to die sooner or later, big guy?”

Mariam fingered the edge of her scarf, voice hollow, “*You* have a plan?”

“Err, stall for time, muddle through, hope something turns up.”

Matt ignored the production crew as he trailed the others on the sandy path that lead to the sea. Adding his sandals to the pile, he noted the wind was fresh here. It began whipping Kalinda’s hair about. Toes squirming in the warm sand, he scanned the beach, *Perfect setting for a boutique rum commercial*. Holly was saying something about this week’s challenge involving a stand-up paddleboard race. *Sea’s a bit choppy*, he thought.

Then, "What's that!" The comedian shielded his eyes from the glare and pointed at the surf zone.

"Is it … are they seals?" said Mariam. She trotted past the waiting paddle boards towards the water. Matt winced at her shriek.

It wasn't seals.

The celebrities stared. Boutique rum adverts were unlikely to feature two sun-and-water damaged, wet-suited bodies. Despite the claims of the lodge's glossy brochures: the commandos' time on the fringes of the Cassowary Ecolodge had done nothing for their complexions.

Kalinda backed away, "That one's been, been—"

"Yeah, he's been a bit nibbled." Matt touched her on the shoulder, and she put her hand over her mouth. "Come on Kal, don't look."

The smell seemed to linger as he reclaimed his footwear and fled the scene with the others.

"Mathew Davis," called the voice of *Siri*.

The vegetal creature held a small cage. It let the wind ruffle itself, "Apologies-regrets, additional sky-mouse deceased, additional humans deceased." Dazed, Matt accepted the dead rodent. "Unfortunate disregard barrier hazard."

Matt's voice wavered, "So not killed on purpose."

"Correct-affirmative."

"Okay, I guess the crew will tell Maggie about the bodies. I might bury this near the little waterfall pond I've found. Err, do you want to come – maybe we can talk?"

"Correct-affirmative."

Away from the sea breeze, Matt heard the creature rustle as they walked. "I was wondering … you know that meditation thing we had, is it really possible for humans to communicate with trees?"

"Negative if light foragers judged mere landscape entities," it twitched its antennae, "achievements of communication, pre-machine age human cultures."

"Are there still, tribes that can talk to trees?"

"Uncertainty. Disruption intact forests, disruption such humans."

They reached the pond.

"Oh. Hi."

Mariam's brief solo retreat to the sanctity of the pond ended. The light-forager hovered at the water's edge, adjusting its leaf-wings in the dappled light. Mariam made anxious circles in the water with her bare feet.

"So, you've found it too." Matt flourished a hand at the alien, "Apparently the frogmen died trying to come through the exclusion barrier – it wasn't like – deliberate."

Mariam nodded and although reluctant to make eye contact with the alien she drew on her interviewer experience and said, "You know I feel many of us are more surprised that plants have communication and intelligence than that extra-terrestrials exist."

"Maze running protocol, poor test planet's photosynthetics' sentience," said the light-forager.

"Obviously, we can appreciate intelligence in yourself," she continued, tracing more nervous feet circles in the water, "but it just wasn't that obvious to us in plants."

"For prosperity your species requires mere outwitting of coconut palms," it spat static, "and yet, you balance on edge self-destruction."

"Err, but many people are into trees big time," said Matt diplomatically. "I mean, you can't go to the wholefoods shop without seeing Tree of Life tattoos."

"Prior time, this tree youthful," said the alien, indicating a towering specimen furry with epiphytes, "humans unaware history own existence. Non-awareness microscopic life form existence."

Matt shrugged, "Yeah, viruses sometimes take us by surprise."

"It's just that to us, trees seem just to stand there. They don't do much," said Mariam.

"Trees have a … a saying, 'Mobility is wasted on the mobile.' Do you disfavour still humans? Those that sleep, those watch the *YouTube*, the *FriendFone*, those infirm, those damaged – be those subtracted worth?"

"No, no," she mumbled.

"Got any prophecies?" said Matt, (Mariam gave him *the* look). "Or recommendations, handy hints if you will?"

"Affirmative. Be still and contemplate – but not of selves." It rippled antennae, "Earth plants non-destructive energy transfer moral and sustained."

Matt peered at himself in the pond, with the qualms common to all sentient species, with both eyes and access to reflective surfaces. "Err right," said he. "No offence, but I sometimes just get the general gist of what you're saying. Bit like reading Shakespeare. Are all types of plants communicating?" He leaned back and gave a patch of moss an affectionate pat. "Like this?"

"Minimal quality sentience."

"And the ferns?" asked Mariam.

"Low networking interaction. Their weft lacks complexity.

"Two ferns don't make a *Ficus*, eh?"

"Self finds humans of more interest."

"Err, right ... that's nice. Whereas this tree?" Matt brushed the stately rainforest specimen the alien had brought to their attention.

"Contrast. Self-knowledge, complex relationship weaving."

"Cool," said Matt, noticing that up close to the alien it smelt of pine forest, with a hint of alcohol. *I could use a drink and a good lie down.*

"You can *talk* to it?" queried Mariam.

At the edge of Matt's vision, it seemed a shrub rustled its leaves disparagingly. He shook his head. *Get a grip*, he told himself, *leaves move in the wind or not – they don't rustle disparagingly.*

But the rustling continued as the other communicative alien – the lethal one – the one Matt and Mariam had overlooked in the shadows, crept next to its companion.

"Trees don't talk. Trees sing," said the aliens in stereo and briefly intertwining eyestalks and antennae in ways beyond the power of narrative word-smithing.

Mariam gasped, "And these?" she queried, poking small mushroomy things growing on a rotten log behind her.

"Not plant. Not photosynthetic. Sentience unintelligible."

Although the tone of the reply didn't and couldn't suggest judgement, Mariam resumed her feet circling, feeling chastened. "So, it's okay to eat mushrooms?"

"Consumption all life forms abhorrent." It made the modem noise. Then: "Don't eat things that don't eat things. However, selves shall conduct code non-interference human affairs; conditional energy source non-plant."

"Yeah, they said that before," said Matt to Mariam. "They'll look the other way if we eat koala steaks barbecued over a pit of flammable baby penguins. Just don't use a bamboo skewer to cook it!"

Mariam rolled her eyes, equilibrium returning. Deciding to open a new topic for discussion, and one close to her heart, she said "What do your, err, *your kind* think of human energy resources and policies?"

"Variousness of primitive technologies. Cessation tree burning imperative."

"Don't burn wood, eh," said Matt. "Hey, it's a consistent world view."

"What *is* your opinion of renewables – wind and solar power et cetera?" said Mariam, her TV persona returning like a penguin to its burrow.

"Indifferent opinion-concern, inefficient science mechanisms. Better humans emulate plants directly," said the non-lethal alien.

"Not sure that's a goer," said Matt with a concerned glance at his co-human.

For if an imposing silence is possible, it was an imposing silence that emanated from the green invaders. The newcomer (the "abrupt" one) twitched its antenna at its comrade and stalked away.

Matt leaned back and rubbed his shoulders against the textured bark of a tree fern. An inkling on an idea, a suspicion flared – nothing you could actually base a conspiracy theory on. He and Mariam exchanged, 'What was that about?' looks.

Mariam breached the silence by asking, somewhat indignantly, "Well, what about coal-fired power stations and global warming – what's your perspective on those issues?"

"Human coal use distasteful."

"Because of the greenhouse effect?"

"Negative. Coal consists ancient deceased photosynthetic life forms – extracted, consumed by fire."

"Err, right," said Matt. "I can see that might seem a bit … unpleasant. And global warming?"

"Enhanced carbon dioxide, enhanced temperature promotes photosynthetic life form abundance. Humans already culturing light foragers in greenhouses."

"So, your kind might welcome global warming then?" said Matt with a slight mischievous glance at Mariam.

"Some would agreement."

"Wow, okay," said the comedian.

Mariam retrieved her feet from the natural pond. She examined them closely, as if they'd disappointed her, and went off to contemplate her world view. Around the world, alone and in groups, humans were doing likewise.

Matt took a fortifying gulp of rainforest air, indicated the trees, and broached a new topic, "We make a lot of buildings from wood ..."

As in the story of the three little pigs and the wolf: the alien concluded that houses of brick (stone, cement or a hole in the ground) were preferable to houses of straw and wood. *Not*, it may be clear, because these materials are inherently flimsy and prone to lupine home invasion. Rather, because the photosynthetic owners of these useful structural elements feel strongly about being killed, dried and re-arranged into various shapes, no matter how Feng Shui compliant.

Matt splashed his feet, more violently than the pond deserved, "What about water – do you need freshwater. Can you use the sea? Is there enough water for all of us?"

The alien adjusted its posture. It complimented Matt on the quality of the pool-side sunshine and said, "Self has freshwater requirement also trace elements. Sea stripped of excess salts – will allow colonisation coastal desert landforms. Awareness humans consume excess water in wasteful dietary production. Plentiful water locked solid form at poles."

Matt plunged his feet into the pond again. Such discussions hadn't previously been part of his ideal career arc. The young comedian had followed a traditional career path: he was a law school dropout; had dabbled in university theatre; achieved success in youth radio; won an emerging comedian award and had just completed his first national stand-up tour: 'Matt not Gloss.' In an era where news and current affairs can't be broadcast without a comedian (or even a whole team) Matt hoped his appearance on CCE would lead to his very own desk seat on the panel show gravy train.

The light-forager interrupted his thoughts, enquiring, "Be you negatively optimal?"

"Nah … it's okay. I might be off. Good talk, though. I'll see you later, yeah."

And with that, he also wandered away to fret, worry and meditate (in the ponder sense) and have a good lie-down.

The alien contemplated the diminishing pond ripples.

Chapter 11 Truth, Proof, Doubt and Dinner

As those of you who'd rushed to join a 'Jain Philosophy for Beginners' class (or, indeed, any philosophy class) can attest, the three great conundrums of human existence are: What is beauty? What is truth? And what's for dinner? Except for those tortured poetic souls, much of the populace prefers to contemplate the first two, after they've satisfactorily answered the third question. Yet, this couldn't be resolved. Not until the truth of the alien incursion and their food directives was determined.

End of the world scenarios brought out the risk-takers. Marriage proposals spiked, people strapped on aerial contrivances and jumped out of perfectly satisfactory aircraft, while others chanced with deadly foodstuffs. As the days went by, culinary-indecision-paralysis affected ever more people (additional to those affected dicing with Japanese fugu pufferfish).

What had started as a metaphorical ripple in the far-away exotic pond of Cairns, had in a week developed into a worldwide tsunami of interest. Media commentators held their collective breath, waiting for the wave to break – so to surf the waters of smug derision back to familiar shores.

Astronomers claimed given the size of the universe, intelligent life forms were a near certainty. However, it's one thing to envisage this as an intellectual possibility, and toy with Drake Equation estimates, and quite another to see that possibility sandwiched between adverts for sports drinks and pet insurance.

Within days of the infamous "ratings spike" there were reports of similar creatures frolicking in forests from Eastern Europe, Brazil, and Canada. Reality TV and the fake news phenomenon of the recent decade had dulled the public's capacity to determine truth, proof, and beauty. FriendFone, Facebook and their competitors spread each new dubious click-farm revelation.

But the number and plausibility of images grew. The public viewed footage of abandoned forestry operations in locations such as Indonesia, The Congo, and Colombia. There was a commonality of downed tools and vanished labourers. Reports of *forest spirits* and *tree demons*.

*

As we've seen, people could in later years recall when they first viewed or heard tell of the CCE arrival. Belief, however, often came later and was a variable personal experience. Rather than document every last individuals' response to events, the narrator has thoughtfully focused on important persons closest to the action for narrative purposes ...

Our Cassowary Lodge celebrities, while stunned and confused, did immediately believe. Jess Kelly, underemployed scientist and abseiler, *was* convinced by the discovery of the alien craft. Niels Larsson, Swedish forester and Saab owner, was *yet* unconvinced. Mike Ross, Canadian conservation campaigner (whom – do not fret – we are about to meet), didn't require proof.

Merely confirmation.

For the majority, proof came from the land of the maple leaf, the world's largest forest producer. For in Gaspe National Park, a busload of visitors on route from the interpretation centre to the trailhead, observed a troupe of aliens admiring the black spruce forests. They did what tourists do best: film their reactions to the phenomenon, record other people's reactions to the phenomenon, almost incidentally record the phenomenon itself, and upload the whole thing to *me2Screen* or *YouTube*.

A vacationing New Yorker took the best of the footage. By an extraordinary coincidence, the fellow was an alien aficionado. Oddly, this convinced the species of people who hadn't believed in corona virus and couldn't understand logarithmic growth if it were festering on their tonsils.

*

Preparations were underway. It was the lunar month anniversary of their "occupation" and the young people thought this important. Beneath the great trees of Giant Sequoia National Monument, Mike Ross listened to birdsong blend with rice boiling and the pounding of chickpeas. Arms folded he watched the newcomer enter the banner and dream-net draped clearing.

"Err hi – is my sister here? Crystal ... Crystal Roche."

She's a hugger, recalled the veteran conservationist.

"Crystal! Thank-God, there you are. Have you heard the news? Has anyone got a phone or a tablet?"

Mike watched his group murmur a collective "No." On its outer edge, that bare-toed fellow explained they'd fled the technological world and its evil 'one device to rule them all' vibe. "... we're not trapped in the algorithm."

"We don't need them, we have the wood wide web," said Crystal.

The brother fidgeted and said, "I know this is gonna to sound crazy, but aliens have appeared on a reality TV show in Australia." Mike quit leaning on the tree and stepped towards the crowd.

"Cool bro', you finally tried the good stuff."

"Crystal, I'm serious, it's been on the news and all over the internet for weeks.

"Hey man, that place is all self-absorption and negative energy," opined one of the group.

Mike hastened closer. Bare-toes had started up again, "Yes! The aliens have been liberated from Area Fifty-One! This could bring the military-industrial complex down." He'd been without alien subreddit for weeks and now began muttering about advanced aviation threat projects (conspiracies were his thing since discovering at age six the tooth fairy and Easter bunny weren't, strictly speaking, real).

The group made room for Mike, "What do they *look* like?"

"They're like plants. Or plant-lobsters. They say they will use the sunshine and protect the forests."

Mike nodded imperceptibly.

"Awesome …"

"So random …"

No, it's really not, thought Mike.

"Well, I don't know, this is quite large news. I think I'd have seen it in the stars," explained a bell-enhanced activist in an apologetic tone.

"There've been sightings worldwide. Look, this is a video some tourist took in Canada." The protestors crowded around the small, world-linking portal that was Crystal's brother's phone …

"Ah, that's black spruce forest," said the veteran conservationist. *At last*, he said to himself.

"From your neck of the woods, Mike," noted a youngster, employing his undoubted ability to state the obvious.

"Amazing …"

"No way …"

"We shall form a gender-neutral interspecies forest protection movement …"

"Oh my gosh. I must compose a melody of solidarity" announced Crystal. She retrieved an ocarina by its thong from the recesses of her unfettered bosom.

Her brother looked askance. "Sis, you don't understand; they're attacking people in forests. It's dangerous here, Crystal – you're all in danger."

"Your astrotheology is all messed up, dude …"

"Attacking people? I don't—" Mike was interrupted. He shrugged and reached for the phone.

"Hey, Crystal, this family intervention is a downer," said the shaggiest protestor. "The tree creatures and we are in solidarity. One forest at a time, tree by tree, the righteous shall protect the earth from the tyranny of the burger." He flicked his long fringe aside and Mike saw the vein in his temple throb. A sure sign he was about to launch into another burger rant.

Mike, followed by the wisest of the protestors, edged away. He tapped replay again and again. He couldn't hear the audio over Shaggy's lecture on the impending danger of Burger Saturation Point. Looking up, the veteran smiled: Crystal had wandered off, and her brother continued to be talked at.

Somebody joined the ocarina with a bongo drum, and a little interpretative dancing begun. *Focus youngsters. It begins.*

A fellow veteran of the movement scratched his white beard. "Mike – you'll remember *Skippy the Bush Kangaroo*?"

The Canadian produced his cool grandpa smile. "Yes Spike, that thing could assemble flat-pack furniture and defuse bombs."

"Exactly! When I was in Oz thirty years ago, half of 'em believed SCUBA divers get routinely scooped from the ocean and dropped on bushfires." He glanced around at the unsinged redwood forest and his companions. He raised his spectacular eyebrows. "So many BBQs ruined by the squelchy thump of plummeting divers or an unexpected rain of luridly coloured snorkels." He grinned. "That's all I'm saying."

"But Spike, the phone footage," said one of the kids.

The tootling of Crystal's clay flute with its mighty one-octave range distracted Shaggy from his theme, and everyone was terribly pleased. Especially the unfortunate brother.

"Crystal," he called plaintively. "You've got to go—"

Now the barefoot fellow with the jacket fashioned from some kind of reptile interrupted. "Crystal's brother dude … It's not just burgers man – it's all agriculture. Yeah, your burger uses more land and water than vegetarian options, but you know what use even *less* – just shooting a deer, just catching a fish."

"I'd better rescue him," said Mike. "Can I have his phone back?" He approached the group. Bare toes was saying, "Doesn't matter whether forests are cleared for burgers or tofu man. It's still forest death. Only by living as our ancestors did, moving through the landscape, hunting, fishing, gathering nuts and berries, fashioning shelter and clothes from—"

A discordant combination of sounds from the ocarina obscured what bare toes was saying about fashioning clothes (but a glance at him provided some clues).

"Perhaps another time," suggested Mike firmly. He returned the phone to the unfortunate brother.

Many of the group couldn't accept the aliens posed any danger to them; others still doubted their very existence.

"But we're like, in neural inter-phase with the forest."

"Do you believe it, Mike?"

"I have no doubts. No doubt at all."

Photons of light danced on ancient sequoia trunks and any Wi-Fi present, which it wasn't, because it wasn't that sort of protest, would have stopped working. Inexplicable alien technology distorted space as the craft manifested between trees with a precision to make grown driving instructors weep.

Behind him Mike heard someone say, "Cool," in an awed tone.

Doubt on where matters stood vanished like cat poo in a sandpit. Crystal flinched as though struck unsuspectingly by a falling snorkel and Mike whispered confidently, "It'll be okay."

Two troupes eyed each other across the small clearing – some of the eyes were on stalks. Silence fell in the forest. Bare toes could hear the voices in his head again.

"Humans leaves now," said a light forager in the voice of the phone-app Siri.

It pointed a wing-leaf.

The protestors gasped and retreated. Mike alone stepped forward. *It's been years.* He glowed like a prophet who'd seen the future – one trodden by hemp sandals. His eyes flashed, "I am your ally, Mike Ross," he declared grandly. Sensing odd glances from the wider group, he said, "*We* are on your side, we protect this forest."

"Instruction repeats: Leaves now." Directing eyestalks at cooking pots, it further declared, "Cease slay-consume vegetable life-forms."

Mike opened his mouth; he peered uncertainly at alien anatomy.

Crystal's wits cowered like the last pufferfish in a restaurant tank trying to hide behind the filter.

They abandoned ideals of collective interspecies workshops in the sudden desire to be elsewhere.

"It wasn't meant to go down like this," sighed another of the troupe, shaking her head and close to tears.

Mute, the protestors and Crystal's brother began the walk out of the forest.

Back to the altered and nervous world.

"Damn it, sis. I left my phone behind."

In times to come the brother, sister and others would join with the extra-terrestrials; contemplate the nature of truth and read Jain philosophy. But for the moment they fled at a brisk walk.

Thirty-minutes up the road, Mike rolled his eyes. Bare toes was prattling again. "Might be time to close the Vegan Academies, yeah. Did anyone else get how leaves on a tree and leave like, well ... *just leave* are the same word? That blows my mind."

"Do please be quiet," said Crystal

Chapter 12 "Go Beavers!"

The puzzle of alien communications and intentions had exercised sharper minds than Mervyn Dyer Jnr and his nemesis: a bunch of giant toothy rodents. Merv parked his white SUV near the riverbank south of Portland. He was intent on a spot of illegal beaver removal. Minutes later he scratched his head … the beasts were already gone.

For in an unfathomable coincidence, the previous evening, when a lone alien appeared on the riverbank and disrupted the communal tree felling with its barked command: "Go Beavers!" a guest scientist on a TV show said just the same thing in a completely different context. This is his tale.

The plague of reality TV and made-for-streaming-service dramas had failed to kill off the long-running *Tonight Show*. Since the great (somebody else's) ratings spike, Megan Allen had entertained her viewers and live audience with jokes about the extra-terrestrial arrival. Alien invasion humour of the:
"Christmas will still happen – but you can't trust the tree!" variety had invaded regular *Tonight Show* segments. And hash-tag gags such as '#Worst vegetable experience ever,' and the more recent '#I hate trees because' had attracted thousands of public responses.

But now, Megan, and worse, the show's advertisers grew concerned. Maybe the world *hadn't* been subjected to the greatest marketing and publicity exercise since the Loch Ness monster was a hatchling. As the show's first female host put it, "We need to scramble a serious response. The public is talking, talking, and uploading videos. We're out of step."

Unfortunately, this would involve dealing with actual scientists rather than lab-coated entertainers modelled on *The Muppet Show*'s boffins. As her staffers began the search for experts in plant communication and intelligence, it became clear this was a small field. Then …

"Yeah, got one."

The pic allayed worry over a guest scientist meeting American TV standards in terms of hair, dentistry, muscle tone, and sheer physical symmetry. Oregon State's faculty page showed the young professor as tall and lean with shaggy dark blonde hair and stubble. He fulfilled all the requirements for Swedish people on television and had agreed to fly to NBC studios in New York.

*

On set, the band struck up *Big Yellow Taxi* by Joni Mitchell.

The announcer said, "Please welcome Professor Niels Larsson," and the audience applauded obediently.

Niels took his seat next to the host's familiar desk and Megan established her guest was a researcher in tree communication. She floundered a little in the non-accustomed, non-celebrity presence. Then *The Tonight Show's* host relaxed. The scientist had that sense of calm competence; without needing to say anything (which so often takes hours in front of the mirror to achieve).

"Thank you so much for coming on the show. Please tell the audience a little about yourself and your work?"

"Well yes, I like to whittle," Niels grinned. "Also, I am two years working at Oregon State University – GO BEAVERS!" Megan chuckled. There was a smattering of cheering and a round of applause from the studio audience.

"And originally from Sweden?" said Megan (of course she already knew this).

"Yes, yes, that is so. From Stockholm and then at Uppsala University."

"I've got to tell you; my family has spent some time in Sweden … had such fun there. So, I'm curious: plant intelligence, you have expertise in this space?"

"Well, Megan, I would say more plant communications. My research deals with *communication* among trees."

The host gave one of her endearing, puzzled frowns of concern – like a panda endeavouring to remember where it had misplaced its cub this time. "My gosh, it's a lot to take in. I know – well, I've heard – there are gardeners who talk or play music to lettuces and tomatoes, but …" Megan gestured with her palms up, and the audience murmured in mutual bafflement. "So how did you get started in this area?"

"Well, yes, I was studying forestry in Sweden but spending a semester break at a marine laboratory in the south of England. Much different to study of trees. A part of what they were doing was growing tiny plants of the sea – microalgae – for the feeding to fish and shellfish. Mariculture purposes, you see. I was most amazed. Many of these plants were so beautiful, but also surprising for me that certain of them were swimming. Gosh, I thought – these most simple of plants swim about, moving towards the light and looking and behaving like animals. If they were big enough to be seeing without a microscope, they could be interesting pets, I am thinking. We have some video of these algae, yes.?"

The house band started up *Rhapsody in Blue*, and the audience murmured as footage of micro-algae with names such as *Chlamydomonas*, *Euglena* and *Tetraselmis* swam about erratically like wind-up toys in a bath full of toddlers.

"Wow. So, they swim with their tails? Tell me, what are *those* things?" said Megan.

"Flagella."

"Flah what?" laughed the host good-naturedly.

The scientist smiled and continued, "Seeing these little plants that look and behave like the simple animals made me think: If primitive things have such abilities, what might higher plants, like trees be capable of?"

"Such as star in a reality TV show and end the madness that is soy latte!"

The audience chucked obediently.

"These beings … they are not trees. Our Earth classifications cannot apply to them. That's like asking, 'How many home runs make up a touchdown?' But they are photosynthetic like our plants and feeling they have an affinity with them."

"And so, after seeing these microscopic plants, this plankton?" queried the host. Niels nodded encouragingly, and Megan continued, "You studied behaviour and communication in plants?"

"Not immediately, no. I completed my forestry studies and worked in that field for a little while. So, I may not be these alien creatures most favourite human!"

There were nervous titters from the audience and the Professor continued, "But I didn't forget the micro-algae – they made me question the limited way we think about plants, and soon my work on forestry production began to investigate how forests are communities not just many individual trees. At first, this research was still, you are understanding, concerned with growing the most lumber. Only later, I began to research the communication between trees."

"In fact, I hear you're something of a tree advocate these days."

"In a way, yes."

"You've branched into a different area," said Megan with a sheepish smirk, to the amusement of her studio audience.

"You could say that … well, you did say that," said Niels amiably.

"So, I'm curious, how *do* trees communicate?" said the host, favouring Niels with one of her serious expressions.

"Well, Megan, it is most intriguing, trees communicate by chemical signals through the air and through their roots, where they may also exchange nutrients and information. On an individual level and a forest level, they sense and respond to their environment with hormonal, chemical and electrical activities, although the electrical activity is slower than ours."

"So interesting. Can you give us some examples of that communication?"

"A famous example is when caterpillars attack oak trees. The trees are surely not enjoying this and are responding by making bitter-tasting chemicals in their leaves. Interestingly, the tree under attack produces chemicals detected by its neighbours, and they also produce the bitter leaf molecules *before* the caterpillars have reached them. In fact, giraffes have discovered this plant signalling before us humans."

"Giraffes!" Megan turned her palms up in surprise.

"Well sure, they have always known more than they reveal," joked the scientist. "Research has shown when giraffes eat acacias, the trees release the signalling chemical ethylene into the air, and other acacias detect this and begin to produce unpleasant leaf chemicals. But the clever giraffes have learned this, and they move upwind where the trees are not being warned."

"Like the trees are *really* trying to help each other out?"

"That may be so, but it's not all the rainbows and unicorns. There is a balance of competition and cooperation between individuals and between species."

The scientist continued, "Research has shown trees redistribute sugar through the roots, reducing the disadvantage of a poor position in the forest. Essential nutrients injected into one tree can be detected, transported to another tree, in more need of them, some distance away."

Megan sensed the studio audience, whose attention generally flitted like a teenager hearing her phone beep, were hushed. Almost tense. A small number walked out. "And professor, can I ask what's your response to scientists that say vegetables, trees, can't have intelligence or feelings as they don't have a nervous system?"

"Well Megan I would make two points: Firstly, it's not I saying our Earth plants are intelligent – rather, it is obviously intelligent aliens that have said so. Secondly, my work is on communication rather than intelligence. However, I do not believe the lack of an animal-model nervous system rules out a type of intelligence. Nature – it is said – finds a way. We do not say ants and plants cannot breathe because they have no lungs. Evolution finds the means to perform the same functions with the different starting materials." (A little political satire was usually as close to controversy as this stalwart of American television came. Mentioning evolution on live television had some viewers reaching for their remote controls.)

"And can I ask you, Professor – the aliens – were you surprised? What happens next?"

"Oh yes, most surprised. It is not so shocking to me that these beings are in some ways like plants and in some like animals. As I said before, they are not of the earth – our labels do not apply. Plants are life forms that produce their food from sunlight – why should that mean they have no intelligence, no sensory apparatus, and no communication?" Megan nodded, and Niels continued, "and so it seems these strange life forms can communicate with the trees of the earth and with us. It is most amazing, and we all need more informations."

"You can say that again," said *The Tonight Show* host, and then turning to the audience, "Please thank Professor Niels Larsson."

Watching the broadcast in a distant office of an organisation that may or may not exist, a black-suited man picked up a phone and dialled a secure number.

Chapter 13 “Fox not Fox?”

“Where’s the vet?” queried one of Jess’ less avid *CCE* watching housemates. “They kill him?”

“Try to keep up mate,” said Rob. “He got voted off last Sunday night. It’s nearly time for the next one.”

“Huh. Aren’t they captive?”

“Nah, the aliens want the show to go on – in its original format – making edicts and shit. Like in the ads.”

“Weird.”

*

The ubiquitous scent of mango lingered on the outdoor dining table and on the juice-sticky fingers of five celebrities. For the uninitiated, watching TV personalities plant avocado and mango seeds seemed an unlikely premise for the world’s most popular show.

Returning with the fruit-stained bucket, Matt remained discouraged by the vet’s elimination. Ironically, it has been Paul’s idea to “Pay the fruit tax.” Now, as Len put it, “We’ve come over all vegetally minded,” and under approving alien supervision, the remaining cast members planted the seeds of their consumed fruits daily.

Matt dropped the bucket at the dining table and wandered off to sit in the shade of one of the lodge’s tasteful low-rise cabins. The one with the matched set of Balinese demon masks. He wasn’t alone with them for long. Trailed by a crew member, the least alarming alien approached.

“How’s it going?” nodded Matt.

"Self enjoyed the fused hydrogen particles of dawn – thanked energy source without slaying it."

"Excellent."

The leaf-creature lowered its synthetic voice, "Strange, yet curiously pleasing humans so enjoy the light-gathers – pay the fruit tithe."

"Yeah, it feels somehow appropriate. Kind of thanking the food."

"Fruits be reproductive parts light-gatherers?"

"Apparently," said Matt idly making patterns in the dirt.

"Additional: eggs, lactation fluids, testicles be reproduction produce?"

"What! Humans don't eat test—" He ceased drawing circles on the ground. *Do you think we have a thing about those bits? Maybe we do.* He changed the subject a little, "Do your youngsters, your babies, look the same as you?"

The alien folded itself on the ground companionably close to him. "Negative in initial instance."

"Oh. What happens?" he said, looking the leaf-creature directly in its eyestalks.

"Metamorphosis following interval aquatic aspect."

"Ok. Like a frog or a mosquito larva?" said Matt. He swallowed, thinking, *Eek! was that insulting?*

But there was no need for alarm.

"No accurate earth-life-form parallels." It paused; it made the static sound: "Sentience emerges following pupae aspect."

"Cool, like a cocoon, right?" said Matt.

"Affirmative," came the reply.

"And what about sex? You know, are there two types? Like I'm different to Kalinda – who is, by the way, a total fox," added the comedian, waving his hands about suggestively for emphasis.

The light-forager rippled its antenna, it directed its eyestalks this way and that. It made the modem noise. "Visual-logical error fox reference." All its eyes now arched towards Matt.

"Sorry, not an actual fox … figure of speech thing. Ignore me. Does your, err species, have two sexes?"

"Inexact parallel. Hermaphrodite mode and parthenogenesis also as ecologically necessitated."

Wish Paul was still here. We need a tree guy. Maybe if I'd paid more attention in science. He continued scratching (different) patterns in the dirt.

"And you live for a real long time? Like long enough to watch every David Attenborough nature documentary ever made?"

"Affirmative." The vegetal creature re-arranged itself, and the conversation continued.

Chapter 14 Coffee to Go?

Ash smiled patiently as the first timer considered the many options. Like the twirly tail of a cat – opting between serious pouncing and a good lie down in an appealing sunbeam – the customer considered.

"Err, I'll have the almond milk decaf cappuccino and a blueberry Danish."

"Sure," said Ash, busying herself with the gleaming steel and copper apparatus behind the counter. The part-time barista, waiter and forestry student glanced at a clock. The décor of the Retro Bean didn't lack for clocks. Pacific Northwest coffee culture was thriving in Corvallis, and the café attracted its share of the university's staff and students.

Including the uni's newly famous academic – Ash's lecturer, Professor Niels. She glanced again at a clock. Since she'd brought Niels' attention to the *Cairns Declaration,* they'd had a few chats about the aliens. Including their potential attitudes to coffee.

Upon hearing *The Declaration* some people feared for civilisation itself, others more narrowly for their own lives. Many wondered simply what they would eat. Whereas Ash had said, "Hey, maybe I'm weird professor, but when I first saw those TV aliens, I was mainly worried about the availability of espresso!"

Niels toyed with the sugar bowl and a faint smile.

Prof, you can be hard to read. "Joke," explained Ash.

"Well Ashley, broadly speaking coffee farming seems to have the necessary *ahimsa*."

"Fingers crossed. But just in case – how about a Caffe Gommosa?"

"Err, which one was that?"

"It's the house special professor: A single espresso shot over a marshmallow."

That last time, just before the Canadian footage release, Niels was unsure whether the alien menace might yet prove to be the marketing work of Aussie brewers. He was, however, sure in his coffee preferences. Niels shuddered, "No thank-you Ashley, just a Caffe latte."

*From an exotic origin story involving Sufi monasteries in Yemen, coffee had spread its charms around the world in the following five hundred years. Less charmingly, mass production in Brazil and elsewhere had involved slavery and more latterly concerns over child labour and economic exploitation. The fair-trade movement, it now appeared, had to contend with yet another moral minefield before enjoying a macchiato, affogato or Caffe Medici**.

With another glance at a clock, Ash made herself a double shot cappuccino in her KeepCup, waved to her co-workers and headed off to catch the professor's lecture. Given recent events, it ought to be huge.

* Another Pacific Northwest speciality comprising a double shot of espresso over chocolate syrup and fresh orange peel topped with whipped cream!

Chapter 15 The Lecture

Niels waited indulgently for the elderly Saab to run through its diagnostic routine. *Perhaps I should cycle.* But it was days since the car's last outing, and it wasn't wise to allow it to lose confidence. Well-practiced fingers tapped at the console, dismissing the usual self-deprecating list of faults.

Minutes later he drove past the red brick extravaganza of the Weatherford Hall student accommodation. The hall's historic poise contrasted with Oregon State's newer, Forestry Faculty buildings. Niels eased the vehicle into its accustomed parking space.

Ah, there's the Dean. He heard a smattering of applause as he exited the car.

The Dean hustled Niels towards the north courtyard entry, the Swede half listening to a tirade on his insufficiency of university promotion. Today's intended lecture was a general intro to botany and plant taxonomy for first-year environmental science students. Niels nodded to the audience, *Gosh, people are standing in the aisles.* He saw a student group filming proceedings. The noise level rose … *Ah, WPL2* (irregular and light, but enthusiastic whooping).

The black-suited man sat in the front row; Ash scurried in clutching her coffee and stood at the back. The Dean hovered importantly.

Niels' footsteps echoed in the lull as he took his position. *Should I acknowledge the many non-students and media presence?*

It was that old 'your dog has its nose in my crotch conundrum'. Ignore the unsought interest, or appreciate the enthusiasm?

Five minutes in, Niels sensed the restlessness. Taxonomic features separating mosses from ferns weren't holding the crowd's interest. Many of the audience appeared confused (although he was familiar with this). Even the fascinating lineage of the Ginkgo failed to excite the crowd.

"Professor," interrupted the black and orange T-shirted student, "do you believe plants have feelings and communication like animals?"

"Well, *my* work concerns communication and interactions among trees of importance in forestry industries," said Niels. "Other researchers have shown *communication* among various plants studied. However, feelings aren't something I try to define or measure in plant interactions – they are so different from us – alien, I might say in present circumstances."

The audience murmured, and Niels continued, "I don't presume that worms or jellyfish or beetles have feelings, or if they do, that I can relate to them, or them to me. These questions are best addressed in other circumstances, yes."

"Oh, given the present state of affairs we can make other arrangements for the introductory taxonomy professor," announced the Dean, with a glance at the cameras. He sensed an opportunity to let his media dependency out and exercise it a bit. "Would you care to talk to your latest research?"

Niels sensed an overwhelming murmur of assent from the audience. "Okay, yes," he nodded. He approached the audio-visual control panel and located a relevant third-year lecture. After a brief struggle with the technology, he recommenced.

"So … the family life of trees. Such an interesting area, as we will see. In species, such as willow, millions of tiny seeds are made, carried by the wind and never seen again by the parent. They are not rearing them, they are not *putting them through college*, no."

"But other trees, for example, the oaks and the beeches, are making larger seeds or nuts," he continued – reaching his arms high. "*Plonk* go these acorns," said Niels, dropping his arms, and mimicking something more akin to a coconut. "Too big to carry on the wind, they land under the parent tree. *In the shade.* And yet," he extended a finger and waved it, "a tree, young or old, needs light to make sugar to fuel its activities." (Plants lacking access to energy drinks and donuts have instead come up with the process of photosynthesis.)

Niels waved his hands at waist level, "In an undisturbed forest, a small tree this high, is a teenager – it's not wanting to borrow the car's keys thankyou – it's just waiting for a chance to grow. Their time scales are not ours."

"Okay, so here's the thing – if we inject the tracer isotopes such as carbon-14 into the parent tree, we can detect them in the offspring trees. We can track the chain of energy transfer from the parent through their roots, into the roots of the young trees, and finally into the fresh growth."

The audience murmured again as Niels displayed the various informational slides. Regression analysis of radioactive tracer molecules is not everyone's cup of tea and following a brief period can reduce the desire to live.

Then the audience sighed with relief. The next slides were images of tree stumps in various states of decrepitude. With this they felt they could cope. The researcher continued, "And eventually, maybe after four or five hundred years … it's sad, but the parent tree dies. It breaks up, it rots, and nothing remains but the stump. Sometimes just a hollow ring of stump. Such as this," said Niels, showing the current slide, "no branches, no leaves, no way to make its food. Ah, but sometimes, just sometimes they are still alive. Kept alive by nutrient flow from the surrounding trees."

"Cool and surprising, yes?" enthused Niels. "Genetic analysis shows these are the offspring of the stump, and as before, tracer chemicals show movement of sugar from tree to tree through roots and interconnecting fungi. And so, there is evidence of intergenerational care through nutrient flow. This has been shown in trees here in North America and Europe. We have done part of this work at the College's McDonald-Dunn Forest Reserve, not far from here. It has enjoyable walks and interesting trees, also an arboretum."

The audience raised a multitude of hands – showing their student owners, like trees, were curious and more responsive to stimuli than often supposed.

"Yes please", said Niels, to a front-row student with the sturdy and well-fed look of an offensive linesman.

"Professor, if trees have families, emotions, and feelings. How do we deal with that?"

"Well, I suggest with respect and an inquiring mind." Niels paused, "You know the Swiss constitution says something like: 'The dignity of plants, animals and other organisms should be considered when handling them'. Personally, I say – don't go cutting down five-thousand-year-old bristlecone pines and don't eat endangered sea turtles. If I shall continue …" continued the lecturer displaying a series of tree images on the screen.

"We have seen examples of communication and sharing among species of the same kind, even the same family, but interestingly here in the Pacific Northwest and in southern Sweden studies have found *interspecies* co-operation. Labelling and tracing molecules through the trees, we discovered these Douglas firs …" said Niels, indicating the slide, "are receiving nutrition from these birches. Wow, seriously – why are they doing this? Perhaps there will be a test later! Actually yes – if you're enrolled in this course."

Niels took a sip of water, "And so, we did more measurements and were more puzzled. But this is how the learnings proceed and we discovered the flow of carbon goes both ways. So that sometimes the Douglas firs are feeding the beeches. Likewise, in Sweden, birch and spruce were shown taking turns to exchange nutrients. Their abilities complement, smoothing out seasonal difficulties. They are like a team – such as Rocky and Bullwinkle or Rocket and Groot. Even more – forests are a network of connections – you have heard of this: 'wood wide web.'"

With an uncertain half raising of his arm, an honours student standing halfway back said, "More an observation than a question Professor Larsson, but speaking to the topic of alien life forms … have you seen the movie *Avatar*!"

"Yes, I know what you are meaning," said Niels, recognising a kindred spirit in the comment. "Although, I do not think our forests can yet summon scary panther creatures or moose beasts to defend them! But, yes, an undisturbed forest is a kind of super-organism. By cooperating, the trees reduce the risks of drying out, soil erosion, temperature fluctuation, wind damage, and so forth – this happens when one of their companions gets damaged, and a gap in the canopy occurs. As in football, if there's a hole in the offensive line the whole team suffers when the quarterback gets squashed by a three-hundred-pound defensive tackle."

"Professor Larsson," began the Dean, who did not care for Niels' sense of humour or indeed humour in any sense. (Sure, he was aware of the concept – but you could say the same for cannibalism.) "Could you talk to plant intelligence?"

Niels explained the term itself was controversial when applied to plants. He pointed out that plants adapting to seasonal changes – by, for instance – dropping and regrowing their leaves, must measure time.

"If I tickle a single trigger hair of my office Venus flytrap, the leaf doesn't close." He lent towards the audience demonstrating correct flytrap tickling technique. "Ah, but if I touch more than one, the trap shuts … so," he said, snapping his hands together. "This means, yes, the plant can count."

Niels heard the audience grow quiet; there were indistinct grumblings, and a few walked out. In an even tone he said, "Much may be new and thought provoking yes?" Niels shook his head, "And there are those that don't care for the provoking of the thoughts."

This was to continue as Niels described classic Pavlovian conditioning with peas, blue light, and air movement instead of the familiar: dog, food, bell arrangement. A shocking paradigm shift for much of the audience.

"It is not so difficult to see the time telling, counting, learning in *relatable* fast-moving plants. Buy a mimosa, play with it at home!" he urged.

"Err," came the query, "Why have we not heard these things before?"

"An interesting question. You know it was one hundred and forty years ago Charles Darwin wrote of plant movement and suggested that the root tip acts like the brain of a simple animal. Some of his other work may have overshadowed this." Niels smiled, "And in the early 1970s there was quite a popular book called *The Secret Life of Plants* … the claims it made regarding plant learning and intelligence were – shall I say – controversial and perhaps made this field of study appear a little crazy."

Niels took another sip of water, "But there's a bias in research against plants unless it involves them *being useful* to us. To many of us, the idea of photosynthetic aliens doesn't seem right." *Although*, he mused, *at least they're not chasing and eating us*. "Also," said Niels, coming around the front of the lecture desk and sitting on it, "scientists haven't been so good at communicating ourselves. The internet is all adorable pandas and puppies … not so much news about plants. It's so difficult to compete for attention with the sports and remakes of superhero movies."

Niels continued his veering from the prepared lecture, "Trees and plants are so different from us, it is difficult to relate … many live so long and so *slowly*. Yet why should greenness, lack of mobility and a rigid cell wall mean no communication and no intelligence? Does what we eat show *our* intelligence? Hmm, well clearly yes, if we are eating nothing but the Cheese Whiz!"

The audience chortled and relaxed.

Diverging yet further from the planned lecture, the professor continued:

"There's a relationship between trees and wisdom in our human cultures. In Scandinavian legends, Odin, the father of the gods, sacrifices himself from a great tree in exchange for wisdom. This is surely against faculty rules," Niels peered at the dean. The audience tittered, and he continued:

"The Garden of Eden had a Tree of Knowledge, and Buddha found wisdom under the Sacred Fig or Bodhi tree. And, in Swedish, we have the same word for both book and for beech." He slid off the swirly grained desk, stood again and said, "Almost, we're out of time. One last question?"

From the front the Dean said, “Professor, what is your perspective on this alien *Declaration*? Can we communicate and negotiate with them? Is it possible for us to survive if they can enforce their conditions?”

“I did not until recently believe this news could be reliable, and our civilisation depends on plants in so many ways. It is plain the aliens – these vegetal beings – can communicate with us if they choose. If this Declaration is enforceable, it will take time for us to adapt. *If* the alien perspective is akin to that of long-lived trees, we may have such time.”

As the applause subsided, Niels rescheduled the taxonomy lecture. The dean and the man in black were the only audience members wearing suits. Their aura of self-importance and faint menace (more from the one than the other) dissuaded others from lingering near the rostrum.

“That went well, Professor Larsson.”

“There came many extra students to the lecture,” said Niels.

“Not only students,” said the man in black, “I’m Agent Peters.”

He produced the smile from the correct anatomical structures – yet somehow it just didn’t work.

Chapter 16 Liberate the Geraniums

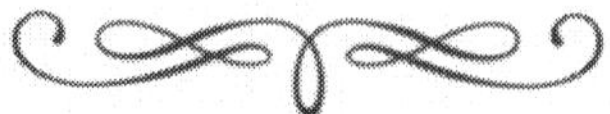

The casual Channel Five viewer might well have wondered why a celebrity carpenter-gardener was delivering plants; plants housed in a diversity of pots, to the Lodge compound. Producer Maggie was nothing if not adaptable. With the demise of the paddleboard race, the backup Week Three plan called for 'survival' contests such as eating toasted, recalcitrant bugs. The idea took flight in much the way that cassowaries don't. The cast proving as recalcitrant as the bugs.

Then, inspiration struck: Since the great ratings spike, homeowners had been abandoning their indoor plants. There was a feeling the inside foliage couldn't be trusted. In the last week, viewers had driven all manner of pot plants to the *CCE* perimeter and abandoned them. Maggie consulted the alien co-stars and made the call. Once more, they lifted the lethal barrier.

In a cross-promotional masterstroke, the liberally muscled and tattooed host of *Tradie Rescue* ('tradie' being Australian slang for a bricklayer, carpenter, electrician, or other worker legitimately requiring the wearing of orange fluoro vests), strode into the *CCE* clearing. Len and the others, except Mariam, recognised a fellow celebrity. But their enthusiasm was short-lived. The producer had forbidden guests from discussing news of the outside world.

"Davo maaate good to see you," boomed Len. "How's the world out there?"

"Ah, youse know the rules, can't be saying much about that." Armed with endless misplaced confidence, 'Davo' Hudson was comfortable in the alien presence. "How're you going?" he asked one.

"Self combines water, light, CO2. Produces oxygen fuels this world."

"Good on ya."

Lenny leaned on a shovel as Davo showed the basics of hole digging, planting, watering, and sundry pot-plant liberating activities. He grinned as Holly explained: "The contestant planting the smallest number of pot plants is eligible for elimination. Begin," she beamed.

"Liberate the captive ones. Let the light foragers weave the earth weft," declared the *hasty* alien.

The idea of competition breaks down somewhat when the prize for losing is removal from TV captivity with lethal alien co-stars. Len and the celebs went to work – without haste. The pile of discarded black plastic tubs, terracotta pots, and repurposed half wine barrels grew, but slowly. Nervous celebrities sought Davo's advice; they wielded digging implements, they puzzled over uncertain shrubberies.

Watched by the aliens, the comedian's nerves shrilled and squeaked like a fearful porpoise. They were nearly halfway through the show's season. *How do we handle the weekly declarations?* he thought, wiping dirt from his knees. The mute alien waved its antennae and twitched its multiple appendages. This Matt took to mean: 'Dig a bigger hole and be careful with that rubber tree.'

Disturbed by the pace of progress and lack of expertise, the vegetal creature dug holes with inhuman strength. Len raised his heavy brows at Matt and muttered, "I didn't sign up to liberate bloody geraniums!"

"Yeah, we need a tree guy."

The hasty alien ceased its leaf-wing twitching and rippled antennae at Matt.

Meanwhile, Kalinda advised, "Vito, I think it's best not to plant ferns in full sun."

He mopped his face with a spotted handkerchief, "I'm more a kitchen gardener."

Len took another rest, and an alien wiped a small leaf wing under its eyestalks. It didn't sweat, but with enough provocation, every species must wipe its furrowed-brow-equivalent. The multiple-eyed beings had seen enough. With their precise gait, Len watched them set off for the production centre.

"You want what?"

The trio's request surprised and delighted Maggie. Her crew looked on fearfully as she negotiated off-camera: insisting only on secrecy from the *CCE* contestants.

The crew filmed the required short promotional segment.

Chapter 17 The Crescent City Incident

Everyone loves Redwood Trees. And cars. Joe McKenna shifted gear. The fog was lifting now. He'd just visited one of those massive trees with a car tunnel. In former times this was someone's idea of nature tourism

To be clear – Joe didn't approve of this. Nor of skiing behind recalcitrant sea turtles or setting off for a spot of weekend whale fishing. After a pleasant winding-road-drive, Joe, an exponent of the simple pleasure of hiking, arrived at his next stop. As he descended the steps, he paused only to contemplate, that whoever had named the Del Norte State Park's Damnation Creek trail was likely unimpressed by the services of marketing consultants.

The thousand-foot descent to the sea and its photogenic rock arch offered neither Wi-Fi nor cappuccino sourcing opportunities. Entire days passed where it seemed to the resident redwoods that nothing much happened. At least nothing much involving humans.

In many-pocketed pants, Joe trod the path.

The air was still, other than the erratic fluttering of butterflies, and there was just the correct quota of morning fog to impart a sense of ancient woody mystery. The hiker was soon out of sight and sound of the twenty-first century.

In a movie version of events, music in a minor key accompanied the sudden absence of butterflies: cueing the audience – if not the proponent – it was time to cling to popcorn or a sweetheart. Butterflies have sensitive dispositions and prefer to avoid conflict (unlike their party-animal moth cousins). But, in this case, they needn't have worried. Joe's mouth gaped unbecomingly; however, the sudden alien didn't react – it's disregard almost insulting.

Humanity still hadn't come up with an agreed name for the vegetal creatures – let alone a collective noun for the hundreds of them standing in the forest ahead. Joe spun round and spotted dozens more. Appalled and bewildered, like a middle-aged man abandoned in a Junior Miss lingerie department, he kept his eyes down and pretended it wasn't happening.

The hiker's heart pounded in his chest – either aiding Joe's body, or possibly attempting to escape it. He retraced his steps at speed.

Not the most interesting of human-forest interactions, thought the closest tree as Joe scurried away.

Nothing like the human-bear encounters of earlier centuries, mused one old timer.

Back at the road, Joe had never been so pleased to be inside a car, nor so eager to embrace top gear.

*

Peace returned to the area.

Until three days later, when a squadron of F-22 Raptors flew low over False Klamath, rattling windows. There hadn't been such excitement in town since a banana slug menaced old Mrs Gibson, near her fridge in the spring of 1998. Meanwhile, an aircraft carrier appeared off Crescent City's Battery Point Light.

Drone surveillance had shown a thousand aliens between the coast and Route 101. Evidently, the extra-terrestrials also loved redwoods, but sadly this wasn't enough for a meaningful relationship. For a few seconds, the planes defended the area for democracy and a free-market economy, producing woodchips at an extraordinary rate*.

*Unknown to the rest of the world, the alien beset dawn redwood groves of western China had been similarly defended into smouldering heaps in the name of a free-market economy and a one-party state

Oh, what's that? mused a startled abalone. It felt a curious electrical tickle in its foot, then an F-22 joined it on the rocky, kelp-stippled seabed. Later one of its fellows commented, "Interesting isn't it: without power ships still float, planes not so much."

Activating the 'Office of Denial and Let's Never Mention This Again' wasn't an option. Covering up a sheepishly drifting Nimitz-class aircraft carrier was rated especially tricky. Instead, following the lead of Australian authorities, the Occupational Health and Reassurance Department swung into action. It established the usual perimeters and reassurances.

Hundreds of agents arrived.

Within hours of the abalone startling events in northern California special agent, Cam Peters of the NSSA (National Shadowy Science Agency) was on the phone to Niels.

"… yes, it will be most interesting. No, no, I will take my car." *And I'd assist without thinly veiled threats of persecution, thank you.* Niels judged the Saab capable of the five-hour trip south. He roused it, and together they left behind Corvallis' city limits the following morning.

Niels passed through compact towns that supplied everything a traveller could need – provided that was a firearm or a wood carving. *Ah, a museum with a café. What's that nice blue and green tree motif flag*? Gravel crunched as he pulled over. *Oh my God*, the scientist barely knew where to look – although the five-metre bear sculpture was an arresting starting point.

"Biggest damn leather bear in Oregon," said a voice with a proprietary air and a nicely faded *Guns 'n Roses* T-shirt.

Wow! Are there additional leather bears striving for the distinction? thought Niels. Followed by, *Damn, so wish I didn't say that out loud.*

But, puzzled by Niels' accent, the keeper of the museum simply said, "Coffee sir?"

"Rather urgently."

Niels was the only customer and sipped his espresso by the display of two-handed sixty-eight-inch crosscut saws. *Rusty but Nice*, he approved, (a regular visitor to all six of Sweden's forestry museums).

The museum and its surrounds housed old tools, tech, and the spoils of a hundred yard sales. He examined displays on the Oregon Trail and the Pacific Northwest independence movement. *Ooh, an early twentieth century whittling set.* And next to that, a corner devoted to local UFO sightings. Niels bent closer: The papier mâché model's peeling label identified it as an alien landing craft, sighted by ten-year-old Billy Jarman in 1997.

*

"Really, all this?" Hours later, issued with a wrist band, a couple of ID lanyards and a biohazard suit, Niels entered the incursion site. He resembled a clean-up crew member at Glastonbury Music Festival. Security admitted him to the similarly attired presence of Special Agent Peters.

Once more Peters had emerged from his laboratory lair – two hundred foot under a sandstone hill in Arizona. Like a movie arch-villain, he paced as he monologued, pausing only to invite minions to agree with his pronouncements.

Niels itched and perspired inside the suit. Disarticulated bits of alien carapace and appendages crunched underfoot. Their blood was pale blue, the flesh white and fibrous – the colour and texture of raw coconut – hard to see against the gloves.

"Have a look at this, Professor."

Extracted from mangled vegetal beings, most of the phones had the sad appearance of a device fished from a back pocket at Glastonbury.

Niels stared.

The alien tendrilled co-opting of human technology was shocking.

"This is what they meant in *CCE* Week Two by 'articulate mechanism assimilation phone app'" said a minion. Her tone suggested recall of each and every televised alien utterance.

Away from the orbit of Special Agent Peters, the mood was more relaxed – resembling an undergraduate field trip. Niels fell into step with a burly, tunelessly humming man, who admitted to working for the Advanced Aviation Threat Identification Project.

"Saw you on the *Tonight Show*, nice ref to confirmation bias by the way."

"Err, thanks."

"Seen any ETs before these?"

"No, these are my first live aliens … well, you know what I am meaning. And you?"

The fellow waved a mysterious looking probe, "Small scale stuff only."

"Um," said Niels, "do you know what they're *doing* with all their camera guys and equipment?"

"The NSSA death eaters? Hah! The usual: tech, weapons, exobiology research … plausible deniability—"

"Deniability?"

"You know, shoot some footage, make it appear the entire thing was deep faked – *if* they decide to go that way."

Niels attempted to scratch his head through the helmet. "That is so wrong, people want certainty and knowledge – anyway it can't work."

The fellow scoffed, "People don't want certainty and knowledge, not if it upsets their existing beliefs. It might work if there's no more aliens – *if* this is all she wrote."

"Err?"

"This is the game-changer – not just food, flowers, building materials and religion." He stopped waving his probe and turned to face Niels. "Purpose, yeah! What if there's more to life than owning the latest sneakers hewn from the blood of third world kiddies?"

Gosh, a philosopher. And a very chatty one – perhaps they don't let him out often. Niels cleared his throat, "Awful to see this," he said as he moved among the burnt and blasted remains of mature coast redwoods collecting alien specimens. His shoes now black with ash. "Are *you* finding what you search for?"

"Not a trace of extra-terrestrial tech." He displayed fragments of phones, "The new opiate of the masses. Wonder how Apple feels about our unearthly visitors using their devices," grinned the fellow.

"You should check out the alien spaceship model I saw on my way here," joked Niels, describing the treasures of the little museum. "Hey, at least you guys will now be having new aliens to put in your secret alien storage facility."

His companion smiled enigmatically and ambled away to search deeper in the remaining forest.

*

Hours later, Niels attended a debriefing session at a lodge near Crescent City's harbour front.

"... Now, this flow chart illustrates the role of the NSSA in liaison with other federal bodies..."

Niels reached for the pad supplied and began doodling a bentwood chair.

Occasionally, a snippet of useful information was revealed. "... we believe their static sound correlates with internet access." Or something such as "... the aliens likely see ultraviolet."

However, it disconcerted the forester to keep hearing the aliens referred to as plants. He tilted his chair back, toying with the balance point.

Buy bread, Niels scribbled as the next speaker began. An inconclusive analysis of electromagnetic activity before, during and after the assault on the unsuspecting light gatherers, had him reaching for the pad again. He started sketching a papier mâché alien transport device.

Ooh, what are those?

Niels suspended the sketch, as the next presenter displayed remnants of alien clawed feet. "Analysis shows calcified keratin combined with a carbon polymer. Note, they are extremely hard and hollow. The aliens push these soft reception tendrils through into the ground ..."

With the misplaced confidence of Napoleon off for the weekend to invade Russia, Special Agent Peters concluded that the might of the combined security services had the situation under control. *You're rather glossing over the aliens arriving and departing without detection,* thought Niels. *And what of disabling fighter planes and an aircraft carrier*? With a flourish, he finished his sketch of the museum's UFO model.

The wise reader will have noted that life is full of extraordinary connections and coincidences.

If Niels hadn't at a whim stopped at a roadside museum, *then* he wouldn't have seen young Billy's model, *and* if the debriefing had been more compelling, *then* the scientist wouldn't have drawn the sketch, but *if* Special Agent Peters had wandered into the audience, *then* he would have recognised the sketch's resemblance to the Wollemi pics supplied by the Australians – which he'd kept secret (just habit). And thus, though a pencil sketch of an alien landing craft was drawn, the conclusion that the extra-terrestrials had visited Earth before was not.

A statement of reassurance was issued mentioning a now-under-control alien incursion "incident" involving minimal casualties (and information release) near Crescent City. In light of the subsequent invasion of the country's great national parks, the government assembled a crack team of experts to keep up with demand for reassurance statements.

Chapter 18 Disturbance of the Sea Lions

A lone Central Park Precinct cop cocked his head and arranged his features into a subtly more annoyed expression. *Stupid fish.* The sea lions were at it again. *Stupid barking. Stupid rain.* 'Easy-going, polite, helpful': such words were not routinely applied to "Big Jim" O'Halloran.

Deep in the winding pathways of the Rambles, Jim tensed, listened again, rounded the path, and in his belligerent tone demanded, "Whaddya think you're doing here?"

The 'out-of-towner' peered disdainfully with multiple eye stalks.

Jim shifted his boot out of a puddle. *Huh – that the best you got? Try talking to the grandkids about music.* With a casual approach to peril he growled, "Wait till the union hears about this."

An hour later, park staff discovered him, unharmed, unbowed, and intricately spun into a cocoon incorporating charming fibre art flourishes and a smattering of park litter.

Calls were made.

By mid-morning, Jim's niece, Ebony, a local blogger, had rushed to the park. She had a great story with a family angle to chase.

"Here you go, honey," she said, reaching down and passing the necessary ice cream. The park was now sunny and stunning. Ebony smiled at the wandering tourists, still secretly hoping to encounter the cast of *Friends*.

"Mom."

"What is it, Anne-Maree?"

"Why are the sea lions unhappy?"

Around them carefree people skated, jogged, and queued to regard the still unsettled sea lions. Wise, indifferent turtles glinted in their ponds. As mid-day approached, couples sat and lay next to each other on the lawns. Some lay more or less on top of each other.

Later, mom and daughter, impossibly cute, skipped towards Strawberry Fields. "Hey! careful please!" squawked Ebony.

She pulled her daughter from his path as the young man shrieked, "Oh my Gosh!" and dashed away in a fashion that didn't suggest regular athletic achievement.

Ebony approached the less excitable but wary crowd.

"I can't see, mom."

Ebony lifted her daughter up, "You're getting *so* big! You see them?"

"Aliens mommy, real TV aliens."

Mom and daughter watched the small group of light gatherers from the edge of the crowd. Confusingly, their visit wasn't to admire the mosaics or pay homage to the slain Beatle. Rather, to commune with the young dawn redwoods and have a pleasant bask in the sun.

Ebony joined the collective texting and selfie taking. Soon the tension eased, and the onlookers became restless. *This* was the first urban sighting, and the light gatherers were a disappointment; failing to work the crowd. The cry went up, 'We're breaking the internet.' Of late, the internet had been much 'broken' by news of alien antics. For many, a welcome change from being 'broken' by shapely portions of celebrity anatomy.

Perfect strangers around Ebony made amiable eye contact and exchanged information: Aliens had appeared across the park, from Harlem Meer to The Pond, and even around the paved, elm-lined Mall.

Not to imply New Yorkers didn't much care about the 'whole alien invasion thing' but there was a notion if the drama wanted to be taken seriously it needed to come to the Big Apple. (Far away Australia … hmm. Remote forests … yeah. The Pacific Northwest … so?) Thousands poured into the park, as did the police and National Guard.

The situation speedily resembled that around the Cassowary Lodge alien incursion site, but with rather more street performers and firearms.

"I can't see mom," complained Anne-Maree.

"Yes, it's getting squishy," Ebony shouldered her bag. "Let's go, we'll come back when it quieter."

*

Scores of guns clicked merrily into unsafe mode as certain folk attacked the aliens with handguns, mace, tasers, small dogs, and whatever else New Yorkers keep in their handbags. Soon the aliens were assaulted with every type of semi-automatic rifle and recreational grenade. Taken by surprise, higher calibre armaments could wound and even kill the visitors. But, in those seconds of mayhem, the indignant leaf creatures unleashed electro-static violence, disrupting nerve pathways. As electric current surged through bodies, those same bodies collapsed (in line with Ohms law pertaining to electricity, rather than his lesser known meditation mantras).

Chaos ensued. The sea lions affronted now by gunfire flapped their flippers and barked; the ground grew sticky with dropped ice creams; scores of people lay unbloodied but lifeless, or terminally befuddled. Others lay more stickily dead – shot by their fellows in secondary disputes and crossfire. When it was over, there wasn't enough chalk to do the traditional outlines and so many bodies lay on grass that it was all deemed too tricky.

Confusion and uncertainty reigned. Certain authorities considered launching an attack on the area with extreme prejudice – but others felt there was already sufficient prejudice. Many preferred the park as it was, not reduced to smouldering rubble.

Ebony's mom love nyc blog surged in popularity. Local news made passing mention of alien visitations in others of the world's great urban parks: Stanley Park, Beihai, Monsanto, Hyde, Ibirapuera, Park Güell, and many more over the coming weeks.

A walk in the park would never be quite the same.

Chapter 19 To the Sun

"We're missing one?"

"Yes, dad, they eliminated the Italian chef* Sunday night."

"Killed him, eh?"

"No," Jess shook her head, "Voted off. After the last edict – the one about firewood."

Bob Kelly grinned, "Just messin' with you. You know Jess, when your Mum and me first started watching, I didn't recognize big Lenny Madden. The blond mullet's gone, thank god."

Jess shrugged, "Before my time."

Once more Jess was tuned to *CCE,* this time at her parents' cane farm. The startling arrival of thousands of mostly mute aliens in the great urban parks of the world had further intensified the focus on the show.

"Have you two seen any aliens?" she asked.

"No dear, but old Sam Martello says he saw one near the river."

"Probably on the turps," said Bob.

*

On set nearest to Matt, two aliens stood with insectile poise. At a conspicuous, cautious distance sat Mariam and Lenny. *Will you stop glaring Len,* thought Matt. Without the edit, *CCE* viewing would've made surprisingly dull television: long awkward pauses punctuated by hesitant interactions, confusion, and occasional alarm.

---

*The chef's bruised ego was tempered by being a thousand kilometres from the Cassowary Lodge. That, and the sense of business opportunity. His alien-compliant food advice *Vito's Veto* soon became the world's most downloaded app.

"So, we're not at war?" Matt's tone suggested an amiable discussion of favourite shared relatives.

"War not mandated."

"But your kind will interfere with human activities when they harm plants?" said Kalinda evenly.

"Affirmative, not necessitated when important persons issue compliance directives." Matt gulped and observed Mariam withdraw further into her headscarf.

The less alarming plant creature: the one with the leaf edge sculpting and the small feathery antennae broke the silence. "Please not to fret. Self is your …" (it made the static noise), "colonisation consultant."

"Invasion consultant more like," muttered Lenny, having trouble with his irregular verb conjugation.

*

The stress of the situation was drawing Kalinda and Matt together. Certain situations draw people together and being held captive on alien-invaded TV shows is numbered among them. The following morning, they sought solace and privacy from the cameras by the pond in the forest.

"Matt, it's kind of strange. I mean, wouldn't you expect alien beings to be better briefed?"

"Yeah, me too, I brought that up with the friendlier one. If I understood, it said their political guys don't listen to the scouts, and IT had a lot on, skipped the last five hundred years and had a pleasant stand around in the suns."

Kalinda smiled, and Matt glimpsed again the cute little gap between her front teeth. "You get on well with them – or at least the *consultant* one," she said, brushing a leaf or two from her T-shirt. "Kind of taking on a leadership role even."

Matt shuddered and pushed back his floppy hair in the way an ex had assured him was adorable. "Kalinda, some people are born to responsibility, they go to private schools, get voted Wi-Fi monitor at an early age, err…"

"Matt, didn't you go to a private school?"

Matt raised his eyebrows and poked at moss. "We need help. These bloody edicts …"

A rustling in the undergrowth broke their privacy. Trailed by a camera crew, the least threatening alien entered the clearing. "Fine quality sunshine." It rippled its antennae. "Are your physiologies optimal and compatible?"

Self-consciously, the two humans wriggled further apart.

"Ah yes, thank-you," began Matt. "Much surplus sunshine here," he waved at the dappled and pond-reflected light. "Enjoy."

The musician smiled at the alien and said, "Think I'll go for a run."

Matt hoped she was out of earshot when the leaf creature remarked: "Untruth spoken language fox observation comrade?"

"Err, yes, that's the one." He recalled her bio:

Kalinda Ryan came to national attention, winning the first season of Channel Five's *Australian Sing Star* by a wide margin. Local fame and success followed. Her stage persona and musical taste weren't exactly old school rock-and-roll. Matt found her uncommonly level-headed. Obviously, he also found her hot.

Matt cupped his hands in the cool water and took a drink. Then another. The leaf-creature extrude a sinuous tendril into the pond. *Must be drinking – Hell! I hope it's drinking.* The celebrity gulped another clumsy mouthful of water. The alien adjusted its posture and began weaving dark grey threads from an organ beneath its eyestalks. Matt stared. The creature completed its task and examined its handiwork.

"Hydration vessel." It gestured at the pond. "Please to utilise."

Matt took the proffered dark-grey, intricately woven bowl. "Err, thanks," he dipped it in the water and sipped. "You said the other week, not just trees, but other plants are important?"

"Affirmative: light-foragers of Earth living beings, not commodities."

The human touched the weave of his T-shirt. Shockingly, the leaf-creature wafting its longer antennae at him and did likewise. Its touch dry and soft.

"Cotton and coal-cloth synthesis."

"Ah, how do you feel about the cloth thing?" said Matt, surprised but oddly calm. This close he was sure of the scent, *Yeah, there's a hint of alcohol: Crème de Menthe.*

It made the static-modem noise and lapsed into silence. Matt directed an uncertain glance at the crew member present. "Complexity," the light-forager announced. "Comrades likely oppose non-essential plant-enslavement: cotton, tobacco, sugar, gluten-bearers."

"Err, non-essential," repeated the comic, out of his depth.

"Comrades hear much informational-matrix discussion of negative human health impacts, negative planet-impacts these plants." It adjusted its larger light-gathering structures and arched more eyestalks at Matt. "Regret-slain comrades declared many negatives of these: human health processes, planet-processes."

"Tayla and Kat said that you mean?" said Matt, sombrely.

"Correct. In spirit compromise and regret, comrades will limit actions to non-essential-harmful: cotton, tobacco, sugar, gluten-bearers initially. Await important persons edict-declarations."

Matt stared at the pond. He splashed his feet. The water prompted memories of childhood sailing outings with his father; of not knowing important stuff: who gives way to who, port, starboard, cleats, and sheets. He had an inkling gluten was essential.

"Yeah, tobacco and sugar, I guess we should give that up. Even origami if we need to, but gluten is like in bread and wheat, right?"

"Affirmative-correct."

"Listen, Kat and Tayla were lovely ladies. Err, but not experts in every way. It's true, some people can't eat wheat – but most can. It's not like smoking, sugary drinks or, err, opium, excess salt, magic mushrooms," concluded Matt with a flourish. "We need bread and wheat."

"Confusion-contradiction human Jains not consuming bread. Comrades will expect important televisual persons communications."

Matt wiped perspiration off his brow. His feet splashed the peaceful pond with more vigour than was fair. "I don't know about that stuff … Kalinda might. She's been doing the whole, 're-discovering the cultural roots thing.' We're not experts on this, this sort of thing."

"Fox, not fox, expertise, not expertise?"

"That's right." Matt took a deep breath. "We need an expert here."

The alien crouched lower, "Expert under arrangement."

"Wow. Great." Matt filled the bowl again. He raised it, "To the sun."

*

Viewing this back at the farm, Bob Kelly finished his beer and said, "What's this fox stuff?"

"Geez dad, you're worried about the fox stuff. There are serious cane and wheat issues."

"Tough times I reckon – might have to listen to that double album of yacht-rock and relax a bit." He opened another beer. "Glad we started on the fruit plantation."

His wife peered over her glasses. "At times dear, your father can be ahead of the curve."

Jess stared pointedly at her dad's faded *Rolling Stones* T-shirt. "Matt Davis is right," she ran her fingernails back and forth over the weave of the rattan chair, "Sugar's not critical but wheat is."

Her Dad selected a couple of almonds and crunched them. "It does my head in. What do *they* want us to eat, what do vegans eat, what do Jains eat …"

"Are you still a vegetarian, Jess?"

"Mainly, yes, but making some changes. Jainism's interesting. One of the, err, prophets – they call them tirthankaras, might have been a woman."

"Well that's different. Any platypus news dear, will you have to look for a new project?

"Probably Mum."

"Ah, something will turn up – remember the corona virus days."

"Yes Dad, I didn't wear a bra for three months and worked part time from home. This is completely different."

With her father rendered briefly speechless, Jess continued, "I think Matt should've pushed for clarity on the alien attitude to wheat."

Bob Kelly swigged his beer again, “I don’t know Jess – I reckon it’s like the Middle East – if you don’t understand it, just don’t poke it.”

Jess drummed her fingers on the bentwood chair’s arm. “What about your sugar cane?”

“Reckon we’re just gonna leave it there.”

“The world might have to get a little skinnier dear.”

Chapter 20 Now Would be a Good Time to Run Around Screaming!

A century after Tesla and Marconi contemplated the role of radio waves in the search for extra-terrestrials, the medium of television had facilitated alien contact. Not before time, alien contact was to be acknowledged.

"Riya Bedi is coming on," called Rob.

"Okay thanks," said Jess. *He's usually not this excited about anything except football and computer games.*

The various housemates present rested their phones, plumped their cushions, and gave Channel Five's post-news panel show *News for Dummies* their full and considered attention.

Care-worn by the burden of office and dwarfed by the UN flag behind her, the secretary-general peered over the Mahogany desk and spoke.

"People of Earth, my fellow humans, since time immemorial we have asked ourselves the question: 'Are we alone in the cosmos?' There is no longer any doubt – we are not. To the visitors, on behalf of humanity, I say welcome. We, Earthlings, have, over time, built a diversity of cultures, increased our knowledge of the world and ourselves, and strived to build a civilisation where all living things are honoured. And so, with good intentions, we anticipate working with you to build a better life for all." With something of the usual twinkle in her eyes she added, "To use a word from my homeland: A more *ahimsa* life."

The remarkable brevity of the statement and the weeks of delay before its delivery were symptoms of the paralysing indecision and disagreement affecting governments of every assortment. Or more accurately, governments of every flavour except one-party states. Where the internet and press are controlled like high-tech greenhouses.

*

In an office in Calgary, a group of young environmental activists gave qualified approval to the statement. Perhaps now humanity would work to reduce its consumptive ways. Perhaps even among countries that swore mutual enmity, if chiefly, as a historical habit.

"Finally!" said Mike Ross, a legend of their movement.

It had been a week since his personal encounter with vegetal creatures in California.

*

Likewise, back in Cairns, Rob remarked, "Well, better late than never,"

"I can't believe she still didn't address the issues around coral conservation!"

Perched on the broad arm of the share house's worn couch, Jess gave Lindsay a sympathetic look. She, in turn, said, "It's a pity she didn't suggest we conserve ahimsa plant crops and reduce meat farming."

"Huh?" said Rob.

"Rob, if we *can* still grow corn and soy, then people need to be eating it – it's not efficient to feed it to cows, then eat them."

"Right," said Rob. "Well, now it's official, hopefully we can start making changes."

"Like on climate change?" grumbled Lindsay.

Don't get him started, thought Jess

"That's right mate," agreed Rob. "Now the UN can take on reporting alien population growth. As well as, you know, *monitoring* genocide, overfishing, human rights abuse, child mortality ..."

But despite the official recognition; in a world awash with divisive algorithms, there were still folks insisting the whole vegetal-creature thing was a mass hallucination: caused by either fluoride in the water or Wi-Fi mind control. More dangerously, there were two sets of people who welcomed the alien invasion. Both existed on campus and wanted the world remade from ruin.

As Rob put it, "You've got your religious nutters who haven't been happy since Copernicus was a boy." He warmed to his theme … "When superstition and blind faith ruled, when evidence-based books and people got toasted—"

"Rob, sometimes, when I hear people say 'evidence-based', I want to scream!"

"Err, Jess, have you considered you might be in the wrong line of work?"

"I *know*, it's just over-used to death. Maybe one day it'll just go without saying. Anyway, you were *saying*?"

"Yeah, and you've got your environmentalist nutters who wánt the Earth cleansed of people."

The segment ended and Jess de-couched herself to make a coffee. Over bubbling water, ex-*CCE* contestant Graeme O'Brien was introduced. He began haranguing the panel, an unfortunate guest politician, and the viewers with demands to 'do something' about the extra-terrestrial visitation. After some minutes of this he switched to another favoured topic: that half of high school students were below average for arithmetic.

Jess turned to face the others, "Is he bitter and twisted from being eliminated?"

"Nah, he's always like that."

Eventually the host muzzled the shock jock and the show's blend of information and entertainment, that may well be the root of all modern evil concluded with the words of the resident comedian:

"So, it's official at last. Now would be a good time to run around screaming!"

Chapter 21 A rose by any other name

Humans do rather like to name, label, and classify: babies, pets, rivers, caffeinated hot drinks. Roses. Things, it seems, must be awarded a name. When Adam found himself unexpectedly created in the Garden of Eden, his first undertaking was to name all the *animals*.

Only later did he say, "Um, Dad, could you rustle me up something in the girlfriend department?"

Yet weeks following invasion by murderous photosynthetic life forms bent on world domination, people remained *stumped* for a label. For most: "Flee, the plant-creatures are upon us!" just felt less than adequate. Scientists tried to muscle in on the area, devising the term, 'Photosynthetic Pseudo-Arthropodal Beings,' which the public abbreviated to P-pabs. Chiefly to mock the scientists involved.

To be fair, in the early days of their residence in the *Celebrity Council* compound, popular TV vet Dr Paul had posed the hesitant question: "Err, so what do you call yourselves?" There was an ominous silence, during which Mariam edged further from Paul.

Then a burst of static and: "Negative context to frame response."

"Err, okay," murmured the veterinarian, relieved to find his heart still beating – if faster than recommended at sea level.

After weeks of the tentative and unconvincing use of *they*, the others, P-pabs, and the completely failed to catch on *Triffids*, humanity, at last, had the required label. The actions of a young girl in New York City resolved the puzzle. We have met her before … but briefly.

*

"NO! NO! Come back!" called the worrisome parent.

Too late.

Skipping across the spacious Central Lawn, the girl dragged her whimpering beagle pup behind her. She halted beside the ominous presence. Central Park had been spacious in recent days since the unfortunate 'thinning out' incident that so troubled the resident sea lions.

"Hello, my name's Anne-Maree. I'm five. Do you love puppies? What's your name? Joey O'Loughlin says, you eat people."

Eyestalks were bent forward and lowered, examining the cowering pup. The alien produced and used a small poking appendage. "Self, no opinion on puppies, human child. Last visitation this planet fifteen hundred years gone, people of Uppsala named self: Yggdrasil and *askr Yggdrasil*. Not eat-consume humans or any flesh. Self eats sunlight. Be not fearful."

Ann-Maree jiggled from foot to foot. She used both hands to adjust her beret and waited to hear if further conversation was forthcoming. When it wasn't, and without apparent disappointment, she concluded: "Well, that's good, isn't it? Bye, Yggdrasil."

And away she skipped.

Into the world of internet sensation and the arms of her relieved mother, New York blogger Ebony Hamilton.

Of mom love nyc fame.

And so, the world acquired the desired label. A name. Members of internet grammar forums had a most excellent time arguing over singular versus plural noun forms. And through an inexplicable, amorphous consensus, 'Yggdrasil' was assigned to the likewise inexplicable: deer, sheep, and fish group of irregular plurals.

Chapter 22 Sugar Kills

Since his *Tonight Show* adventure, the professor had become a celebrity in Corvallis. Enough to attract those 'Where do I know him from?' looks in the street, and to turn heads in his local coffee shop. Presently so located, latte in one hand and sourdough doughnut at the ready, he was being outmanoeuvred by a table.

Ash spotted this and moved to the rescue. She crouched and shoved a folded napkin under the shortest leg. She slipped into the chair opposite Niels.

"Thanks, Ashley. The tables seem restless of late!"

Ash grinned. "Hi, professor." She picked up a sugar sachet from the recycled tea chest tabletop. "Did you look at the New York lady's blog – the mom of the little girl who spoke to the alien? The yggdrasil, right?"

"The World Tree from Norse mythology, yes, like wow," confirmed the academic who had learned his English from American teen movies.

"Her blog said there'd been attacks on sugar plantations in Brazil. Have you seen it?"

"No – but perhaps I am about to?" smiled Niels. *Hmm, here comes another unscheduled alien implications coffee house chat.*

"Yeah, I'll just bring it up again." Ash toyed with her phone and slid it past the bicycle headlamp that someone with too much time on their hands had thought to fashion into a sugar bowl.

October 9
mom love nyc
SPECIAL TREES AND SUGAR

first, a ginormous thank you for the support our family has received. uncle jim is fine and out of hospital now. no harm done from being spun into the cocoon, and his skin looks just amazing! now, did you see reports on the web of fighting on sugar farms in brazil? i was so freakin scared but I felt i had to ask 'our yggdrasil' what's going on.

so, we set off this morning with our hot drink thermoses. anne-maree looking very grown up in her plum felt coat with the toggles. momma wearing a merino knit bobble hat, fake fur scarf and down jacket. [Pic 1. drinks on the bench seat].

sadly, central park is still so quiet. the three of us went for a walk, what a sight! [Video] the fall leaves are so pretty and anne-maree and the yggdrasil chatted about their most special trees. it took us to visit the old black tupelo in the rambles. miss five told it the american elms were her favourites. i am so proud of her, our young diplomat.

so, after summoning up the courage i asked: is it true about the deaths in brazil? 'our yggdrasil' said it was true. and not just in brazil, AND that its friends were disappointed with progress on plant rights on *CCE*! OMG IT'S LIKE THE YGGDRASIL THINK THOSE PEOPLE HAVE THE POWER TO MAKE LAWS! anyway, it says sugar cane farming is the world's biggest crop and that it's unnecessary and not good for anyone.

so that's the blog for today. stay safe and thank you all once more for the love.

Niels tapped replay and watched the blog video again. "Yes, I am seeing that girl on another video where she asks the alien if it likes puppies. That's not a sentence I imagined I'd ever say. I wasn't knowing she was part of a blog. And what's happens with the clothing talk?"

"We-ell, it's her family and Central Park and fashion. She's been sharing that stuff for years – it's gone crazy now." Ash toyed with the sugar, "You can tell she's excited when the blog goes upper case."

"It's charming where the girl and the yggdrasil are pointing at trees."

"Oh, for sure," said Ash. "It's that emotion you get watching FriendFone videos when different animals are friends. You know, like a beaver and a bunny, or a porpoise and an octopus.

"Err, yes," said Niels doubtfully, "shall we not check the web for sugar production figures?"

"Yeah, I have," she nodded. "Sugar cane *is* the biggest crop by world tonnage and right up there for acreage and monetary value."

"Well, we are knowing already the yggdrasil can access the internet, although how well they filter informations is another question ..."

"Any more news on the 'phone assimilation thing' Professor?"

"Oh, that's most secret. You know how it works – if I tell you, then the US government must kill me, then maybe the Swedish Government gets upset and stops exporting our excellent automobiles. But there were yggdrasil killed in New York and other places. So that secret cat will soon be out of the bag."

Like Ash before him, he picked a sachet out of the bowl and wafted it around for a bit before continuing, "But it's concerning, yes. Perhaps these attacks are symbolic, but sugar cane is a grass – it regrows. Why not disapprove of the sugar beet industry instead? That involves harvesting a root vegetable."

Ash shrugged, "Perhaps because that industry isn't so large."

"Maybe, but it worries me, yes."

"Because the yggdrasil might oppose essential grain crops?"

"Yes, Ashley. Did you catch the *CCE* episode where the comic person ... is it, Len? He talks of wheat."

"It's Matt," she grinned. "You need to catch up, Professor."

He nodded. "The alien, the yggdrasil supposed wheat was non-essential."

"It's a worry." Ash glanced at the expresso machine, "Well, I better get back to it. Enjoy the donut. See you next week, I guess."

As circumstances unfolded, she did see the professor the following week. Although not at the Retro Bean, nor in her university class. As for the sourdough blackberry and vanilla donut – it's time had come. Not one to over analyse food, Niels sensed any health benefit accrued from the sourdough flour was negated by the ample sprinkling of sugar coupled to that housed in the squishy interior.

With the appearance of a Minnesotan country singer, down to the three-day stubble look, which so often fails to be achieved with spray-on products, Niels was not of the over-sugared majority. Despite his origin in a country whose idea of food convenience is combining aquatic creatures with cheese in a tube, he'd resisted the thrall of North American food fashion. The diversity of sugar options: white, cane, Demerara, and brown remained undissolved in his latte.

Somewhat paralleling the story of coffee; sugar cane originated in mysterious, far away south-east Asia. Nature's earlier major supplier of sweetness: namely honeybees – jiggled with relief as sugar cane production exploded across the globe over the most recent four centuries. Twelve million African slaves were loaded into ships, cumulating centuries later in strangely coloured and flavoured water loaded with nine teaspoons of sugar per can shipped around the world – including back to Africa.

What the yggdrasil thought of all this, Niels soon discovered for himself.

Chapter 23 The Surprise Intruder

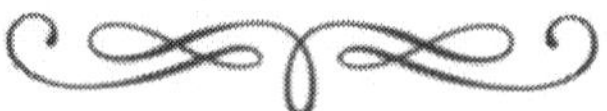

Niels *had* been pre-warned by the texts and calls.

None the less his hand shook and there was minor coffee spillage as the light gatherer filled his TV screen and invited him to join *Celebrity Council Elimination*. Rather like the Saab refusing to go into gear, his thoughts raced but went nowhere. *Do I have a choice? Should I tell the yggdrasil this show is nonsense? Am I the man who didn't want to help save mankind? Where's my whittling knife?*

Following a frantic few days of research and meetings, he made his way to Portland's airport. The first and inconvenient leg: New York.

Later, settling down for the interminable stretch across the Pacific, Niels reached for his reading material, forsaking the in-flight magazine for a crash course in Australian botany and national parks.

He read and the two children sitting alongside studiously ignored him. They appeared to be excess members of an extensive family. Approaching the International Date Line, all was well; the young girl playing interminable games of *Candy Crush* while her brother slaughtered an unlikely multitude of digital enemies.

Niels switched focus and opened the preliminary yggdrasil autopsy findings yielded by the NSSA.

Project Audrey
Chem. & Anatom. Report Del Norte State Park specimens.
... cellular structure contains polysaccharide chitin ... surface tissue organelles analogous chloroplasts ... segmented body plan ... multiple respiratory sacs ... genetic material: terrestrial & novel nucleic acids ... respiratory pigment haemocyanin variation ...

Further reading became difficult as the novelty of air-borne gaming diminished.

Time slowed ...

"Who'd win a fight between a polecat and a giant squid," said the unattended boy by the window, rather to Niels' surprise. A discussion involving terrain considerations and motivations ranged back and forth between the boy's father in the forward row and various other siblings. They were clearly familiar with such conundrums.

"Who'd win a fight between an alligator and a polar bear?"

Even Niels' considerable ability to concentrate was under siege by the fourth query. However, the family became testy, and peace was restored.

Not for long.

Niels' eyes widened as the boy leaned across his sister and said, "You're clever, we saw you on television. Who'd win a fight between a gorilla and hundred poisonous frogs?"

"Err, so the frogs are venomous young man?"

"Arrow frogs."

Time wavered at that point and may have gone into reverse. Or so Niels thought on landing and discovering he'd somehow misplaced a day in transit.

*

After customs and de-briefing, he found himself delivered to the Cassowary Lodge, accompanied by a military convoy, and trailed by the media. *CCE* host, Holly met Niels at the temporarily non-lethal perimeter and escorted him through the vegetated compound, clutching only a bag of borrowed non-plant fibre clothes.

Off to save the world.

Holly beamed and said, "Please welcome Professor Niels Larsson."

Niels thought, *My God, the heat, the humidity – nice hibiscus*. He strode into the clearing.

"All right!" cheered an athletic-looking, dark-haired fellow pumping his fist.

Ah, that's *Matt*, recalled Niels (for he'd been studying).

Recognition turned to alarm.

Niels tensed as the stranger rushed towards him … stuck out his hand and withdrew it.

"Manly hug!" Matt declared. He pounced. "Right then, I'm outta here …"

Chapter 24 Naming the Yggdrasil

Not so far away, Jess and the students waited for the much-promised, much-advertised episode to begin.

"Kalinda should have *more* camera time," said Leong. Jess smiled at him. He was definitely out of his room more these days. Dramatic music played and, wearing an *I Love NY* T-shirt and many-pocketed shorts, the much-hyped mystery intruder emerged.

The door creaked and thumped shut. Rob rushed in, "Ah, the new guy."

"Look there's Kalinda," enthused Leong.

Rob flopped into a seat. "Are you okay?" said Jess.

"Bit shook up, I went to the gardens. The curve's not flattening. Did you know we've got yggdrasil here in Cairns now? Tell you later …"

*

On set, Niels gave the cast a sheepish wave and said somewhat predictably:

"Hello, I'm Niels," and less so, "the yggdrasil invited me to join you."

"Hi. What's a yggdrasil?" said the long-haired woman whom the scientist remembered was the pop star.

"Nobody knew what to call the visitors. Then one of them in New York said people used to call it a yggdrasil or askr yggdrasil."

The celebrities stared.

"The name's from Norse mythology: The World Tree."
"So, there're more of them?"
"Used to call it?"
"What's happening in the world?"

"Err—" began Niels.

"Professor!" shrilled Maggie, approaching and waving her arms. "Guests don't discuss what happens outside the show!"

They suspended further debate on the point as Matt said, "Call them what you will, but here's some we prepared earlier."

The three aliens approached.

The Swede took a tentative step towards them. In a deliberate, measured tone, as if ringing the university's IT department, he said, "Hello, my name is Niels Larsson. I am the tree researcher. You asked me to join you."

*

The show continued, peppered by exquisitely expensive advertising. During a break for the latest in low orbit space flight, Lindsay arrived home.

"Hey all, you'll never guess what I've seen."

Two metres, green, lots of feelers, thought Jess.

"Was it in the Botanic Gardens by any chance?" said Rob. "Geez, they have a lot of ads in this show."

Jess sensed Lindsay deflate. "What have I missed?" he said.

"Well, turns out the intruder is a forester," began Jess.

"No way."

"So … Matt pretended to run away. The so-called intruder's Swedish, um, he called them yggdrasil. And he just asked them to choose personal names," she shrugged, "it'll make it easier to talk." The final ad in the break was a promotion for the show. Jess continued, "So the one that made the declaration is Sif Acer, the one that killed the girls is Tek Alnus and the other one's called Ret Moitch."

"Did it talk?"

"Yeah, turns out 'Harpo' *can* talk – said nothing else, mind," said Rob.

*

Back at the lodge, Niels sat at the table while a small, not terribly important part of his mind (in charge of recognising not terribly important things) registered he'd seen this very table daily on TV.

"I have the advantages – watching everybody on TV. If I have it correct: Mariam, Matt, Kalinda, and Len," he recited, giving each a small nod.

"Good-oh, that'll save playing one of those awful 'What's your favourite cheese games?'" said Len with feeling.

"Sorry, I don't follow …"

"He means a getting to know you – a break the ice activity," said Mariam.

Niels detected scorn for Len bubbling away under the surface. "Yes, I see. Jarlsberg, by the way. Sometimes it's what's missing that makes things interesting."

From behind the crew Maggie said, "Can I ask you three to talk to each other in English sometimes … so the viewers get more sense of the alien personalities behind the enigma."

"Yggdrasil not persons-alities," said Tek Alnus. "Will compromise communicate."

"And you're a professor of forestry?" said Mariam.

"Ah yes," said Niels, taken aback by her interrogatory TV-journalist-manner. "I am with Oregon State—"

"Seriously? You get these guys love trees, right?" said Len with a nod and a glance at the yggdrasil (which suggested nothing a pint of weed-killer wouldn't fix).

"I expect because of my researches into tree communication."

"Either that or they're planning a public execution," murmured Matt. Niels missed Kalinda's discrete prod under the table, but he heard Mariam's disapproving hiss.

"Sorry," said Matt to the newcomer.

"That was a concern I don't mind telling you," said Niels, raising his eyebrows, "but what an invitation. I had to come." *Then there's my fear of being trapped with people who might have no life interests beyond team sports, star signs and celebrity gossip.*

"I still don't understand. *How* were you invited?" said Kalinda with a shrug and sampling an unknown tropical fruit.

"Well it was through the show, Sif Acer I believe it was, said—"

"We don't discuss the show's production, or what happens outside it, thank you," said Maggie, wanting off-camera time with Niels at the first opportunity.

"That is not acceptable to me," replied the professor calmly, "now shall we go for a walk." He turned to the yggdrasil, "Perhaps you can show me the forest, I'd very much like to view it. *If* I return, we'll have things to discuss in private," he said to Maggie.

Niels grinned at Matt, pounced on an unfamiliar fruit, and strolled into the tangle of unfamiliar forest with Sif Acer; intent on untangling and surviving the misconceptions, assumptions, and half-truths that led to his presence here.

Lenny shrugged and resumed consuming barbequed meats as if cholesterol had never been invented.

*

The episode ended, and the students faced each other.

"Were they doing anything, the aliens … the yggdrasil you saw?" said Jess.

Rob glanced at Lindsay, "Just standing there – adjusting a bit."

"Not talking?"

Rob shrugged, "The cops had everyone well back."

"Weird isn't it," said Lindsay. "Hundreds of them in Botanical Gardens down south; in famous parks all over, and only *those*," he nodded at the TV, "and the one that talks to the New York kiddie, communicate."

"Mostly they're just not that into us," said Jess.

"Leong and me were talking about this before," said Rob to Jess. "Just quietly, *CCE* should've asked for you."

"You have alien understanding," explained Leong.

Jess felt herself blush. *That's sweet, but I wish you'd do more housework and leave my falafels alone.* She said, "Actually, the government *has* asked me to join an advisory panel."

*

By evening the jet lag, discussions, and the onslaught of unaccustomed tropical insects took their toll. Niels, sluggish, and reclining by the swimming pool listened to the resident fruit bats chitter their news and opinions. Matt sensed the newcomer needed a break from end of the world scenarios. "So how was your trip?"

The comic considered the reply rather fraught: "Young man on the plane … trapped … very much interested in the poisonous frogs ... and the formalities at your customs, most difficult … understanding emergency visa arranged … but no. Am I on holiday, am I working, am I having a criminal history?"

"Ah, well, you didn't know you still need one to come here eh?" quipped Matt.

Mariam rolled her eyes, unseen in the fading light. The comment ended the newcomer's account of his flight and associated misfortunes.

"Does anyone have knowledge of Shark Bay?" Niels said, returning (albeit cryptically) to present circumstances.

"Oh yeah … it's like a new thing, the government's experimenting with rounding up all the sharks and keeping 'em in one place."

"Geez, give it a rest mate," advised Len, feet dangling in the pool. "We've only just got the new bloke, don't go breaking him."

"But it's my purpose to spread fun and mirth and really good times," explained Matt. "But yeah, there have been occasional protestations."

"I can see that might be the case," commented Kalinda, her eyes bemused. She said, "It's the place in Western Australia where dolphins come up close to the beach. Why do you ask, Niels?"

"We need to impress the yggdrasil. There's something there, although not the dolphins. But now I feel I must go to bed."

"Yeah, I'll show you the hut," said Matt. "You'll love it." The *CCE* cast dispersed, leaving the poolside to the small creatures of the night.

Chapter 25 Eir Nyssa

October 15
Mom love nyc
SURPRISE VISITOR

i do try my hardest to respond to the comments and DMs on instagram, (thanks so much for following) and i've been itching to jump on here, but i had to keep the secret for a few days.

dear readers, we've had a surprise visitor! so anne-maree and me and james and billy and PROFESSOR NIELS LARSSON went to the park to see 'our' yggdrasil! i'm wearing a leather coat and light wool vintage slacks with hand-painted silk scarf; anne-maree again in her felt coat and the cutest little synthetic pink boots [Pic 1]. as we all now know the professor was on his way to australia when he called by. he has such a charming accent! and he has been following the blog!

now as you can well imagine dear readers i didn't wanna exactly tell professor niels what to wear … and he was travelling light … so we had a chat about what might be considered diplomatic … and here's niels wearing james' teal sweater and standing next to EIR NYSSA! [Pic 2] that's right we walked into the ramble and niels explained that people have spoken names and he introduced anne-maree and me. he was so CHARMING and european. and then he introduced himself and suggested 'our' alien might choose a name for itself! gosh, it was so strange to hear that phone voice speak our names. the professor whispered that the first name might be from VIKING legends and the second part of the name was from the tupelo tree. later I googled the first name while we admired the cougar statue and EIR means a goddess of healing and medicine. i don't mind telling you all I said a little prayer to Jesus that this might be good news. [Pic 3 niels, anne-maree and eir nyssa by the statue].

thank you so much for your continued support, many of you i know have been following this blog for such a long time that it seems we are all going on this adventure together!
good-luck professor.

Chapter 26 Niels Bore

It was Niels' first full day at the weathered table.

"… and so, you agree what *they*, what the yggdrasil say about eating plants is true and that they're like animals, thinking, communicating, having feelings?" said Mariam.

"There're several issues," said Niels, picking up a banana and wafting it. "Our alien colleagues say consuming *any* living thing is unethical and uncivilised—"

"Easy for them to say – they don't need to," growled Len.

"Oh yes," agreed the Swede. "Our definitions of plants and animals are based on how they get their energy and cell chemistry. Feelings, communications, even intelligence, are not so much part of those definitions. If you are recalling high school biology?"

"Ah," said Matt. "Not so much. I don't reckon any of us, well except Paul, did much science." He turned to his left, "Mariam?"

"Political Science," she said curtly. It seemed this, her talent for interrogating politicians and seeking 1990s movies on VHS wasn't presently of great utility.

He likes to play the peacemaker, mused Niels as Matt continued.

"My family is in the doctoring business, they rather expected me to follow suit." He went on to explain his formal education in biological sciences had been limited – deliberately so by his private school, after certain hi-jinx involving rodents.

Niels acknowledged the story with a grin. "As to intelligence and feelings – this is a controversial field. I mean, are we really having agreed definitions of these for animals? And among humans, it's a most contentious area."

In the production centre Maggie growled, "Oh God, save us all from Niels Bore." Her crew didn't respond to her science-themed derision – you just couldn't get the staff.

On the set, the forester leaned back and rested the banana, "I don't know if plants have *feelings,* but I know they have senses: light sensation, dissolved and airborne chemical detection (equivalent to our taste and smell), touch … I don't know if most *animals* have feelings – many invertebrates have nothing resembling a brain. It seems that mammals, or at least those I relate to, have feelings. I prefer moose to mice – don't ask me why."

Niels leaned back. The timber seat wobbled a little, and he summoned the patience of someone who'd just realised he was going to have to do a lot of the conversational legwork. With a nod at Mariam, he continued: "As we know, many peoples believe a deity created the Earth's life forms. And for *our* benefit. And you, Kalinda," (nodded Niels), "brought to our attention an ancient religion saying almost the opposite: concerned to kill neither plants nor animals." Niels tapped the banana but resisted picking it up again. "There are some few of us that eat only the fruits; more that say it's wrong to eat animals, even lower animals. Plants and jellyfish, clams, and mussels, for instance, *have* sense organs, but none have a brain. Is consciousness, are feelings, in the brain? I don't know…" Niels shook his head, "Here's me studying tree communications these years and giving no consideration to eating potatoes."

"Chips," sighed Len.

"Yeah," sighed Matt. "It's a total perspective reset. Maybe not the whole 'visit to paediatric oncology ward thing,' but pretty damn close."

Niels ruffled his hair, "The world finds this situation thought-provoking, and many don't want the thoughts provoked."

"Nice," said Matt.

"I think I'll make it my catchphrase."

Kalinda rested her face on both hands, obscured behind her hair. Niels observed Matt give her a sympathetic look. As no-one but the rainforest parrots said anything, he leaned in. "*Now,* I must tell what's been happening in the world …"

And so, in this way, the celebrities learned of their immense fame and the full extent of the alien arrival. Of these, it was difficult to say which had the greater impact.

"Okay then, who wants to look at interesting stuff in the forest?" the researcher asked. He nodded at an approaching alien.

"Always" volunteered Matt rising from the bench seat.

"Self will accompany – important learnings," spoke Sif Acer, arriving and directing its eyestalks at Niels and the young comedian.

*

"Hey Jess, how'd it go today?" said Rob. "There's left-over vegetarian pizza that Allison made."

"Ta," she yawned, "It was interesting – can't say much – but I met Paul McKay!"

"Makes sense, he'd be on an alien advisory group," nodded Rob.

"So jealous, he's gorgeous. Such a nice smile … and shoulders," enthused a housemate.

Jess smiled, "And I might be on an episode of that TV panel show *Questions Without Notice*. There wasn't anything mentioned on the news in the car – what happened on *CCE* today?"

"No contests or real inanities," said Lindsay. "The new guy talked about tree communication, err, volatile organic compounds and such. Mariam's maybe not dealing so well with aliens existing and plants having communication. Oh, and she was incredulous the yggdrasil invited a forester."

"I've looked at his stuff online – he's kind of a tree advocate these days," said Jess. "And they … the yggdrasil still don't realise it's just a show?"

"Nope."

Chapter 27 What's the Plan?

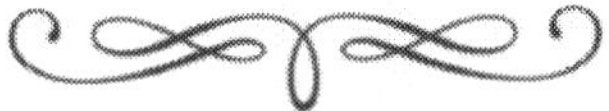

"Professor, what are you attempting to achieve here? What's your idea of the endgame?" Mariam asked in accustomed interview-speak.

"Yeah, what's the plan, Doc?" added Lenny, from his pool side chair.

Niels kept his voice low, "Save what we can and buy time."

"That's not terrible specific."

Well madam, I didn't ask to be here, nor advise the country my presence on a TV show would solve its problems. "Oh look, here come Matt and Kalinda," he observed. "My idea is to show we human types in a good way. The yggdrasil are expecting us to make these edicts." He nodded at the newcomers, "Like Matt did with the carrots and then the firewood. They expect a tremendous proclamation at the end of the show – they think the world will follow."

"No-one will listen to us."

"We'll be public enemy number one."

"This is messed up! If they just landed and said, you know: 'Take us to your leader …'" Matt trailed off.

"Yes, always ask for the directions," agreed Niels.

These terse responses were a far cry from both the premise of the show and its early days. In those sunny, simpler times, the celebrities were only too eager to share their declarations. Opinions and proclamations on public education, welfare, refugees, and quinoa had been freely volunteered.

Kalinda shed her towel revealing a one-piece swimsuit and flung herself at a flamingo pool toy that was unsuspectingly bobbing about. There were no yggdrasil in view, but a camera crew now approached. "Matt has been getting on well with the one called Sif Acer," she called from the pool.

"Yes, the aliens appear to have variable attitudes—"

"Yeah, that big one can't be arsed talking to us," said Lenny, nodding as Ret Moitch led its companions out of the forest edge near the tennis court.

Niels lowered his voice further and said rapidly, "We need to show them that animals are useful to plants, that we people respect the plants. Also, we need to end this isolation, we need informations … I will speak with the producer." Niels glanced up at the approaching aliens. "I believe the producer should tell them the truth of this show, end this misunderstanding." He shrugged, "But perhaps that's dangerous …"

"Yeah, don't wanna be trending on twitter for the wrong reasons," said Len.

The crew and two aliens were almost at the pool.

Niels stood and said, "We should make an announcement on forestry." Then whispered, "A sign of good faith, yes?"

"Reciprocal greetings," said Sif Acer.

Kalinda emerged from the pool. Sif Acer twitched its feelers, appeared to find human skin drying procedures fascinating. As did Matt in this case.

"Time of weekly edict approaches. Time one person terminated," said Tek Alnus.

"Jesus," muttered Len.

Sif Acer waved its feelers and made its static sound. Perhaps detecting apprehension in the air, it said, "Comrade inadvertently ominous. Meaning: Vote terminated."

To the surprise of the massed ranks of remaining cast members, Niels the newcomer announced: "I don't want to be your Yoko …" and speculated that it might be better if no one else was sent home – maintaining a wider parliament of views and experiences.

"Agreed," said the yggdrasil in unison.

The cast directed glum looks at blameless pool furniture. In the awkward silence, Matt pointed at Ret Moitch behind the camera crew. "Does your kind have different roles, different professions?" As a comic, Matt was familiar with imposed leisure betwixt engagements. And with family advice to 'get a real job.' Hence, he chose other examples for clarity: "You know, how Niels is a scientist and Kalinda is a musician."

Sif Acer extended eyestalks at Niels and towards the young woman drying her hair. Its segmented antennae quivered, it emitted the odd raspy modem noise and declared, "Self resembles colonisation consultant, diplomat-explorer; this companion," (touching Tek Alnus with a dexterous leaf-wing) "resembles political representative."

"Right," said Matt. "And Ret Moitch?"

"Common settler-warrior clade."

"Is that so," said Niels.

"Right," repeated Matt, this time more grimly.

"Oh," said Kalinda.

The responses were becoming shorter. Len completed the series with a remarkably porcine snort.

Chapter 28 Excrement

Flip-flops, shorts, borrowed T-shirt; Niels had established a routine. Rising before the others, he explored the tangled pathways of the lodge's acreage, probing its botanical mysteries.

He tensed as the undergrowth rustled.

A bird hopped onto the path.

Silly me. The dreams are making me jumpy. It was a well-rounded specimen of the pigeon variety. Niels watched it womble the narrow path. "Hmm," he said to it kindly. "Do you lack the capacity to fly, or just the inclination?"

With a squawk of surprise, or possibly indignation, it made a deposit on the path and thus lightened took to the air. Niels peered at the offering and marked the area with a stick. After a promising start, peering at pigeon poo, the scientist's morning deteriorated.

As Niels strolled towards breakfast, he fell into conversation with the audio technician known to all as 'AB.' He now learned *CCE* had disgruntled crew the way other shows had donuts and muffins. The stress, isolation, and long hours were taking their toll.

"This is a shit job! What are *they* going to do to us when they realise you lot don't have any power?"

"I know—"

"Bugger! They're so hard to notice when they don't move. I need a break." He turned around and bustled away.

Even at a distance and across species lines, Niels sensed tension. He attempted a casual saunter, leaning on the porch of an expensively rusticised hut. There was certainly extensive antennae thrashing going on. He was momentarily distracted by the decorative penis sheath gourd someone had thought to hang at eye level.

"… self hates worlds infested with sentient non-light gatherers."

"Incorrect protocols adherence …"

Niels observed Sif Acer twitch its eye stalks towards him. *It knows I'm here. It's an argument*, he decided. But not of the 'stick your fingers in your ears and pretend it's not happening type' – Niels edged closer. More the 'whip out your phone and start recording for posterity variety.'

Sif Acer continued, "Correct action: withdrawal, emphasize edicts. Humans begin change, reduce consumptive ways, respect photosynthetics."

With additional antennae thrashing, its companion said, "Negative. Comrades promised this world now. Televisual experience eight-week season – humans must begin at conclusion-finale."

Niels stepped still closer and crouched – taking a sudden inordinate interest in a lone sundew plant. It was a struggle to overhear: the distance, sameness of the phone-app voices, the odd phrasing. The reader can be assured that essentially the yggdrasil were under pressure to open new worlds for colonisation; there had been errors made, guidelines flouted and directives to muddle through, regardless.

*

"This is the place. I was here this morning, and a bird pooped on the path." Niels noted a lack of response from his fellows. He pointed, "Right there, as you can see. If you look closely, there are seeds in the excrement."

"We'll take your word for it, Doc," said Matt. The group moved aside for the yggdrasil. Matt felt the brush of Sif Acer's various leaf-wings as they swapped places.

"So, a bird ate a fruit. The flesh gets consumed but the seeds, they pass through yes, and with luck germinate and grow another plant. The tree benefits: its seeds get dispersed, and the bird has a meal. This is a common relationship involving the flowering plants."

"Discovery of interest," said Sif Acer, drawing itself up to its full height.

"Now, I suggest we view some unusual little plants in the swampy ground near the stream," suggested Niels. A flying insect or ten joined them. The clouds of air-borne nuisance grew denser and developed a closer personal interest as the ground grew softer and wetter. Rediscovering another marker stick and using it as an informal pointer Niels enthused, "So these plants are *sundews*, see how light glistens on the little droplets – they are sticky. Many of these plants are here scattered, and there are tiny flies stuck to some. The soil is poor, and the plants are absorbing extra nutrients from the insects. Yes, feeding on them."

"Cool," said Matt on his hands and knees, "Look at me taking an interest in science. So, it's like a Venus fly trap."

"Yes, Matt. And on the stream's other bank, there's quite a large pitcher plant.

The intrepid group crossed the stream.

"Here at the top," continued the guide, "a chemical scent attracts insects, and they fall into the trap and digest in the bottom water. And so, a plant is eating animals, just as animals eat plants."

"I've seen these for sale at markets," noted Kalinda, not quite poking the anomalous herbage with a stick.

"Ah-ha, yes, carnivorous plants are popular – they are so different from what we expect a plant to be. There may be more species of sundews here we could search for—"

"Err, do we need to?" said Matt.

"I was trying to make the point," explained Niels.

"Consider the point well made, finely honed and sharp, my friend," said Matt with a raised eyebrow. "I mean there's a lot to take in … on both sides. Spare a thought for Tek Alnus here. He's all—"

"It's all."

"Sorry Kalinda, unconscious gender bias strikes again. It's all, 'Plants don't need animals, plants don't kill', and now this – probably needs a good lie down or a pleasant stand in the sun. As do we all." He grinned at Niels. "Also, I reckon our colleagues here can check these things for themselves on the internet now that they know about them."

"Correct Matt Davis/Correct Matt Davis," came the stereo reply.

"Cool. The new improved me, twice as correct as before."

Kalinda sensed a theme might develop. She prodded him playfully in the ribs with her poking stick. In companionable but learned silence, the group returned to the lodge.

Chapter 29 Maggie

Once more Niels rose before the others of the Cassowary Lodge's assorted inmates. He strolled the vegetation lined pathway, strategizing. Likewise, tropical insects gnashed their mandibles as they contemplated their various tasks. They had their own agendas – as did Niels.

As did the producer.

"Ms Reynolds," began Niels, on the veranda, at the production centre. "I must tell you there are now *thousands* of yggdrasil in the parks of the world; forestry industries are much affected; there are attacks on agriculture and early military interventions failed."

The producer shrugged at him and flicked fearlessly at a passing gecko with oversized feet. To be clear: it was the lizard that had the oversized feet. *You are not used to talking with contestants*, mused Niels.

He continued: "Security analysts are believing the alien's natural communication is direct; deception might not be possible. They took your advertisings about celebrity influence at face value. You understand, yes – they believe reality TV is real! The yggdrasil are expecting the celebrities to issue rulings in line with their declarations. Now called the Cairns Declaration."

Maggie had surmised as much. "Professor, I'm more than happy for you and the cast to issue edicts, it's good for ratings – and it was the original basis of the show that they do so." (Admittedly, it hadn't been anticipated this might include human-alien relations).

Niels gazed wistfully at a Fijian war club fixed to the wall. Maggie was unmoved by appeals for either a sense of perspective or a feeling for the greater good. Niels was incredulous but hid it behind a stoic Nordic demeanour and three-day stubble. In her time, Maggie had been lectured ineffectually on the greater good by experts in the field.

"Ok, then. Well, *I* may tell the yggdrasil the truth, but it's surely better if *you* explain the misunderstanding. And consider ... what will happen in four weeks when the world doesn't follow our celebrity advices? *Okay, next topic.*

The compound was isolated from events by the blend of the yggdrasil's unfathomable motivations grafted to the TV show's original premise. The newcomer sought to end this.

"To achieve our important task here – to attempt the negotiations and conciliation we need access to informations—"

"We focus grouped this until it bled – we change nothing."

Breathe and admire the elegant whorls of the ferns, Niels told himself. Her manner was that of a surgeon disconcerted to find the patient wanting to chat of risk analysis and such, rather than being nicely unconscious. "And it's important to show the yggdrasil we humans do protect some forests. Take them to your excellent Australian National Parks."

Outside field trip ... interesting, thought Maggie. But Niels just heard the derisive snort and: "Professor, you've got thirty hectares of rainforest, streams, and beach – how much more do you need!"

Niels' fingers sought wood to drum. In his best academic manner, he argued, "Ms Reynolds, having a group of people make important pronouncements affecting the state of the world, while deliberately isolating them from the state of the world isn't an ideal strategy, yes."

There was a chilly pause considering the air temperature. "Well, clearly, you've never been to Canberra!" The producer made a half-hearted try at gecko abuse, causing it to regard her with contempt and scurry out of range.

"Ok Ms Reynolds, I am abandoning the conciliation." There was steel in his manner – you could have stuck fridge magnets to him if so inclined. "I spoke to the aliens – they *agree* we can have web access, and we *are* going on a day trip from the compound in their transport craft, which will be most exciting. We shall view important botanical treasures together." Maggie's jaw dropped. "And we *shall* return. You might care to send a camera person along, yes."

The producer grimaced and stalked off, pausing only to glare at another gecko. And a tree frog.

Chapter 30 Plant Free Fashion

October 15
mom love nyc
PLANT FREE FASHION

sharing a few photos today of yours truly and the kiddos in fall fashions. lately I've got to wondering what the family's clothes would look like without plant products. gosh i've learned so much. big thanks to eir nyssa. billy and ann-maree have had to drag me away from the tablet at times, SORRY kiddos mom's back now! so say goodbye to denim jeans and jackets people, no linen shirts, no funky hemp capes, banish cotton in all its forms and get this: even rayon. wow, i kinda thought rayon was made from gasoline. But no, it starts with wood fibre! oh, also, no rubber. so there go the kiddos' gumboots and raincoats! [Picture 1 billy splashing in muddy puddle]

ok so what could we wear? back to the research (sorry kiddos!). well, wool from many critters: but usually sheep, alpaca, mohair, or cashmere goats. and yes, hand knitted bobble caps like nanna used to make. love this look! [Pic 2 mom and daughter in matching caps] and not forgetting felt! [Pic 3 ann-maree looking adorable in felt coat].

well I can tell you dear readers all that reading about wool made my fingers kinda twitchy. so into the cupboard under the stairs (OMG, another day!) and hey presto: the knitting bag! ok I admit I might have just needed a break from the research, and maybe trying to teach miss five to knit was kinda over ambitious. the tangles, the dropped stiches, oh the frustration but that adorable look of concentration made it so worthwhile [Pic 4 three rows of stiches with the ladybird tipped needles].

ok, other traditional clothing materials from animals are silk and leather [Pic 5 college days: red biker jacket over cashmere sweater with silk scarf] and dare I mention this dear reader... yes, fur! wow! so that just leaves synthetic fibres, now these are the ones made from coal or oil or gas and many can blend with cotton or wool. so, in a more plant friendly world we could all be wearing: nylon, polyester, acrylic or lycra [Pic 5 James looking very fit biking in C park]. something to consider dear readers. have a great weekend now.

Chapter 31 Day Trip to Shark Bay

Kalinda hadn't visited the beach since the occasion of the dead commandos.

Yet the mood was oddly festive. Expendable young camera wrangler Jaspa Dench had joined them. *We're out of here – at least for a while*, she thought. The alien craft's sculpted exterior resembled shoe tread from the glory days of sneaker manufacture.

"What is it, Niels?" *You've gone pale.*

"Kalinda, I've seen one of these before – a model of one – in a small museum in southern Oregon."

She skipped back as the thing hummed in a friendly tone. Interlocked plates or segments parted, and the yggdrasil duo entered. Sif Acer directed a jointed eyestalk at her and said: "Welcoming."

As the humans stepped in eyes widened (metaphorically at least, they were on stalks). Kalinda heard the massed breath intake and Matt gasp, "No way."

"Please to make destination entry Niels Larsson," said Sif Acer with a flourish.

"It's a laptop or tablet," said Kalinda in wonder.

Yes, it was: one embedded and enmeshed with tendrils in the fibrous sticky walls. Niels typed: 'Hamelin Pool, Shark Bay, Western Australia.'

Kalinda peered around Mariam. The destination was over two thousand kilometres away. The device estimated driving and flying times (there was, however, no estimate of travel time by extra-terrestrial transport device). As far as earth science could later determine, travel between location and the destination was instantaneous.

Exposed to infinite time and space, six human minds reeled. Incomprehensible energies whirled and spat outside the shell of the pod, and human consciousness cowered and shivered. Not an out-of-body experience – although discussing it later, the pop-singer suggested that might've been a welcome alternative. Then, whatever had just happened, ceased to do so and appalling nausea replaced it.

The sun sparkled on the rippling wavelets, and a light wind assisted their passage to the beach. Back at the Cassowary Lodge, a pod-shaped part of the world vanished, leaving a sphere, black with absence. The most theoretical of theoretical physicists, if present, would have flung down their favourite pencil and trotted outside.

Even during daylight.

Kalinda and the arrival party weren't alone. The tourists present hadn't seen live yggdrasil before, and the appearance of two such divided the crowd: many fled, preferring to do their alien watching on TV. Others moved closer: intent on a little DIY natural selection, and more thrilled by the celebrity sighting than the aliens themselves. Tek Alnus made a firm suggestion they keep their distance.

Still dazed, Kalinda said, "Where are they – the Stromatolites? Oh, Lenny, you poor thing!"

He was vomiting.

Stromatolites: Variably shaped aggregations of minerals such as limestone blended with blue-green algae have cheerfully produced oxygen for three and a half billion years. Consistent with Australia's proud history of either losing or failing to notice important stuff, they remained undiscovered until 1961. Even standing on a labelled and designated stromatolite viewing platform, Kalinda wasn't sure where to look.

"What, those dull lumpy things?" whispered Matt.

Niels launched into his lecture: "Here we are praising the role of the first photosynthetic organisms and their crucial activities in supporting life on earth …"

A minute in, Kalinda concluded her elementary school leaf-tracing-activities weren't the best preparation for the avalanche of information. The sun beat down: on her, on Niels, on Lenny's bald spot. It beat down on the stromatolites and the yggdrasil – but only they – clever things, could turn it into energy.

I get it, thought Kalinda as Niels said, "What respect people have for these simple photosynthetic life forms, protecting them, building the infrastructure to allow visits of appreciation without damage."

Ignoring the infrastructure, the aliens climbed from the platform, antennae rippling. The celebrities, after a moment's hesitation, followed them, the Swede last.

"Are there … any sharks?"

Her eyes sparkled, "No, Niels," smiled Kalinda.

Something that a visit to a stromatolite reserve soon establishes is that for the average punter there's only so much interest to be derived from them, (in the absence of, say, a giant fibreglass and cement model replete with gift shop; on which Australian tourism destinations so pride themselves).

Accordingly, after some dutiful splashing around, Kalinda waded up to Niels and Sif Acer and queried, "Is this the same beach where wild dolphins swim into the shallows?"

"Yes, I read that on the plane – it's in the bay but a distance away. This is a super salty part. I don't know if dolphins visit here."

"These the predatory water animals humans exhibit a preference for?" asked Sif Acer, keeping its leaf-wings out of the water.

"Ah, yes, you could say that, I guess," said the songstress as the increasing sea breeze played havoc with her hair.

"Perhaps some will venture," said the yggdrasil, craning its eye stalks this way and that.

Soon, wandering among the stromatolites in an increasingly desultory manner, Kalinda and the others directed surreptitious *have we admired the sacred algae enough yet*? glances at Niels.

Rarely used parts of her brain analysed the shape of sudden dorsal fins and their movement through the water.

Dolphins.

"Matt look," she called. He was conferring with Niels on the 'positive people-plant interactions strategy'. Matt's eyes widened, and he splashed towards her. Niels, less practiced in shark identification, hung back.

Kalinda giggled as she caught, "Good talk, Doc. Great trip, and it's excellent to have a purpose … but it's even better to pat a porpoise!"

And with that, Matt waded towards her.

Chapter 32 “Have you seen how many followers …”

“Hello, you two,” Niels attempted a playful tone, “what are you doing?”

“Reciprocal greetings,” said Sif Acer.

Matt grinned, “Err, I’m trying to teach Sif A jokes.”

For real. But before Niels could explore this theme further, the rest of the cast, Tek Alnus and a camera crew arrived at the breakfast table. Under alien supervision, the cast demurely nibbled a range of tropical fruits.

Except Big Len, who stuck to grilled bacon, tomatoes, and mushrooms on toast. This didn’t prevent him saying, “The new guy’s a real strong candidate for fruit-tax-bucket-monitor.” He wafted a meaty hand towards it.

Gosh, I saw it on television, now I’m smelling it. “A question,” said Niels. “Before I am flying to join the show, there were reports of conflict on sugar farms. Can you explain, please?”

“Sugar cane production cessation,” stated Tek Alnus in the impassive voice of the phone app.

The celebrities directed by now, well-practiced, wary glances at each other.

There was the characteristic static rasp, then the creature said, “Simple light-gatherers crushed, boiled, filtered, burnt. Additional information: humans mix remains unwanted with soil, culture unfortunate generation above. This will cease. Likewise, cotton and tobacco, light-gatherers to be unmolested.”

Combining nervous and sheepish looks, the humans kept their eyes down as the yggdrasil continued, "Such activity wrought environment destruction tropical landscapes, native forests killed and replaced, native humans replaced, others transported forth in slavery." Like Siri reading a poorly edited Wikipedia entry, the alien said, "Additional information: consumption develops sub-optimal health processes. Examples: irregular glucose metabolism, obesity, damage of dentition, irregular cell growth cancers, undesirable others."

"Well, thanks for your clarity and concern on those points." said Niels with a deep breath.

Next to him, Matt spoke up, addressing Sif Acer, "You mentioned this before as a compromise – these being less *essential* crops." He casually relocated empty sugar sachets behind his coffee.

"Affirmative. When televisually important persons issue directives consistent with ahimsa principles such conflicts eliminated," said Sif Acer directing its eyestalks this way and that.

The celebrities exchanged appalled looks as the enormity of the misunderstanding hit home.

"Why did I let my agent, talk me into this," murmured Mariam, who'd maintained her privacy, but not her opinions, more than the others. (Rather defeating the show's purpose in the watching producer's view.) The rainforest parrots heard a muttering of agreement about the failings of agents. "I could've been on Heron Island watching the turtles come up to lay their eggs," she continued. "It's my happy place."

"Sounds cool," said Matt kindly and happy to change the topic away from the perils of sugar consumption. Wistfully, he reflected on pre-ratings surge conversations concerning astrology and activated turmeric colonics.

"Query: Heron Island location pictured on human sun-metal disc message?" said Sif Acer.

There were a few blank looks.

"I think in the 1970s there was a space probe with a gold record containing images and audio. Does anyone recall? Niels looked around the table and at the crew recording proceedings.

"Seriously, Doc? I was listening to AC/DC and trying to have sex with the girl at the next desk. It's not my thing," concluded Lenny.

"Gold, affirmative. Multiple 79 Hydrogen unity," said Tek Alnus.

"Is that how you discovered us – the Earth – from the record some boffin sent into space?" said Len, his tone indignant.

"Negative. Spectra chemicals of life detected. Planet visited previously. Many planets of suitable light intensity, gravitation, water, known to us," explained Sif Acer.

"Did you enjoy the Island picture?" asked Mariam.

"Affirmative, many trees. Light gatherers under-represented remainder disc." The alien tweaked its configuration to maximise sunlight capture.

"Was there anything else on the disc you liked. I mean, other than trees?" said Matt, eyes bright with interest. "Not that trees aren't great!"

"Some music," ventured Sif Acer.

"Affirmative" added its companion.

"Who decided what to include," wondered Kalinda aloud.

"Is it not your purpose: human leaders, human experts having this knowledge?" said Sif Acer peering at Kalinda and the others.

She nibbled her lip and said, "What is it, Matt?" concerned by his new-record-level of befuddlement.

He shook his head, "It's like this recurring dream: I'm naked in an exam for a subject I'm not enrolled in and know nothing about."

Niels nodded, "I'm afraid as excellent as we are in many ways, there are gaps in our knowledge and our power …" *God, I'm sounding like Matt.* "And that's why I like to store my extra knowledge on the internet."

*

A few hours later, Matt entered the production centre, "So, the magic happens here ..."

Maggie had grudgingly returned the casts' phones. "*Do not*,' she ordered, investigate you own popularity or interact with the fans."

Upon her leaving, Matt and Lenny immediately did so. Mariam researched the coral cay, and Kalinda, the contents of the Voyager space probe gold record.

"Geez," said Matt, "five weeks of email, frequent shopper points, penis reductions, bank statements, gig invites. What is it with shoe shops?" continued Matt, developing a theme, "you buy a pair of socks and that magical spray-on micro particle stuff, and they think you're in a serious relationship with them!"

Kalinda laughed, and shortly afterward exclaimed, "Matt, did you see how many followers you've got?"

"How many?" said Len.

"Forty million," she reported, excited for Matt.

"Yeah, I saw it, thanks. I'm trying to be cool!

"Would you all, oh, I don't know, care to do some research," said Mariam.

"Sorry, Miss," said the comic, with a discrete eye-rolling.

Chapter 33 Heron Island

Niels, Mariam and Sif Acer approached the pool.

"Hi, everyone, I've just seen Maggie—"

"Bad luck Doc, but sometimes in a show like this, well we just can't avoid it," grinned Matt. "But, hey, isn't great seeing a woman in the media burst through the glass ceiling."

Niels ignored this. "So, we thought," (indicating his companions) "to spend the afternoon at Heron Island, viewing the trees and the corals."

Kalinda flicked her hair aside and said, "But we'd have to come back here again afterward?"

Niels nodded sympathetically, catching Mariam's 'not in front of the alien look.'

As before, the cast filed into the pod with a crew member. Where they confirmed instant transport by alien tech reduces the sense of anticipation and distance. But not the frog-on-rotating-garden-sprinkler sense of vertigo.

Tropical light fell on Heron Island's trees, noddy terns, and gorgeous blue-green reef shallows. The light fell on tourists sipping cocktails by the pool and fending off voracious chip-stealing gulls. The light continued falling at a predictable, earthly 300 000 000 metres per second, and then unexpectedly, a pod-shaped hole in accustomed reality appeared. And was filled – a moment later – by the pod itself. The earthly sunlight, its confidence shaken, but bravely carrying on, continued to shine – illuminating the hats, headscarf, and bald spot of an ex-cricketer as the owners of these staggered forth.

Len lurched and swayed. He sank to his knees in ankle-deep water and vomited on coral rubble and a surprised blue sea-star. The sea-star or starfish was having a trying day. Only moments before a human had picked it up, turned it over, poked its tube-feet and generally displayed its person to a group of tourists.

This unsought sea-star wrangler was mere metres from the pod when it materialised, causing him to stagger and gulp in shock. He recovered himself, (for he was an Outdoor Education graduate); swallowed in the speculative manner of someone eating unfamiliar street food with too many legs, and said, "Welcome, my name's Brad. You've come to see the reef?"

"Seriously, a Pom!" exclaimed Lenny.

What is the meaning of this strange greeting? wondered Niels. None-the-less he engaged the sun-bleached, tanned, and muscled guide with the disreputable sneakers in conversation. And after a brief planning meeting, the reef guide went off to gather his fearful, scattered flock. Meanwhile, the *CCE* cast and crew member headed inland to the island's forest. Their intention: to partake in Brad's reef tour on their return.

*

Heron Island on the Great Barrier Reef is only eight hundred metres long, appears forested from the air, and unlike most land bodies nervously surrounded by water – consists of coral. The *CCE* cast didn't know exactly why its image appeared on the Voyager gold record (although to be fair, the same might be said of the copious imagery of human reproductive anatomy included). Regardless: Niels found no trouble lauding the island's attributes to the yggdrasil.

"As you are knowing, the island is heavily forested, and yet here is a resort where people come to enjoy the beauty and also a research station."

The party moved under cover of the trees themselves. Away from the moderating influence of the sea, the sheltered, humid air hit the academic like a physical force. In his well-honed field-trip style, he continued, "This island has scarce nutrients for the plants. Fortunately, thousands of birds visit here, fertilising the ground with their droppings."

Lenny muttered, "What is it with this fellow and bird shit! Err, Doc," he said, stepping forward, "what if you show the aliens the trees and such, take in the research station and I'll drop by the resort; reassure everybody, maybe check out what's good on the reef, what to avoid."

"Avoid!" said Mariam, oozing contempt.

"Oh yeah, giant clams, jellyfish … *sharks*," said Lenny, with a significant glance at Niels.

"Fine," said Mariam, "don't engage with the process. We'll pick you up later."

"These shady trees are of the bougainvillea family." Niels pointed at the forest floor. It was almost without undergrowth, but well-endowed with bird life. The terns, having regular exposure to guides, were barely interested, as he said, "The tree seeds are sticky with little … little barbs, yes. They fasten to the feathers of the birds. So, in this way, they disperse seeds from island to island. Once again, an example of plants and animals needing each other and of humans protecting and admiring a forest."

Well said Doc. Go us! thought Matt.

Around them, resort visitors and staff vanished like ice creams eaten with insufficient urgency. A ten-minute walk, with pauses and questions from human and alien alike, was enough to take the group across the island.

"We could visit the research station before picking up Lenny and meeting Brad," said Matt. "I'm feeling sciencey again – it strikes me at times."

And so, they followed the sandy path through the trees to the Research Station turn off. Where a hastily arranged and undaunted researcher told the yggdrasil more tales of forest-bird interactions. The second topic: coral bleaching – caused an abundance of antennae thrashing.

*

At the same time, entering the cane and rattan furnished main bar with an expectant stride, the recoil of the crowd disappointed Lenny (he considered that if his appearance wasn't as well-proportioned as some; in dull light, at least, could be described as ruggedly intriguing). A few pointed questions on yggdrasil whereabouts soon allayed his concerns about the warmth of the welcome.

"Oh, so you're here on the island then?" said a relaxed fellow in a turtle-motif T-shirt.

"Yeah, mate," said Len, establishing this was the case.

This settled – he settled into the Bar – conveniently supplied with a public happy to buy drinks for the celebrity. He basked in the attention, heroically downplaying the dangers dodged daily. As is usual for Australians of the tropics, they exchanged tall tales of deadly local creatures. It was an hour before the others returned to retrieve him (parking the yggdrasil outside). By then, the public's exposure was twice that recommended by authorities such as ex-teammates.

On their return to the beach, Niels observed his reclaimed co-star seemed relaxed – liberally so. Lenny was intent on pre-warning him of the reef's many perils. For not only does Australia boast more slot machines per head of population than other continents, but – as the forester was now learning – a generous-over supply of lethal creatures.

Ret Moitch remained on the beach – the threat of menace keeping the on-lookers at bay. Niels performed introductions, and those with people-feet were fitted with well-worn sneakers. The dreadlocked Englishman lead the party into the shallows. Reassured that the sharks were small and harmless; the deadly jellyfish out of season; the sea snakes merely curious, the fire corals in deeper waters, Niels relaxed. He hadn't seen such tropical fish since the waiting room of a childhood dentist in Stockholm.

"Here in the intertidal zone," said Brad, "the corals are prone to wave and tourist damage." He led them to peer into deeper rock pools nearer the reef edge. "Careful please, not to damage the reef."

For their part, Mariam and Niels were more concerned with damage the reef might inflict on them. Although their guide had allayed Len's jovial warnings concerning a host of malcontent fauna (of which Niels had been happily unaware), he kept a close eye on his feet. *Is it worse to stand on something squishy or something spiky?*

"Are there any biting, stinging animals that affect you err, yggdrasil?" said Lenny, lacking subtly as banded sea snakes lack legs.

"Prior testing suggests no requirement for concern," responded Tek Alnus. It arched its eyestalks towards the cricketer and held its light-gathering structures above the water.

"Ah."

Brad halted the aquamble* near a branched pink coral that met his exacting standards. Niels steered the guide's spiel towards the perspective he wanted the yggdrasil to hear, "So even though many corals are resembling plants, they are really animals?"

"Yes, that's correct. Related to jellyfish," said Brad.

"And yet while they are animals, they contain plant cells?"

"Yeah, yeah, I just learned this," said Len, slurring, "... zu-zu-phalli," he announced, with a grin at Mariam.

She glared.

Brad raised an eyebrow, "Sir is quite the scholar: Zooxanthellae."

"And these are single-celled photosynthetic algae in a mutually beneficial relationship with the coral animals?" queried Niels for the benefit of the yggdrasil.

"That's correct, a dinoflagellate. They give the corals their colour and bleaching occurs when the algae leave the host coral."

"So, people come to see this protected island of coral, with its trees and soil enriched by the birds and the living coral reef," asked Niels.

Brad thought this was an unusual perspective but guessed what lay behind it. "Absolutely! Including yours truly. Came for a week, been here seven months."

---

*aquatic amble.

"Sif Acer, is this what you meant when you said, 'Humans should like corals more,'" said the forester.

"Negative. Miscommunication," said the alien. "Meaning intention: Humans should be more like corals."

"I don't understand."

"Emulation. Humans should emulate corals."

"Cease discussion of corals," said Tek Alnus, its antennae thrashing.

As a trained outdoor education graduate, Brad sensed tension in the group. He attempted a distraction, "Giant clams also contain zooxathanthallae – it gives them that fluorescent appearance."

"Cool," said Matt, "another animal-plant team-up."

Niels turned as Lenny announced, "I don't reckon anyone could get trapped in one of these things." Recalling adventure stories of his youth, Niels agreed, but he hadn't attempted to his insert a foot in the molluscan menace. "See, they close real slow, and not all that tight," showed the cricketer learnedly.

"Please, sir, leave the clams alone," instructed Brad.

By mutual consent, the reef-shallows tour over, the group wound its way back – dodging sea-cucumbers of both the slimy-black and knobbly orange breeds.

The daylight was fading, and clam abuse forgiven, Brad showed the *CCE* party more of the island's natural treasures. The guide suggested they sit on a beach and watch stingrays jumping out of the water as the sun set. Matt and Kalinda thought this an excellent idea, but not so the yggdrasil. And so, the party once more entered the hovering pod. Niels made a mental note to discover what became of the yggdrasil after dark and another to discover the significance of the coral dispute.

The pod hummed and vanished, tangling earth physics in its wake – like kittens playing with string theory. Tourist phone-shot footage of the pod vanishing wasn't great quality. Yet it inspired an inordinate number of alien technology conferences on the island in years to come.

Chapter 34 Vibrating Strings and Leaf Wings

Soon after their return, as the fruit bats whirled overhead, Niels approached Matt and Kalinda chatting by the pool.

"Hi. Kalinda, can you spare me a moment?"

"Sure. What is it, Niels?"

"The afternoon went well. And earlier, when talking of that gold record sent into space, our alien colleagues said they liked certain music. Maybe the day completes well if you'd like to play something?"

"Well, Niels, I would, but I didn't bring my guitar."

This surprised the scientist. With limited exposure to Reality TV shows, his understanding was that instrument strumming was standard behaviour at some point.

"You know AB, the audio dude," said Matt, "he has a ukulele if that's any use to you. We had a chat about it. I do a little three-chord uke strumming myself – four counting A minor."

"Great, I'll find AB," Kalinda said brightly.

"I'll supervise," said Matt.

"Perhaps after dinner, although I think it rains soon," observed Niels uncertainly.

Dinner comprised BBQ fish and the usual tropical fruits, moodily lit under flickering fuel torchlights (and the trinkets from the Pacific so necessary for reality TV). After their day trip, the cast was in fine spirits. The least alarming of the yggdrasil was present. Not only was the scientist's prediction of rain incorrect, but he didn't anticipate the conversation turning to turtles.

"Pity we didn't see any turtles today, eh Mariam," said Matt.

"It would have been nice," she agreed. "But too early for the egg-laying season."

"Turtles-animals …" began Sif Acer and then lapsed into suspenseful silence for a longish moment. Following the familiar burst of white noise, the plant-creature observed, "Larger varieties having elongated life spans."

"Yes, not so many animals live for hundreds of years. Turtles, tortoises, Greenland sharks, if I remember correctly. Trees live slower and longer than animals," said Niels, pouncing on the topic.

"Clams today were of interest," said Sif Acer, directing most of its eyestalks at Niels and a few at Lenny. "Additional observation: perhaps turtles should control resource allocation."

As usual, subtly of expression was lacking in communication by phone app. Still, Matt was sure: the creature had made its first joke. He turned as Mariam said: "Yes, having longer fixed terms of government means politicians could plan properly for the future, instead of focusing on a three-year election cycle."

"We'd get stuck with the bastards for longer," scoffed Len.

Kalinda stood. "I'll tune-up. The crew's set up in the meditation clearing. Just give me a few minutes."

Niels nodded and tried steering the conversation.

"The changes we humans need to live, err, harmoniously with your kind, will take time. I'm sure this can happen within the life of these trees." He waved at larger specimens near the clearing's edge.

"Self-adjudicates: Humans more interesting beings than grasses," the vegetal-being ventured by way of reply.

Although a compliment, of sorts, reflected the forester – it was not an answer to the question. He chomped on prawn tails in an unsatisfied way.

Soon enough Matt announced, "I reckon she'll be ready by now. We should head over."

"Will she just sing? Is there a backing track?" said Mariam.

"One of the crew has a uke …"

"God no!"

"It'll be great … it's a blackwood tenor with pickup – Kalinda used to play classical guitar. No need for alarm!"

"Are you trying to get into her pants or something, mate?" snorted Len. "Pretty sure Maggie Reynolds would be rapt with that!"

In the clearing, the *CCE* crew were present. They'd arranged chairs for the cast and stayed to watch the show. Sif Acer stood behind the chairs, and Niels further back with the crew. Kalinda explained to the camera that since there'd been an appreciation of recorded music launched into space decades before, she intended to play a few tunes.

The creatures of the night hovered in the lights, and the trees loomed evocatively at the clearing's edge. Kalinda plucked a few strings; then, almost shyly, a couple more (as if she were a lone musician, representing humanity to an uncertain audience). Her pure high voice soared out into the night, as reprising her church performance days she played Amazing Grace – coaxing the small instrument to sustain long plaintive notes.

Stood next to Maggie behind the crew, Niels heard the rustle of the remaining alien pair. They lurched to stand beside their companion. The two humans shared a rare moment of bonhomie as the night sky, flickering lights, and music mix worked its ancient magic. The performance continued, sampling folk music standards, and then something Niels didn't recognise. Something classical and complex, without vocals, notes slipping over each other like running water. The yggdrasil stilled their usual busy adjustment of appendages. With a nod and a sign of his finger, Niels signalled to the show's producer.

Unseen by the camera, the aliens vibrated slightly but distinctly.

"Is it a sex thing?" rasped Maggie, somewhat ruining the mood.

The performance ended with an up-tempo pop song that the forester understood to be one of Kalinda's own. Again, unobserved by the camera, the alien audience came out of their vibratory state before the last note; before the humans applauded. Then, for the first time, an alien made a show of deliberately touching a person as Sif Acer brushed Kalinda's shoulder with its leaf-wing.

Chapter 35 Cousin Benji – The Prepper

October 25
mom love nyc
AWAY IN A BUNKER

I'm back dear readers! been such an interesting week with james and the kiddos. we've been staying with james' cousin in the pacific north west. cousin benji is very much the prepper. here I am in borrowed camo vest (so many pockets!), tactical belt, woollen pants, shooting a few cans [Pic 1]. benji and family have been prepping seriously for five years. now the yggdrasil have arrived they feel it's time to leave town and bunker down. here's anne-maree and me making brownies and vacuum packing them [Pic 2] while james and benji prepare home-smoked salmon (cherry wood fire, thyme and black pepper seasoning) [Pic 3]. the kiddos had a great time climbing in and out of the bunker, feeding the chickens and spying through the periscope! but can I just say dear reader that I pray all this won't be necessary!

In other news today eir nyssa said anne-maree was like a sapling. so, it has learned a figure of speech, so interesting. until next time peeps!

Chapter 36 Tall Trees

Niels squatted, wobbled, then sat on the spongy grass, having trouble with gravity, equilibrium, and such. He gulped, "From Sweden, this is the world's end."

"That's harsh, Doc," joked Matt. "But sure – on a day with the wind in the south-west, you can smell it from here."

The yggdrasil examined the translocated European trees, waiting for their travelling companions to recuperate. Soon the bracing spring air of the southern capital worked its charms. Clouds lurked around the mountain, akin to adult children reluctant to leave the family nest, as the group set off to collect their minibus.

Left to its own devices, the pod vanished. It left a blacker than black swirling pod-shaped void in contemporary physics – and more locally – next to the bandstand, in St. David's Park, Hobart. The claws of the yggdrasil scratched and scraped on the city's hard surfaces as they left the gardens behind.

"Agreeable to view person habitations stone and brick alternative to unfortunate trees," said Sif Acer.

At the rear of the group with Kalinda, Matt said, "Yeah, we talked about that before. Any preferred housing options?"

Niels observed Sif Acer ripple its feelers. Its companion said, "Humans belong in caves."

As they walked, a wary crowd shadowed them, and Sif Acer revealed unguessed at earlier visits to the planet. Niels thought, *it seems chatty ... is it nervous? Maybe it doesn't care for the pavement.*

However, as the party drew closer to a morning street market, he understood.

"Bugger," exclaimed Lenny, selecting one of his milder but still handy expletives. Even he of the unhurried thought processes realised the potential for unpleasantness given Tek Alnus' proximity to hundreds of people buying fruit, vegetables, flowers, and other fine Tasmanian produce.

The crowd moved back in a wave. Urban alien sightings were still a rarity. But there was little panic. *Wow*, thought Niels, *I've never seen so many woollen jumpers – more than Stockholm. Oh, there's a reindeer.*

"Jesus, it's like a homeless convention, said Matt.

"Shh," said Kalinda, poking him.

"Look, kids are wearing feelers!"

Niels hadn't much-considered clothing implications of the Cairns Declaration before meeting Ebony Hamilton in New York. Clearly others had. There was an awful lot of non-plant fibre clothing on display: woollen hats everywhere, jackets of real and synthetic goose-down … leather coats. Fashion trend? yggdrasil-supportive political statement? The forester was uncertain.

Scattered members of the crowd applauded, and the *CCE* cast relaxed, or at least shifted down a gear in tension.

"Smile and wave," advised Matt.

"I need a coffee," grumbled Mariam, and joined a queue in front of a converted 1950s era caravan.

Small hand-knitted children stared, and a busker ceased strumming as the yggdrasil made their way past honey kombucha, vegan coconut ice cream and a hundred kinds of bread. Niels and Kalinda exchanged significant glances and wove through the crowd, nonchalantly blocking Tek Alnus' view of offending produce. A difficult task when a being has multiple telescopic eyestalks and quite the propensity for offence. (A difficulty akin to discovering an un-whiskered market barista.)

"Oh dear," whispered Kalinda.

The alien lurched to a halt. The stall sold fresh carrots, white radishes, and beetroots: roots and leaves still provocatively attached. Tek Alnus vibrated ominously, but its companion led it away.

Its annoyance was matched by Mariam's.

She explained to buy a coffee she had to engage a bearded beverage guardian in negotiation. "First, he chastised me for not having a reusable cup …" she shook her head, "then he wanted to write my name on the cup. Then he debated the spelling and made me wait five and a half minutes."

Matt, meanwhile, through the exercise of more charm, had secured free drinks for all. The group sat around repurposed cable reel tables.

"Let me tell you how coffee is farmed," began Niels. Nearer locals ceased their discussions of the perils posed by the world's discovery of their city in recent years and listened in. Neither tales of coffee production nor the crowd itself appeared to agitate the yggdrasil pair. But the scientist was keen to take them away.

"So … we meet the guide at the hire place, do the road trip to the national park and later shortcut by pod to the west coast. Shall we stop at that historic winery?" His calm surety wavered for a second. *And we must come up with a proclamation by tomorrow.*

The cast considered the winery an excellent suggestion. Even so, the rapidity with which Matt stood displayed an excess of enthusiasm.

"You okay, Matt," said Kalinda, brushing his arm.

"Yeah, yeah, no worries, bit hyper. Feels as if I've had five coffees, but I've only had three – and one of those papaya energy drink bubble teas."

"Can't take you anywhere eh," scoffed Len, and the party set off to the vehicle hire business.

The establishment's junior employee soon concluded dealing with alien tourists was beyond her pay scale. Her expression barely altered when, with unnatural strength, the yggdrasil tore the backs from two seats. That was the simple part; Niels was reminded of the complex articulation of the Saab roof, as the aliens folded their jointed bodies into the vehicle.

"Call me BJ," said their waiting, sturdy-boots-and-shorts-clad guide. Like many of his ilk, BJ appeared shy of the brush and comb.

Len regarded him from beneath heavy brows. "I'll drive."

At the helm of the electric minibus, Lenny regaled the others with tales of his former cricketing exploits in Hobart. Niels had a vague awareness of cricket's importance as a summer sport down under. He knew there was a major match that started just after Christmas and finished shortly before Easter, but he had no clue as to "… took eight for one hundred and thirty for the match – was over by tea on day four."

Mariam had been to their next location before, but her focus had been the renowned Museum of Old and New Art (MONA) rather than the historic winery on the same site.

"I don't really drink," admitted Kalinda as they parked.

"Nor I," asserted Mariam.

"Jesus," said Lenny. Unlike the aliens, he had but one pair of eyes and so didn't detect Mariam's glare.

Wine tourism was not a major industry in the Sweden of Niels' youth. And the group's visit soon established wineries were unlikely to be overrun by alien tourists. But many a reader will be pleased to know – at least the yggdrasil didn't object.

BJ took over the driving. They headed north, and Niels saw a picturesque landscape of wattle and eucalypt forest, agricultural pursuits, and transplanted European trees in towns, and by narrow roadsides. He also observed an excess number of flattened marsupials.

On route to their destination, Niels addressed the yggdrasil and Jaspa's camera: "Russell Falls in Mount Field National Park is the oldest reserve in the state. Tasmania has almost half its area assigned to forest reserves."

"That's right," called BJ. "But disputes over exactly what can occur in the various reservation categories keep us locals busy on long winter nights."

"Err, BJ, *what is it* with all these dead animals?" asked Niels. He couldn't identify the crumpled creatures scattered like confetti across the bitumen – but it was difficult to miss the unnecessary abundance of them.

"Well, we have a lot of wildlife: pademelons, wallabies, brush-tailed possums. There are adverts to drive slow at night when the wildlife is up and about." BJ glanced at Niels in the rear vision mirror.

A glimmer of an idea for broaching an awkward subject occurred to Niels. *Using already dead life-forms is a tricky topic to casually introduce*, thought he. It requires a certain amount of lead work. Turning to Sif Acer, Niels said, "I am knowing you have declared eating animals is immoral, uncivilised and so forth …" He paused and with increased confidence said, "But, despite this, the yggdrasil can tolerate it. What, however, if the animal is already dead? As we see here?" he waved at the passing carnage. The alien didn't respond, Niels hurried on.

"In times past, if a whale beached and died, the local people would eat it. Or in places where thousands of salmon swim upstream to spawn and die – not so much now with the environmental degradations, yes – but what is your view on eating them? Do you understand my meaning?"

Matt added helpfully, "It's important to arrange death and sex in the correct order."

There were disdainful noises from the others.

Sif Acer said, "Distasteful prospect. Negative immoral prospect."

Questions from Niels' co-humans came rapidly:

"What are you saying, Doc?"

"What do the Jains say?"

"Geez, the yggdrasil already said we could still eat meat – why bring this up?"

"I wish," continued Niels calmly, "to establish how far we can apply this idea of non-harm. I am knowing this may be uncomfortable, but trees are killed by natural events: strong winds, floods, an avalanche of snow, and so I am wondering whether we humans could use such timber for certain needs." He paused, "Or is there an inconsistency between using dead animals and plants."

"Not one that's been keeping me awake, Doc," said Matt.

“Consultation necessary/consultation necessary.” The yggdrasil lapsed into silence. Len and Mariam filled the void. They’d much to say: both simultaneously and at volume.

BJ hurled the bus up and around the narrow fern strewn road – the wheels sampling the gravel surface from time to time. As they filed from the vehicle in the Tall Trees Walk car park, mischievous spring winds snuck up sleeves and down collars. The visitors were glad to follow BJ, all bare legs and ligaments, into the shelter of the trees.

After a few minutes’ walk, enormous, tall gum trees appeared in the forest. They had smooth, straight upper trunks that contrasted with the lower, untidy, shaggy-bark-effect. These: the Mountain Ash.

BJ patted one such, “They’re the second tallest tree in the world, growing to a hundred metres and living between three and four centuries.”

“And not only here but across the state, the grandest specimens are protected?” said Niels strategically.

“Yep.”

“Gotta love big trees,” said Matt.

The group stood by an enormous log, carpeted with moss, adorned with fungi, and older than European settlement. The thump of a startled pademelon broke the quiet, followed by the sound of small, running feet. Sif Acer perceived, craning its eyestalks forwards and down, that a human child had fastened itself to its lower regions.

“Mummy, Mummy! I found one, like on the TV!” the creature called.

Simultaneously, three strange yggdrasil strode through the sparse undergrowth into view. With stamping thuds, more marsupials scattered. Tek Alnus stepped towards the newcomers. And then, out of sight, came the plaintive cry of a bushwalker calling for its young. The Mountain Ash hadn’t seen such excitement since the pale people first came to the forest.

In contrast, three-years-old today, Cate lived in a whirl-wind of questioning excitement: “This mud sticks. Presents. Presents. Presents. This cake’s got fire. Mummy, can I keep this one?”

The light-forager regarded the small creature, sensing something of its thoughts. Sif Acer covered the child with a wing-leaf. It giggled. The alien removed the appendage. The girl giggled once more.

Kalinda took advantage of a loosening grip, as the child turned to look at her stricken parent. She said, "Let go, sweetie," and peeled Cate from Sif Acer's hard cool limb.

The alien stepped off the path, motioning for the now firmly supervised child and its parent pass. "Please to proceed." And with predatory grace, it sauntered off to join its companions.

Other than Jaspa, who aimed his camera at the group of yggdrasil, the others stood about feeling redundant. Hush voiced, BJ said, "They're getting common in the parks now – lots in the south-west too."

Niels nodded grimly. *Our next destination.*

Chapter 37 Ancient Trees of Gondwana

Shaking his head in disbelief, BJ steered the bus into a large, marrow-shaped craft.

Shortly after this, it re-appeared on the outskirts of Strahan.

"Worst uber ever," moaned Len, staggering out. "Better run me through the plan again."

"We take the Gordon River cruise to the Heritage Landing boardwalk." With a glance at Sif Acer, Niels continued, "There we admire the celebrated huon pines. Then, we are in BJ's hands, rafting upstream and spending the night on the riverbank. Jaspa will record this, yes."

"Important personages edict-command will follow," said Tek Alnus.

Niels scratched his stubble, *we haven't forgotten.*

Certain *CCE* celebrities were not much drawn to outdoor pursuits or adventure tourism. The closest Mariam had been to wilderness was spotting David Attenborough at Heathrow baggage collection five years earlier. Meanwhile, Matt appraised the loaded red raft with mock horror. He regaled the others with tales of capsizing, punctures, pirate attacks, and other maritime ordeals – a few even outside the confines of his childhood swimming pool.

"Err, Matt …" whispered Niels, boarding the cruise boat, "do you think you can keep the yggdrasil away from the dining room."

It was soon apparent the tourists preferred their photosynthetic life forms conventionally attached to the ground, rather than striding their holiday transport with an air of menace. They hovered in the buffet's vicinity, keeping away from the yggdrasil and watching the ancient forest glide past.

"Step aside people, let me show you how it's done," said Len, lumbering towards the buffet.

"Hey – just a sec! I know you. Yeah, didn't you once take eight wickets at Bellerive?"

"Yeah, that was me." Deprived of deep-fried potato wedges for a month, he made the most of a brief alien-free feeding opportunity. "Just doing my bit, don't want the yggs to see all this," muttered Len warily, between bites.

*

Later, when the cruise reached its destination, Len peered warily into the gloom of the trees. However, the odds of being lunch to escaped convicts with a lust for human flesh had been much reduced in the recent century. The most dangerous creatures of the forests were yggdrasil: the self-appointed tree wardens.

Over the tour boat's PA system, the celebrities heard: "Strahan was founded as a base for timber cutters or 'piners' in 1887. Early European visitors were much appreciative of huon pine as a boat building timber." (So appreciative axe-wielding convicts soon cut most of it.)

The party examined the mossy, dripping forest from the comfort of the boardwalk, Niels said, "No-one has cut living pines for decades. They are fully protected." (Be assured, any pepper grinders or boats the adventurous reader might fancy are fashioned from long-dead wood.)

"The air smells amazing, said Kalinda."

"That's the smell of time," said BJ, who fancied himself a poet.

They halted by the largest tree. Niels turned to the camera, "This one's estimated at three thousand years. These pines are the second oldest living things on earth. In the past there were terrible errors, but we humans are learning."

*

On their return, the *CCE* party had the boat to themselves as they changed into wetsuits. Loops of rope and carabineers glinting in the sun always add an air of authority – and so equipped, BJ organised the unorthodox crew.

Please separate Mariam and Len thought Niels.

The raft began its stately progress upriver. After twenty minutes of watching the myrtle beech forest glide past, the two yggdrasil by unspoken communication grasped and examined the paddles.

BJ looked back at the wake wearing a: *can't believe this, but I'm way too cool to acknowledge it* expression.

"No hands!" called Matt, waving his blade in the air as the inhuman power of the yggdrasil moved the raft faster than any previously paddled red raft.

It was no accident had Niels thought to issue the *CCE* 'proclamation' from the south-west wilderness. No stranger to political controversy; the region's trees were again in the public consciousness. Radio shock-jock and former *CCE* contestant, Graeme O'Brien's advice to eat more vegetables and don more plant fibre clothing (even hemp), as protest had bemused much of the country. Yet, O'Brien's strategic suggestion to threaten the South-West World Heritage area *had* gained a degree of public and political support. Elsewhere, similar threats had been made by the former owners of mossy skeletons and their rusting chainsaws.

As the distance between the raft and the nearest espresso machine increased, the cast grew quiet. Meanwhile, the light-gathers paddled like a party of five-year-old's over-stimulated by red cordial. The tea-coloured river narrowed. Time and black river rocks slid by; cliff faces, caves, and small islands appeared. Unknown yggdrasil watched from the banks. The ungainly raft danced on the water; the expertise of the guide coupled to the power of the aliens.

At the bow of the raft, rope in hand, Niels had that ubiquitous TV Viking look: firm unshaven jawline, wind tousled fair hair – blue eyes alive with curiosity. He leaped and secured the raft. Lenny followed, but slipped on a rock and splashed into the chilly water. He surfaced and stood waist-deep, with the sad-eyed look of a baby seal. One with a deep personal sense of misfortune.

Mariam slapped the raft, "Oh, come on, this isn't *Heart of Darkness* somebody lure him out with a sausage or something." Removed and dried in the Lower Gordon campsite's rustic hut, Lenny and the rest explored the campsite and surrounds.

"It's so quiet," said Kalinda. There was no wind and no animal cries, just a pervasive mossy muffling of sound. The celebrities kept their voices down.

"Yeah," agreed BJ. "But you'll see a few of the locals once it gets dark." He took a frozen hamburger from the watertight blue food barrel, clipped it to a thin cord and tossed it in the river, "Might stir something up with this."

"Any deadly serpents?" said the Swede.

"Mate … it's simple, you see a snake in Tassie – it's poisonous!" clarified BJ with unnecessary enthusiasm. "It saves all that: Is it a python? Is it harmless? Should I be worried bullshit? you get with mainland snakes."

Matt didn't share Niels' concern with toothy local wildlife. But slapping at a leech on the back of his calf, he stumbled and sprained his ankle. He hobbled away for BJ to examine him, with Kalinda offering moral support.

"Yep, got it," The guide removed the unnecessary leech. "The river's cold – stick your foot in it – it'll reduce the swelling."

Soon, three metres upstream, BJ pounced on his fishing line. With a cautious firm hand, he removed two kilos of recalcitrant snapping crustacean. Matt hastily removed his foot from the water. "Cool, giant Tasmanian freshwater lobster," said the guide, beginning a brief lecture. "Anyone want to poke it?"

Other than Niels and Lenny, the group kept a wary distance.

"Haven't seen a platypus on the river for nearly two months," BJ continued, releasing the lobster. It vanished in the dark water, and he lowered his voice. "You see the news they vanished when the yggdrasil arrived?"

Niels nodded.

"Oh my God," groaned Matt, focusing the wider group's attention. He'd attracted the attention of many happily swollen additional leaches – and not just on his legs. Kalinda moved sympathetically closer. BJ, with well-practiced techniques, swung into action.

"Small creatures devouring you?" said Sif Acer, small antennae rippling.

Matt whimpered. "Ahh, there's one near my area. Bugger off Jaspa, you're not filming this."

Tek Alnus' static burst was eerie in the failing light. "A feeder becomes the feedee," it said (unhelpfully in Matt's view).

The songstress excused herself.

"Nasty …" said BJ, applying his removal techniques with skill and a grin.

After this brief brush with somebody else's crisis, the humans gathered round the light and heat from the fuel stove. They donned extra clothing layers and head torches as the river mirrored the flickering stars.

Inevitably, someone waxed philosophical.

BJ said, "It just blew my mind when I watched what you guys were saying about the wood web connections. So many nights in this forest and others, don't you get that sense of being connected to everything. Of what it feels to be a tree, a tree among many, the cycle of day and night, winter–summer …" he trailed off, overcome with mystical feelings.

The darkness hid the rolling of several human eyes. Niels nodded, *I've heard similar sentiments, better expressed perhaps and often in Swedish.* For such feelings were not unheard among northern European nature lovers. Niels liked to keep them in a lesser-used part of his mind labelled 'unscientific thoughts.

"I know what you mean," said Niels hesitantly, tearing the label off. "I have experienced that in the forests of my homeland, and elsewhere, even in dreams … I think it's partly why I began tree communications research. Lately, around the yggdrasil, I feel it most strong."

"Geez, Doc!" said Lenny. "You should meet that tree mediatation woman we had on the show."

A screech echoed from the forest. The noise – which meant some poor creature's evening was ruined, shattered the campsite's ambience. The visitors looked to their guide for reassurance.

"Maybe a devil," (In the sense of the world's largest marsupial carnivore – rather than the Lord of all Evil, or a tech company CEO), shrugged BJ unconcerned.

Likewise unconcerned, the trees continued their soft rustlings. But an unseen bird flapped and squawked nervously, and a little higher up the evolutionary ladder, Lenny edged away from the forest. "Hey, since you yggdrasil don't run around hunting, eating, making stuff – just standing around gathering sunlight – what do you do with your time?"

"Weave songs of consciousness," responded Sif Acer.

"Wicked," said BJ.

"Improper statement," said Tek Alnus. "Yggdrasil possess manufacturing ability."

"The transport pods, for instance," said Mariam, speaking with exaggerated slowness and clarity for Len's benefit.

"Preferable be gathered-sunlight-standing than human pursued ambition of ever-increasing consumption," concluded Tek Alnus in that disparaging, antennae thrashing way, which is so unwelcome after dinner.

BJ sensed the metaphorical atmosphere had become chilly and the actual atmosphere was now producing fine misty rain. He said, "It might be bedtime people."

"Yeah ... looking forward to crawling into my sleeping bag with my complementary mint," announced Matt attempting a chirpy tone.

"Remember, we must have *the* talk" said Niels.

Chapter 38 The Strahan Proclamation

Grey light snuck through slits in the rough timbered hut, luring Niels from his bunk. BJ had already risen and seen to the boiling of water.

"Thanks," said Niels. He accepted a mug of hot chocolate and took it to the riverbank. He sighed and watched his breath condense. The forest was peaceful, the rich earthy scent in the air mingled agreeably with his drink; the river was adorned with precisely the correct quantity of mist; he hadn't seen Maggie for twenty-four hours *and* they'd drafted the proclamation.

*

And yet how fraught were the hushed conversations of the night. Niels' a week ago arrival at the Cassowary Lodge had sparked a series of whispered discussions that Matt had likened to arguments in a library (although not the modern multi-media games arcade crossed with childcare centre variety). With some species of edict, proclamation or announcement expected on the morrow, matters came to a head.

In the hut's darkness Niels said, "You are knowing the alien presence on your TV show is a misunderstanding."

"Yeah, could we try explaining everything to Sif Acer? Maggie Reynolds isn't here," said Matt uncertainly.

"Even if *you* try that mate – Tek Alnus *is* here. If it goes pear-shaped, you put us all at risk," said Len.

"Shh."

I'm herding kittens, thought Niels, but there was an uneasy consensus that not producing an edict would be akin to removing Wi-Fi from a temperamental, currently Wi-Fi'd adolescent. He forced himself to unclench his jaw. "We must try. Maybe people will follow, perhaps countries, even the UN …"

"They'll just laugh."

"Who knows? But I never appeared on television promising to solve my country's problems between commercials for, what is that show … *Whoops! I Married a Stranger*, yes."

*

The scientist took another sip of hot chocolate and wiggled his bare toes. The mist was lifting, he peered at the riverbank and removed his left foot from the path of a leech of an uncertain disposition. A pair of black cockatoos flew over-head, squawking in accord or hostility, breaking the silence. He shuddered, reflecting on last night's tense discussions. Fragments of the views aired, swirled in his head, and pressed replay:

"I'm so going to change my agent …"

"It'll look like collaboration …"

"My agent sucks."

"At least this has given colonising nations a taste of their own medicine."

It *might be nice to have a little farm: fruit trees, chickens, a pond of krafta (freshwater crayfish),* thought Niels. Further musings were interrupted as the camp stirred. More cast members accepted hot drinks, and the aliens crept from the forest into the regrowth zone around the hut.

All bare legs and leather wrist-thongs, BJ called, "Got some damper and vegemite on the go."

Given the context, Niels suspected, *these might well be foodstuffs.* In the spirit of adventure and scientific inquiry, he abandoned the river's reflections and approached breakfast.

Hours of downstream travel later – first by raft and now by cruise boat – Niels again studied ever-shifting riverbank reflections. Huon pines, he'd come to know, came in a variety of shapes. None he'd seen, however, could match the splendour of the large boardwalk specimen. The 'Proclamation Tree' as the *CCE* publicity machine was to designate it. Niels delivered the negotiated word form at Heritage Landing on the return trip. The first six words made the difference in the end.

With light drizzle spotting Jaspa's camera and the great pine adding gravitas in the background, he said:

"By the power vested in us, we of the Celebrity Council declare a stop to lethal forestry activities and those inconsistent with the principles of ahimsa. Likewise, production and destruction of root vegetable life forms must cease forthwith."

"Well done, Doc, I do love an edict that ends with *forthwith* – gives it a nice olde-world feel," said Matt, giving him a friendly pat on the shoulder.

Chapter 39 Days at the Farm

November 3
mom love nyc
DAYS AT THE FARM

hey, it's me dear readers. as usual, sharing way too many pictures! as you know i love to try and respond to your lovely comments and suggestions. so … we're all just back from a week in california. oh my gosh, how AWESOME is it that california has just banned forestry.

here's james and me and the kiddos (adorable in synthetic gumboots) with 'bear' browning at his farm [Pic 1]. bear follows the blog and invited us all to see what he has learned WORKING TOGETHER with sri achras the local yggdrasil ambassador! [Pic 2]. kiddos just loving collecting eggs [Pic 3], helping with the cows [Pic 4], checking pumpkins [Pic 5], jumping in muddy puddles [Pic 6], more muddy puddles [Pics 7-9] just keep scrolling!

so awesome what sri achras and bear and the volunteers: crystal and the gang [Pic 10] are doing here. bear plants sample crops and he and the yggdrasil discuss how the aliens feel about using the food. he says this has all been quite an adventure and hopes it will reduce conflict between out kinds.

amen to that. in the evenings, the volunteers would play and sing [Pic 11] the kiddos would join in until they fell asleep. so tired so blessed [Pic 12].

i'm just so fricking INSPIRED. so full of plans for what we can grow in our apartment. stay tuned!

Chapter 40 Gobekli Tepe: The Beginning of the End

Lenny strode into the clearing. *Where is everyone? It's like aliens have taken them.* He rethought this. *Worse – it's like aliens have released them – without me.* Then he spotted a camera crew and advanced, using a line of palm trees for cover. Sneaking closer, he heard phone app voices. And peering around a trunk, he realised the aliens were talking to each other. Lenny slapped his head as realization dawned. *Bugger! I forgot. Matt and the others will be meeting at the forest pond.* As Lenny plotted how to join his co-stars without being seen, he heard:

"Sif Acer, you cannot protect your pets forever."

"Not pets, sentient beings worthy respect."

"When humans adopt light gathering or cease molesting photosynthetics."

"Selves could accelerate learnings."

"Not worthy. And forbidden ..."

*

The sportsman's co-stars sat around the natural pool. A rustling in the undergrowth curtailed hushed discussions of the world's reaction to the weekend's 'Strahan Declaration.'

"It's only me – slept in," said Lenny.

"A few countries have banned forestry," said Mariam tersely.

"It's only weeks to the show's end. What will happen when—"

"Yeah, Kalinda," said Len. "Gotta tell you what I just heard ..."

And he did.

"... so, off to Turkey" concluded Len, "hope we've got our passports."

"Um, how did Tek Alnus put it: '... we venture where your species began unweaving the Earth,'" recalled Matt. "It's different – *them* picking the destination. Given what Len just heard, it doesn't really bode well."

"It barely bodes at all," said Mariam.

*

In an archaeological site's carpark, an alien craft rearranged matter to its liking. The visitors looked out on the timeless, dry, and evocative landscape of Gobekli Tepe. A straggler among them, a large ex-cricketer, reached the viewing barrier. The nausea was clearing, and he felt peckish. He gazed upon extraordinary carved rock pillars and an abundance of rocks. Shrewd questions sprang to mind: *What is this? Where am I? Is that a doner kebab stall?*

As his mental fog lifted, he realised Tek Alnus had begun a lecture. A lecture, or possibly a rant. Lenny heard:

"... something, something, something ... signifies termination low impact hunter-gatherer lifestyle ... monumental architecture shows humans elevating selves above nature ... agriculture and its attendant horrors ... fanciful creation stories ... inexorable population increment ... enslavement wild grass species ..."

A stranger interrupted the alien's remarks. The sole crew member, Jaspa, swept his camera around as the man hustled past the forbidding figure of Ret Moitch.

"Welcome, sirs and madam, selam. I am Professor Demir."

A guide of more fearful disposition would not have approached the group. The professor was not such a guide.

"Welcome to the most ancient, the most excellent archaeological site in the world – the pride of Turkey!"

Len turned to him, thinking, *you've got guts mate*. "Like what you've done with the place," he said, impressed by the fellow's audacity and taken aback by a strong New York accent.

"Thank-you sir, what you see before you is seven thousand years older than the pyramids of Egypt and the Stonehenge of England. Built without pack animals, using only stone tools, the largest blocks weigh ten tons."

Matt leaned towards Lenny and whispered, "He's gonna be so pissed if it turns out the yggdrasil built it."

The newcomer continued, "I am former student of Dr Schmidt, who first excavated this site. Will you all view our work?"

"Agreeable, proceed," said Sif Acer. It tweaked its configuration.

"We are here on the northern edge of the famous fertile crescent. You know of this, yes, from history books?"

"No," said Lenny, who did not.

"Sir, it was here between the mountains of Turkey and the desert that great civilisations and religions developed five thousand years ago. Local tradition says Abraham was born in Urfa, near to here."

Lenny whispered to Matt, "It's always the shepherds and the virgins—"

"Within memory, elder trees of planet. Abundant are changes endured," said Sif Acer.

The professor mopped his brow with a handkerchief, "We date the oldest parts of the site to almost twelve thousand years ago when the ice age was ending. There is no evidence of habitation and no water." Professor Demir patted a twenty-foot T shaped pillar proprietarily. "This is a new paradigm – built by hunter-gatherers, before farming, before settlements. A monumental ceremonial site."

"Cool scary cat creature," said Matt to Lenny approvingly of a spectacular pillar carving.

"… and see here we have hands carved. Here the arms and a belt. These colossal figures represent stylised humans or deities," continued the archaeologist. "This is a contrasting aesthetic to that of ice age cave paintings. These people looked at the natural world differently."

"Affirmative. Interpretation: humans view selves not integral with nature, began attempted mastery nature," said Tek Alnus scraping a blade-tipped leaf-wing audibly over the surface of a limestone monolith.

A career of fearsome Archaeological Department machinations had taught the professor excellent survival instincts.

He said nothing.

The group roamed the site, the Turkish professor outlining the alternative theory of cultural evolution: where hunter-gatherers developed organised religions before settlement and agriculture.

There goes half an hour of my life, thought Lenny, looking at carven boars, snakes, scorpions, foxes, and spiders. *Geez, it's hot.* The yggdrasil, meanwhile, enjoyed the bright light and heat – adjusting their many appendages to maximise solar exposure. Like the cricketer, they had little interest in the timing niceties involving ancient ceremonial sites.

"Human creation myths unconstructive," observed Tek Alnus.

The lecture tour continued, and it startled the visitors to learn the stone-age builders had not invented the wheel, nor developed pottery, writing, (or even a single, humble reality TV franchise). Professor Demir charted the highlights of the Neolithic revolution (a major human milestone: right up there with the taming of fire and the recording of *Dark Side Of The Moon*).

"By eight thousand years ago, peoples of this area had transitioned from harvesting wild grains to domesticating wild grains."

Or alternatively, as Tek Alnus put it: "Rye, barley, wheat, enslavement began this prior place and time."

Steady on, Tekky, thought Len as the alien began another semi-rant. To summarise: the yggdrasil resented control of plant reproduction; they didn't care for the spread of this depravity worldwide, but what really made their chitinous antennae twitch, was clearing of woodland and jungle tree communities to farm ever-increasing quantities of enslaved plant crops.

"Oh dear, how would you have us live?" asked Kalinda, arms crossed.

"Negative yggdrasil concern. Perhaps live as ancestors: hunter-gatherer mindset. Ideal ahimsa relations with wild undomesticated plants. Negative land clearance. Negative exponential population increment, negative resource consumption increment. Non-light gathering lifestyles rarely moral, at least minimise damages ecological."

CCE viewers reacted to Tek Alnus' statement with degrees of alarm. But there were some exceptions: 'paleo dieters' pumped their fists, stroked their beards and cast smug, disparaging glances at their girl-friends' falafels. Survivalists gave their hunting knives one final honing, knotted their favourite bandana, and headed their palaeolithically designed bodies for the woods. Previously unbunkered preppers loaded their kids into the SUV and proceeded to the bunkered hinterland of Maine and Washington State.

Mariam stirred into action. "Yes, well, obviously the wisdom of indigenous peoples has been long ignored by the west. Political leaders should consult with first nations peoples on sustainable resource use." Mariam continued in this vein. Lenny edged away like a lone uncle who'd unwisely attended an elementary school concert-prize night extravaganza.

The planet's tiny populations of indigenous peoples still living ancestral lifestyles were necessarily unaware of Mariam's commendation and support. Their cousins, familiar with electricity, television, social media, non-potable water, diabetes, and shanty-town poverty, glanced at their humble surroundings and in a multitude of endangered languages thought something equivalent to: "Yay – go us!" and as an afterthought, "... someone should really get that diseased dog out of here."

"But," said farm raised Kalinda, "farming is about growing plants and animals sustainably. So we don't just keep taking them from the wild."

Sif Acer focused its eye stalks on her, "Surplus foodstuffs favoured population increment and displacements hunter-gatherers." It rippled its feelers and said, "Agriculture, both plants and animal life forms requirement broad-scale complex-habitat extinction. Ultimate replacement with monoculture, lacking weft plant mind web."

"Peak oil, peak water, peak human reached," said Tek Alnus.

Len exchanged concerned looks with Matt. The comic said, "So a few thousand years later these dudes were growing wheat, making bread and farming goats, sheep, whatever, yeah?"

"Regrettable affirmative," said Tek Alnus. "Non-consistency with ahimsa principle. Jains not consuming breads, goats, sheeps."

Uneasy conversational exchanges continued. Len and Matt slunk further from the group.

"Is that right: Jains and bread?"

"I'll check it now, Len." Matt stared at his phone. "Nah, it's stuffed – it won't do anything except stream Canadian ice hockey games."

"Nice hit."

"Yeah. I was gonna buy a fridge magnet, but I'm going off the place."

*

Tropical parrots flew off in alarm. A pod-shaped void in the Cassowary Lodge universe filled. Soon, celebrity-alien TV normality resumed. The cast recuperated. Promotional teasers appeared on social media; Facebook likers continued to like Matt and find Mariam tiresome.

Hours later Mariam said, "Did anyone notice just before we took off to return, Sif Acer opened a panel in the pod wall?"

"I was looking at the control screen device," said Niels.

"I was just sucking in a couple of big ones," explained Matt.

"It did the same. A tentacle thing came out of its body."

"Yeah, I've seen that before at the pond. But still, it was an interesting trip. All those pillars and carvings, I'd never heard of the place."

"Matt," said Kalinda gently, "the yggdrasil didn't approve, especially Tek Alnus … it was all, 'buildings are bad, farming is bad, we should be running around chasing wild boars or kangaroos and eating berries.'"

"Yeah, I know, I just thought … well, the temple was interesting."

The celebrities turned their heads as Sif Acer, trailed by AB, Jaspa, and another crew member approached.

“Regrettable, negative feedback reactions reported,” announced Sif Acer without pre-amble. “Colleagues have departed. Self must follow presently.”

The celebrities made a variety of disquieted communal noises.

“Why? This is most sudden. What’s wrong?” said Niels uneasily.

“Several days since issue forestry termination edict. Self-ruthful, this ignored. Multitude colleagues forcefully protecting forest webs. Much conflict, forests conflagrated. Yggdrasil outrage.”

“Confa what?” said Len.

“Burnt, set on fire,” explained Mariam.

“Bastards!” exclaimed Matt, “I’m sorry, that’s so not good,” he said, standing and moving to touch the plant-creature on its upper body.

Sif Acer twitched its antenna. It said, “Self-expresses hope for species co-existence. Some humans possess regard other life forms. Will attempt interspecies consultation body future time.”

The humans in question exchanged glances. Kalinda stood and moved next to Matt. Their hands brushed, then clasped.

The three-day stubbled Swede said, “Err, let me give you an advice. This experience we had together was based on error. The TV show that you and I joined here is just for entertainments. People watching the show are knowing this, but we have here, between our kinds, a misunderstanding.”

The creature produced its static squawk. “Question: fox, not fox situation?”

“I am having no clue what you mean but it’s sometimes difficult for us to know what is real and what isn’t. Not to criticize my colleagues here, but being popular … widely known, being celebrity doesn’t mean persons have expertise. I mean for governing a country, making complex decisions.” The Swede glanced at the others.

Mariam made the amused, startled noise of the urban seagull trying to swallow a chip sideways.

“It’s just that celebrities don’t make important decisions, run the world, and so forth,” explained Niels. Matt and Kalinda avoided mutual eye contact, Mariam made another involuntary noise like another seagull trying to swallow a larger chip and perhaps some tartare sauce.

"Self shall depart, before current footage transmitted, before light's end," said the remaining yggdrasil. "Do not approach barrier yet." It twitched its feelers, "There are regrets."

One last awkward *CCE* silence developed. Thinking on his feet (as required occasionally of comedians finding themselves booked in error for events such as the Bendigo Terrapin Fanciers Annual Dinner), Matt raised his banana-mango-rum cocktail and said, "To the sun."

Sif Acer borrowed Lenny's half consumed can, raised it high and declared, "To the sun!" It poured beer over its segmented feet.

"Hey," objected Lenny.

This was the final *CCE* footage and an iconic image of the times. The remaining alien strode away into the gathering tropical twilight.

As it approached the forest edge it called, "Niels Larsson, Mathew Davis, please to approach."

Curious, the duo did so.

"Self-number is ..." announced the plant creature, reeling off a string of digits.

Niels sought clarification, "For what purpose is that number?"

"Numerals of phone device."

"You have a phone," began Matt and trailed off sheepishly as the alien directed eyestalks at its thorax region. "Yeah, of course."

"Device performs functions no rational species requires. Also, distance communication."

"So, we can communicate with you in future?" said Niels.

"Affirmative."

"Err ... okay, thanks," said Matt – uncertain he would require further yggdrasil company or even *CCE* reunion events.

"Night always ends. Reverse greetings," said Sif Acer, stepping into the gloom of the forest edge. As it disappeared, it wiggled its antennae and called, "Successful courting rituals Matt Davis."

*

The cast and crew mingled uncertainly in the departure's aftermath. Confusion mixed with relief and they raided the kitchens. There was a substantial mixing and consumption of drinks. They exchanged stories under the stars and contemplated the unsettling future.

Maggie had disappeared, and Matt brought her director's chair to the pool side. Eventually he announced, "There's nothing left to drink except Crème de Menthe."

Soon, one of the crew added, "There's nothing left to eat except capsicum dip." More people drifted away to sleep, many slept where they lay. No-one yet dared approach the barrier.

CCE's last morning hadn't yet had time to dawn. Matt slept and ignored the rainforest waking.

As usual.

His subconscious registered a certain tenseness, a certain excitement in the locality. This was highly usual for his subconscious of late. His sluggish, now waking senses detected himself sleeping low on the floor, in unaccustomed comfort … on a futon in the control centre. He felt a tickle on his cheek and turning his head, saw her long dark hair over his shoulder and bare chest. *Not* usual, and so wonderfully welcome.

There was distant shouting and then heavy boots thudded on timber. Torch in one hand, weapon in the other, Corporal Rocca flung open the door.

The yggdrasil were gone. History's highest rating show had ended.

Matt was terribly, terribly glad.

Chapter 41 Questions Without Notice

"Lindsay? Allison? Are you home, Leong, are you still awake?" called Rob. "Anybody want to see Jess on TV?"

*

It was a period of global suffering. Every plane landed additional throngs of alien experts, media-savvy Norsemen, and celebrity chefs. All heading directly to the chat-show production studios. Australia's public broadcaster was not immune. In a major coup, before his departure, Niels Larsson had agreed to appear on *Questions without Notice*.

This, the scientist learned, was a public forum style chat show. But not, we can be assured, of the variety that sees enraged homeowners: whose vegetable beds had been defiled by the deposits of neighbouring cats, confronting those same unrepentant felines.

Tonight's special episode featured legendary retired TV host Terry Bedford. Hailing from the far south, he was, like aged single malt Tasmanian whisky, the thinking woman's tipple. Craggy and twinkle-eyed, he donned a trademark cardigan and polished his spectacles.

Terry had seldom experienced such energy in the studio. Elsewhere, Jess' housemates; a late-night hipster demographic and women of a certain maturity made cups of tea and settled down with their cats. After introducing Jess and the other panellists, the host turned to Niels.

"Thanks very much for coming on the panel, professor. How are you finding the world outside the *CCE* compound?"

"Hello, Terry. Well, it ended so suddenly. A misunderstanding brought the aliens to the show and after the edict we made was ignored, they ended it. I'm not sure I am processing it yet. But it's a relief not feeling tense always. And I learn to wear the socks again."

Terry gave a low chuckle and twirled his pencil. "And the yggdrasil? Can you describe the experience of alien intelligence?"

"At first, especially, it was so visceral. You sense their strangeness in your stomach, your skin. But it was more difficult for the others who were present when their colleagues were killed." He nodded at ex-contestant Vito, seated next to the host. "I just tried to engage. Sif Acer at least was approachable but so very enigmatic. We couldn't always figure their meaning and intentions – the lack of the tone variation made communication difficult."

"Such as the difference between a statement and a question," remarked the panel host, in his customary timbre (that set so many mature, cat-owning hearts a-flutter).

"Yes, or the distinction between those and a command. Or even a joke."

"I'm not sure I noticed many of the latter."

"No. Only from Matt Davis," smiled the guest.

"Now, the big question," said veteran comic Susan Q, "that we're all dying to know the answer to: Were there any *CCE* romances?"

The audience tittered. Terry twirled his pencil.

The Swede's eyes twinkled, "I am saying nothing."

Next to Susan and looking across at Terry, Jess thought, *can't believe I'm here*.

The host said, "And professor, I understand you've a keen interest in Norse mythology. What is the significance of Yggdrasil?"

"Terry, I am no expert, but the World Tree is said to unite the heavens, the earth, the underworld. The name is often interpreted as Odin's Horse in the sense of a gallows. Odin sacrificed himself on it in his search for knowledge. In another story, Odin sacrificed his eye in a well contained within a world of the great tree. We see an association between yggdrasil and wisdom and sacrifice."

Jess folded her hands and studied Niels. *This is so weird. On CCE he wore a singlet, a bead around his neck and not much else. But he sounded as though he was wearing a turtle-neck jumper and corduroy pants. And now he is – nice colour too.*

Terry twirled his pencil, "I'm reminded of what Oppenheimer said of the atomic bomb. That: 'I am become death, the destroyer of worlds' idea, linking knowledge and destruction.'"

Elsewhere in the country, non-ABC viewers were spared such philosophical speculations tuning into *Whoops! I Married a Stranger* and repeats of *Emergency Puppy Rescue.*

The host peered over his spectacles. "Please, an opening question from the audience … perhaps the lady in the second row."

"Are we now at war with the yggs?"

Terry turned and suggested shadow defence minister Julee Murray might care to take the question.

"I don't believe so, not in any formal sense either as a nation or as a species. But the public deserves a defence, and this government has yet to explain its policy regarding the alien incursion."

The veteran presenter nodded and continued. "Yet, there are reports of conflict and deliberate burning of forests across the world."

"That may be so. The minister needs to address this situation."

Terry Bedford sensed this was one of those rare moments when politicians might prefer *not* to hold office. He glanced at his notepad.

"I might bring you in here too, Vito. What do you make of your former colleague, Graeme O'Brien's recent suggestions to threaten forests or burn the Melbourne Botanical Gardens?"

Jess knew the radio star's tweets and verbal rants were not, as surmised, by many an ABC viewer, like cyclones or deadly reptile incursions, merely unfortunate acts of god – he crafted them on purpose. And sometimes entire weeks went by without one.

"Well, Graeme says many things," said Vito diplomatically and stroking his waistcoat.

Host Terry persisted: "None the less, does this suggestion of leverage over the yggdrasil have merit?"

The audience murmured, Jess shifted in her seat, *someone say something.*

"It would be a serious mistake to cede the moral high ground and issue the threats," said Niels, breaking the silence.

"I might bring you in here, Jess Kelly. You were in the public eye during the mass platypus deaths in July. And now we're talking of an alien presence. Remarkably, it seems the two are connected?"

"Yes, Terry, the evidence suggests the yggdrasil arrived in large numbers well before the TV show started." She heard the host do a little light pencil tapping work.

"And the platypuses died?"

"Not platypi?" said Susan Q, sitting next to Jess.

"Don't get me started," Jess joked.

The comedian rocked back, palms up.

Jess continued, "There's no reason to suspect the deaths were deliberate … perhaps the yggdrasil were testing their defences, or a large transportation event caused electromagnetic interference. We realise now, there were mass electroreceptive fish deaths in many river systems. This suggests they moved into various forests before they announced themselves."

"And I understand you were instrumental in determining this?"

"Well Terry, seeing those drones drop out of the air got me thinking," Jess said modestly.

"And again, you had a role in confirming the alien presence outside of *CCE* here in Australia?"

"Based on what the aliens said Day One, I thought it possible to guess what they might do next …"

"Well done you," said Susan, "smashing through the glass test tube."

"I'm sure we'd all appreciate insight into what might happen next," said the host. With a tap of his glasses and a cursory pencil twirling, Terry raised his voice and said, "Can I ask with a show of hands, who in the audience has seen a live alien?" Half rising from his seat and peering over his lenses, Terry announced, "Perhaps a third … thank-you"

The show's host, with a subtle pencil pointing, said, "I'll take a comment from the audience … the young lady with the green shirt."

How does he choose? wondered Jess.

"I don't want to criticise on him, but that was one of the worst things ever when Kat and Tayla got killed. Those beautiful girls. I mean, where's the justice?"

"Thank-you. I'm sure no-one's condoning the deaths of Kat Adamson and Tayla Brooke. I might bring you in here, Allan la Fontaine. What does philosophy say concerning morality, justice, and extra-terrestrial actions?"

Jess had heard of the controversial French professor, best known for his animal rights philosophy, and popular book, *Eating Bambi.*

"Such interesting times we are living in! The business of philosophy is often said to be: How shall we live? What is truth? What is moral behaviour, and what is its source? Alien life and its implications have not much occupied the attention of philosophers." The guest folded his hands and looked into the camera as if observing events only he could discern. "There are several aspects to consider with these unfortunate killings: Our species develops our laws – can we apply them to other species? If a bull kills a person – do we consider this murder?" He paused and peered wisely at the camera.

He's a bit of a character, thought Jess.

"As a utilitarian, I argue risking billions of lives to avenge two deaths is not a correct action. Regrettably, first contact experiences across a cultural gulf are often marred by violence."

"It appears," observed Terry, "that conflict we've seen is due to difference in cultural values and moralities. Not on resource competition."

"Too right, Terry," chimed Susan Q. "These aliens are not after our coal or our uranium. But if you're watching guys – you're welcome to my share. They don't even want to eat us! But can I say, just in case … I'm one tough and stringy old duck. Not prime dining. No offence Terry, but I reckon you'd be pretty safe too." The host smiled indulgently, and the audience chuckled – pleased to relieve some tension.

On a roll, the veteran comic continued, "Back in my old dad's day, if a fellow walked down the street holding a brace of dead bunnies, nobody batted an eyelid. Imagine that now, people would be aghast – aghast I say. Small children would whimper. But that's the thing. My poor brain's fluttering like a moth in a lamp, but that's how the yggs feel about a bunch of uprooted parsnips."

With a subtle piece of pencil work, the moderator indicated Niels, "Is that your perspective, professor?"

"Yes, I can agree. The yggdrasil require certain parameters of gravity, temperature … atmospheric gases. We share a Goldilocks zone, but little competition is needed." He continued: "There is enough sunlight for both our species. They have a hierarchy of concerns we need to negotiate. Chief among them as Tek Alnus said: 'eating living things bad, eating living things that *don't* eat living things most bad.'"

Jess followed Terry Bedford's glance as he peered over his spectacles and selected a youthful fellow wearing a suit jacket over a superhero T-shirt for his next question.

"Professor la Fontaine, your writings deal with animal rights. How do you suggest vegetarians such as me reconcile the yggdrasil's existence and their directives with our past and future practices?"

Jess looked up. There was a mass murmuring from the audience, a smattering of applause, a few interjections. *Good question*.

The ABC stalwart said, "Your response, professor?"

"My writing on animal rights does not assign their lives value *per se* because they are animals, but rather, because they have a capacity for suffering." With the smugness of someone who had risen before dawn and completed a five-mile run (when they could just as easily have not), he said, "It is sensory awareness, communication, capacity for distress that's crucial. We must extend rights to every life form that exhibits these."

"Perhaps a comment from the gentleman by the aisle," said the host.

"So, you were wrong?" said the selected participant (he wasn't one to call a fence a 'boundary enclosing fabrication of security'). "All that: 'Oh, you own a pet dog, so how can you eat a burger? Now has to include: 'Oh, you love trees – how can you sit on a timber seat? How can you eat potatoes?'"

The audience consisting as it did of the curious, the fearful, entry-level vegans, philosophy fans, and paleo-dieters mumbled and grumbled. They couldn't castigate nervous disquiet, so they castigated themselves and one another.

"I have expanded my world view in light of the alien arrival," explained the philosophy professor in a sure tone. "To paraphrase, 'When the facts change – I change my mind, sir. What do you do?'"

This is intense, thought Jess. The audience was buzzing. Host Terry signalled a large suit-clad man in the front row.

"Isn't this just bunkum: philosophy, animal rights, plant rights, they're just our own mental constructs?"

"I'll take that as a question," said the moderator, a hint of amusement in his eyes. "Professor le Fontaine?"

"Yes, these are mental constructs, as are God and money. Ideas are powerful."

Terry peered studiously at his notepad. "Professor Larsson, if you don't mind: Your perception of the alien interpretation of the ahimsa principle."

"There is much difficulty, Terry. It's a general principle and as the saying says, 'The devil is in the detail.'" The audience murmured again. Niels sampled the local water, "As we know, the yggdrasil don't eat or kill for food. They consider they are being conciliatory, referencing the ahimsa tradition. It is not so difficult to understand whether we've ended our food's life, but how do we define *harm* or violence or exploitation?"

Niels waved his hands, "If we humans are plucking leaves from a tea bush – is that distressing? How will the British survive if they cannot drink tea? Can we mow the lawns or cut a stem of rhubarb? These aren't death, but are they harm? I do not know. The yggdrasil have a broad sympathy for our planet's vegetation, but not expert knowledge of this. They are still learning – as are we." Niels paused and concluded, "It's clear at least: they declare unicellular life forms having no sentience."

"Professor, can you define those for us … and what is their significance going forward?"

"Well examples are bacteria and single-celled photosynthetic organisms: these micro-algae may be crucial. We culture them to produce carbohydrates, protein, oils, vitamins and even those excellent blue Spirulina smoothies. It is now possible to grow animal protein without an animal."

Susan Q snorted, "I'm sure someone will correct me, but aren't there millions of bugs on our skin and in our tummies?"

"Yes, billions even," confirmed Jess with a nod.

"So, I'm inhumanely slaughtering billions of them when I wash my once-firm epidermis? Although, (she dropped her voice) in the interests of humanity – mine mainly – I prefer to close my eyes when I get naked." She tossed her head, and with mock horror, began, "And don't even get me started on pooping. Can I say poop on telly?"

Allan la Fontaine sagely rested his chin on his hand and commented, "Ms Quade makes the point: Where do we draw the line? Which lives are important, and *who* decides?

Terry Bedford nodded at the guest philosopher, peered at the camera and said, "There's been much discussion of this term *Ahimsa* since it was first used on *Celebrity Council Elimination*. Can I call on Dilip Jain, an Australian Jain, to give his perspective?"

"Yes, thank-you Terry." Dilip, a well-groomed, media-savvy IT specialist from Melbourne with a golf handicap of fifteen, stood and beaming gave a brief wave. "Please, everyone, take a good look if you wish!" he joked. "Hello, mother." He sat and continued, "As you know, there's been tremendous interest in ahimsa in the last month or two.

Our local website is quite overwhelmed with queries. May I take this opportunity to say there's more to Jain philosophy than ahimsa or non-violence – although this is important."

"And" he continued, playfully waving his finger at the panel, "ahimsa does not relate solely to the dietary but to our *thoughts, words* and *deeds*. To continue … another important concept is *anekantavada*: that reality is multi-sided, that truth and reality are complex – we've heard examples tonight." He paused and said, "May I tell the famous story of the elephant and the six blind men?"

"Oh goody," said Susan Quade.

"Please …" said Terry.

As he did so Jess thought, *I can't pronounce it ... but it's similar to science – the idea that knowledge is provisional not absolute. Like the whole: is light a wave or a particle thing.*

Dilip placed his hand on his chest, "And we're not, each of us, the same – Jains in India may think differently than those brought up in the west." He turned to the panel, "Professor Larsson may be interested that Jains don't cut down trees."

Celebrity chef Vito caught his host's eye. "Ah, Dilip, what's the Jain perspective on bread? I understand it's not eaten. I have been developing a yggdrasil compliant diet."

"Like other peoples, Jains may have different interpretations on principles of faith," said Dilip. "Last Christmas, my neighbouring children showed me the nativity scene they'd made. And I had *no* idea that dinosaurs attended the birth of the baby Jesus!"

The audience chortled and the resident comedian said, "Oh, go on, Terry, give that man his own show!"

Dilip smiled and continued, "Many Jains eat bread, but not breads that contain yeast; other fermented foods or even alcohol."

"Because yeast is a living thing with its own soul or spiritual essence?" said Allan.

His accent is strong, but his English is perfect. Better than Niels, thought Jess.

"Something like that, yes. In the past, we filtered water to avoid consuming tiny life-forms. Also, more hygienic."

"Oh, my head hurts again, yeast is a plant right," said Susan Q to the panel.

Niels smiled sympathetically, "Well, no actually – it's a simple member of the fungi kingdom – as are mushrooms."

"Not eaten by traditional Jains," added Dilip.

"So, in certain respects, Jainism is more extreme in protecting life forms than the yggdrasil," said Allan in a tone that suggested he was the first person to notice this.

Niels ignored the tone, if not the comment. "The distinction is that the yggdrasil are especially protective of photosynthetic life forms. Although it may be their discomfort with wheat and cereal farming is based on opposition to landscape clearance and broad acre farming."

"Got to tell you … I'm more concerned by any unfortunate uber-vegan misinterpretations of alcohol," began Susan Q, "because I reckon, I'll need it!"

The audience chuckled and Vito said theatrically, "I have news."

"No! What?" she said, sensing peril – like a ship meeting a playful iceberg.

"Ah … alcohol, not so vegan. Isinglass: the clarifying agent added to beer and wine comes from dried fish swim bladders – sturgeon traditionally."

"Need to know basis Vito, need to know." She continued. "So, wine's okay if you don't mind the bladders. Any issues with chocolate, oh, and coffee?"

Jess looked towards the forester for reassurance on this crucial point.

"Ah, yes – a question of importance," grinned Niels in his best media performer manner. "Don't worry, both coffee and chocolate derive from fruit pods, trees are not killed."

"Such a relief," breathed the shadow minister attempting to convince the audience she was a regular, everyday 'person of the people'.

"Although, from a water usage viewpoint, chocolate production uses more than other foods," added the celebrity chef sternly, to the discomfort of many.

"Would you care to talk to food concerns going forward? You mentioned working on yggdrasil-compliant diets?"

"Yes, Terry, we have an app under development and a book due out for Christmas. If I may …" he paused grandly. "I call it the '3F' diet: Fish, fruit and fungi. By this I refer to seafood generally – this reduces land use conflicts with the yggdrasil; the second 'F' includes those vegetables that are really fruits – egg plant, pumpkin and so forth. And the final 'F': mushrooms and the glorious truffle."

"Thank you. I might now take audience commentary on visions of the future," said Terry Bedford with more decisive pencil tapping.

While a less discerning audience remained beholden to shows such as *Divorced at First Sight* and *Celebrity Pet Swap*, the ABC studio audience raised their hands in the air. Jess Kelly, panellist, unemployed platypus researcher and daughter of cane farmers facing an uncertain future, listened as a young man outlined his vision of arcadian living. *I wonder if I can speak to Niels privately.*

With more piercings than a farm fencepost, the earnest fellow described a low-tech vision of fruit trees, compost, gendered labour division, alien-wariness, and a minimum of consumer durables.

Susan Q's comment: "Ah, Australia in the 1950s," established that the gentleman aspired to self-sufficiency, but not to a sense of humour.

The Nation's public broadcaster doesn't inflict advertisements for foot massagers or discount vitamins on its devotees. It does, however, promote its shows to its audience of hipsters, grandmas, and as Susan Q had it: hipster grandmas. While the host called a break and wandered off to chat with the audience, Jess waved and leaned towards Niels.

"Niels are you in the country for much longer?"

"No, just a few days. I shall return to the US and discover if I'm still employed." He shrugged, "I also wish to see my family in Sweden."

"I wonder if I could have a word after the show. My parents own a cane farm – they won't risk cutting it this season. Like that last audience person, they have an idea of integrating fruit trees and maybe algae, fish, yabbies, chickens and using renewable energy sources."

"That will be fine. I am curious to discover what a yabby might be!"

Terry strolled back, engaging in a minor cardigan adjustment.

"Thanks, talk to you later," said Jess.

Chapter 42 Meeting Jess

Niels agreed to meet the platypus researcher in a fashionably unkempt area of Sydney. He'd assumed Jess was familiar with the location. But, as they wandered the street, past the sounds of early morning beard trimmings, and the whine of tattoo needles applying World Tree motifs, he thought, *this isn't really her thing.*

Niels had found little prior opportunity to discuss the alien situation with other scientists.

"So, you deduced they guarded that canyon?"

Jess smiled, "Maybe I got lucky."

"I don't think so …"

The two talked alien tech, work histories, and yggdrasil intentions, as they strolled the hipster-ridden street. They passed tai chi wine bars, in search of a conventional coffee source. Drifting by yet more tattoo parlours, vinyl record stores, and then an academic book shop, the pair were reminded of their career uncertainties. Ahead, they spotted a café, and stepping around an intense local bard (rather heavy on the down strum), found seats at a sidewalk table. As Niels and Jess discussed now stalled platypus research, she regarded him with an odd expression.

"Is everything okay, Jess." She had an interesting voice, a little husky – like an aged jazz singer – but she could only be in her late twenties.

"Sorry, silly habit … I was waiting to see if you'd say platypi. It's a kind of test."

"Oh dear."

She grinned, "I have a weird thing about the correct plural."

"Ah, good to know. What then of your farm?"

Conversation switched to the issues faced by Jess' sugar-cane-farming parents. The café's other clientele: survivors of all-night dance music venues, early morning dog walkers, and their pooches had other concerns. Accustomed in recent years to US service industry standards, the lack of attentive staff puzzled Niels. He peered hopefully into the interior gloom. "This café is decorated with stuff my parents threw away thirty years ago."

"I realise you're tired of the question," her eyes smiled at him, "but what happens now?"

"The yggdrasil will end forestry operations – if we don't do so."

"No doubt. Do you think root vegetable growing will also end?" Jess turned and looked at the disinterested man lurking near the register and the cake displays.

"Probably, it's very confusing … the aliens are *very* alien." Niels grinned. "I am meaning, they didn't realise it was a TV show! Sif Acer said they hadn't sent large numbers of scouts for hundreds of years, and, well … things had changed more than they were knowing. But with enough time, we can adapt."

"Niels, many people speculate they have a collective mind. Any ideas. Do you understand their social structure?"

"I am understanding they communicate in a network through the ground, and other means; directly exchanging thoughts to reach collective decisions. But I'm sure they are separate personalities."

Jess signalled to a waitress, "Is there a leader, a ruling elite or something?"

"On *CCE,* Mariam and I likened it to a settler society … individuals finding their way in a new world. They have some agreed ideals and a few specialists, but not as many rules and bureaucracy as we might expect. Their few *ambassadors* are here to protect our interests up to a point."

"At first," said Jess, "they seemed hostile, then sort of indifferent."

The indifferent man by the register tinkered with his curls again – it was too soon to tell whether he was bettering them, or indeed, whether he worked at the establishment. Just then, an employee carelessly happened by and Jess snared her.

"Those killings were unplanned. The ahimsa thing was a type of guilt compromise, likewise the initial targeting of non-essential tobacco, sugar, cotton …"

Other than the occasional wofflesome noise from the dogs, the surrounding tables became quiet. Patrons even stopped manipulating their phones. Many hadn't come to terms with the whole 'plants have feelings too' paradigm. Two doors down, the busker, misinterpreting the café's hush as enthusiasm, began another tune.

Niels said, "There is an opposition to our industrial-scale farming – even if the crops are harvested dry and dead."

Jess nodded, "A few yggdrasil just messed with harvest machinery near my parent's place.

"Have you talked to one, Jess?"

"No, I saw one in the Botanical Gardens, but it didn't speak."

Jess outlined her family's plans to convert the cane farm to a mixed tree companion-planting system.

"A variation of syntropic farming," said Niels. "I am also interested in this idea, where trees may harmonise and support each other – as in a natural wood. The yggdrasil find monoculture plantations disturbing – Sif Acer says the trees barely communicate – 'their ability to weave the song weft' gets damaged if I understood. Likewise, plants in pots."

The waitress returned with their monstrously overpriced drinks. Waffles of exhausted appearance, cowering beneath soy ice cream.

"Ah, it's a while since I smelled maple syrup."

"It never occurred to me before," said Jess. "But *they* might be unhappy with maple syrup. Like an involuntary blood donation, maybe?"

Niels laughed, "Yes, I suppose. And rubber. There are so many things to consider."

"So, my Dad has this idea from south-east Asia: farming chickens over a pond, their waste fertilises algae, which then feeds fish."

Niels poked at the waffle and nodded, "Interesting. Best if the fish are omnivorous species, and you know, it is possible to farm algae directly for human consumption."

Jess saw other diners directing curious glances at Niels. The waitress and the guardian of the cake display had an animated but hushed conversation.

"Hey, man." The presumed proprietor approached with an unrequested blueberry Danish he had sequestered about his person. "Love your work … so intense. *Hafgufa World* … awesome debut album."

Jess looked on confused as Niels successfully denied he was the bass player of the Norwegian black metal outfit Kraken.

He shrugged, "This has happened before."

"Told you he was Tree Jesus," said the waitress smugly to her boss – confirming what the onlookers had suspected.

"Cool. I love trees. I love all plants."

Judging from a distinctive aroma and lack of personal energy, Jess surmised he especially loved one plant. She felt the yggdrasil might consider he'd an odd way of showing it. After this minor brush with the café's service standards, conversation resumed until interrupted by a phone beep. Unfortunately, as Niels suspected – he was most likely overdue contact with Special Agent Cam Peters of the US Government:

Return at once.

Niels formed the impression standard niceties weren't expected:

No.

He turned the device off.

But so prompted, Niels said, "Security people have called the yggdrasil a threat multiplier: Their presence increases the potential for conflict of every sort between us humans. Something we must consider."

Jess nodded. "Niels, would you consider returning to Cairns?" And looking at Niels with a speculative expression, she invited him to visit the family farm.

Chapter 43 Mir Arauca

A day and a half later, Niels found himself returned unexpectedly to Cairns. Jess had shapely almond eyes. But … *generally, I like to know a lady a little better before I agree to meet her parents.*

As Jess drove west from Cairns, the engine noise of the battered vehicle and the gravel road made conversation difficult. This is the Australia visitors expect to see, thought Niels: big sky, heat, dusty roads. He glanced at Jess' profile, *she seems more comfortable here than in Sydney.*

Occasionally the radio became static-free enough for Niels to hear something such as, "… Worple is caught at silly mid-leg for a duck off Aldrin's arm ball and so, an early tea break …" and similar snatches of early cricket season commentary.

The vehicle slowed and conversation was possible again. Jess turned into a sagging-gated long driveway. "Niels, can you get the gate?"

The dusty vehicle approached the farmhouse. In a faded check-shirt minus its sleeves, Bob Kelly sat on a sun-bleached plastic chair, watching. It had been an interesting morning. Now he stood as the latest visitor – a lithe and lightly freckled young woman – leapt from what locals call a flat tray ute.

"Hi, Dad," said Jess uncertainly.

"Barb," he called, "Jess and the fellow are here." Jess took an uncertain step towards her father as the yggdrasil standing companionably beside him roused itself.

"This here's Mir Arauca, says he's – *it's* been waiting for you two."

"Greetings and pleasantries Niels Larsson, Jess Kelly. Self fulfills local explorer-emissary function."

Barbara Kelly came out of the house and introduced herself. Her checked shirt had intact sleeves. "Right then, anyone for a beer?" asked Bob.

"Sure, okay, thank you," said Niels, who knew a social convention when he saw one.

Soon the screen door banged. The farmer returned, and they passed cans around. "Mir's been having a look at the farm – seen the solar panels, the generator, the cane ..."

"When did Mir Arauca arrive, Dad?"

"Not long after dawn. I was down in the orchard and found Mir bonding with my lunch. The dog went a bit wonky … howled, did a lap of the yard, tried to climb the windmill. You should see the spaceship – it's behind the shed."

"It's terribly interesting, dear," said Jess' mum. Her daughter smiled, stunned by the unconventional homecoming.

"Well then, shall we have a toast?" suggested Niels.

The leaf-creature said, "To the sun," raised the beer and poured the contents over its feet.

The others followed suit, more conventionally sipping their beers. After a brief chat in the dusty yard, the group toured the farm. Observing Mir Arauca and Jess chat, Niels was struck by the creature's motion. The other yggdrasil he'd met moved with a prim predatory gait – this one galumphed like it had precisely the incorrect number of legs.

The alien visit was the most extraordinary things to happen locally since old Nugget Roberts had discovered half a dinosaur skeleton while putting in a new dam. This wasn't obvious as the unflappable couple showed the alien and Niels around the farm.

"We're real proud of her," said Bob to Niels with a nod at Jess. "Figured out where the aliens were hiding, was on the news, the Facebook, always reading when she was little. Pity about them platypuses, eh?"

Niels nodded. He was struggling with Bob's broad accent. *He doesn't much open his mouth when he talks.* They continued the tour. *Maybe it stops the flies getting in.* Niels waved them away from his face. He heard the expansion plans for nuts, mango, banana, and native tree syntropic farming. He said, "Would coconuts palms grow here?"

"Ah, coconut: the food that just keeps giving. We should look into that, Dad," said Jess.

Moving between the trees, the yggdrasil declared: "Excellent, let them weave tangled threads of community." Stopping by the drying cane, the creature said: "Minimal self-reflective feelings and thinklings … humans more interesting companions."

It adjusted its larger leaf wings and said, "Note that the light gatherers' roots still live.

"The vegetative brain equivalent," said Niels for the benefit of the others.

The party visited the various sheds; they discussed algae culture and off-grid power generation, greeted the nervous livestock, and headed for the dam. The dog (over its fright) tagged along. The alien complimented its hosts on the quality of the local sunlight. Bob reached the dam edge and explained his joint chicken-algae-fish farming master plan to the visitors.

"Reckon I'll use silver perch, might throw in yabbies too."

"I am hearing this name before," said Niels. "What animal is it?"

"There's a string on that post … just pull it in."

With a glance at Jess, Niels did as instructed and hauled in a battered old tin housing some variety of roadkill and half a dozen snapping crustaceans. These he carefully tipped out.

"Ah, krafta." He told the family of the similar, larger creature he'd seen in Tasmania, and with reciprocated interest of Swedish kraftskiva parties.

"Observe them disport," remarked the yggdrasil.

"Have a go picking one up, mate."

The dog barked with excitement.

"Bob" said Barb, with motherly disapproval.

Niels, sensing a local induction ritual, crouched and approached the escapees.

"Mate, you've gotta be more positive – choose one and really commit to it."

Despite the heat, dust and muddy water, Niels was incongruously reminded of sisterly relationship advice at the last family kraftskiva.

"Just grab it nearer that join on the shell," advised Jess, squatting beside him.

"That's it, you're good with yabbies," approved Bob.

Ah, a rating system for crustacean wrangling, mused Niels.

At the tour's end, they returned to the home paddock and its Jurassic windmill. Past the house and the second shed where farmers keep their less functional motor vehicles, Barb said, "The flying saucer is just behind here."

"Ah, it's the same as the Wollemi one," said Jess.

The craft lacked a human device, co-opted and be-tendrilled. In the spirit of relaxed interspecies exchange, Niels asked whether the pod contained water and equipment. Mir Arauca confirmed that it did.

In a further spirit of adventure, the Swede accepted the family's invitation to stay the night. His last evening before returning from the land of the outback to the land of the quarterback.

In my parents' time, reflected Niels, a visitor could assess their hosts by observing books, records, and movies on VHS. Whereas now, we store these on devices and phones. (And yet, uninvited phone viewing remains a major social-norm violator!) Niels glanced at the alien and thought twice about trying to explain all this. The living room of the Kelly home overflowed with traditional indicators of cultural and personal preference. The two visitors perused these with interest.

"So much vinyl," said Niels, edging past Bach, Beethoven and Brahms.

"Yeah, mate. I'm cool again – not so much the wife – but she's a keeper," grinned Bob Kelly.

Niels smiled and peeked at fifty-year-old record sleeves.

"Ah," nodded Bob, "Question: Which is the best Led Zep album?"

"Err, four ..."

"Correct—"

"I am thinking," said the forester "that since James Cook University has studies in marine biology and aquaculture, there'd be expert advice on equipment, gaining pure strain cultures of algae ..."

"I am thinking," said Mir Arauca in imitation, "these carbon polymer discs store human musical patterns?"

"Oh yes, come and look." Barb showed the alien the family's record player.

Meanwhile, Jess invited Niels to view her childhood room. Betraying, unsurprisingly, a scientific bent, the bookcases held volumes by Dawkins and Jared Diamond lurking between the Harry Potters. From the bookcase tops peered two dozen plush toys: bears, crocodiles, sharks, and all manner of cats. A disassembled pump or two somewhat spoiled the childhood museum ambience.

"Still got 'em," said Bob, appearing in the doorway and taking in Niels' perusal of the fluffy menagerie. "When Jess was a little'un, she spent half her time crawling around the floor with a sock hanging out of her pants for a tail – pretending to be a horse or a cat or something."

"Thanks, Dad."

"Are you still a vegetarian, dear?" came the call from the kitchen.

"Mum, it's only a couple of weeks since you saw me. Perhaps I'll call myself a secular Jain," Jess said in a bemused tone. "Does everything have to have a label?"

Later, Mir Arauca folded itself into a rocking chair and sampled the family's music collection. Barb established it preferred this, to joining them at the dinner table. It did, however, accept the offer of water. None-the-less, the hostess was a trifle tense. She hovered fretfully as the alien manipulated the LPs with its scratchy looking appendages.

The creature sat in the corner, conversing with the family. Occasionally a slurping tentacle noisily entered its *Maroons* stubby holder. Simultaneously, headphones draped over the base of its antennas, it worked its way through the offerings of Johnny Cash. Niels led the discussion, engaging the affable plant-creature on the crucial issue of food supply.

"Yggdrasil have agreed to tolerate use of already dried timber. But how will your species feel regarding the frozen and dried and tinned plant foodstuffs that now exist."

"Yes, is it the ivory conundrum? I mean, some people say it's best to burn not only poached tusks but ban the ivory artefact trade and even destroy most things made from it," said Jess.

Mir Arauca made a short discordant sound – rather like a record being scratched – but fortunately not in this case. "Dissimilar. Yggdrasil possesses strength of will to protect light-foragers. Humans have not such will to protect elephant creatures. In spirit of tolerance and accord, yggdrasil kind will ignore use current stored human nutritions from slain plants."

"So, these baked beans will be okay, dear?" queried Jess's mum.

"Affirmative."

"And the breakfast cereal?" asked Barb, opening another cupboard and showing the packet to the alien.

"Also, affirmative."

The humans glanced at each other, reassured. "I was wondering about clothes," began Jess, but trailed off as the creature quivered, sending waves through its leaf-wings.

"What's up, Mir?" quizzed Bob, unconcerned.

"What manner of sound this," said the visitor, removing the headphones and waving the record sleeve.

"That's bagpipe music," explained Bob – a little defensively some might have judged. "In the old days, the warriors followed the piper into battle."

Niels nodded. *Bagpipes make me want to kill someone too. Generally, the piper.*

The extra-terrestrial replaced the record.

"Try these dear," said Barb, distributing Dylan, and Neil Young.

"So back to clothing then," said Jess. "Are your companions going to object if people keep wearing their old plant fibre clothes?"

The light forager made the static sound again and after a few seconds delay replied: "Negative views regard new cotton. Advise: recycle, repair, reduce waste of existing fibres. Advise discretion wearing the blue cotton jeans."

"Many people don't think we should farm cotton in Australia. Or rice either – uses too much water – better to farm it elsewhere," Jess informed Mir Arauca and Niels.

"Yggdrasil maximum opposition to cotton, tobacco, sugar cane, every location. Multiple negatives." The helpful, un-nuanced tone of the phone-app softened the blow, but there was little doubt the yggdrasil opposed several agricultural norms.

Conversation restarted, taking in local, international, and interspecies topics of interest. Mir Arauca did its party trick: turning off living room lights and appliances without leaving its seat.

"Reckon you could make good money on stage," grinned Bob.

More beers were drunk, and Niels was not displeased when the alien interrupted unsought offers to explain the rules of cricket

"What are these creative algorithms?"

"Can I see the cover, dear," said Barb.

"That's Bach. *Cello Suite No. 2 in D minor*," confirmed the local enthusiast.

The Mir Arauca lapsed into silence for a minute, then said, "Hear Bach plait the ether; weave the universal fabric, plot the dance of the matter particle harmonies."

Bob choked on his beer and said to his wife, "You've got another fan, Barb."

"Be there additional?"

"Oh yes," enthused Mrs Kelly, rising and selecting a sample of records from the bookcases.

"There sure are …" added her husband, eyebrows elevated.

"Try these Mir," said Barb, bringing a selection over and relieving the alien of the yet unplayed *Scorching Hits of Summer 1975* (an unfortunate relic of her husband's youth).

"On your show, Niels," said Barb, "young Kalinda played *Air on the G string* by Bach, you know … that night you had the concert."

The visitor nodded, "Oh, right. I know little of classical music – they seemed to enjoy the show."

Later, the group trooped outside under the bright moon.

"Well bye, then, Mir," said Bob.

"Reverse greetings, may you prosper until the suns burn out."

"Will we meet you again?" asked Jess, eyes bright with curiosity.

"Affirmative," it folded its leaf wings and traipsed to its pod. "Time cycle prophecy-algorithm declares self will remain." It gestured at the night, "Never returning though blue windows behind the stars."

Bob Kelly looked quizzically at his wife. Then the family and Niels watched the yggdrasil pod rotate through interstices of matter and vanish. Back inside, Jess and Niels talked long into the night. Eventually, the Kelly homestead put the cat out and dimmed the lights.

*

Air travel was to become uncommon in times to come. The ominous darkness of deliberately lit forest fires framed Niels' departure from Australia and arrival in Oregon.

Chapter 44 Catch Up Time.

Faced with the prospect of giving up forestry, potato crisps, blue jeans, tobacco – and having a good long think about complex stuff, humankind reacted by threatening, and indeed, applying their underused cigarette lighters to the forests. The so-called forestry wars raged for 15 months. But oddly, it seemed no number of Marvel Universe movies had prepared the populace for what it's like when gods go to war.

Every species, in every tongue; even species without tongues, has the equivalent of the expression: "It's a funny old world" (including gas cloud worlds, lonely meteors, geothermal vents, and feathery pigeon armpits).The yggdrasil found FriendFone ("Making the world of YOU") and its competitors' business model of divisive algorithms, endless consumption and the primacy of opinion "funny" to say the least. It was therefore feeler-twitching ironic that the yggdrasil-internet-hiatus-punishment-of-humanity was in a sense beneficial.

In our era of unreliable news and alternative facts the reader can be assured that although many trees were burned, many others survived; the internet is about to work again; and fortunately, as multinational tech companies weren't paying tax anyway, their demise had little impact on government-funded infrastructure. However, it is true plus sized clothing manufacturers struggled as starvation stalked the earth. Likewise, true: Matt and Kalinda are now a couple; the icecaps are melting, and the moon landings were real.

*

An elusive, surviving city pigeon landed on a windowsill; the building only five-blocks from Central Park West. It peered at banked tubs containing growing mushrooms, a room of restless chickens and a door. On the other side sat a woman. The screen of her device showed it had achieved the much-desired internet connection. She gave it a brief pat. For the first time in fifteen months Ebony Hamilton had a connection for two consecutive days.

She pressed post.

March 4

mom love nyc
CATCH UP TIME!

it's over a year dear readers but I'm back. 2 days connectivity in a row. awesome. so definitely time to jump on here. eir nyssa says it thinks the www will stay working working working now. the fighting has stopped and with the winter the fires are out. i pray you have all been ok.

so much change, so much news. sharing a few too many pics (SORRY) … just keep scrolling! another year older, more tired but oh so energised. gotta say - so much fricking energy in our amazing resilient city. like the world's biggest battery. OR DONUT!

here's James and me and the kiddos in C park [Pics 1-3: the family clothing line]. yes, i've finally done it dear readers - launched GREEN PROMISE my clothing line. but more of that another time!

many of the neighbours have moved out of the city: some to their bunkers, others to stay with relatives in the country. and so, we are using (with permission!) the apartment next door. [Pics 4-7: #THE FARM NEXT DOOR] so good for anne-maree to help with the chickens and billy loves collecting the eggs.

big shout out to the truly inspiring folk of the local gardening cooperative. with the advice of the many park yggdrasil we have been busily planting fruit and nut trees for the years ahead [Pics 8-12]. hard times but good times. the days of throwing out the ugly fruit are gone folks!

only having the cell phone to take pics sure has been different! last summer we welcomed our neighbour KEVEN LEAHY to the production team. You might know kevin. He filmed that famous yggdrasil footage in canada that convinced most of us they were real (just before anne-maree talked to eir nyssa). he's been so great filming the blog and our crazy activities: making all the 'how to' segments and anne-maree's 'ask the askr yggdrasil' videos [see links below]. No more jump drive sharing people! talk soon, have a great day.

*

On the other side of that wall sat another woman. She finished stripping to her underwear, dimmed the lights, lit a scented candle, then turned on her video cam and gave it a brief pat. She began whispering urgent flat pack furniture assembly instructions into cyberspace. (Some of us make a living in the darndest ways – but this is not her story.)

Chapter 45 Return of the Web

Hoping for an act of feeding kindness, the pigeon perched outside another window. Behind the glass and behind a further, substantial thickness of glass, Kevin Leahy's eyes swam in and out of focus like sharks in a horror movie. He, too, still had connection: two days in a row. The maintenance of a zombie-culture, crypto-zoology, historical-alien-encounter website in the web's absence was problematic. Sometimes the fifteen dollars to buy the domain name seemed excessive.

His *Monsters and Aliens* site had surged in popularity after the yggdrasil invasion – more so after *he'd* shot and posted the iconic Gaspe National Park footage, taken during a rare venture into nature. The webmaster reached for another drink. His apartment was vast yet cluttered and well supplied with energy drinks. An effect achieved without the help of an interior designer, live-in partner, or in fact, any partner. In the corner behind the floor lamp lurked a pile of deceased and discouraged beetles – the parental influence had been absent for some time.

With the demise of the web, under-exercised gamers, and bloggers, who'd spent years secreted in basements emerged. Nervous as cicadas in non-prime number years, they greeted the sunshine. During such an emergence, he had met Ebony Hamilton and family. The apartment block's blogging celebrities.

The parental Leah's were uncertain if the yggdrasil or their fellow citizens alarmed them more. After months of fires, fighting, food deprivation, irregular Wi-Fi, and the uncertain hazards of wearing cotton, Kevin's parents had retreated to a communal bunker in the Catskills. Similarly, to others of the *prepared,* they'd taken a shrewd look at the unfolding yggdrasil apocalypse and fancied, on balance, they'd rather it befell others. Hence, they'd left New York, by-passed the unhappy crowds, the economic and cultural turmoil. (Rather like the narrator, Kevin's folks preferred to skip these tiresome details.)

The webmaster took another sip of canned energy. *Two years ago, the highlight of my weekend would've been re-organising the vinyl collection from the alphabetical to the chronological.* [A few years before that; in his late teens, as Covid-19 had its way with the world, Kevin's lifestyle was barely affected.] Now, he ran a successful website and was preparing to scope locations with one of the nation's most pervasive bloggers. It wasn't easy to blog based on USB-stick distribution – but she was one determined lady.

*

There was a knock on the door, and Anne-Maree skipped in with a basket and her usual self-confidence.

Can she only move by skipping?

"Hi, Kevin, eggs. Eggs for you. We're going to the park …"

With winter's end, the new growth fascinated the yggdrasil. Tens of thousands of the light foragers were now resident. Kevin filmed his fellow humans attempting to interact with the aliens.

Toasts of: "To the sun" and "To the Spring" rang out, and locals poured drinks over alien feet. Mostly, the yggdrasil ignored humans. It was an odd sort of invasion. Occasionally, a misguided soul might launch an attack and be met with lethal electrical violence. But rarely.

The trio strolled between the recently planted fruit and nut trees of the Great Lawn. The mood was festive, families played games and consumed snacks. Even with the recovery of FriendFone, people chatted to strangers holding opinions different to their own. Kevin swung the camcorder around, filming the musicians: jazz ensembles, 12-string guitar folk-rock and massed ukuleles honked and strummed.

He noted, "Since Kalinda Ryan on *CCE,* every busker's been testing their stuff on the aliens."

"Everyone says the yggdrasil love ukuleles," said Ebony.

Anne-Maree dashed towards a copse of fifty or more yggdrasil, a cello player, and a crowd of curious humans. Eir Nyssa was present; scarf adorned, the fabric faded and weather ravaged. The child had tied it on a year before as a kind of inter-species friendship bracelet.

Eir Nyssa patted Anne-Maree with intricate wing-leaf movements.

"Looks like everyone loves the music," enthused Ebony.

"Affirmative, much reflective patterning in the vibrations."

"Ah," said Kevin, studying the crowd. He disappeared into the throng.

"It's called Elgar's Cello concerto," he soon reported. "Can we shoot this again? Where you mentioned the vibrations," he asked the alien.

"Repeat self for recording purpose?"

"Yeah, that's it."

This done, the group refocused their attention on the cellist. She didn't hold the child's attention for long. With a little foot-shuffling and grasping of the parental hand, Anne-Maree said, "Mom, tell Kevin who's visiting."

"Yes," she smiled at her daughter, "we had a message from Niels Larsson, he's arriving on Tuesday.

"And mom, mom, we could have a concert – like at school. So, people and yggdrasil can enjoy the music."

"Great idea, honey. A good-will concert." She turned her attention to some-time assistant Kevin, and said, "Building on that … today we'll shoot footage of the city reconnecting with the world, reactions to that, how people feel about having the internet again. And I'll make a few calls. There are singers in the planting team and musicians."

"Should we set boundaries on musical genres and talents?"

"Oh, really Kevin? Let's just let it develop organically."

*

Two days later, Kevin waited in the Park with Ebony's family. Anne-Maree and her little brother crafted 'grass angels' in the long growth. Then a squirrel ran down a tree trunk, chittering in alarm. Eyes bulging in fright, it swirled its tail and squeaked its unease to the world.

To Kevin too, it seemed the air went swirly and ominous. Time slowed, the squirrel's call froze, and then he remembered to breathe again. A hole in space-time appeared, and the blogger of all things peculiar realised there were more important agendas afoot than monitoring squirrel calls.

Alien tech appeared: the intelligence directing the landing beyond miscalculation. Petal-like structures opened, and a yggdrasil emerged. Its longer antennae sampled the air as it waited for its companion human to overcome his travel sickness. Time continued its uncertain pause as a small crowd eyed the pod with curiosity and apprehension. The spell broke as Anne-Maree skipped towards the alien craft. She claimed and hugged a nauseous Swedish scientist.

Sif Acer introduced itself to Ebony and her family.

"Pardon, I'm sitting on the ground a moment," said Niels wobbly. The child crouched with him, chatting of an afternoon concert and the doings of the apartment poultry. Eir Nyssa joined the group and made more introductions.

"Splendid sunlight quality," announced Sif Acer. "Query: Companions of Niels Larsson observe transport interior?"

Kevin raised his hand.

"Totally neat," enthused Ebony. They stepped into the sickly pale green interior, the shade of a hundred hospital corridors. "This is *so* going in the Christmas newsletter!"

Niels kept his expression carefully neutral when told of the concert. Later, he and the two yggdrasil walked along West 72nd Street. As in Europe, the ever-increasing arrivals occupied positions on grassy verges and clustered around the city's plane trees. As in his homeland, fruit café-bars scrambled for position, and urban rats found themselves served up by street vendors.

"What manner creature be sky rat," asked Sif Acer.

"Err, I don't know," said Niels. He approached the cart and after a brief non-purchasing chat reported: "pigeon."

Chapter 46 Concert and Congress

Hastening to the Sheep Meadow and its makeshift stage, Niels joined the largest group of aliens the world had yet seen. He glanced at shadings of olive, grass and tree-frog green; at diversities of leaf-wing size and number. He sniffed. *It smells of spilled cider.* With the New York City skyline as a backdrop, the forester shivered at the premonition of the Earth to come.

Surrounded by wool and synthetic fibre, Niels listened as Ebony and park management delivered introductory remarks of the 'goodwill to all' variety. His face flushed as the blogger singled him out. Niels waved politely at the applause, *Whooping Level 3* he estimated. A stern representative of the gardening liaison committee ordered the crowd not to interfere with the fruit trees. Then, attired in a chic vampire length leather coat, the master of ceremonies claimed the microphone.

The noise scattered a phalanx of elderly Iowans crossing the stage front. The sound scattered the tree-birds and the half-mile distant sea lions. The awful work of amateur musicality commenced …

A lone bagpiper, an older gentleman, begun proceedings. Soon, and seemingly chosen for chronological contrast, a fourth-grade elementary school choir – accompanied by their teacher herself on guitar, replaced him. A glance at the human audience suggested they enjoyed '*This Land is Your Land*' and its foresty references more than the alien vegetal beings.

Niels phoned a friend.

"Telephonic greetings, Niels Larsson," came the response from the cell-phone-integrated alien.

"Hi, where are you?"

"Thirty of metres east direction. Self-adorned with coal-cloth decorative item."

"Ok." *That's good.* Not wanting to be speciest about matters, Niels suspected identifying Sif Acer among a crowd of thousands was beyond him. Soon, with a little waving, the two found each other. The alien folded its jointed limbs and sat beside Niels.

It showed off one of its upper appendages and said, "Human child Anne-Maree Hamilton constructed item for self."

"Yes, I supposed she did," smiled Niels.

There was a brief delay as the next act prepared. Then, "Hey guys," said Kevin, who moving with all the clamour and presence of a sea-sponge joined Niels and the alien ambassador.

The would-be vampire ushered nine members of the Staten Island Strummers on stage. Two tunes later, Niels ran his hand through his hair as a dozen Hawaiian shirt-clad members of the Brooklyn Ukes replaced them. He detected a ukulele motif in proceedings and was alarmed by the tireless fervour of the strumming.

"Ah … are you enjoying the performance?" he asked Sif Acer.

"Indifference."

"Yes, I am thinking as such. Excuse me back soon." And with that, he wandered off, three-hundred yards to the north-east. Soon confirming this was an optimal listening position. The scientist suspected erroneous assumptions at play: the tendency to find patterns where there are none. That three aliens once enjoyed a solo ukulele gig didn't mean more ukes were desirable. Niels thought, *these small instruments are like vitamin tablets: more may not be better. And with a balanced diet, simply not required.*

Gusts and zephyrs of recollection buffeted him. An incongruous image of a rocking-chair-seated alien listening to vinyl records came to mind.

He made another call.

"Hello Matt, this is Niels Larsson, sorry to be waking you. Did I wake you?"

"It's four in the morning, Doc."

"So sorry, Matt, I assure you it's important. Do you know the classical music Kalinda played that night on the show?

"Seriously?"

Discussion established Matt hadn't yet attained ideal fiancée status. He agreed to ring the pop princess. While Niels waited, he recalled that Kalinda had achieved a world-wide hit in recent months.

Mere minutes later, "Yeah, you there?"

"Hi Matt," said Niels, marching back towards the sea of confused and restless yggdrasil.

"Chopin and Bach, she thinks."

"Yes, that was it, Bach. Thanks very much."

"Later, Niels. Much later."

Niels pocketed the phone and re-joined Sif Acer and Kevin. With a glance at the latter, he said, "They're still playing …"

"Actually, no. Look closely, and you'll discern the shirts are different." This was indeed the case – Central Park had ukuleles, as other parks had Dutch elm disease.

"Still, give them a participation ribbon and get them off stage," continued Kevin "I never thought I'd hear myself say this, but bring on the cellist."

"I am also agreeing."

Kevin and Niels reached the backstage as the latest of the entertainers finished.

Sif Acer ventured off to have a strategic conference with a copse of healthy elms it rather liked the look of. Niels spied clusters of yggdrasil detaching from the main mass and making their escape.

"Ebony," said Kevin, "call a time out we need to order off-menu."

The MC announced the strategic pause in activities to the audience.

Backstage Niels observed an encouraging number of violins, violas and additional timbery serious-looking instruments. "They like *Bach*," the Swede explained to Ebony and the musicians.

"Everyone likes Bach," said a bowtie adorned violinist in his east coast drawl.

"There *is* some programmed," said Ebony defensively. She nodded at the woman in the long dress, "Mindy's set is next up."

Kevin recognised yesterday's cello player. "Mindy can you go on now, keep them busy, yeah."

As the first notes of Cello Suite No. 1, The Prelude, rang out, the musicians clustered into urgent discussion groups. The many three-cord uke and guitar strummers departed. However, there were serious players among their number who joined the classically instrumented.

Niels felt the uncertain hush. The music continued, but the murmur of outdoor picnicking, concert-going humans quietened. They stared transfixed at thousands of yggdrasil standing immobile, vibrating in unison, absorbed by the soloist. Niels gave a nod and thumbs up, 'it's all good' signal to the puzzled MC.

When the Bach-filtered musicians exhausted their repertoire, Sif Acer ceased its subtle movement and adjusted its segmented eyestalks at Niels. It dug its claws in the ground and sampled the feelings of its fellows.

Niels looked at it and raised his eyebrows.

"This the greatest of human undertakings … mimics the mathematical ambiguities of tree song, reflects the vibrations of cosmos."

Eir Nyssa, Ebony, the MC, and an unfamiliar yggdrasil ascended the stage.

"Who's that?" asked the forester of his companion.

"Comrade not chosen human identifier. Comrade, not your ally."

Eir Nyssa approached the microphone, thanked the musicians and organisers, and made positive inter-species relation remarks. Around Niels, the crowd clapped. He studied the unknown yggdrasil onstage. *What is the meaning of these eerie alien gestures*? Its companions plunged into stillness. Again, Niels tilted his head and peered at his companion.

Sif Acer directed a single eye stalk in his direction, "Consensus interaction."
As the minutes passed, some in the human audience rolled up their tartan picnic rugs and left.

Then, with a static rasp, the figure nearest the microphone announced, "Unexpected excellence of human vibration patterns. Request arrange additional …" it paused, "concerts."

The creature continued to speak. It insisted, "Humans cease slay light-foragers." In the spirit of inter-species tolerance, it announced the collective yggdrasil would appoint "suitable-adequate" humans to represent their "cultural-geographic areas."

Sif Acer said to Niels, "Comrades possess severe-reduced human tolerance following unfortunate forest attacks. Musical patterning's have …" it rippled its antennae at Niels, apparently stuck for words.

"You mean … given us another chance," he proposed hopefully.

"Affirmative."

On stage, Eir Nyssa moved to the microphone.

"Western Europe and additional English-speaking countries appoint Congress members: Professor Niels Larsson, Miss Anne-Maree Hamilton, Professor Allan la Fontaine, Mr Mike Ross, Mr Matt Davis, Ms Jess Kelly, Mr Tyson K Whitney.

Anne-Maree gave a shy wave.

Niels took a deep breath. He wondered who Tyson K Whitney was, and whether Matt had gone back to sleep.

Chapter 47 Monsters and Aliens

That night after the goodwill concert, Ebony's family, Niels, and Sif Acer debriefed at Kevin's apartment. The yggdrasil's antennae twitched as it roamed the unaccustomed indoor space. The apartment's Lego Star Wars theme park aesthetic was under siege as Anne-Maree and her little brother were loosed into it; Kevin's relief obvious to Niels when James Hamilton eventually took the youngster home to bed.

"Kevin's not a good sharer," Anne-Maree whispered with concern to her mom.

"The things I could do in this space with some ethnic rugs and cushions," whispered Ebony to her daughter.

Niels had accepted Kevin's offer to stay during his New York visit. Once they were alone, the host began conversation with, "We should swap origin stories."

If not for his iron self-control, the scientist's eyebrows wouldn't have merely twitched but risen. With all the introspection of an eight-hours-a-day facebooker Kevin continued in this vein for some time.

"How do you come to live in such a large apartment and convenient apartment by yourself?" said Niels.

"Well, there's Gustav and Natasha, the tree frogs …"

"Frogs are cool."

"Absolutely. My brother Ben comes and goes, but the parents went to their bunker community eight months ago. During the virus outbreak a few years back, they just bought extra ammo and kept going to church. But this is different."

"I am hearing such things, but …" Niels trailed off.

"Oh yeah, have heard nothing since. And mother hasn't eaten carbohydrates since the millennium. Things must be testy down there by now."

Niels nodded. He peeked at books with titles such as *Sasquatch* and *Who built the Pyramids?* He glanced at a model of Thor's hammer. "And you didn't want to go?"

"Lord no! Eating tinned food, playing endless *Monopoly* with my parents' friends. Either that, or staring at the metal ceiling, the couch … the filing cabinet, the other couch with the rip in the arm." He adjusted his glasses, and in defence of some implied criticism said, "They're not total pre-enlightenment values nutters. They do have books!" (If, housed in a straw-walled library – just in case.) "Anyway, it's not like the yggs were going to wipe us out."

Niels stroked his couch's aged timber arm. "Kevin, how's it been in New York the last eighteen months?"

"Tense, real tense. I mean a city swarming with people deprived of sugar, tobacco, fries, communications, and online games. Things got a little lively."

So desperate, video stores had enjoyed a resurgence. People were even eating the irregular-shaped fruit and veg previously discarded.

Niels shook his head, "We were so much dependent on electricity, the internet and the tech economy."

Kevin said, "It was all bound to come to a head, eventually …"

"Yes, just a matter of time before another Carrington event brought it all down—"

"Huh? Oh right," said Kevin, "that 1850s solar flare thing." He grinned inanely, "I meant, they were just asking for trouble: FriendFone, Apple, Pageface, Nile, me2Screen … once they started installing dolphins in their moats and conducting meetings on volleyball courts."

Niels didn't much care for Kevin's grin – he glanced speculatively at the replica hammer.

His host continued, "It's not the initial outlay of your basic freshwater dolphin moat that's the killer – it's the maintenance."

"Please, do you mind if I watch the news?" said Niels.

"Carry on. Time to check the website for posts – it's been ages since we had hours of connectivity at a time." Kevin crossed to his enormous timber desk. "So, what happens now? With the whole inter-species congress-committee?"

Niels glanced at the TV and said, "It seems music has saved us, bought us time at least. I'm thinking, as before on *CCE* we meet and visit enterprises showing us in the positive light. And broadcast this. Also, we try to establish clarity on plant ahimsa."

"Don't get me wrong, professor, I understand why they selected you. But the others? The comedian? Our young celebrity now tucked up in bed."

"Sif Acer says chosen for curious minds, having empathy." He scratched his stubble. "It said species differences are about ways of thinking, not how many feelers you have."

"Well, professor, how do you *feel* about being back in the human envoy game?"

"Please, call me Niels. You know … I am thinking it might be nice to have a quiet Swedish language bookshop in Barcelona or perhaps Prague. Or a farm."

"Bookshop, eh. Interesting."

"Ebony says that you shot that famous Canadian footage and run an alien visit website?"

"Oh yeah, for sure, 'Monsters and Aliens', it started more with cryptozoology – you know unknown species, dinosaur carvings at Angkor Wat, mythical creatures …"

"Griffins, giants, err, house-elves?"

"Well, less Harry Potter, more yetis, lake monsters, how did our lone pet wildebeest get pregnant? That sort of thing."

"Right, okay."

"Then there's a smattering of contemporary zombie culture – all good fun." Kevin began scrolling through new posts. "Still nothing from Russia, China and other countries of the one-party state experience." He kept clicking, "Last year there were reports from Siberia of alien building activity. I've seen descriptions of water transported in a 'force ring' and dumped on fires, and of stirring up volcanoes."

Meanwhile, the TV news continued its summary of the last year's economic devastation. Niels reflected: *yes, we can't eat money.* Even less so: cryptocurrencies. Apparently, folks who'd stashed their Ethereum and Bitcoins under the mattress had misplaced them. TikTok had stopped, and the blockchain had seized up.

Niels turned as Kevin started up again: "These days, I'm more into previous ygg visits. Had to go real old school this last year, checking out libraries, historical accounts of indigenous legends." He sipped an energy drink. "Doc, do you know if your semi-immortal pal has visited before?"

"Sif Acer told me it lived in Scandinavia about fifteen hundred years ago."

"Ah, so perhaps the talking ones have visited before. Eir Nyssa says it couldn't speak to people in ancient Sweden – at least not directly. *Not in spoken language*."

"Interesting," nodded the visitor.

"The website's, well, it's a tricky balance. A lot of interesting stuff gets posted – including the resistance guys."

"The *who* guys?"

"Doc, there's a network, not the government – they're keeping what they know to themselves. Just ordinary people who share intel, ygg hacks, weaknesses, tech ..."

"Not so surprising."

"No, but stupid. I mean, they think the yggs can't access the internet! I take down their stuff. Keep track of it, though."

Kevin wandered from the desk to adjust previously disturbed collectibles. The TV continued spewing out news: continued lack of phone connection to major parts of the world; yggdrasil rampages through a market garden in southern California, and pro-alien rallies in northern California.

On the flat screen an advertisement advised an elegant but funky peeler, corer, and blender of fruit could be the very cornerstone of a cheery modern family dynamic.

"Seems the General Sherman* tree actually survived," commented Kevin, scrolling through website posts.

"I visited it once. Wonderful news if it wasn't burned – if reports were inaccurate."

"Not misreported. *Faked.* One government causing trouble for another, using fake news to stir up the yggs. If the Feds can weaponize the aliens or their tech, they will – surprised they haven't tried to snatch one of our talking dudes yet."

Niels stretched his legs. *Such a generous quantity of non-empirically tested views.* He prowled the room, checking on the activities of the frogs. This didn't save him from Kevin's speculations.

"Doc, Niels, I mean. About those previous yggdrasil trips to Earth. Why did they come, and why did they leave?"

"Eir Nyssa said they didn't enjoy the weather in Sweden … climate scientists report that was an especially cold period." Niels stroked the couch arm and said, "Maybe they do the forest tourism, or surveying before colonisation."

"Yeah. There's an awful lot of *world tree, knowledge tree* myths around the place. And *malevolent* tree spirits and the like." He peered over his thick lenses, "This'll sound out of left field, but what if ancient peoples drove the yggs away, locally defeated them?"

"Kevin, your speculations are most thorough and wide-ranging. However, I am thinking I must be getting to bed – things to do in the days ahead. Tomorrow I go to view the Oregon forests with Sif Acer and drop in at my University."

"Cool. Going anywhere near Portland?"

"I could," Niels shrugged.

"If you could pick up an old and fragile book. My optometrist's sister – also an optometrist, by the way – has a sideline in historical books …"

---

* A Giant Sequoia, the largest tree in the world.

Chapter 48 TK Whitney

Tyson K. Whitney and his knit cap sauntered through Washington DCs Eastern Market. The DJ's walk was as loose as his late 1980s hammer pants, and he projected self-confidence like a force of nature. He couldn't saunter a dozen steps without enjoying greetings from well-wishers. Tyson had been a local celebrity for a year following *his* yggdrasil encounter. Now, like Niels, he'd experienced the full surreality enchilada: being drafted to join an ill-defined Congress by alien spokes-creatures.

And he'd just spoken to the Swedish dude, Niels, by phone.

Since the *Cairns Declaration* eighteen months before: wool-knit caps, beanies, bobble hats, call them what you will had become ubiquitous, even in climates too warm to wear them. Exactly what the beanie meant was difficult to say – though many had tried. In the complex world of alien-politico-fashion, an aggressively woolly, pop-pom adorned knit cap might suggest: 'I am not now, and never have, subsisted solely on a plant-based diet.'

Greeting another knit-cap adorned fan, Tyson K mused that headwear comprised little of his discussion with the forester.

"Forest protection is the great alien priority," began Niels. "Then they focused on what they consider non-essential but widespread crops: sugar cane, tobacco and later, rubber and cotton. We've wasted any goodwill with the fighting and attacks on the forests. But now Tyson, the discovery of our music by the yggdrasil, has given us another chance."

"Great Doc ..." Here, Tyson K felt in his comfort zone.

Humans are nothing if not adaptable, as the range of clothing and food displayed at Eastern Market showed. Wool and nylon, polyester and leather blended in ways not formerly seen outside those old Mad Max films. As he strolled, Tyson caressed lumpy, textured tropical fruits. His nostrils quivered at the distinctive odour of barbeque rat on a stick. In the last year it had been embraced with defiant humour, and not only by survivors of the all-night EDM venues that Tyson presided over.

Tyson K, as known on his fashion, food, and yggdrasil survival blog, was in his way just as influential as the lawmakers of the Capital. For the DJ was one of those rare souls with the curiosity and courage to approach and question an alien. And one of even fewer to receive a reply. Tyson first encountered "his" yggdrasil in Lincoln Park a month after the startling events of *CCE*. On the otherwise ordinary fall day, the public met the arrival of the alien with panicked enthusiasm to be somewhere other than Lincoln Park.

Tyson had approached the green menace as it fine-tuned its wing-leaves on the grass edge near the Mary McLeod Bethune Memorial.

"Yo, how's it goin' man?"

A feeler twitched.

"Hey, I figure you're not from around here … these people usually they be picnicking, tossing the Frisbee, playin' with their kids – having a fine time here, you know. So, I figure all this running and screaming … well, it's good to try something different, yeah!"

The creature focused its jointed eye stalks on the knit-cap clad human.

"That was a joke, man. You have jokes where you come from, yeah?"

"Concept awareness, comprehension optimal negative."

"Hey, you can *talk*! Not so good, but … cool."

And so began the relationship between the DJ and alien light-forager. Over a year and more Tau Ulmus, (as it came to identify itself), became the Capital's chief yggdrasil-liaison. A minor local DJ figure before the fateful encounter, the opportunity had been firmly and entrepreneurially grasped. And now Tyson K would join a team tasked with finding a way for the yggdrasil to tolerate humanity.

Chapter 49 Tripping to Portland

Kevin stayed up late, aided by energy drinks. His followers were now informed of the website's narrowing of focus: from the former generous range of cat-bear sightings, killer freshwater squids, and first-person-shooter zombie game reviews. His guest Niels had risen early, dreams again disturbed by blood-spattered gothi*, of offerings heaped in sacred groves.

Niels drank coffee, looked around and perused the frogs; *these I can relate to*. Soon, he entered the softly humming transport device in the park. By the time the sea lion pups had detected its movement and were preparing to bark, the pod was in Portland. It hung above the street, a narrow, retro PC game and fruitarian café lined affair. Niels stared down at the bronze statues thoughtfully embedded in the sidewalk. Cautiously, the pod descended.

Sif Acer and a queasy Niels entered the optometry clinic. The staff hadn't seen such excitement since management repositioned their brand from Portland Vision to Vision Portland (resulting in a copse of trees repurposed into new stationery). The scientist explained their mission to the startled opticians.

"Miss Pert," called an underling.

---

*Gothi: Norse priest-chieftain

An aged woman of severe appearance appeared and barely glanced at the alien. Indeed, it appeared she'd barely responded to stimuli since about the time laser printing was invented. The visitors opened an adjoining brass door into an alternative world of low lighting, dark wood and mustiness.

A bookshop without paperbacks and self-help manuals.

The staff stared at Sif Acer. Not so much with trepidation, the alien simply seemed incompatible with an optometry-bookshop enterprise. Unaware of these musings, the plant-creature crept past slumbering books. Its antennae and eyestalks twitched.

"Pre electronic human informational storage."

"Yes," said Niels, sensing a question.

"Constructed from light-forager structural elements?"

"Yes," said Niels, but more sheepishly.

"All species construct errors former times."

After further explanations, the pair secured the battered two-hundred-year-old prize. Minutes later, there was little to remind the befuddled employees of Vision Portland (and Historical Books Portland) of the unlikely manifestation.

*

The next stop was the professor's first visit to Oregon State's Forestry School by alien transport craft. The resulting stomach-churning unease suited the mood. The refurbished shine had dulled. There was a feeling of gloom, of uncertainty, of cutting-edge equipment pushed into corners, bubble-wrap still un-popped.

If there was one profession not required in the new alien paradigmed world – then forestry was a leading candidate. Sif Acer took itself off to explore the local woods and Niels met with the Dean. The man had lost his former zip – the usual flood of management clichés had dried to mere puddle-splatter.

The two discussed Niels' potential return. He said, "I have ideas … moving into algae research; mushroom farming; specialise in fruit tree culture; rename the School Plant Science …"

Exchanging the Dean's stylish office for the strictly functional laboratory, Niels encountered a familiar face.

"Professor Niels!" exclaimed Ash, with a brief hug. "Hi," she added.

"Hello, Ashley, nice to see you again. Is Andrew present?"

"He sure is my friend," said the lab manager in question, approaching in his usual bulky way. "The TV star returns. You've been a busy man," he added, grasping Niels' hand.

Andrew had found himself less than busy in recent times. Everywhere the economy had taken a massive hit. The lab's mighty plant genome sequencer had found alternative uses.

"… we've developed mail out kits for those anxious not to marry their sisters … we can assist you to make a copy of dearly departed Princess Fluffy Tail." Andrew lost the grin, "We've worked in the morally dubious field of assisting health insurers raise premiums for the genetically unfortunate." He wiped his brow. "So, the yggdrasil samples … epic biochemistry! Let's go across to the cafeteria and debrief. I'll get the laptop. Oh, how was the Dean – no visible claw marks," he joked in his deep voice.

The trio exited the laboratory. The contrast between the buildings and the disarray of the lawns and gardens was stark. Gardening hadn't seen such peril since nineteenth-century plant collectors set out into the Amazon. Shrubberies were exuberant and messy; lawns unevenly shaved (all the prim and jolly, 'Keep off the Grass', signs redundant). In the café, Niels observed, student numbers had declined. Those present looked at him with unusual interest.

Andrew began, "We managed to culture tissue from the fragments you collected from Crescent City the year before last. They died after nine weeks, but I dare say we could improve on that if needed. Anyways …" he continued, "keratin cell walls, but calcium in the epidermis too … big numbers of mitochondria-like organelles, nucleic acids similar to ours, and novel ones. Weirdly: found carbon fibre microtubule structures without organelles."

"So non-living?"

"Yeah, seems so. Maybe remains of clothes, armour, equipment?" he shrugged, "who knows."

"And photosynthetic organelles?"

"For sure, be a shock if there weren't. But Niels here's the thing: there's little genetic variation in the chloroplast homologues despite considerable variation in other tissues from a range of specimens."

Niels experienced a brief flashback to *CCE* at Heron Island and big Lenny poking at a giant clam. He took a sip of coffee, "Any signs of reproduction … eggs, foetuses, larvae?"

"Well, Niels, your samples were pretty beat up, toasty in parts… so difficult to say. Not that we'd necessarily recognise it."

Ash, critically examining her coffee, asked, "Anything new there, professor? Does that tally with what secret government types told you?"

"Broadly yes, Ashley, but they are not the best sharers," he said, quoting Anne-Maree.

"And what now, professor – with this new panel or congress," she shrugged, "whatever it is."

"We meet and try again and hope to buy time to make changes the yggdrasil insist on." There was a hush from the nearer tables. He continued, "I have met or spoken to many of them, these Congress persons. Also, I have tried to contact the Australian comedian Matt Davis – but he pretends his car is in the tunnel."

"One of them is a DJ and blogger from Washington DC – posts about the yggdrasil, food, music and fashion. He designed the beanies with a pocket everyone wears."

Do they? "Yes, Ashley, I've spoken to Tyson K by phone."

"But one Congress member's a child!" said Andrew, incredulous.

Niels shrugged, "She has a curious mind. It was she who first learned the name *yggdrasil*."

"Her mom posted from the concert in Central Park the other day," said Ash.

"Yes, the yggdrasil appreciate the music of the composer Bach. Something we can use as a means of reconciliation. There will be a grand concert in the summer."

"Bach in Central Park," grinned Ash.

Chapter 50 Meetings, Museums, and more History

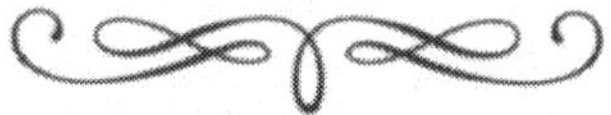

Niels' day had been eventful. His pod-travel nausea was easing, but his phone had been quicker to recover. In Corvallis, it paired itself to a robot vacuum cleaner. But on his return, it informed him Jess had landed at JFK *and* that Special Agent Cam Peters was insisting on a meeting.

For Niels, an advantage of living in Sweden while the yggdrasil had their way with the planet's telecommunication systems, was lack of contact with the special agent. Oddly, today's earlier texts attempted a casual tone (as if Peters were re-imagining a childhood when friends called him 'CP'. This was self-delusion. Psychologists who've run the numbers assure us that folk who thrive in senior security advisory roles have a degree of psychopathy that prevents friendship).

Already present in New York, Agent Peters agreed to meet at the nearby Natural History Museum. He soon launched into a set of instructions concerning the new Congress and ordered Niels to investigate an alliance with the aliens. A scenario where the US might be left alone; in exchange for ceding the rest of the planet to the green menace.

"Do they have a weakness, Professor?"

"Their mindset."

"Explain," barked the Secret Science Agency's finest.

"Err, they are not interesting in anything but our plants and trees – they don't see the complexity. The few, we might call scientists, are now leaving. Except for linguist-ambassadors, they have not the curiosity. They are like us – shocked when a virus jumps species and dares to infect. There is an arrogance, yes."

Peters dismissed this. And Niels himself.

Yet Niels lingered, finding himself intrigued by a jar of bleached coral rubble.

*

From the vast apartment's kitchen, Kevin beamed at his guests. *What a day.* (He'd been appointed the informal recorder of the Interspecies Committee's activities.) "Hey. My place is becoming the unofficial save-the-world Bat Cave. Might have to wear my underwear on the outside!"

Niels and the recently arrived Australian Jess Kelly smiled politely. In anticipation, Kevin had worn his best shiny vinyl jacket and track pants combination (the one with the lime green stripe). But soon, with a well-practiced shrug of resignation, he realised Jess' attention was rather more drawn to Niels.

The evening TV news was on. The feature story describing the recent trend of making offerings of olive oil and beer to the aliens. Local practices were compared to the new cult of yggdrasil worship developing or *reviving* in northern Europe.

"This is an exaggeration," said Niels. Then recalling recent dreams, he flinched. *At least they're not sacrificing horses yet.* "I don't believe so many of my countrymen really worship our aliens – just as many conceal the carrots inside their buildings."

The knock on the door signified food delivery. The Australian and the Swede exchanged bemused glances as Kevin located a space not occupied by pop culture collectibles to rest the pizzas.

"Hope it's okay – I ordered a seafood, and I don't know about this one."

"I wonder if the pod travel makes me hungry, the pizza's smell is excellent," said Niels.

He glanced at Jess, her nose wrinkled endearingly as she said, "Is it still Margherita if it doesn't have basil?"

"Gotta make compromises," shrugged Kevin. "What are we drinking? Got a Californian chardonnay and cider." He peered through his lenses at his guests and distributed drinks and pizza. "Cheers."

"Cheers," said Jess and Niels together, echoing the occasional stereo utterances of the yggdrasil.

"No need to pour anything on the floor," Kevin advised. He turned to Niels, "It's weird, you were there when that toasting trend started, and here you are … *here*," he concluded astutely. Kevin continued, "Now here's an idea: What if Sif Acer made that gesture because that's how the locals treated them back in Viking days? That earlier ygg visits influenced the culture of those times."

"Yes, Kevin, I am hearing that speculation before – you know I wonder if that 'drinks on the feet' toast is functional – maybe the yggdrasil can absorb useful nutrients that way."

Jess nodded. "I'll just move this." She re-located a weirdly prescient tree creature from Tolkien's oeuvre out of the way of pizza activities for its safety. "Yeah, that makes sense – even if they can take nitrogen out of the air, they will have to get phosphorus, metal ions, other elements they need, from somewhere."

"Jumping back in," said Kevin, "When you consider historic yggdrasil visits, they must have gone to the Amazon – that's the 'to die for' forest, right?"

Jess nodded and Niels said, somewhat defensively, "Yes, but they also appreciate the conifer forests of the far north and deciduous trees fascinate them."

Not to be side-tracked, Kevin related that for centuries, explorers armed only with reluctant horses, near-total ignorance, and smallpox had plunged into the Amazon jungle. Their search for: gold, fabulous rivers, eternal life, endless free sex, and minimal taxation.

"Not forgetting the hunt for rare orchids," joked Niels, inspecting an uneven distribution of pizza-shrimps, and thinking *I may need a stress-relieving whittling session if this continues*.

"We used to believe," continued the host without pause, "that the jungle had only hunter-gatherers and simple agriculture. But now, with satellite photography, clearing and drought, there's evidence of widespread monumental building structures."

Niels observed Jess arrange her shapely legs under herself, and he reached for another cider.

"I'll show you pics," said Kevin, warming to his topic. He clunked a laptop key and exploding unicorns vanished. "So, these are aerial shots of pyramids and mounds in the jungle, and here the footprint of extensive buildings in land cleared for cattle ranching."

The visitors moved comfortably together, sharing the device.

"When I was young," said Jess, "we used to hear of the Amazon's destruction. I can't believe it's *worse* now. Much worse these last five years with deliberate fires and clearing—"

"Yeah. Tragic right. Now this bas relief carving was lost in the Brazil National Museum fire years ago. It's identified as the Feathered Serpent – *but* now that we've seen the yggs (he stood and performed a little leaf-wing mimicry) … you get what I mean?"

Niels made a barely encouraging nod, but none-the-less encouraged Kevin continued. "Here's the thing. There are maybe fifty aliens worldwide that can or *will* talk. And we've asked most of them: 'Have you been here before? Where did you go?' – that type of thing. Well, I don't know of a single one that says it's been to the Amazon." He nodded significantly, "I say they're hiding something!" Kevin relieved Jess of the tablet and left the room.

Niels had a sense of missing something significant. Then he spotted it. The bottle opener. He glanced apprehensively at Jess as Kevin returned with a generously proportioned book; akin to volume three of *Critters That Will Ruin Your Picnic in Australia.*

Kevin sidled over and sat between them.

"I secured this at an antiquarian bookshop closing down sale. Kind of kick-started my interest in the topic." He wrangled open the heavy, ornate cover: an account of a seventeenth-century Portuguese expedition.

"Of course, they were searching for the usual: legendary lands; The Fountain of Youth, for …" The resolute tone with which their host related conquistador adventures troubled the guests. "My ancient Portuguese isn't so great," Kevin grinned. "But this man: Father Cristobal de Acuna," (he pointed but didn't quite touch) "was a missionary. Now see *this* illustration," he enthused, delicately turning a page, "the children are kind of scary looking and wearing *strapped on leaves*."

"Looks like my nieces' fairy parties – just gone a bit feral," joked Jess.

"And here, in the background," motioned Kevin, "these remind me of the cocoons the yggs spin."

"Hmm," said Jess, in the cautious tone of one who hoped this might shield her from enthusiasms to come. "Any relevance to now, Kevin?"

There was a brief, polite negotiation over the last piece of pizza.

"Oh definitely," said Kevin, trotting to the kitchen with the remains of dinner. "Back in a moment."

"Niels, what first with this panel-committee thing?" asked Jess, in the temporary absence of Kevin and his props.

"I am thinking, visit specific farms and try to establish certainty around agricultural practices the yggdrasil will tolerate."

"Will that be hazardous? I mean, especially if they don't approve!"

"I'm sorry, Jess. None of us volunteered for this. In this circumstance, I assume it's safe – there may be disapproval, but I trust Eir Nyssa wouldn't let harm come to Ann-Maree. For our situation, the instructions aren't on the backside."

"And Matt Davis?"

"*So* the best thing on that show. Barring yourself, of course," added Kevin, re-joining them with another book.

"I haven't been able to reach him since I called during the concert." For Jess' benefit, Niels explained: "I remembered Mir Arauca liking classical music at your parent's farm, but I was not knowing you or your mother so well to ring early in the morning." he shrugged. "It might be helpful if he joined. He has a certain, err … quality."

"Yeah, yeah, I know what you mean. Can the yggdrasil make him join?"

"No idea. Anyway, I'll go to Australia and try to persuade him."

"Thanks again for collecting this, Doc," said Kevin. He flourished the account of the English adventurer, Algernon Whittington-Hortle's 1821 expedition to Peru. "Hardly anyone's heard of him now. Back in the day he was controversial: went looking for the cities the Portuguese described centuries earlier. He said they were still there, reclaimed by the jungle. And he found local tribes that maintained connections to the ruins. But when professional archaeologists passed that way, decades later – they couldn't find what 'WH' had described.

Jess sneaked a covert look at her phone.

"There was a young architect from New York on the expedition, and he sketched their finds. See here – there's a plaza built around a pool. The children are wearing leaves tied to their arms and backs. And here," he said, flipping another page, "is a sketch of a tomb … they said the mummy had leather *wings* attached to his back, and a skull elongated by head binding."

"Ah", said Jess, still non-committal. She ceased her surreptitious phone checking and made it overt, "Golly, is that the time!"

Niels was likewise stunned – having thought the hour later still.

"Gosh, the jetlag's really kicking in. Best be off, but thanks for today – both of you. See you later, yeah."

"I'll walk you down," said Kevin.

Niels fondled his necklace bead. *Perhaps the break in proceedings will halt the onslaught of yggdrasil-in-the-Amazon speculations.* However, he might just have well roamed the apartment block inviting the residents to deposit their firearms in a large, embroidered disposal receptacle he'd prepared earlier.

For, after some desultory chatter about the state of the evening outside, Kevin continued. "Not so long before the yggs arrived, a site was found near the border of Colombia and Ecuador. The graves were looted of gold and artefacts, but …"

"I see. Two questions Kevin: Do I need to know and is there more to drink?"

Kevin reported from the kitchen, "Have got nothing cold."

"It'll be okay," Niels assured him in an urgent tone.

"The thing is – among the so-called non-valuable items – there were artefacts that seem to me to include ygg body parts, like weapon handles. That grave contained hundreds of frog skeletons and arrowheads: The 'Frog Chief.'"

"So … the 'Frog Chief,' tell me more," Niels said.

But not, as it happened, until months later.

Chapter 51 Retrieving Matt

An alarm rang out, just audible above the maelstrom. Surfacing, like a kraken from the deep, a foam-clad appendage, reached for its prey. Matt blew bubbles from the phone, revealing another message from Niels Larsson. Clearly changing sims couldn't save a fellow from being on the receiving ends of texts from Swedish foresters. Nor retailing loyalty-programs. It was a hot tub of the large, sumptuous variety – occupying the third-floor balcony, and Matt had settled in for some serious relaxing.

"Hello Niels," he began tentatively.

The week had been trying. Matt considered his moral compass abandoned; most likely, in the clutter of the third drawer down. Now, all manner of people (and non-people) were trying to insert it in him. Whereas all he required inserted, presently, was a mango and coffee panna cotta. He replaced the phone. *Why can't a man be left alone with his girlish collection of dissolvable bath products to eat deserts in the hot tub and watch televised sport?*

*

Matt strolled back from the shops the next morning, too lost in thought to notice a new 'Grow your own algae and bugs' shop in the high street. He barely noticed the black-market potato dealers lurking in the shadows. He eyed one of those cars the unwary may observe on billboards: the type that provoke angst and resentment in old school enemies. *Look at that car – owner must be a wanker.*

Then he remembered it was his.

He gave it a proprietary pat and scurried up the steps. Niels had threatened to visit this very morning – with reinforcements. The comedian had a pretty shrewd idea what the Swede wanted.

*

Niels valued Jess' easy-going enthusiasm, so he asked her to come along and help entice Matt from his Melbourne lair.

"Err, Niels, I only just arrived in New York!"

"Sorry, I know, but I don't think travel time need be an issue."

Niels discussed the problem with Sif Acer …

"Thanks. Awesome …" *Such goodwill, so generous.*

When offered the alien travel-pod, memories of driving-lessons on icy, moose-infested roads at the family's northern retreat came to mind.

One of the odder parts of the experience for the human flying solo was the security system. As the green light flickered over him, he thought, *ah, this is how an unnecessarily plastic-wrapped and bar-coded banana feels.*

Later, after practice, and attempting nonchalance, the forester entered the pod trailed by Jess. "Jess, that's the *satnav*." They approached the embedded device.

She put her hands on her hips, "Looks as though a spider, a fungus and an iPad had a really good time together."

Not wishing to startle the locals by materialising inside the Number 78 Tram, Niels directed the pod to appear in a park near Matt's home. When their nausea passed, the pair set off, guided by a functioning cell phone network. They passed boarded up herbal remedy apothecaries, a working public transport system, and waste food distribution centres. Yggdrasil stood alone and in clusters. In gardens and grassy road verges.

Jess and Niels climbed the red-brick steps to the small landing. The Swede wasn't one to judge another by their recycling accessories, but he'd never before seen empty beer cans and a succulent residing in a giant clamshell.

They crossed the threshold. Matt's smile was warily hospitable. On balance, he considered it too late to hide behind the couch.

"Manly hug?" he suggested after an awkward pause while Niels, and he considered their greeting options. This accomplished, the forester introduced Jess. Matt's place was a narrow, disused factory to inner-city living affair, spread over three floors. The entrance led into a games room.

"So, congratulations," said Niels. "Just fantastic …"

"Yeah, ah, thanks," said Matt with a disarming smile. It surprised him as much as anyone – his parents remained shocked by their youngest son's success.

"Yeah, just finished a tour and a book. Did you see the phone advert?"

Niels was momentarily at a loss. "Err, Matt, I was talking of your engagement. To Kalinda," he added, to clarify the matter.

"Of course, sorry mate," began Matt flustered and suitably embarrassed. "Yeah, thanks a lot, she's great … like cocktails by the pool, like summer at the beach! Jesus, what am I saying? I was thinking earlier – I might have become a bit of a dick since I saw you last."

The three remained standing awkwardly. The room had a bar, and Niels advanced on it hopefully. Soon there was nothing between them except for a rather hideous brown and gold, striped, and shaggy rug. Well, that and a drink invitation. *This is the longest I've ever been in Australia without a beer offered.*

"Do you hang out with the other ex-*CCE people*?" Jess asked, attempting to stimulate a little conversation. "Other than your fiancée, I mean."

"Nah, not much. See them on telly sometimes. Other night, I was knocking back a cold one in the hot tub, and Mariam was on the news – lecturing about something. I even had a text from Sif Acer a few months ago. But we haven't organised a reunion or anything."

"You *are* knowing of this advisory group or Congress that the aliens in New York selected you for?"

"Yeah, heard I got a guernsey. About that – got your messages, but every time I thought, *should get back to the Doc*, something came up."

Niels regarded him impassively with pale blue eyes – hinting further information would be welcome.

Matt paused, detecting the unsettled feeling that occasionally swept over him in the presence of people with purpose. "My old man had to go to hospital."

The visitors made simultaneous noises of sympathy and enquiry.

"He, uh, broke his ankle tripping over a dog while trying to kick a football. An Australian Rules footy," he added as if this clarified things. "Silly old git!"

For Dr Davis, orthopaedic surgeon, the embarrassment of the situation wasn't helped, being called by all and sundry: "Matt Davis, the comedian's father."

Niels continued to gaze steadily at the younger Davis.

In such circumstances, trapped by earnest well-meaning ex-colleagues, Matt wished for the easy evasiveness of his first manager (now completing the tenth month of his involuntary community service).

"And I was gonna call after dad's crisis. But next thing I know, two police and a national parks ranger knock at the door …"

Niels raised an eyebrow.

"And they're like, 'Mr Davis We found your jet-ski damaged and abandoned at the site on an *illegal* jet-ski jousting tournament. During which a group of novice stand up paddle boarders were scattered, and damage sustained to a passing dugong.'"

Niels edged towards the Whack-A-Mole table. He took an exploratory grip on the tethered mallet as Matt continued.

"Turns out the thing had been stolen – probably while I was at the hospital."

"Wow, that is unfortunate … and barely credible," said Niels. *Put down the mallet – not very ahimsa of me*!

"Don't I know it," agreed Matt, running his fingers through his hair.

Jess crossed her arms. "You're joking. This is a routine, isn't it?"

"Yeah," admitted the comedian, "… anyways, you better have a look at the place. The living room's up here."

Niels clattered up the transparent staircase to a modernist and austere room, his subconscious poking at him urgently.

Chapter 52 Lichen, clams, and corals

“Have a seat,” Matt said, indicating a range of seating options – one unorthodox.

“I am interesting in this one,” said Niels. He advanced on a sofa someone had thought to construct from a granite boulder, timber, and stainless-steel rods.

“Not my best thought-out purchase,” Matt shrugged. “Try it – it’s surprisingly comfortable.”

Jess moved closer, “It has lichen growing on it.”

Sitting on the thing, Niels regarded the crusty growth. As is often observed, a subconscious can be a tricky and persistent thing.

“Are you okay, Niels?” asked Jess, feeling her companion’s interest was beyond that required, even for unconventional furniture.

“Lichens are a symbiosis of a fungus and an alga … also that giant clamshell on the step … when we were on Heron Island, the guide said the clams have algae in their tissues …”

“As do corals,” added Jess, eyes alive with curiosity.

“Exactly! coral: another animal with photosynthesis.”

“This is connected with yggdrasil concerns or their biology?”

“Oh yes, for sure and certain.” He faced Matt, “Do you have episodes of *CCE* recorded?”

“Doc, they’re online again now. Do you want them on the big screen?”

“Please, if you would.”

“Here’s the remote. Go for it. I’ll call Kal, she’ll come over.”

"So, you want to find the Heron Island episode?" asked Jess.

"Yes, but first can we go to the episode the aliens arrived."

It didn't take them long to find the shocking footage that began with Tek Alnus emerging and killing the two young women. It was after all the most viewed event in the history of viewing.

"Gee, I remember where I was when I first saw this," Jess commented. Niels nodded in agreement, and they both glanced with concern at Matt. He sat on a conventionally fabricated couch at the end of the long narrow room, whispering on his phone.

The footage proceeded to the *Cairns Declaration.* Sif Acer filled the shot, and from the wall mounted screen, the creature once more said: "Advise humans enhance like corals."

"This is about the chloroplast DNA you mentioned the other day.

"Yes," nodded the Swede. The subconscious had completed its task – the mental cogs were whirring.

"So, the Island episode then?" suggested Jess.

"Sure …"

As the footage started, Matt raised his voice. He looked across the room at Niels and said into the phone: "Yeah, Niels is here, and Jess Kelly, the platypus scientist. He brought her along to make her watch videos of himself. Oh – and he's got a thing for clams. Giant ones. You sure you want to come? Ah, apparently, it's getting to a good bit. Until soon. Bye."

With a glance at Matt, Niels said, "So, on the island, Sif Acer says, 'Humans should emulate corals.'"

"Whatever that means," added the host, moving back to join the visitors.

"And after that," Niels continued, "Tek Alnus said, 'Cease discussion of corals.'"

"It's a dispute, isn't it? Tek Alnus didn't want you to know something," said Jess.

"You were totally stressed about sea snakes and stonefish," reminisced Matt smugly.

"That is true – terrifying creatures," he agreed, to Jess' amusement. "Now go forward to that evening. See how Sif Acer comments on the Giant Clams again."

Turning to Matt, Niels explained, "Before joining *CCE,* I took samples from a battle site in northern California. I couldn't hear of the analysis until last week." He glanced at Jess, "As I mentioned before, there was diversity in their cellular DNA equivalent and their mitochondrial DNA, but a very little in their chloroplasts."

"And that's important, because?"

"It means the photosynthetic organelles are recent – they've had less time to evolve. They're the same, Sif Acer told us to emulate corals—"

"They made themselves photosynthetic!" exclaimed Jess.

"Yes."

"Err, what?" said Matt.

Niels examined the supplied TV snacks. "Imagine their general DNA is this bowl of M&M's …"

"Right," said Matt.

"And the DNA in their light-making cells is this …"

"Bowl of chocolate-coated almonds," confirmed Matt taking one and examining it speculatively.

Niels stared at the bowls, "Sorry, I can't think how to explain it with snacks."

"So they made themselves," repeated Matt.

"Yes," confirmed Jess and Niels – together.

There was a reflective pause, Matt crunched the almond, "You know, I almost missed this – learning some new alien weirdness – not so much the sense of menace though."

"This changes things – it will take thinking through," said Niels. "So, you'll join us on this new Congress the yggdrasil announced?"

"It's not that I have the conscience of one of those things that lays its eggs in caterpillars—" began Matt.

"What, parasitic wasps?" said Jess incredulously.

"That's it," he said, "I do have a rudimentary sense of morality. But I'm not qualified at important stuff – other people are better at fighting cancer, inventing ahimsa duck pate, ruining our shared sense of community with toxic FriendFone posts. And to quote George Washington, 'I've taken leave of this public life'".

"Well, hardly Matt, you have your own show, you're on TV panels constantly, you're a major celebrity," argued Jess.

"Yeah, thanks, but it's not the same. I don't have to fix anything. I just play the clown or the angry amusing prophet, denouncing the hypocrisies of our times – piece of cake."

"No-one's qualified for *this*. Not me, not Jess, not a six-year-old."

There was a reflective pause, during which Matt again felt the stirrings of the moral compass. A tenseness began in his gut, enlarging until a lump formed. He sensed the lump might prove soluble in alcohol. Consequently, if a mite tardily, drink-serving-duties began.

Matt began downing drinks at a startling pace. "*Celebrity Council Elimination* was awesome for my career," he said, gesturing at the surroundings. "But it hasn't all been 'beer and skittles,' to quote grandma. I once had a pint of strong Cornish cider poured over me, I've been sent threatening vegetables in the mail, I've been stalked through my shoe-store loyalty card. I could go on …"

"Yes, well, if you prefer the monotony of a *less-menacing* lifestyle," said Jess airily.

Niels laughed and Matt grinned, "Yeah, maybe I do. It's like in that excellent old kid's movie where the hero says, 'I save the world, and it just gets messed up again …' or something."

Niels nodded, *ah, the tone of opposition softens*. "Matt," he said, "the yggdrasil asked for you, but you don't have to save the world by yourself. There are others: Jess, me and J. S. Bach will lend a hand.

The group heard the door open downstairs, footsteps ascended the semi-invisible stairs, and Kalinda emerged. Her hair was shorter now, Niels noted. He crossed the room, and they exchanged greetings and hugs. He introduced Jess and then said, "Matt's thinking whether to join this new yggdrasil Congress."

Kalinda put down a shoulder bag. "Thinking," she said, turning to the fiancée, eyebrows vanishing under her fringe, "of course, he'll join it."

"Sometimes Matt just needs a little enabling!"

Chapter 53 The Congress Meets

Crystal shook her head in wonder. It *was a year ago today I accidentally rang Rehn's old cell number.* Her brother's phone: the one forgotten in the general rush to 'leave' the Sequoia Forest protest site.

"Telephonic greetings! Former device Rehn Roche. Presently location William Browning agriculture. Self has identified as Sri Achras."

So had begun the brief life-changing conversation.

Crystal had soon ventured north to Fresno County. She smiled as the now-familiar yggdrasil ambassador approached and executed a brief scratchy hug, "Good morning, Sri Achras. How's the sunlight today?"

"Quality exemplary Crystal Roche. And your health processes?"

"Great, just great. Looking forward to seeing Mike Ross again and dear little Anne-Maree. I'll help Bear show the Congress visitors around … show other yggdrasil and people how we do things here. Take it to the world, yeah!"

*

Across the country, Professor Allan la Fontaine greeted *his* first-ever yggdrasil. After meeting Niels, the two Australians (Matt and Jess), and the two Hamiltons (Ebony and Anne-Maree) in the apartment of their tame cameraman (Kevin), they strolled to Central Park.

Anne-Maree ran to greet Eir Nyssa – latching on to the creature's lower limbs with a dull thud. Kevin filmed the meeting between the alien and the Frenchman. The former resembled a cross between an oversized prawn and a banana palm, whereas the latter was one of those narrow, angular fellows with the look of a ruffled ibis. It rather surprised the group that the philosopher hadn't spoken to a yggdrasil before. In this age of the dementia scourge, a gentle prompt will remind the reader Jess and Niels *had* met Allan before – on the same Australian TV panel show where they'd met each other.

Ebony explained to the others, "Anne-Maree, and I stayed at Bear's farm before the dreadful forest fires. We did a blog …"

As the party walked towards the reservoir Allan said to Eir Nyssa, "My *previous* worldview was that moral requirements must be extended to encompass animals, I find this must now be extended to *every living thing*. I thank your kind and Niels for this enlightenment."

"Not weakness to grow new direction, towards light," said the alien.

"I once cut down trees, and you argued people should only eat plants. Yet here we are," shrugged Niels. (Previously he'd asked the absent Sif Acer's opinion of his past. The creature had waved some antennae at him and casually dismissed the past. Something Niels much appreciated in an invading alien.)

*

On arrival Allan staggered first from the pod, knelt, then sat on the loamy soil. With this unpropitious entrance, Crystal realised the main group of guests had arrived. Earlier, she'd greeted Tyson K, who turned out to be a tall, athletic man of the variety commonly used in advertisements. And not just advertisements for tall, athletic men. She'd kept him company until the next guest's entrance. Crystal rushed towards the celebrity conservationist, before pulling up short, remembering *Mike's not a hugger*!

Forewarned and thus doped up on anti-nausea drugs and antihistamines (to ward off the effects of livestock) Kevin watched the pod doors unfold. He filmed the Congress' exit and Alan looking pale on the grass. Then the world tilted, and Kevin felt the need to join him down there. From this vantage point he registered a pair of sizeable, battered boots. Kevin warily observed they were attached to tree-trunk sized legs enclosed in faded overalls.

"Welcome all. That's some arrival. I'm Bill Browning," began the owner of the boots. He stooped and helped Kevin to his feet with one enormous hand and the Frenchman with the other.

"Rough trip eh!" Bill continued, "You might call me the proprietor of this here enterprise slash lifestyle. But most folk call me Bear. Nice to see you, ladies, again," he added with a nod to Anne-Maree and her mom.

Kevin began wobbly recording proceedings. As Bear's deep, slow voice continued, he took in barns, workshops, crop fields, the many odours of agriculture and two-dozen workers. His eyes, sandwiched between the thick glass of his spectacles and that of the camcorder lens, widened with what might have been love at first sight. To confirm, given future developments and the need for narrative clarity – it was indeed love at first sight.

For among the welcoming committee, next to the cement Buddha (thoughtfully arrayed with solar lights), was the most beautiful girl in the world. He realised with a start that his nausea had vanished. Moments later, the pod vanished and was replaced with … nothing – a churning vortex of nothing. Kevin filmed the nothing, prudently backing away from it.

Seconds later, another pod replaced the appalling nothing. An alien emerged and said simply: "Hatl Thuja."

Kevin's eyes narrowed. *I've seen you before.* This was the light-gatherer with the lower limb spikes that spoke at the Central Park Concert. Bill Browning's size and presence had come as a shock. Despite that, he held all the menace of a basket of golden retriever puppies. But, in the company of this latest alien, Kevin's peril detector gave an unmistakable ping. The newcomer, Eir Nyssa, and the local light gatherer, Sri Achras moved together, feelers quivering.

"Originally," Bear continued, "this was a family farm …" But, unfortunately, poorly maintained battery hens, drought, taxes, imports, and madness had taken their toll on the family's numbers and finances. Bear concluded with the story of his army service, his IT fortune, and the soil-toiling lifestyle change. He introduced the gorgeous girl as Crystal. Kevin moved his camera strap to the other shoulder in what he considered was a pretty dynamic fashion. The goddess smiled at him and began offering homegrown coffee to the visitors.

Kevin's eyes narrowed behind the viewfinder. He perceived that Matt (though a fiancée whose training was proceeding well) had straightened his shoulders, smiled with his baby-seal-eyes, and run his fingers through his floppy hair in a sinister female enticing fashion. Distracted, Kevin missed Niels suggest the group delay the farm tour while they introduced themselves. Hence, he was briefly puzzled when Bear abandoned them and sauntered off to view the exhibition of media personnel accumulating by the farm's gate.

*

With the yggdrasil arrival and attacks on human communications the previous year, the reset button had been pressed. Even the frivolity of entertainment in general had reduced (tawdry affairs such as 'My naked date on a curiously well-provisioned deserted island', which may well have blurred the yggdrasil perception of man as the Earth's most sentient animal; had vanished like undergarments nearing the show's cameras). With all due respect to other malevolent social media platforms, FriendFone's news feeds, tailored to prejudice and sales targets were falling from favour. Undermining of the shared sense of reality was reversing. Verification had value once more. The media contingent continued to swell.

Assembled by alien whim, the group sat uneasily on the bench seats of the long, weathered outdoor dining table. For Matt, the reminder of the *CCE* setting was poignant. Bypassing textured breads and a multitude of dips, he offloaded scrambled eggs, added mushrooms, and passed the plate to Niels.

"Ah, that creature of myth – a living forester," said the Canadian Mike to Niels by way of opening conversation. The Swede attempted one of his casual 'it's going to be all right' grins and passed on the plate – he was not in the market for an egg and mushroom toasty. "You are a former vegan then?" said Mike Ross in a conspiratorial tone.

"No," said Niels matter-of-factly.

"Vegetarian?"

There was a strained pause. Niels experienced another of his recent inexplicable visions of Viking sacrifices: household goods, horses, honey and sometimes beer lain at the feet of sacred trees. He much preferred the beer version – as did the horses. "No, no. I don't think those terms are useful anymore, in living with the yggdrasil. As for me, I am allergic to the eggs."

Jess gave Mike Ross a curt, not much impressed 'where is this going?' sort of nod, followed by a brief glance at Anne-Maree. Just then, a child of indeterminate gender approached Anne-Maree. It was obvious the two had met on an earlier trip. The newcomer enthused about recent improvements to the communal worm farm and led her away to tour its many attractions.

"You know," said Jess, in a chirpy tone. "Being a vegetarian since the yggdrasil arrived feels like being a living Rorschach test for *dickheads*." There was a momentary, stunned silence. Matt grinned, and Allan nodded in agreement.

"I never met so many vegetarians," said TK. "You guys are common as seeds in squashes."

"Anyone have any kiddos?" asked Ebony, in the tone of a parent for whom the novelty of offspring hadn't yet lost its gloss.

There were various murmured and head-shaken denials from the group. "There is, unfortunately, a view," began Mike, "that a lack of descendants disqualifies a person from having a view on the planet's future."

"Speaking of the future," said Niels smoothly before another awkward silence developed, "Perhaps we should make a few remarks around what we hope to achieve in these meetings with the yggdrasil."

"Heavy! You don't want to play *What's your favourite cheese*?" joked Matt.

"I don't consume cheese," noted Mike. Allan looked intrigued. Jess' look, might just possibly have unsettled a baby bird.

Matt shrugged, "It's a thing," he protested.

"We should start over," said Tyson. "Write our own name tags*, someone tells a joke, breaks the ice. Hey, funny man …" said Tyson with a gesture at Matt.

"Thanks mate. *So, three cats walk into a bar with a piccolo …*" He changed his tone. "Just kidding. I think it's what Niels said back in the day on *CCE*. You might have seen it?" he raised his eyebrows. "I'm here to … well anyway, I'm *here*. So, muddle through, save the world, that's the plan."

"Nice plan," said Tyson K. There was a general agreement with Matt's statement – perhaps put more eloquently by others.

"What's your daughter think of everything?" Jess asked the New York blogger.

"Bless, she just loves all God's creations."

"Vraiment," said Allan la Fontaine, peering over his spectacles. He peered further into the mid distance, "Is that a pig?"

"Oh yeah," confirmed Tyson ("call me TK").

The philosopher nodded, "Surprising."

"Well, that's the thing," said Jess, toying with the table's basket of decorative pinecones in a troubled manner. "Expectations and assumptions. What will *they* tolerate, and for how long?"

"So true, as I've said on the blog, Eir Nyssa doesn't even approve of fish. But as long as we don't *slay* plants, it looks the other way," said Ebony.

"Yeah, like black on black crime," quipped Tyson out of the side of his mouth and finishing his coffee.

Awkward silences were accumulating at quite a rate.

The yggdrasil trio broke their silent communicative huddle. By now the visitors were eager to disperse and view cabbages or chickens. *This is the trouble with mornings*, thought Matt. Stuff that was possible in mornings just vanished by elevenses. The farm's composting facility was looking tempting compared to the present charged atmosphere.

---

* The name cards would have read: Matt Davis, Niels Larsson, Tyson K Whitney, Jess Kelly, Mike Ross, Allan la Fontaine, Ebony and Anne Maree Hamilton, and cameraperson Kevin Leahy.

Chapter 54 Bear and the Carrots

"We generally start with the carrot patch, don't we, Sri Achras?" said Bear, a trifle theatrically.

"Carrots?" repeated Allan, as Anne-Maree and her new companion joined the group.

"I keep 'em as a kind of penance," he grinned, "it's how Sri Achras and me met."

A casual observer would've seen a large man on his knees obscured by a growth of carrot tops. He struggled comically with a battered straw hat in the frisky wind. The sequence of events went: pull carrot, adjust hat, brush soil off carrot, adjust hat, add carrot to pile, and so forth. In a break with this routine, an alien creature happened by. Uninvited, it spun the large protesting man into a fibrous cocoon from which part of the hat protruded. Then, examining its creation and making minor adjustments, it addressed the cocoon at length. The gist of what it said was that vegetables very much preferred their nether regions safely tucked into a nice loam soil.

Anne-Maree chirped excitedly, but her mom interrupted.

"Oh my gosh, that happened to Uncle Jim too," related Ebony to Bear and the group, "and you know … his complexion was amazing afterward."

The big man nodded thoughtfully (recalling that time of dermatological excellence). "There's a misconception that the cocoon is a punishment, but that's not right, what did you call it, Sri?"

"Restraint and educative process."

"That's it," said the big man. "You feel much closer to the vegetative world and the yggdrasil once you've been in one of those things."

"So less, rather than more *alienated*," grinned Matt.

Anne-Maree jiggled with enthusiasm and opened her mouth again. "I—"

"That's right," said Ebony, "Uncle Jim now runs a sanctuary for abandoned houseplants and rescue trees."

Sri Achras twitched its leaf wings, "Perhaps larval humans should incubate in yggdrasil cocoons."

Hatl Thuja thrashed its antennae in agitation.

Interesting, thought Niels – with a glance at Kevin. *But nothing you could base a conspiracy theory on.*

Behind the camera, Kevin thought otherwise.

"Old Jay Nichols, two farms over, spent so long in a cocoon he had to send out for pizza," joked Bear. As they walked, he continued, "These are remnant patches of turnips, beets, onions, parsnips, rutabaga and then some."

Niels said, "To be clear: there's a consistent yggdrasil opinion on these vegetable types?"

"Sure, sure, if it grows under the ground, if it has roots on it, if digging it up and eating it kills the plant, that's a no. Agreed Sri Achras?"

"Affirmative William Browning. Human Jains practicing such vegetable ahimsa excess one hundred generations," said the alien ambassador, directing its eyestalks to take in the entire group.

"Why not more humans learned this?" queried Hatl Thuja.

"Well, we could talk dissemination and persistence of belief until the cows come home," suggested Allan.

Niels feared he might do exactly this, "Root vegetable ahimsa was obvious from prior statements on *Celebrity Council Elimination*. But, botanically, a carrot taproot isn't a potato tuber. So, can we be clear and understanding please of the yggdrasil opinion on potatoes?"

"Potatoes over there," waved the farmer, "shall we walk that way."

They passed through a gate into another field. A donkey leaned over the fence. Jess patted its coarse coat and said, "People have been asking: since potatoes can be dug after the plant's died down … is that okay?" she chewed her lip.

"Ah, we've had that discussion, haven't we, Sri Achras?"

"Frequently, William Browning."

"The Jains consider tubers to have *ananthkay* – the potential for future lives. When the leaves and stems die back: the potato lives on – they may even sprout in the pantry, clever little things. So, it's just not the same as picking an apple, or soybeans, or wheat, or maize."

Sri Achras said, "Immoral taking lives for food, additional so eating things that don't eat things!"

"Kind of like making a point of culling Quakers," noted Matt.

"My understanding," began Allan grandly, "is that the Jain philosophers ascribe a hierarchy of *sense* reception to life forms – higher life forms may have three, four or five senses and hence harm to them should be avoided—"

"So not solely trees but all plants have senses, communication and memory," said Mike Ross, turning to the forestry professor, rather than the philosophy version of the species.

"That's so. I conduct my researches on trees; but others study seemingly less impressive plants: short-lived crop species and weeds. This reminds me," enthused Niels, "we should discuss parasitic plants another time."

"So, science says there's no difference between senses or feelings of a thousand-year-old tree and a cabbage?" the lawyer-conservationist continued sceptically.

Jess tickled the donkey between its ears and peeked at Mike Ross. The lawyer had an affable, tufty-haired teddy bear quality until you looked deep into his eyes. Then one speculated on a dark past as a minor Eastern European dictator or a mid-1970s record producer. *The poor man's clearly struggling with his world view.*

The donkey twitched as Hatl Thuja barked static, then: "Life has complexity, life uncommonly binary …" The light forager continued at length. The narrator has once more helpfully thought to record the proper gist of its declaration. This ranged through topics such as gender and identity; the percentage of DNA humans share with bananas; spurious differences between humans and other animals … spurious differences between trees and other photosynthetics (*plants* – sorry, forgot to paraphrase).

Watching Mike, Jess saw his eyes narrow as he attempted to take this exchange in a spirit of well-meant, good-natured-exploratory-interspecies-dialogue. He said, "I understood we will examine the important issue of grain crops." (From Kansas to North Dakota, farmers rested their issue of the *Wheat Growers Gazette*.)

Jess turned to Bear, "I imagine you and Sri Achras have discussed wheat farming at length?"

"Yes, Miss, we sure have. Basically, if wheat, barley, oats, rye, maize, or rice plants are dry and dead at harvest – then it minimises problems."

The humans relaxed visibly.

"Why," said Hatl Thuja, "humans speak: Harvest crop, not kill wheat. Speak: eat beef, not eat cow." It waggled antennae, its leaf wings quivered, radiating annoyance and green light (or more pedantically: reflecting the latter). "Exist issues, additional. Example: reproduction control. Example: disrespectful automation and commodifying production."

"Yeah, Sri Achras and me often discuss large scale, mechanistic horticulture. They don't care for it. Even if the soy or maize is dry, the sight of a monoculture crop to the horizon harvested by enormous impersonal machines. Yeah, not so much," Bear said with a slow shake of the head.

Niels took a deep breath, "Breeding, DNA manipulation, how are you feeling about *that*?" Then fearing he sounded like something from his last performance review, he said, "I am meaning, what is the yggdrasil view on genetic manipulation of food, of living things?"

Jointed eyestalks focused and Hatl Thuja said, "Life forms no moral right alteration other life forms genomic selves."

Niels and Jess exchanged significant, 'we know you made yourselves photosynthetic glances' and making every attempt at a light and easy tone the Swede followed up with, "I see … and what is the view on genetic manipulation of *one's own species*?"

In the silence, Jess heard the ominous rustle of dry wheat.

Chapter 55 Conciliating the Legumes

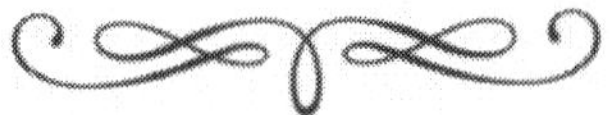

"Well, moving right along," said Bear, glancing hopefully at his ally Sri Achras.

"Suggestion now conciliate the legumes," said the light forager.

Two minutes of wandering betwixt rows of soybeans soon established the visiting humans hadn't before seen the source of tofu, that chameleon of the kitchen. Or as Matt had put it, in a pre-emptive strike aimed at lightening the mood, "Ah, my nemesis … we meet at last."

Delving into his pockets, Bear produced a half-inch metal washer, bailing twine, an interesting stone, and samples of dried pods. He used the latter, but not the former, to explain, "So we can pick when dry and dead like wheat."

TK turned to Matt and made a show of checking his pockets, "Hmm, flash drive, pocket fluff, gum … ketamine."

Matt grinned, and the party rambled among the farm's display plots of chickpeas, snow peas, lentils, kidney beans, and their leguminous allies. Anne-Maree's interest wavered, and she skipped off to commune with the farm's rescue donkey, now peering over the fence. Niels consulted the three yggdrasil, and other than Hatl Thuja's grumblings on subjects of crop monoculture and mechanistic worldviews, they concluded legume farming was potentially yggdrasil-*compliant*.

*

Niels whispered to Bear, "I am wishing we could leave things on this positive note and visit the nearest bar." But he knew the vexed issue of leaf, stem and inflorescent vegetables needed raising.

"Plenty to see Niels – we can swing by the dairy too." He waved to a distant truck that seemed part of the landscape. "Might thumb a lift."

Kevin was pleased to see the approaching dust-covered vehicle. The camera man-blogger wasn't especially blessed in the way of physical attributes; except such a precocious talent for bunions, the family podiatrist had talked of assigning him to a secret research institute in Florida. He climbed into the truck with Jess.

"Nice ute," she said as they squashed into the back. She gave it an appreciative pat.

"Yep, yep nineteen fifty-four Chevy," confirmed Bear. The group began bouncing their way across the farm. "Stateside, we call it a pickup. When I started here, I went high-tech – the background in IT and all. Had drones mapping the dry areas, computerised drip lines, every variety of sensor you can imagine. And sure, you can get real *efficient* that way – particularly in a greenhouse, artificial substrates, that type of thing. Now, though, we're going more traditional, not the whole Amish enchilada," he gave the cabin roof a meaty-palm-slap, "but more of a balance. Helps if three-quarters of your workforce are volunteers. Happy with wholesome self-grown food, a bed, and the lifestyle experience. Even got working horses. Horses make more horses. Drones don't build themselves," he chuckled.

"Not yet, man," said Tyson K as the truck rolled to a halt.

*

"Ah, the cows have come home," noted Matt.

The group toured the dairy, then admired composting activities. Ann-Maree captured the most fearsome of the resident worms and another ancient pickup truck arrived. It took away the small dairy herd's latest steaming offerings.

"Do yggdrasil have an opinion on whether organic fertilizer or pure minerals, err chemical nutrition, are more desirable?" asked Jess.

Sri Achras reported no particular view on organic versus inorganic nutrient chemistry. It did, however, stress that grass would gladly exchange the posterior end of cow offerings for the relief of not being nibbled by the anterior end.

With cows in the air, so to speak, Eir Nyssa asked, "You do not slay-consume these spotted life-forms?"

"That's right," said the burly proprietor. He presented a summary of cow-related activities.

"Humans consume their female fluids?"

"Err, yes," said Niels. "Or make into cheeses. Although some peoples are allergic to sugar in cow's milk; others have evolved to tolerate it and so to eat the cheeses." Casually, in the manner of a tree – or an iceberg – where most of the activity happens below the surface, he said: "Can I ask your opinions of beings changing their genetics to enhance themselves?"

Hatl Thuja thrashed its antennae.

Niels glanced at Jess. Soon it was obvious there'd be no response. It was also plain there are only so many times a Swedish forester can nonchalantly mention the topic of genetic manipulation, while still maintaining a nonchalant quality.

"And so, this way to the veggie plots," directed Bear – maintaining a tenuous grip on his positive attitude.

"Not you, mister," he said to the donkey that Anne-Maree had coaxed into following the group. To Crystal, he said, "Shut the gate please, if that donkey gets in here, we're gonna have an unregulated buffet of doom on our hands."

"If we don't already," muttered Matt under his breath.

Chapter 56 Meanwhile in Melbourne

By unfathomable coincidence and the wonders of the International Date Line, food security, and related topics were being discussed: both simultaneously *and* a day in the future. In a TV studio in Melbourne, Australia, former *CCE* participant Mariam Turner was earnestly holding forth. She was present on one of those breakfast entertainment affairs where the hosts aspire to bear the tag of *serious journalists,* despite the news being edited to fit the themes and rhythms of the advertisements.

Moments earlier, while she waited in the green room, the earlier segment ended with footage of a little yggdrasil-assisted mayhem.

"Yeah, people get totally freaked out being killed by aliens."

"Personally, Bruce, I get freaked out by being killed by anything!"

"Sure, you say that now!"

Following this witty exchange, they introduced Mariam.

"So, two Aussies on this Ygg-Human Congress thing – we're really punching above our weight there," said aspiring journalist number one (balding, mid-fifties, male) leading with a sporting metaphor.

"That's correct, based on colonial history, we've been grouped with Western Europe and the English-speaking democracies from New Zealand to the Caribbean," said Mariam.

"And there're other Committees or Congresses elsewhere in the world?" said aspiring journalist number two (early thirties, blonde, female, fixed smile) brimming with attention. She pretended to check her notepad, "We hear that the Dominican Republic has its own Congress?"

"That's so, likewise, Gabon in West Africa."

"But that's madness, surely. Most of Asia has only two, South America, only one. What's your take on this?" said AJ1 in his 'no-nonsense every-day bloke' tone.

"Colonisation always plays by its own rules. The European powers contrived random borders alternatively dividing first nations peoples while simultaneously creating unstable confederations of disparate parts. The consensus around the small single country congresses is that they've kept a high proportion of forests. Historically the terrain of the Dominican Republic favoured family farms instead of industrial-scale agriculture. The aliens are rewarding them for excellent conservation practices."

"You know the yggs better than most – are you hopeful these congresses can negotiate a treaty, especially around food security?" queried AJ2.

"No," said Mariam bluntly with a slight shake of her head. "The yggdrasil don't judge us worthy of the respect that's a prerequisite for negotiation. We recognise ants and termites are social, city-building creatures – yet we pay no heed to their concerns."

"Yet individual aliens appear more, more kindly disposed," suggested AJ1, stroking his jacket lapel.

Mariam nodded, "Yes, as in any invading colonial force. Some of their individual equivalents of explorers, diplomats, or local governors, may have an empathy for us. But those few have little proper authority, and most of the ever-increasing yggdrasil are at best indifferent to our concerns since the forest wars."

The co-hosts exchanged their best serious journalist expressions.

"As a parent, I'd say they asked us to clean up our room, get our act together, and we responded by kicking them in the shin," said Mariam in a firm tone. "Because they've discovered they appreciate our classical music, they're at least going to listen to our concerns – but that may be as far as it goes…"

Mariam was allowed to air her views for a solid three minutes until the next advertisement break. After the break, normal service returned in the form of short snappy stories: an alien 'pitch invasion' ruining a children's soccer game and the ever-popular topic of yggdrasil-gardening hazards.

Chapter 57 New Land

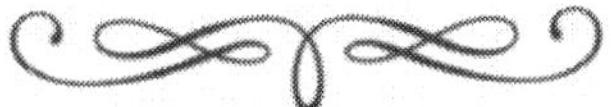

You will have heard it remarked that distance and time may offer a sense of perspective. And so, it was a week later that Tyson K Whitney floated a thousand feet of perspective above the waves; south of the Big Island of Hawaii; headed further south-west and discussing aliens, leafy vegetables, and other themes of interest.

Soon after concluding his tour of Bear's farm and exiting the pod-contrived maelstrom of space-time; Special Agent Peters had summoned Tyson, where he joined Niels and Jess Kelly in the agent's whirlpool of self-importance. The conference room table was of a length to require your passport at the far end. The current issue: yggdrasil misbehaviour near the Hawaiian military bases.

"So, you want us to ask the yggs what goes down?" said TK.

This, he soon established, was not the way of the Secret Science Agency. With reliable communications restored, enormous alien watercraft and new islands hadn't escaped notice. Attempts to observe the phenomena less than two hundred kilometres from Cape Kumukahi had led to mechanical impotence: the destruction or disappearance of flying assets and the hapless drifting of the water-borne variety. But, cutting-edge eighteenth-century flight technology, the agency came to realise, wasn't susceptible to vexing alien electromagnetic interference.

The trio were ferried to the floating city that constitutes a Nimitz-class aircraft carrier. Meeting Lt Keenan of the Navy Balloon Club, TK noted the contrast with his charge, semi-inflated on the deck. The colourful, billowing contraption lacked rigidity and formality.

"Who's in command?" barked Keenan. The pilot exhibited such a remote manner, TK peered at him for signs of an USB port.

"It's a flat team structure," explained TK. The flat team structure looked on as the blue and yellow panels took shape.

Later, the Lieutenant piloted their craft south-west. The passengers smelled their quarry before they saw it. The balloon drifted through pockets of sulphurous fumes. Turbulence jolted it and radio communication with the base ceased. Below, clusters of large alien craft, like textured cigars, floated on the waves. Under the belly of the balloon, the basket swung exuberantly, as though held by a child collecting mushrooms.

The balloonists were silent. They drifted over the hellish landscape of black smoking rock punctuated by rivers of lava. Time passed, tiny sprays of volcanic rock hit the basket, and thermals tossed the balloon. Tyson was well aware a mere skin of balloon nylon kept them floating above a landscape of toasty death. As he braced himself against the scratchy basket, a sudden lurch threw Niels and Jess together in a soft and intimate tangle. They sprang apart and began hurriedly discussing the final, leafy-vegetable part of Bear Browning's farm tour.

"Mir Arauca, that you met at my parent's farm is so much more approachable, just plain nicer than Hatl Thuja," said Jess, not quite making eye contact with Niels.

"Oh, yes, for certain," he replied, "the ambassadors are trying to help us." Niels realised his likewise lowered eyes were directed at her chest. He took a deep breath and elevated his gaze. Tyson looked on impassively, amused. *Oh yeah, they keen, only they don't know it.*

Lieutenant Keenan was simply impassive.

*

The Congress-humans and yggdrasil had gathered among Bear's sample-plots. Since the invasion, people were better informed on vegetal matters than they'd been for decades. Even at the less educationally inclined end of the spectrum, competitive reality TV gardening shows had replaced competitive life-partner snaring entertainments. Although great skin tone, tattoos, and no self-filter were still highly prized.

Jess and Mike had tried to quantify the degree of harvesting harm the yggdrasil might accept. Suspended now over a landscape that lacked vegetables, and in fact, any living things, TK reflected on the incident when taking the minimal harm argument to a logical extreme Mike had broken a sprig of rosemary from a bush. There'd been an edgy hush as he suggested such a tiny portion couldn't be harmful.

TK tensed, recalling: "Negative negotiate with species immoral reckless slay-consuming other life forms."

In the balloon now, recounting their first Congress meeting, TK said, "Well, at least we've met everybody."

"It was a bit awkward at first," said Jess. "I didn't warm to Mike Ross."

"Yeah, what's with him? He takes it so personally, as if *they* owe him," said TK. "He's … 'Dudes I campaigned to save the forests; don't tell me I can't eat lettuce.'"

"We're all on the same side," suggested Niels.

"You think?" said TK. A rattle of tiny rocks hit the balloon, bouncing into the basket. The pilot announced he was dropping ballast and taking the craft higher.

"This was not," said Niels. "What I was suspecting when they say: Come ballooning in Hawaii!" He continued, "Yes, I am knowing there was no certainty established in every area, but overall, it was positive. Let me tell you …"

He recounted how wandering from the group with Eir Nyssa, and the two Hamiltons the discussion became light-hearted. Crouched low, examining silver beet, while Anne-Maree held a leaf wing companionably, Eir Nyssa said:

"Don't dig it up, make a clean cut with a sharp knife, thank the plant, and don't ask me to watch you consume it, please."

"Err, great," Niels had said, with a surprised look at Ebony.

"Many comrades don't want you to eat anything."

"So, they want us to die out?"

"No, not die out as such, but not to kill, or harm and eat." Eir Nyssa made a near-human sigh, "It takes time to find the wisdom of self-discovery and move to a real ahimsa, light-gathering lifestyle. Each species must find its way."

*

Reviewing these discussions with Niels and TK suspended over a landscape intermittently hurling things at them, Jess felt her perspective shift. *Niels is right, things are fairly positive.*

"How come that little girl's yggdrasil can sometimes talk," began TK.

But then, disaster struck – specifically, it struck TK's 1990s puffer jacket. "Man, that's hot," he exclaimed, beating at his sleeve.

The trio refocused their attention on the forbidding landscape below.

As they watched, shades of darkest grey and black, more usually seen in an angst-ridden youngster's bedroom, slide by, Jess said, "No one or nothing can live on that for ages."

"*They* think long term," said Niels. He searched in his thick jacket's pocket. "If we want to know what they're doing, let's ask …"

"That won't function," declared their pilot, glancing dismissively at the civilian's device.

"Perhaps not," said Niels, tapping at his cell phone.

Yet, only three seconds of piano concerto music had played before Niels heard: "Telephonic greetings, Niels Larsson."

His companions listened to Niels' side of the brief conversation and heard him thank Sif Acer before he disconnected. He peered over the side of the basket and said, "Yes, they are deliberately making more land over the tropical latitudes. They use the volcanic hot spots and the edges of tectonic plates. It says they are creating without destroying." Which was ironic, because below the apocalypse had come to tea.

Jess shrugged, "It's bound to add to climate change, have effects on ocean currents, fishing, whale beachings ..." (Unfortunately, in an underfed world, running aground was the least of cetacean calamities. The borderless and increasingly lawless oceans were no safer than the land for the planet's largest living protein source.)

Eventually, the end of the new island was in sight, and beyond that lay the bulk of their launch ship. As one last piece of fist-sized pumice went whizzing past, the balloon fled before any more of the vigorous local geology assaulted it.

Chapter 58 Salad Ahimsa

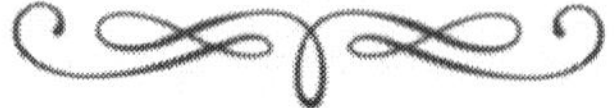

May 3
mom love nyc
SALAD AHIMSA

dear readers, back again from bear browning's farm in california (Pic 1 eva-maree and dermie the donkey). and as usual it feels like we've all been on this adventure together. so many DMs, so much love. now I know we all crave certainty in this uncertain world, and I do so hope the new yggdrasil-people congress will help. If you haven't seen the report here's the link [congressepisode1].

but today people i want to talk leafy vegetables: kale, lettuce, spinach, basil, silver beet, basil (love my basil) … all those good greens. how often do we see them plastic wrapped roots and all? LAZINESS PEOPLE. gosh we don't cut down the tree to eat an apple! grow them dear readers, do it yourself, nurture, take what you need: don't take their lives. #saladahimsa

Chapter 59 The Red Rose and the Bee

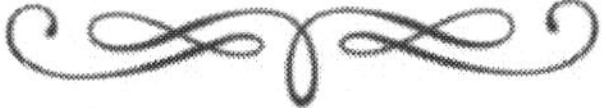

The difficulties of gardening in the yggdrasil age had exercised greener thumbs than Manchester resident Max Greig. He heard another of the street's surplus of terriers yap and grey-muzzled Mr Tuggles next door answer. The neighbours lived in hope Max might tame the suburban wilderness he called a garden. *They* were old-fashioned and unaware that many now discussed pruning as earlier generations had discussed birth control. Printed on recycled paper, their latest offering lurked untouched on his desk. Between the headlines promising fruit preservation tips and warning of the hybrid-super slug hazard, ran the title: Yggdrasil Compliant Gardening – Banish the Uncertainties.

Max observed his neighbour in the adjoining front garden: stripped to a singlet and resplendent in towelling hat and grey chest hairs. Although only ten years apart in age, it was as if Max and Reg came from different centuries (they did, however, have cricket in common).

Across Manchester, people were out enjoying the warmest spring in living memory. Next door Reg Hall amiably waited for a bee to finish its business. He continued his snipping, his adjusting, his pruning. Reg's red standard roses were, in the opinion of many, the pride of the street. Standards must be maintained and sometimes sacrifices made.

There were five of them. The stems more than an inch thick in the old measure, spaced across the yard front. The gardener ceased operations again to admire the dynamic tension between symmetry and exuberance. Light danced on leaves. He tip-pruned around more bees, squished a rare aphid, and admired his handiwork from various angles. The approaching yggdrasil's claws scraped the pavement. Its sensory antennae danced this way and that.

Terriers like their routines. Mr Tuggles gave a practiced short bark and dashed next door, through the hole in the fence. A nice enough fellow lived there, but with a very ragged garden. Very ragged indeed.

The leaf-creature focused its eyestalks and spun Reg Hall, the middle rose bush, and a passing bee into an ornate cocoon. From which a single red rose, in the splendour of full bloom protruded. Just to make the point.

"Mary, are you there, Mary?" Reg called to his wife "A fellow could easily take against these alien chaps. Oh, heck, there's a bee in here!"

Its work complete, the alien departed. Alerted by the terrier, before Mrs Hall rapped on his door, Max opened it and peered out.

"So sorry, Mr Greig, it's happened again."

"Don't worry, Mrs Hall. We'll get him out – no hurry – might as well wait for the fibres to dry."

"Thank you, dear, it's just with my carpal tunnel …"

Chapter 60 Heating the Tundra

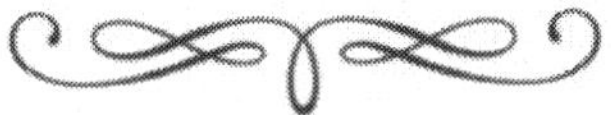

The thing that most startles the casual observer charged by walruses is the odour.

Matt's nose wrinkled as the creatures approached. He gripped the hockey stick tighter. *Strewth! That 'left-over seafood-baking-in-Christmas Day-heat' smell.* What had begun with cautious grumbling and snorting soon increased in volume as the tusked ones surmised the alien pod was in no hurry to leave.

"Hrrumpff," roared the walruses from the moral high ground that comes so readily to endangered species. What with the vanishing sea-ice, ground-shaking explosions, and occasional column of fire, the Yamal Peninsula walruses were cantankerous of late. The alien lurched past Matt and his recently acquired hockey stick into the narrowing gap between belligerent pinnipeds and humans.

Kevin recorded the action as Sif Acer began performing vaguely threatening yggdrasil Tai-Chi. The advance party of walruses settled down with a series of snorts and whistles to watch events unfold. It'd been months since the last compelling display of the aurora borealis.

"Happy now, Matt?" said Niels – head tilted, eyebrow raised. With the danger passed, Niels reflected on the last week's negotiations. A trip to the Siberian tundra – even in summer hadn't appealed to most members of the newly appointed human Congress.

*

"Like herding the cats," Niels muttered, organising the trip to satisfy the preferences of Sif Acer, Matt, and Mike. Another factor was his preference to limit awareness of private pod access. The humans met at Whitehorse in the Yukon and drove to meet the alien in Alaska's Denali National Park.

"I suppose there won't be any ski-lodges," Matt speculated glumly but accurately when informed of the trip. [What passes for a ski season in Australia had failed to eventuate.] It was only the promise of a little walrus viewing that clinched the deal.

The comedian maintained a low level of disgruntled-bemused commentary of the: "Yeah, Siberia has a real low rating on trip advisor …" variety during the three-day road trip. By the time of the happy discovery of top gear, his interest in the distinctions between tundra and taiga had waned. Other than the exciting potential of "zombie diseases," such as smallpox and the 1918 Spanish flu released from corpses in the thawing permafrost, the Australian ignored many of the vehicle's conversations.

Later he claimed the trip's highlight was an abandoned fridge on the side of the road. Stopping and observing it topped with both a hockey stick and a birdcage containing a book of German verbs, the comedian began hours of intermittent, amusing speculations. As we've discovered, he also souvenired the hockey stick.

The contrast with Kevin's attitude was as stark as the polar-edge landscape. Informed by Special Agent Peters of yet more possible yggdrasil-associated geologic misbehaviour, Niels had consulted the *Monsters and Aliens* blogger. He'd found Kevin absorbed in an illustrated tome that dealt with management of the domestic frog and raised the topic of supposed yggdrasil cities in the far north.

Blurred images and poorly spelled reports appeared as the blogger scrolled through the posts: Dmitri – brother of a minor Russian oligarch owned the world's northernmost dacha. The long-term follower of Kevin's blog reported a country in turmoil and believed the yggdrasil were working on an engineering project within fifty kilometres of his summer home in Siberia.

*

With the walruses viewed as promised, the party prepared to move inland and meet Dmitri. Sif Acer tracked Kevin's contact by his phone signal. An unseen hound woofed ominously as the pod arrived at the modest dacha.

"Is your father home?" asked Kevin of the teenager who appeared and slumped against the door frame.

"Yes," she muttered with finely calibrated indifference.

"Hi, I'm Kevin, please tell him we're here?"

She sighed.

By contrast with his daughter, Dmitri greeted the visitors effusively. He considered it a tad late for his morning drink but had deemed it polite to wait for the expected guests. Now he distributed vodka, and toasts were made. Their host was a cropped haired, fit-looking fellow in the tight black T-shirt and neck tattoo combination that and so often suggests a dubious ethical code. The assumption of an outdoorsy customer was soon confirmed.

Niels sipped his mid-morning vodka and asked, "Dmitri, the yggdrasil city – it's near to here?"

"Less than an hour to drive. Close to where I killed the bear."

"The bear!" said Matt, concerned, and for a range of reasons. "What bear?"

"Just bear. Not koala bear, no. Manly Russian bear, you not knowing such bear."

Matt blinked, unsure whether to be amused or offended. He changed the topic and learned even at this distance, the ground would sometimes shudder. As Dmitri put it, "Land it shakes, at night, sometime the flames. With south wind sometime compost smell."

Theories and mystery abounded, and some who'd ventured close hadn't returned. Matt glanced warily at the others. On balance, he favoured joining the group of those who'd returned mystified rather than those who'd simply never returned.

"Negative danger," said Sif Acer. It invited the teen, Elena, and her father to visit the mysterious installation. The near twenty-four daylight felt like a generous thirty to the Muscovite youngster deprived of a social life. She shed the slouch and agreed to accompany the group.

Only the sense of vertigo told the humans they'd moved. The girl gasped as Sif Acer touched the textured wall, and the pod-bottom swirled, becoming transparent. The ground unexpectedly located itself a hundred metres below them. Yet more unexpected – the things embedded in the ground, south to the horizon.

"Wow, it's like, like nothing on earth," said Matt with a grin once the first shock passed. "What the hell are those enormous black tentacley things?"

Black, gleaming tubes – something between tentacles and pipework crisscrossed below them. At chaotic intervals, the structures disappeared into craters. An aesthetic of the grown, and the constructed.

*

The pod landed, and the party exited into the chilly bright day. Into the *least* militant weather the region had ever seen. Other than the wind, the site was eerily quiet. Sif Acer probed the soft wet ground with its clawed feet and extruded its earth-antenna. Dozens of yggdrasil crept from the large nodes forming the tube-junctions.

Sif Acer wafted a leaf-wing at the human group, "Companion persons have questionings?"

Kevin hoisted his camcorder and turned to Niels.

The Swede stroked his stubble, "Greetings. No offence is meant by our presence." He paused, "Would it be okay to explain your work here?"

Sif Acer reported: "Comrade says 'yggdrasil will grace the spinning Earth with mighty forests.'"

"By altering the climate?" asked Niels in a subdued tone.

"Comrade affirms," said Sif Acer.

"So, all this ..." continued the Swede waving an arm, "is to *heat the permafrost on purpose*?"

Sif Acer re-arranged its upper appendages to its liking, "Comrades affirm. Intention – banish glaciers return entire planet to optimum light-gatherer conditions."

Niels reeled. "Is there a target, do you have that level of control?"

The gathered yggdrasil exchanged unspoken communications, and a few strode closer to Sif Acer – touching it. "Comrades chosen no human language. Comrades will speak through self." The familiar synthetic voice continued, but the group now understood they heard the thoughts of the gathered yggdrasil.

"Effect: Thawing frozen grounds release organic carbon material and favour decomposition … enhance carbon dioxide and gaseous methane compounds … fifty million planet cycles around sun previous, blue planet ten degrees thermal enhanced … intention enhance carbon dioxide four hundred parts per million to excess one thousand part per million … intention increase water vapour … intention increase gaseous methane form."

There was a static rasp, then: "Light-foragers will re-cover entire lands."

More static and Sif Acer twitched its longer antennae at another of its kind:

"Reforest frozen southern continent, additional: most oddly named Greenland island."

"Humans may possess the oceans."

"Complete the human greenhouse."

"Geez, and I worry about *my* carbon footprint," muttered Matt.

Mike's eyes narrowed. He had a Roman nose, and he gazed over it, like one of the less benevolent emperors, "Our modelling says the world will get hotter and *dryer*. That's not good for forests."

"Liberate water from ice glaciers, extinguish fires, water deserts, moisten atmosphere, desalinate ocean water: climate enhance warmer and wetter."

"Release the greenhouse!" became the meme of the week.

Matt sensed the need for a change of topic and mood, "These, err, crater things, are you digging them?"

Through Sif Acer, Matt learned the holes weren't dug. Rather, the unstable ground collapsed as frozen methane melted and was released. Mike added a few extra pointers to further the comedian's education in this aspect of earth science. Dmitri produced a lighter and set fire to a hole in the ice to complete it.

"Don't suppose you found any mammoths?" said Matt – breaking new ground as it were.

"Yes." "Affirmative." "Several," came the replies.

"Cool. Please point me in the dead mammoths' direction."

The Russian teen said, "I come with you."

As they passed out of camcorder range, Matt explained to her, "The very best guitar and ukulele nuts come from mammoth ivory."

"C'mon mate – they're already dead," he rolled his eyes at Kevin's look of reproach. In a whisper, Matt said, "Fortunately I brought my pliers – just in case!"

Niels touched the amber bead he wore around his neck. *They won't listen to a plea for our crops, or the survival of polar bears and walruses.* He turned as the Russian enthused about the spread of the snow forest; year-round hunting possibilities, longer growing seasons and baring his chest outside more often.

"So, in future, you are buying Russian coffee!" Dmitri boasted.

Is he joking? "And also, our excellent Swedish coffee," grinned Niels. "I am much concerned though, as the climate warms the cold-adapted forests will die. The evergreen pine, spruce, larch forests; the wonderful deciduous forests to the south of them and the splendid redwood trees."

Niels ran his fingers through his hair. The wind was relenting, and a few small flying insects buzzed past. Kevin swung his recording device from Niels to take in the gathered aliens. They were at their most plant-like: lower appendages immobile, the twitching of their light-catching structures stalled.

"If the world returns to the dinosaur days, or something similar, yes, then tropical forests *only* will cover the lands, but many ancient, wonderful, complex forests and trees will be extinct. Together, can we make a preservation plan?"

There was a brief pause. Then through the conduit of Sif Acer: "Life-form matrices feature much complexity. Majority light gatherers enhance from heating strategy. We thankful your consideration."

Squelching back through the melting ground, Mike said hush-voiced, "There's no going back once the methane's released."

Chapter 61 Day at the cricket

"Don't get me wrong," said Kevin, back in his apartment, adjusting his glasses and discussing the Siberia trip with Jess and Niels, "it's a gruesome crime against nature as we know it. But crazy-awesome applied science."

"Yes, just when I convince myself things are going okay." Niels sighed. "Maybe we can discuss it at the big solstice concert. After that Bill Browning and I are planning a yggdrasil-friendly tech expo at his farm, spread the goodwill and hopefully persuade them to reduce the speed of global warming."

"Great, Doc – now you remember the sketches in Whittington-Hortle's journal?"

"The children with leaves?"

"Right. A young architect named Gould; Northrup J Gould drew them. Turns out a descendant still lives in New York and saw the blog. And this," said Kevin, producing the small time-worn trunk with a flourish, "was his." He began leafing through drawings, journal notes, and letters. "It's not all from South America but hey, look at this …" Brown and brittle with age, the artefact had been used to wrap a collection of blow darts. "Gotta be part of a leaf wing."

But Jess had other interests.

"Kevin, you should definitely have it tested." She turned to Niels, asking in her husky voice, "Did you see what happened in the cricket? Lenny Madden, from *CCE,* was on the news trying to help."

Niels shook his head.

Jess brought the two men up to speed on the cultural importance of, and disruption to, a game of cricket underway in northern England. She enthused on helping resolve the yggdrasil interference issue.

The Swede and the American commiserated. But barely.

"It would be a good precedent, peaceful negotiations, exchange of viewpoints ..."

"Okay Jess. If it's important to you," agreed Niels.

*

The next day, Day Three of the Old Trafford test match saw Manchester neighbours Reg Hall and Max Greig in attendance. In the stands, the teacher reflected, he and Reg had chosen the wrong day to attend. Day One had seen the Australian captain send the opposition in. With England none for a hundred and ten approaching lunch, the Aussie chieftain had left the field early – so the wags in the crowd had speculated – to catch the next flight back to Sydney!

Day Two, the pod arrived. Just before tea, the crowd at the James Anderson end reeled as the swirling space-time anomaly opened near the sightscreen.

The umpires halted play and attempts by celebrity ex-player Lenny Madden and others to converse with the vegetal beings failed. Curiously, the longer nothing happened on the ground, the merrier the crowd became (a manifestation of another of those inverse square laws – such as 'the duller the accountant, the brighter the tie'). The crisis was deemed so serious that the *Complete Rules of Cricket* were packed up and delivered to the ground by a small fleet of minivans.

*

A sole plant-creature now moved from a deep long-on position to stand tweaking its light-gathering structures at wide mid-on. Play halted again. Once more, the retired fast bowler lumbered into action. And again, not for the first time in his career, Len Madden left the field with a sense of things failing to go his way. An element among the spectators jeered.

"Pour another beer on its feet, mate!" came a merry suggestion from behind the pickets.

"Hope Doc Larsson gets here soon," he muttered to a security guard.

In the stands, Max hadn't much speculated before today's activities (or lack of them) on yggdrasil attitudes to sport. He clutched a beer, and applied his intellect to this issue, "I imagine competitive wood chopping, Canadian log rolling, and such are pretty quiet now, eh Reg?"

"Don't see no real interference here," observed the older man, "no-one's been spun in cocoon. Just get on with it, lads!"

Soon the lone yggdrasil wandered behind the boundary rope, and play resumed. An over or two were completed when, "Speak of the devil," enthused Lenny on the edge of the playing arena.

Niels smiled and shook hands with the big cricketer. "My cricket consultant," he joked of Jess by way of introductions.

Jess and Niels strode through the sacred player's gate. The crowd was in a jovial mood, thought Niels, as he followed the Australian around the boundary rope. He observed two sets of parallel sticks and a dozen or so fellows in white milling around as they watched a tall man wander towards the boundary rubbing his trousers. *So, this is cricket.* It seemed the only thing that could further slow proceedings would be a set of outdoor furniture.

He and Jess approached the aliens. The commentators hadn't seen such excitement since*... well, since the morning session, when Smythe had driven straight down the ground for four and the ball had disappeared into a space-time void (rather putting the mysteries of reverse-swing into perspective).

---

* Cricket has a long and venerable history, punctuated by intermittent excitement. The loss of the ball had had the most senior commentators rummaging in the cobwebbed attics of memory. Balls, they reflected, are often misplaced in cricket games – and have even known assault with sandpaper, been scratched with bottle caps, and smeared with confectionary enhanced saliva. However, they concluded this specific lost ball had no precedent.

The nearer creature swivelled its sensory antennae as Niels approached and formally addressed it. There was no response. The forester looked around. Play such as it was continued, Niels tried again.

Without success.

He directed a: *What now*? glance at Jess.

Equipped only with shorts and a floral T-shirt, she approached even nearer the leafy presence. The crowd hushed at this development and then resumed its muttering as the alien ignored Jess. Hands-on hips, she regarded it and the state of the game.

"Niels," she smiled sweetly, "Can you actually call Sif Acer and see if *it* can talk to them?"

"Okay," shrugged Niels. He made the call, explaining the circumstances to the alien mind. Instructed to hold the "communication device" aloft, the phone emitted a series of staccato bursts.

"Companion will communicate," said Sif Acer. It explained what to do …

"For real, yes?" exclaimed the startled Niels.

The alien ambassador repeated the instructions.

*

A part of Niels' mind was bemused that his hand clutched a cell phone snugly inserted inside an unknown yggdrasil. The hand itself was less pleased by its predicament and objected to control by the 'so-called brain'. Now brushing intimately against several living leaf-wings, the forester found he agreed with Kevin's identification of the dried specimen in the explorer's collection.

A prolonged burst of white noise issued from the vegetal creature. Then, "Greetings, Niels Larsson human."

Under Jess' guidance, he asked the creature a series of questions on alien attitudes to willow cricket bats; a trophy of timber bail-ash; mowing, walking on, and rolling grass.

"Matters minimal concern."

"Err, can I ask why you and your comrades *are* here?"

"Fine quality sunshine and soil nutrient flavours."

There was a smattering of applause, and the ball thudded into the fence near where Niels stood – arm inserted in the extra-terrestrial.

Ah, something has happened, Niels mused. A player approached the boundary, but none too closely. Jess and the nearer security guard exchanged glances, and she retrieved the ball. Niels watched his companion beam and throw the red ball to the fieldsman. The crowd applauded. The fielder tossed the ball to a companion who did likewise – they rubbed the ball on their pants for a bit and returned it to a tall, angular fellow.

Ten minutes of action crammed into five days, said Niels to himself.

Unusual human activity lacks brevity.

It sure does.

Initially, self and comrades did not perceive this was purposeful undertaking.

Niels smiled at this and then shivered in the anomalous Manchester heat. The hairs on the half arm *not* stuck in an alien stood on end. Recognition dawned.

The yggdrasil hadn't spoken aloud, and neither had he.

He closed his eyes and forced himself calm, *what's going on?*

He perceived: Direct neural interphase transfer.

Niels was lost for words (and thoughts). Jess stared at him. He marshalled his thoughts and tried to direct them. Other than a vague mental tinnitus-hum, nothing happened – he glanced at the crowd, at the slow pace of cricket proceedings, at his forearm buried inside the alien. He felt the sun on the back of his neck and a flash-back of pod-travel nausea. Were *all* the thoughts his own? Feelings of fear joined with heat and travel sickness?

No need for fear.

The thought, or rather the feeling, appeared in his mind. Niels visualised Sif Acer and realised he could detect *that* alien's conflicted, passionate, and rebellious presence in a complex web of distributed intelligence. His brain buzzed with random thoughts such as *the trees are chatty today*, and *this makes SnapChat look like two cans and a length of string.*

Niels focused on the matter in hand and said aloud for Jess' benefit, "I am thinking you didn't realise they played a game here?"

"Affirmative."

"So, you don't have any particular objection to this recreation?"

"Affirmative. No recreation objection."

The alien waved feelers at Jess as she stepped to Niels' side. A quick verbal consultation ensued, and the senior curator stepped warily closer. A quick, *silent* consultation also ensued. The orifice in the alien's carapace opened and Niels removed the sticky hand that clutched his phone.

"So …" began Jess, raising her voice for the benefit of the nearer reporters and addressing the alien. "So, we're agreed, if the yggdrasil wouldn't mind staying outside the rope, just while the people in white clothes are using the grass area. And please, can you stop the ball getting lost in the, in the hole," she concluded.

The senior curator gave Jess a nod of acknowledgement and a rare half-smile. "While you're at it, love. Ask 'em to keep off the wicket!"

Chapter 62 Summer Fashions

July 8
mom love nyc
SUMMER FASHIONS

the hot sunshiney days are here dear reader! late in the fashion season I know: but SO excited by the new fabrics! no cheap shiny badness in these artificial fibres [Pic 1 miss-six and me in matching olive-green skirts] and james and billy scooting, skating and rock clambering in lightweight wool blend active wear [Pic 2]. big shout out to the guys at *Water Weed Tech* that have collaborated in these fibres made from MICRO-ALGAE!

not long now to the big solstice concert. gonna be great. and in a little secret, just between us, the wonderful KALINDA RYAN will be opening the show!

sorry to end on a downer but not so good news from brazil and elsewhere today. just when you think it's sorted, widespread disruption to soy harvesting is being reported. #tryanstaypositive

Chapter 63 The Wicket

The crowd applauded Jess and Niels from the ground.

Further, Len applauded Niels' suggestion: "Shall we go for an afterwork?"

Len ducked his large head, avoiding low hanging sports memorabilia as the trio entered *The Wicket*. The cricketer needed refreshment. Being ignored by yggdrasil in public view was taxing work, not good for the reputation. Fortunately, he knew a 'good pub around the corner.' Lenny was acquainted with good pubs around most corners in the known world, proximal to cricket grounds.

Niels sat on the dark wooden bench with the two Australians and realised he was in error, supposing his annual cricket quota attained. A portrait of a rotund, roguish, and be-whiskered man attired in a striped cap stared at him. His companions dissected the failings of their national team. Fleetingly, the twenty-first century intruded: the phone beep alerted him to a message from Ebony Hamilton. For the moment, he ignored it.

Niels waited politely for a chance to steer the conversation towards the celebrity cricketer's recent travels to India. Failing to share in the excitement of being surrounded by mounted cricket bats used by W. G. Waddlehouse and company, his eyes glazed over. The Swede dealt decisively with his drink. If cricket anecdotes were in the offing, he'd need help. Jess perceived this and approached the bar.

"You two together then?" said Lenny, once Jess was out of earshot.

"What! No!" Niels shook his head.

"Pity – she's got guts that one. Throws better than some blokes," he gave Niels a knowing look, "is she batting for the other team?"

"Excuse me?"

"I mean," said the cricketer in measured tones, "Is she a lesbian?"

"What, no … I don't know – it hasn't come up!" Niels was pleased to see the object of this discussion return – both to silence his former *CCE* comrade and because she was bearing drinks.

But less pleased when the topic returned to sport.

Glass in hand, he rose and examined the aged-timber décor. Ebony messaged again. Niels peered expertly at the wood grain and realised the patina was limited to the front. An odd idea entered his head: *this pub is like those Amazon peoples Kevin studies*. Tribes who believed time was circular, and they could travel back to avoid the modern era and its encroachments. *Here it seems the interior designers have returned to about nineteen-ten*. Staring at his phone, it occurred to him the subject line of the blogger's text had prompted these strange musings:

SOY FARMS IN THE AMAZON ATTACKED.

Niels swore quietly and bilingually. This halted the need for the Australian team to unearth a new spin bowler (or, at least, for that to be debated presently).

The genteel surroundings seemed to have affected Lenny. He explained, "We paceman rather disparage the spinners, poor buggers." He supposed Niels had learned words like those just used, fraternising with lumberjacks and students.

"Niels, what is it?" asked Jess.

"Bad news in South America – no details but Ebony – Ebony Hamilton," he added for Lenny's benefit. "She says there's been disruption to soy harvesting."

"That's tofu, right?" said the cricketer with a shudder, "I thought we *could* grow that."

"Yes, we all did. It's important that we *can* grow it," said Niels.

Across Manchester, the city simmered under the unaccustomed late afternoon sun. Whilst in *The Wicket's* gloom, the trio talked of soy and the implications of the tundra trip.

"Sif Acer says its comrades want to use the water locked up in glaciers to *awaken* the deserts." Niels explained.

"Yes, I heard. They can what? Slice bits off glaciers and move them?"

"That's right, Jess. Kevin showed me images and reports of many things: icebergs moved through the air, massive desalination …"

"Niels, it's Kevin's website!" She raised her eyebrows, "Living Neanderthals, time travel zombies, the fifth column yggdrasil invasion plan – that we're both part of by the way – don't know about you, Len. Need I go on?"

Niels laughed. The two scientists agreed attempting to counter the warming plan head-on would be ineffective. The forester said, "Any hope of reviewing the greenhouse plan comes from emphasizing the threat to cold-adapted forests.

"Surely, they must have realised this will affect those forests," said Jess.

"Who knows? Their scientists have left. They may see it as a 'greater good' situation. Something to discuss at the solstice concert," added Niels, scratching his jaw.

"And the yggdrasil making themselves photosynthetic?" said Jess quietly.

Fast bowlers famously find it difficult to both walk and think. Fortunately, Len was seated. "What!" he exploded, peering at his companions to see if he'd understood. Their expressions told him he had.

"The hyp, the hypocritical bastards, with their *trees good, animals bad* malarkey."

Heads at other tables turned. The trio's faces were not unfamiliar to those at the bar. The cricketer ignored a near synchronised pinging of phone messages and continued at reduced volume.

"So, it's a secret, then?"

"Well, not exactly," said Niels with a confirmatory look at Jess. "But few are aware. We are thinking of the best time to use the informations."

The scientists glanced at their phones and each other, confirming the same message from Mike Ross. For Lenny, Jess summarised the lengthy text:

"Soy farms affected at multiple locations, small groups of yggdrasil involved. And oh," she said, "dozens of cattle dead."

Soon, there was an orchestra of message pings: Ebony Hamilton (again), Mike (again), Kevin. Then Allan La Fontaine rang. Shortly into the conversation, Niels said, "Allan, if you are agreeable, I might collect you ..."

"Does anyone want to come?" Niels asked of his companions.

"I call shotgun," declared Len – rising a trifle unsteadily.

Chapter 64 Sacred cows

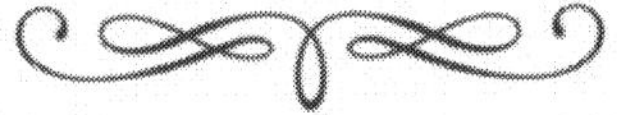

With near precision, the pod materialised partly in Allan's London sitting room, and partly in a surprised neighbour's kitchen. Her cat attempted a superior cat-look and fled. During the walk back to *The Wicket* from the pod's hiding place, Allan veered drunkenly, recovering from the effects of the spatial leap.

The expanded party halted before the main bar's wall-mounted TV. The sports news featured footage of Lenny, Jess, Niels, and their interactions with the Old Trafford yggdrasil. Heads turned, there were acknowledgments from the patrons and many an offer of drinks. Then, the newsreader looked grave and said, "In news just in …" and reported widespread prevention of soybean harvests across Brazil. In accordance with fashionable notions of news, she imbued the statement with the desirable mix of mystery and menace.

By now, Len's speech had gained the slowed-down newsreader articulation of the experienced drinker. The early evening continued still and balmy, and the quartet moved to *The Wicket's* beer garden. The early twentieth-century theme didn't extend this far. Jess gave what might have been a muted growl as they sat.

"What is it, Jess? asked Niels with concern.

"Oh, nothing," she laughed, embarrassed. "It's just that I loathe this plastic stuff!" For enjoying, in many respects, a rational and even-tempered approach to life, the young woman possessed a deep loathing for mock cane furniture.

"Mademoiselle may be wise to avoid Boulevard Saint-Germain in the foreseeable future," said Allan with an amused smile.

Niels stroked the plastic chair. "Bamboo … it's fast-growing; cut without killing the plant, light and strong. I am liking bamboo. Perhaps we should try to make subcommittees for the various agricultural industries to liaise with the yggdrasil, yes. As Bill Browning has done with his crops?"

The others nodded.

"And for sports too," Lenny said. "Reckon we should order snacks, eh? And talk about tofu – never thought I'd say that!"

"It's a worry, with potatoes and sweet potatoes, those dense, energy-rich crops off-menu the legumes are even more important," said Jess.

The pub's patrons regarded the group with curiosity, and a steady supply of free drinks gathered at their table. "No worries, I'll take a few for the team," vowed the cricketer generously.

"And yet the excursion to the … model farm, if I may use that term, established the yggdrasil didn't think soybean production *was* in breach of plant ahimsa," puzzled Allan La Fontaine.

Jess nodded. "What do you think's happening, Niels?"

"I, I speculate that soy *per se* is not the issue, it's clearing the tropical forests to grow it.

"Len, you've been to India in the last few months?" said Niels.

"Yeah, Doc went by ship. Not my thing, but cotton farming's over. But yeah, I heard the family-farm scale set up was unaffected – if the crops were okay, ahimsa types of crops."

Jess nodded. The food arrived, and they swapped it for empty glasses. She snared a fried pumpkin wedge and said, "If they reduce the soybean harvest, its vital people get to eat what remains."

"Well, I'm no greenie, but it sucks the Amazon is cleared to make tofu," declared Len, articulating the words with care. He was by no means a fussy eater – drawing the line only at tofu and sandstone. He passed the former with caution to the far side of the table, "What was that advert … 'Rubbery, tasteless and just a little slimy – it's all about the sauce, it's all about the sauce,'" he sang merrily to the amusement of the nearby tables. He waggled his finger at Jess, "You don't want to be sounding like a Tofu Nazi."

Jess shook her head, “Lenny, there’s a bloody big grey area between advocating for reduced meat consumption and invading Poland. Besides: most soy goes to make livestock feed, as does lots of maize – what we call corn – gets used for animal feed. She passed the curry tofu dish to Allan on her left.

“We could feed many more with the same crops if people ate them, instead of feeding them to cattle – then eating the cattle,” explained the Frenchman, peering over his glasses at Lenny.

The cricketer grunted, reached for a prawn, and said, “Speaking of food – why is all the food orange? Even the cheese is orange!”

“Ah, one of the great conundrums of the human condition! We are hard-wired to identify patterns: see cave bear faeces – don’t enter cave. But, Leonard, what is chance, and what is a pattern? What is the nature of truth?” The Frenchman pointedly chose a piece of cheese. “Red Leicester, I believe.” He swallowed it.

Lenny regarded him with anti-intellectual hostility and vague alcohol-enhanced muddle. “You’re saying cows are bad? Try telling a billion Hindus to get rid of their cows’ mate. They’re sacred over there, you know.”

“An interesting point, Len,” said Niels. “We often hear the environmental benefits of reducing cattle numbers. But, yes, it’s complicated; India has the most cows and they’re not eaten. But feedlot cattle *are* an inefficient means of protein production,” Niels sipped a cider.

“Exactly, even without the yggdrasil, we’d be better off eating soybeans et cetera directly rather than eating them via the burger chain. I don’t eat meat myself,” Jess continued, “But to be fair, in much of Australia we grow beef cattle on land too dry to grow crops … so it’s complicated,” she concluded, brushing a hand over plastic-cane.

“Yeah, might be better off eating Skippy*, but that’s a whole other story,” said Lenny, knocking over an empty bottle.

---

*Whom the reader may recall is a TV kangaroo

Allan nodded magnanimously, "Since *the arrival*, I have been studying Jain philosophy. And it strikes me we might pay more heed to the law or tenet of *anekantavada*." The philosopher expressed himself unstintingly on the subject and with a liberal sprinkling of words in italics.

Big Lenny yawned, spilled a drink, and helped himself to another free beer. He ritually ogled the young women at nearby tables. Increasingly, he and his immediate surrounds were subject to the *second law of thermodynamics*. The conversational themes were not what he might have chosen himself, but it was a change from dining companions discussing the evils of short-form cricket, 'alcohol-free Mondays,' and similar nonsense.

"Speaking of complexity," said Jess, "what of Mike's' most recent text suggesting we should ask the yggdrasil to eliminate cattle? I doubt they killed those cattle on purpose."

The group emitted a series of hesitant "ah, um," variety vowel sounds that imparted little extra insight.

"That is one serious can of worms," noted Lenny sagely. "What, what," he repeated, his speech slurred and raising his finger in the manner of a cricket umpire adjudging a dismissal, "… if cows ask the yggs to eliminate us!"

And with this last remark, he slid with surprising grace under the table.

Chapter 65 Iquitos

"… but Matt – remember how you found Siberia."

"Piece of cake Kal – we just turned left at Alaska."

She gave him *the look*.

"Well, okay, why not Rio or Buenos Aires or even Lima? – lemurs are cool!" Matt pretended to read from his phone. "Spend the days swimming in the river avoiding those little fish that swim right up you; as night approaches, have a gin and tonic (don't spare the quinine) on the deck, overlooking the mighty Amazon. Share your bodily fluids with the mosquitoes. Then for your evening's entertainment watch resentful natives do a dance and roast a hyena or something, take your antihistamines, and climb into your scratchy hemp hammock."

Kalinda tried out a sympathetic smile, "Matt, is it because it's at an eco-lodge again?"

"Well yeah, go to Peru, try and save tofu. Geez, I thought I'd already saved it. An eco-lodge *again* with *dozens* of yggdrasil. What could go wrong?"

"Iquitos has a famous floating market," replied his fiancée, ignoring these dramatics and reading a genuine description from her phone.

"It sounds like a godforsaken nest of humid villainy. I should've become a movement and wellness teacher."

"Then we wouldn't have met …"

*

A week after this domestic discussion, Matt prowled the after-party with Niels, grasping stick-impaled-tofu. The South American division, Human-Yggdrasil Congress, had chosen the last major port on the Amazon for the urgent three-day food security conference. Every Western Congress human attended (the youngest member accompanied by her mom, Ebony). There were a dozen alien ambassadors present, including Sif Acer, Eir Nyssa, and Mir Arauca.

"Niels, she's got her eye on you, mate!" grinned the comedian. Across the vast conference room prowled the unofficial head of the South American contingent – Marina: flirting, planning, networking. Earlier, she'd presented the final version of the *Iquitos Agreement.*

Whereby:

1) The yggdrasil agreed to reduce the rate of soybean farm reclamation.

2) Humanity through a mix of forestry expertise and indigenous knowledge undertook to help reforest the former cleared areas to avoid weed infestation.

Matt, although not stalked by gorgeous Brazilians, was finding the 'The Jungle Room' unsettling. In post-yggdrasil Peru, he felt a low simmering level of guilt – nothing specific – just a diffuse guilt that came with being a fair-skinned person, on a junket, in a world of deprivation. The mounted jaguar head, however, glared with explicit disapproval; the stuffed capybara observed him with mild admonition. As for the enormous snake: nothing stares likes a stuffed reptile with button eyes.

Niels, meanwhile, stepped deftly behind an especially 'leafy' alien, one eye on Marina. *I think Matt's correct.* Allan was present, chatting to the presenter who'd made good on his threat to talk at length on similarities between Jain philosophy and sumac kausai, alli kausai (the good and harmonious life). Focused on the hum of urgent conversations, Niels ignored the décor. He wandered overhearing snatches of discussion in English, Spanish and Portuguese from humans and yggdrasil:

"… it'd be easier if they just claimed to be gods and said, don't grow cows; bonsai bad et cetera."

"They don't care enough to want to rule us – we don't seek to rule bugs."

"You can't just tell indigenous peoples not to eat meat. You can't tell people of completely different cultural norms in this post-colonial era what to do."

"… surely, the U. N. must now make a directive to reduce meat consumption."

"Observation your species consumptive ways with despondency."

"It will be a shocking paradox if they drive the peoples with the least impact on the forests out of them …"

Niels paused in his casual avoidance of Marina, took a coffee, and listened to a three-way conversation in English.

"… there is disharmony between we yggdrasil."

"Over your impacts on our human activities?"

"Affirmative. Human impact on light gatherers lesser, prior planet visitations. We selves failed expect these changes. Errors have been performed."

Niels edged closer. This was the *best* conference coffee he had ever tasted, the other alien said:

"Differential tolerance among comrades for recent century's human activities."

Niels resumed his wanderings, casually avoiding Marina. W*here's Jess*?

He overheard:

"… yeah, I heard the yggdrasil have shut down rubber farming and palm oil in Indonesia and Malaysia."

"Good."

Gratuitously female and showing more cleavage than strictly required for saving the world, Marina spotted Niels and wove towards him. The grand windows on the balcony were open. Kevin was there recording proceedings:

"… non-ambassador comrades decide correct measure of antagonism toward humans – not humans."

"Hi, Kevin, just stepping out."

Niels rested the coffee and stepped through the window.

*

On the street, he'd been expected.

The stranger spoke. Niels shrugged.

The fellow tried again. In heavily accented English saying, "They have weakness." He mimed a yggdrasil adjusting its leaf wings. "Are you for men, professor? For humans?" he peered at Niels.

"Of course, yes."

The little man appeared satisfied. He nodded, "Puede usted venir. Come."

Wandering off with a strange man in an unfamiliar city for an ill-defined purpose didn't seem wise to Niels. But the man was aged, leather-skinned, and there was very little of him. The scientist found this encouraging in a potential assailant.

Further from the conference, the streets became less salubrious. The pair reached the water's edge, and the guide stepped into a canoe. He conversed with the stocky man at the stern and gestured to Niels with a gnarled hand. The Swede had seldom met a timber watercraft he didn't care for. None-the-less, he hesitated stepping aboard this one.

The canoe made its way to and through the shantytown. The helmsman spat a wad of coca leaves into the reeking water and they docked at a market. Although not wishing to offend other muddy, mosquito-infested shantytowns Niels had met in his travels; this was by far the worst. He passed laneways crowded with distressed buildings, tables of glassy-eyed fish, armadillos for purchase or hire, and all manner of unfamiliar smells. The guides argued, a blindfold was produced, and Niels was encouraged to cover his eyes.

*

Later, he stood as they removed the cloth in dim surroundings. Focusing, Niels' eyes were drawn to a mask. He flinched, *that's not a mask.* Dark brown, leathery, hung by its black hair; the visitor stepped back from the artefact of legend: a string of shrunken human heads.

The shutters were drawn, but dust motes danced in musty light through gaps in walls: part apothecary, part museum. A room cluttered with quivers of long arrows, stuffed caimans, glass jars of native herbs, gourds, and terracotta pots with markings strange enough to enthuse Kevin for hours.

"Aquél," pointed the old man.

His secretive hosts watched him examine the artefact: a metre long, the colour changed from green to darkly brown, the edges curled and frayed. Yet it was undoubtedly a yggdrasil leaf wing of some antiquity. Another man entered the hut. His ragged shorts and battered flip flops did nothing to raise the tone of the place.

"Hola, mi nombre es Angelo," he touched his chest.

Niels nodded as Angelo joined him, examining the alien body-part. Then Angelo led Niels to a dusty jar on a rough-hewn shelf.

"Anguila diablo."

Through the discoloured preservative, Niels counted a half-dozen elongated and segmented creatures. Eyeless with teeth, their mouths agape in death. The wizened little man joined them.

"Yggdrasil."

He did the pantomime alien again and stared into Niels' eyes – determined the visitor understand him. Niels nodded; *well this is weird.* The sheer incongruity of this word from his homeland's mythology, uttered under present circumstances.

Through Angelo and the old man's uncertain English, and Niels' even less certain Spanish, the trio talked. Niels learned Angelo had encountered a yggdrasil group months before their ratings-surge-debut on *CCE*. And in his home village (hundreds of kilometres to the west), the elders recounted legends of earlier "forest spirit" invasions. Nearby, indigenous people were fighting a guerrilla war against the yggdrasil.

Niels had wondered if local peoples and the aliens might have a common cause. Now he learned this wasn't so. The reserved areas where they lived near traditional lives contained the most intact forests. And these, many aliens believed, were best preserved by removing all humans. Hence, an indigenous resistance had been exchanging information. The elder added that there were stories of peaceful relations with the yggdrasil – but centuries past.

Now, it was … "Time to gather the arrow frogs."

Chapter 66 Darkest Peru

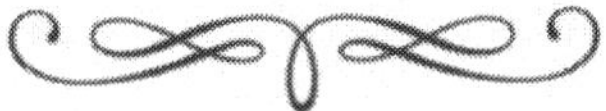

July 10
mom love nyc
DARKEST PERU

on the road this week dear readers. here with all the congress gang [Pic 1] in deepest darkest peru! no sign of paddington bear yet but here's anne-maree [Pic 2] in her yellow paddington rain-boots (non-rubber!). it sure does rain a lot. took some time out from supporting our little delegate to tour food and fashion at the amazing belen mercado [Pic 3]. and supporting a local women's cooperative and their truly amazing hand-stitched traditional hats (see website link). jess kelly, anne-maree and me in matching plum bowler hats in the plaza de armas! [Pic 4].

it's only the second day of the congress. but it does seem plain we are going to have to get by with fewer soybeans from the amazon in the coming years. and most folk are saying we can't waste it on cattle. looks like FEWER BURGERS for all dear readers.

Chapter 67 The Amazon

It is an inconvenient truth that sometimes things are complicated: the rules of cricket, the nature of proof and truth. Many readers might even attest that not all problems can be solved by on-line trolling and the wearing of T-shirt slogans.

Niels brushed his algae-tech T-shirt and said to Matt and Jess, "So you are understanding my thinking? We need to learn what these people know of past yggdrasil visits, the current fighting … alien weaknesses. *But* we can't travel there unless our ambassadors come along." Niels ran his hand through his hair, "And *they* wish to visit pre-agricultural peoples, so we must restrict certain informations."

"A tough position, yes?" he concluded.

In contrast to this convoluted strategy, travel to Angelo's people near the Colombia-Ecuador border was direct from the Iquitos meeting. There were no witnesses as the group of jungle-kitted humans, and yggdrasil spilled from the alien craft. Of the Congress attendees, only Allan La Fontaine declined the visit. Angelo and a local: Maria-Theresa Alonso joined the others. From the Department of Indigenous affairs, she spoke English, Spanish, Portuguese, and several west Amazon languages.

Three of our little group's familiar yggdrasil joined Iae Hevea from the South American Congress. Angelo led the way, setting out for the last semi-permanent village before the hunter-collectors of the deep reserve. The aliens could communicate with him in Spanish, but not his native tongue.

For Ebony (hovering near Eir Nyssa), the decision to bring Ann-Maree to such isolation had been difficult. Like the others, she *had* assumed the alien transport pods moved directly from place to place. However, Sif Acer now explained that the pods actually travelled to their locations via a terminus on a mother ship in deep-earth orbit.

"As human train machine journeys location on differential line," it said, using its improving ability at metaphor.

The upshot was the group couldn't return for three days. That this was because the mother ship was busy receiving arrivals from deep space was a separate concern.

The jungle had a vulgar, over-ripe smell, nothing like the deodorant scent of northern pine forests. Thorny ferns, with no resemblance to city-office varieties, scratched at legs, and air-borne pests shadowed them in a militant fog. There was much re-application of repellent as perspiration poured off them.

Not far along the narrow, barely a path, walk to the village, TK announced to Matt, "I'm stayin' near you, man."

"Me, why me?"

"I'm an artist – I don't have health benefits.

"Ah-huh?"

"Well, aren't you Aussies used to trampin' around with things trying to kill you, living on wild mushrooms and such?"

"Nah – spent six months in the boy scouts – once tramped around the Dandenongs with a faulty compass and a coke.

"Huh."

Walking ahead of the American and ineffectually clearing the path, Matt sensed TK wasn't convinced.

"Seriously, my childhood was quiet and safe. If I played a CD after dark, dogs barked, and old Mrs Lynch next door phoned for an armed response!"

"Ah-huh."

"What I'm saying is: You have a giant snake needs wrangling – give Jess a yell – it's more her thing. Besides, we have four tame yggdrasil, what could go wrong?" Matt swatted away an insect tickling his neck, "Geez, I hope these soybeans are sorted – I don't want to come back and save the world *again*."

TK applied more bug repellent and contemplated this. "If this was a video game, who dies first?"

Matt didn't have time to reply to this decisive change of topic …

"Well, not me … they wouldn't kill the black guy first. Not one of the ladies; Niels is safe I reckon. Mike … *too* obvious. So that leaves you, or Kevin!

Matt laughed, and they squeezed by Angelo, who waited to check on the stragglers.

Coincidentally, at the back of the group Kevin was panting, sweating, and wearing his 'Just kill me now' look. Ahead of him, Mike knew enough Spanish to take offence, after overhearing the guides' reference to "the old man." The Canadian's eyes flashed under bushy eyebrows and he lost the harmless teddy bear look.

The forest seemed far too quiet to Kevin, as Mike increased his stride. Accustomed to obtaining his vitamin D from a bottle, the webmaster rubbed at what he believed to be his hamstrings, trying to motivate them a little. His bunions throbbed. Even before the unknown yggdrasil stepped onto the path, Angelo, too, had sensed the silence. The local recalled that dread 'not the hush of sleeping puppies' feeling.

Then running feet and Jess calling for Mir Arauca broke the quiet.

*

The group gathered as best the track permitted.

Kevin could hear, but not see, his companions. In the forest, the yggdrasil ambassadors communicated with a score of their compatriots. The latter fixed the humans with mute, multiple-eyed suspicion.

Kevin ground his teeth hearing Matt observe, "Ah, Kevin got spun into a cocoon."

Of the bits that weren't, TK said, "Man, those white high-tops are ruined."

"This happened to Bear Browning," said Mike.

"Yes, and also—"

"Uncle Jim. That's right, sweetie. We visited him in the hospital," said Ebony to Anne-Maree.

"Bear said he could somehow sense the plants—" began Jess.

"Yeah ... Kevin, Kevin, can you hear me," yelled Matt. "Nothing to worry about mate – happens all the time. We'll get you out. But can you kinda sense the trees talking or anything?"

The 'not-quite-a crisis' state of affairs continued until Eir Nyssa returned. It reported that the local yggdrasil were "conciliated." The intrusion of non-local humans had alarmed them. Eir Nyssa cut the hapless Kevin from the hardening cocoon.

"Oh man, you're ruining the science," muttered Matt.

The rest of the walk was an unremarkably, wet, warm, scratchy, and insect plagued venture. Ebony took an inordinate interest in her cameraman's complexion. As they pushed through rampant foliage, she mused on jackets for the fall line and considered the many possibilities of yggdrasil 'cocoon goo' cosmetics.

Anne-Maree asked, "Mom, why are the people chewing those leaves."

"Never you mind."

"Kevin," said Matt. "How're you going? Have you come over vegetally aware?" The comedian was unaware Kevin wasn't the first cocooned group member.

*

Cloud wreathed forest later thinned, and through the reduced canopy, light poured into the village's clearing. An escort of small boys armed with slingshots announced their arrival. The garden plots suggested the tribe had been here for several months. Filed-teeth warriors gathered around Angelo and children smiled excitedly at Ann-Maree. The hubbub ceased as the four yggdrasil entered the village.

"PAZ, PEACE," they said in unison ...

Late afternoon became evening, and food preparation began. Niels and Jess sampled the proffered tuberous vegetable gruel. The children of the tribe who'd accompanied the visitors on their tour of the village and jungle sat with Anne-Maree and Eir Nyssa.

"I think these are underground vegetables," whispered the child.

There was a short static burst, then, "Not to worry, too late now."

Jess, Matt, and Niels, who were closest, turned and stared at the yggdrasil. *Again*, thought Niels – the girl was casually holding one of the alien's jointed limbs. A boy, naked except for too-large flip flops, said something unintelligible to the visitors.

One of the young warriors strutted towards Eir Nyssa and addressed it in his tongue. Jess, through the interpreter Maria-Theresa, explained to him the lack of a common language. Up close, she noticed his cheeks tattooed with blue dots. He offered her a bowl of something she suspected included fish. As the sky darkened, attempted communications filled the air. The villager registered Jess' expression when she realised the bowl was the principal part of an armadillo. An amused conversation between the tattooed tribesman and his friends ensued.

Maria-Theresa explained: "He make joke … says he has never known one to come back to life."

Across the cultural and language gap, Jess couldn't explain she would've been happy if it did so. Not a 'totally strict vegetarian' and not across wide cultural gaps. She tried the dish and smiled.

Across the flickering fire, Niels brushed his amber amulet and gazed at Jess: he considered the smile, the almond-shaped eyes, her mixture of wit and kindness ...

Observing this, she gave him a quizzical smile and nodded at Kevin, who exhausted from the assaults on his senses and his person slept.

*

In the morning, Kevin rose with the early worms – hoping in part to avoid them and their invertebrate friends. Despite yesterday's adventure, he still chose to journey to the territory of the rarely contacted tribe. The yggdrasil in the forest reported to Sif Acer that the trail and territory were unsafe. The villagers meanwhile warned that those same aliens were unsafe.

Accordingly, Ebony said, "Ann-Maree and I will stay here in the village with Eir Nyssa."

The remaining ambassadors agreed to go with the group *most* of the way to the neighbouring territory.

As they walked, the rain thrummed against the large leaves that Angelo and the villagers held above their heads. Matt's feet picked their way over the ground.

It writhed and wriggled: its layers of leaves, worms, and fungi like the back of a vast mythical beast. Following the barefoot chief, it occurred to him that whereas once humanity had chosen its leaders for their wisdom, their ability with a spear, or because their great-great-grandmother had 'entertained' the king – we now choose them for their entertainment value. The rain stopped, and the air became dense with humidity. Matt continued to watch the headman's mud-stained heels.

Later, the path joined a stream. The riverbank rocks and logs promised relative comfort for a few minutes. Determined to keep at the head of the visitor group, Kevin had exhausted himself. The avoidance of dehydration, giardia, malaria, and parasitic zombie wasps was tiring but motivating work. He flopped onto a muddy log, dizzy with fatigue. A guide gestured to Angelo, but Jess had already seen it.

Little escaped her in the field of carnivorous aquatic reptiles: "Kevin, don't step on that little caiman, you'll hurt it."

Kevin jumped.

"And watch the electric eel."

"Told you she was good," said Matt to TK. "You know," he continued, "before we came here, I was reading they have little fishes in the water—"

"Piranhas?"

"Nah, worse than that – tiny fishes: you don't feel 'em until they attach to an extremity, or worse … swim right up one!"

TK looked at him speculatively. Matt nodded and made confirmatory hand gestures. The American shuffled further from the river.

The path found and lost the inconveniently arranged river. Behind Angelo and Kevin, Matt pondered, then stepped over a red-feathered arrow laid across the path. *Not a double yellow safety line in sight.*

Dozens of scratches later, the group rounded a bend and sighted the waterfall that marked the territory of the reclusive tribe. An enormous Ceibo tree dominated the riverbank. The lead visitor, Kevin, halted, reluctant to approach the water.

"Amazing, colossal, giant …" he removed his glasses, wiped, and replaced them. "Err, arrow?" he added uncertainly.

"Are you," said Matt, bending to slap at an insect, with designs of the back of his left knee, "just going to stand there naming types of squids?" The semi-crouch saved the comedian's life as the next arrow whirred over his head and struck Iae Hevea. A shower of arrows accompanied by blowgun darts punctured trees and backpacks. The thick air stunk of shredded leaves and fear. An arrow pierced a Sif Acer leaf wing.

"Get down!" yelled Jess.

"Vete! Ir embora! Cease ammunitional devices. Go!" commanded Sif Acer as it hustled towards the threat.

The alien trio planted their clawed feet in the earth. There issued a deep resonant chord such as to make a soft-metal guitarist weep. Then came a cacophony from unseen jungle creatures; a half glimpse of bow-carrying warriors and silence. Iae Hevea tore a long arrow from its upper body.

"Be humans damaged?" called Mir Arauca.

The humans glanced wide-eyed at each other.

Matt groaned in response, "I knew I should have picked a non-playable character." He sat up and displayed a deep gash in his upper arm. It bled freely and attracted invertebrate interest.

Maria-Theresa found the cause to be impalement by projecting tree root rather than airborne weaponry. She paled, "I don't believe an artery is hurt, but it's deep and dirty." Opening her first aid kit, she poured water and disinfectant over the gash. She looked at Sif Acer, "Can we, err, pod transport him from here?"

"Regrets. Not at presently."

"Oh man, can we bind it together?" said TK with a worried look at Niels.

"Mathew Davis, self can optimize injury. Do you show entrustment?" asked Mir Arauca.

"What do you mean … have you, you know, fixed people before?" He shuddered and stared away from the wound at the river.

"Affirmative."

The group glanced at each other, but no one spoke.

Matt took another deep breath. "Yeah, okay, then." Inexplicably, he found a profound sense of trust in this alien being.

The yggdrasil crouched beside the stricken comedian. It extruded a near-black fluid from spinnerets below its sensory antenna. Then, with intricate movements, Mir Arauca spun the goo into cotton-candy threads. It filled and covered the wound with the dark grey material. The group watched the sticky threads dry and set.

"Please to recuperate."

The village guides exchanged concerned comments.

Niels touched his wounded comrade on the shoulder, "Matt?"

"It's weird, but good-weird. I don't know. I mean, I'd rather be floating in a rooftop spa. But I feel kinda good. Am I a tad high?"

Mir Arauca remained mute on this point.

"Are *you two* okay?" Niels asked Iae Hevea and Sif Acer.

"Likely affirmative."

"What now?" continued Niels, glancing warily at the forest. "Are we safe here?"

Angelo conferred with Maria-Theresa.

She said, "We must go, it was error to bring yggdrasil this far. I shall leave the gifts. If they accept, it may be possible to gain trust and visit another time." She hoisted her pack and the party prepared to retrace their steps.

Niels removed the dart that had punctured his pack and stowed it in one of the many pockets. The last to move off, he picked up the red-feathered arrow and snapped off the tip.

He lingered, scavenging more arrows and darts.

Chapter 68 Ayahuasca

Waving her arm around Jess said, "I'd been hoping to see an opossum or something – I've never seen a *non*-Australian marsupial."

However, Angelo had devised other plans for their last night.

From his hammock, Matt viewed the actions of his countrywoman. *Quite a talent.* Despite the fading light, Jess hit the enormous bird-eating-spider of legend with forceful wristy topspin. A feat rendered no less impressive by the arachnid's non-existence.

*

The afternoon had started conventionally; the visitors observing a range of inexplicable activities: poundings with wooden mallets, stirrings … weavings. Matt studied a girl repair a reed trap with a level of manual skill to make an electronic games athlete weep. Anne-Maree and Eir Nyssa sat on the ground, warm limbs and cool leaf wings entwined. Younger members of the tribe joined them.

"What you doing, kiddo?" asked Matt.

"Quiet please," said the child, serious faced.

"The youngsters are listening to the trees sing," explained Eir Nyssa.

"Cool."

The clearing didn't lack for odd sights. Mir Arauca stood with headphones hooked over its antennae, clutching the Canadian's vintage Sony Walkman.

Later they stared into the flickering fire as a shaman sang Tree of Life creation stories. It was all splendidly atmospheric; more so, after the elders invited the visitors to try the local ayahuasca.

"Dream the forest, hear the trees sing … get in touch with the ancestors, meet your spirit guide." And great things might be expected too – but for the moment Matt didn't recall them.

TK said, "Guy I know tried it in Brazil, maybe, anyways didn't enjoy it none. Spent an evening patting an armadillo, turned out to be a rock. Dude was just oozing fluids."

Despite this recommendation, the visitors except Maria-Theresa and the two Hamilton's sampled the concoction. Matt sipped the bitter brew and gagged, unsure which was worse: the taste; the 'worst-hospital-soup ever' odour, or the lack of basic filtration.

"The badness *will* increase," the translator assured him.

A curious crowd assembled in anticipation.

Matt, finally succumbing to the spirit vine, speculated, *perhaps watching drugged gringos is the local entertainment. Maybe someone will go loco and befriend a caiman.*

*

The last of the visitors to stir the next morning, Matt woke with the sun in his eyes. As it had come a long way, it also shone on cooking bowls and detritus; it was absorbed by plants and yggdrasil, except the green wavelengths of light, which reflected off them – and from sickly looking human colleagues.

"Geez, the tree meditation on *CCE* had *nothing* on that," groaned Matt. Anne-Maree sat nearby playing with a beetle. Matt listened to fragments of conversations …

"Well, vomiting *is* part of the ritual – it releases the negativity."

And what sounded like grim, new-age poetry:

"I recall the gravitas of the forest; I heard the Ceibo sing and the dark plotting of the fungi." (This from the Canadian).

"… there were huts, but not these huts. I was in Africa. Maybe me, maybe ancestor me. I don't know, man. And I was a shaman, a medicine man, and there were yggdrasil, kind of friendly. Before that, just colours and lights and weird shit and, and I remember an idea for a VR knit cap!"

Kevin groaned, "Yeah, I wish …" The chaos alkaloids and local secret ingredient of dried leaf-wing had quite a different effect on the New Yorker. "Headache, vomiting, sweating … hot flushes, cold flushes, tremors, numbness … like *Monopoly* I guess: 'Don't pass go, *don't* have a fun time – go straight to consequences.'"

Matt cracked his eyes open again, rolled over, smiled cautiously at Anne-Maree and her beetle. It directed him a knowing look – as if they'd met before. *Kevin sure looks green,* thought Matt. His skin showed every abuse; you just couldn't take it out in the sun or use it to mask your emotions. *He looks how I feel.* Ebony stepped past her daughter and thoughtfully provided the Australian with a disapproving look and an instant coffee.

Not prone to metaphysical speculations or excess sharing of feelings, Niels listened to the others relate their experiences. His trip to the spirit realm had begun with oddly familiar tree communication. Then, beyond the fractal shapes, beyond the odd vision of him and Jess embracing in a dilapidated fountain – the stone carvings of skin-flaying, heart-removing unfriendliness; beyond all these, he had seen, or *been*, an ancestor. Unlike TK, in Niels' visions he could semi-comprehend the speech of the pagan Norse. The forester shivered in the steaming jungle heat. Shivered in remembrance: the awful reek of the sacrifices laid at the clawed feet of the askr yggdrasil.

Angelo beckoned Niels to the clearing's edge. It was plain the indigenous man wanted to hear of his visitor's visions. They tried, but their shared languages were too basic. A little hazy, still a little jungle soiled, the Swede called for the translator.

"He says," (translated Maria-Theresa) "did you speak with them?"

"I'm not sure – it was more I could sense their thoughts."

"He says," (translated Maria-Theresa) "were you for them, or against them: the tree demons, the yggdrasil."

"It was difficult, complex. I tried the peacemaking, but something was changing, something bad." Niels spoke directly to Angelo, "What do you see?"

The local man guessed at or understood the question. Through the linguist, he said, "Always same: fighting in jungle … in future, in past. I die, we die, they die, they return. Always return of the yggdrasil."

As Niels returned to the group, Jess said to him, "Sometimes I wonder if we're missing something obvious."

"Yep, I reckon you probably are," began Matt.

Then he noticed the aliens were absent – except Mir Arauca, apparently supervising the recovering humans. The leaf creature crouched, sensory feelers at rest, listening to the Walkman again. Matt waved at it.

"How's it going?"

Eyestalks twitched and directed at him.

"Apprehension. Poignancy. Self-suspects premature ambassador recall."

The seedy, 'high-school kids on poorly supervised camp,' vibe ended abruptly.

Iae Hevea had died in the night.

The mood was uneasy and sombre as the humans helped bury the alien beneath large leaves and fallen branches.

*

Matt continued to have ayahuasca flashbacks for days, and both Niels and Jess accompanied him home. Surprised by the guests, Kalinda didn't at first notice her fiancée's arm. Not being one to judge (or at least not in company) her first reaction was*: Gee Matt, a less thorough tourist would've taken a few selfies and bought a carved gourd – not return with a tribal tattoo.*

In fact, the charcoal-hard and coloured, yet flexible scar was the reason Niels had made the journey. The comedian felt sheepish returning thus damaged. Niels was apologetic about the comedian's wound and believed he should deliver Matt in person. Jess reckoned she'd just come along.

"Oh, Matt," said Kalinda. "Does it hurt?"

"Nah. It's pretty good now. Reckon I could bowl a few overs of harmless left-arm orthodox."

Jess sat with Kalinda chatting of the upcoming solstice concert and recalling the grim mood of the alien's burial.

"But now it seems Iquitos, and the jungle trip were positive – overall, I mean. We're finding ways to co-exist."

Matt sat next to them on a comfortable chair. He glanced at the granite couch – it was the oddest thing in the room, and it wasn't doing anything weird. He was terribly glad. He reached across and gave it a brief pat.

Chapter 69 Solstice

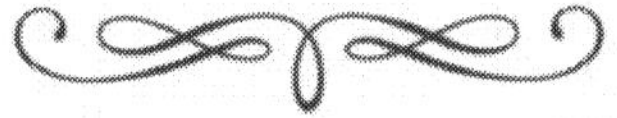

It was the summer solstice, and across Europe, from Estonia to Uppsala and the Black Forest, the neo-pagans gathered. In the new paradigm, a range of divisions lay broken or blurred: political left and right; animal and plant … religious faith. Some saw the aliens as loathsome perversions of God's blueprint, where 'plants' should not walk and reason. And others sought to worship them (or at least feature them prominently in revived DIY nature-worshipping traditions). A budding faith of the young and dissident; of the evidence-based and the unknowable.

Across the Atlantic, in New York, alternative solstice activities were underway. A pioneer 'on-trend' few among the hordes pouring into Central Park saw fit to paint themselves green. Niels weaved his way between these and light gatherers who'd hung *I Love New York* caps from their antennae. There was a spirit of goodwill in the warm afternoon air.

He passed into the VIP area and approached the North Meadow stage. Niels peered curiously at enormous speakers, (the size of European pagan-prancing-stones) and detected a friendly poke in the ribs. The forester turned. Kalinda smiled her shy, mischievous smile with its measure of 'don't bullshit me' directness (which is an excellent trick if you can pull it off). They hugged.

"Have you seen Matt?" she said, "I lost him after I reported backstage."

"Not yet, no, but there's a chair with his name on it. Is Matt okay with the arm and everything? No strange diseases or symptoms?"

"No, he's fine. He said you had a weird ancestor-vision thing."

"Yes, Kalinda most strange, I am having a few flashbacks – but it's okay."

The musician gave him a concerned look. "I had an odd conversation earlier with that science agency man you and Matt meet with – he's at the back over there," she indicated, tossing her hair. "He wanted to know what I feel from the yggdrasil when I play. Whether they're weaker when they listen. Almost as if… could music be a weapon instead of a bridge?"

Members of the orchestra were gathering. The concert's musical director emerged and met Niels.

She fretted, "The maestro is late again."

"He has a reputation," commiserated Kalinda.

"Yes dear, he once famously missed three-quarters of a performance of Wagner's Ring Cycle." Addressing Niels, she continued, "His instrument is so very famous: A 1705 Stradivarius from the golden period."

Niels nodded, "I wonder if our aliens understand this music is produced from the dead trees."

The director's eyes widened at this. And further still, as Matt reappeared and joined the conversation. "They're making violins out of carbon fibre these days. I've got a resin uke with a timber top – sounds great and it's pretty much indestructible!"

The director shuddered, clarified final details with Kalinda, and disappeared to continue her fretting.

Observing Niels' interest in the stage audio tech, Kalinda pointed out the chief sound engineer's tent and its vast, minion-commanding presence. Members of the Dominican Republic and the South American Congress strolled past with Mike Ross and Allan La Fontaine. Jess arrived, kissed Kalinda and distributed an unsought beer and a pear cider to Matt and Niels, respectively.

"Thanks," they murmured with precision yggdrasil stereo.

"We are spending too much time together," joked Matt with a speculative glance at Niels and Jess.

“Ebony’s over there with the yggdrasil,” waved Jess. “She’s into teaching them non-literal language. TK’s helping her out – mainly to avoid Cameron Peters. As the only adult American on the Congress, the special agent was keen to make Tyson his pet project.

“Is he that horrible?” said Kalinda.

“Well,” said Matt, “It’s a full moon tonight, yeah? For the summer solstice. That’s how it works? So … he doesn’t *always* go the full werewolf, but you’d want to keep a wary distance!

Kalinda smiled, “Gotta go.”

“Over here champ,” called Matt, waving to Kevin, who peered myopically towards the call. The two had an edgy relationship, in part, because during *CCE* filming, the comedian had achieved ‘camera-person sticking to him like a poultice’ saturation point.

Of ukuleles, that bane of the first Park concert, there was but one. The photographers massed their black-snouted cameras as Kalinda took the stage. Although her classical training featured piano, and her pop-music career piano and guitar; in the public mind there was no escaping the uke association.

Her arrangement of *Air on the G String* delighted human and yggdrasil alike.

Matt squeezed her hand as she re-joined them, “Awesome,” he whispered.

Fortunately, the maestro was found, now replacing Kalinda in front of the orchestra. The first violin wore the shoulder-length hair that so arouses suspicion attached to a male of four-decades life experience. Bach’s Prelude rang out, and the yggdrasil crowd stilled as the full might of the New York Philharmonic hit them. Sensory antennae rippled; leaf-wings vibrated in subtle unison.

At the end of the afternoon session, some two hours later, the vegetal beings stirred. The musical director reappeared among the VIPs. She reported, “They’re saying the crowd’s maybe half a million people and three million yggdrasil.”

There was still no sign of ‘flattening of the curve’. With no ticket sales and many aliens standing among the park’s trees, estimation was fraught with difficulty. Humans show a range of behaviours confronted with the unknown: Niels, for instance, preferred an awareness of that he didn't know; Matt was cheerfully unconcerned by ignorance, and Special Agent Cameron Peters' chief concern was to hide his lack of knowledge from others.

Failing to uncover yggdrasil weaknesses other than the slim potential of playing Bach at them against their will, the agency chief had changed tack in recent months. Mike Ross' previous activities, in opposing a US-Canada gas pipeline, had attracted interest from other government agencies. Now a photograph, taken at dusk *ten* years before; at a meditation retreat in Grand Sur had surfaced. It showed a certain Canadian environmentalist *and* a possible space-time hole. Cam Peters' focus had now shifted to career-saving investigations of collusion and fifth-column activity among the Congress members.

Unaware of this, Niels wandered among the snack and merchandise seeking audience, overhearing conversations:

Kalinda and Tyson K Whitney discussing TK's ideas for a synthesis of EDM (electronic dance music) and classical that humans and yggdrasil might enjoy together.

Ebony talking to Kevin of Kevin's cocoon-improved complexion, his unpleasant ayahuasca experience, indigenous legends, and the organisation of the upcoming expo.

Niels joined the coffee queue with Jess, where he met and chatted to "Chuck" Li, the celebrated Chinese tech billionaire (the founder of Plum and "the man who put the dot com in communism"). Chuck's finances mysteriously survived the eighteen-month yggdrasil-wreaked internet havoc.

Their discussion was interrupted when: "Damn!" said Jess, with a grin. "I finally *remembered* to bring one of my many KeepCups somewhere, and I've left it on the seat."

"I'll get it," said Niels.

As he returned to the VIP section, the Swede was alarmed to discover special agent Peters' infiltration of the area. A terse conversation between Peters and Mike Ross was underway. Ross, who'd often crossed swords with politicians and captains of industry, wasn't intimidated.

Examining his antagonist closely, the conservationist concluded the agent had not the deadeye look of the political or religious fanatic but rather the bird of prey visage of the self-interested office psychopath.

As Niels secured the cup and retreated, he heard topics of discussion range over respective personal moralities, dietary habits, sexual proclivities, and dedication to the cause.

"I doubt I serve the same cause as you," said Mike evenly.

"I do not doubt *that* Mr Ross."

KeepCup returned, Niels observed the city's Mayor preparing to speak. Soon, as the sky darkened, and now supplied with coffee, Jess and he strolled to their seats.

Angela Sutton spoke with pride of the way her city had moved to reduce food waste. The city's first female mayor urged the human crowd to view vegetal life as allies, not as a mere passive exploitable resource. She foreshadowed the symbolic tree-planting ceremony to follow the concert. As Niels had so often done, Mayor Sutton asked the aliens for time to make the necessary ahimsa changes.

From a copse of yggdrasil by the stage, the familiar individual that spoke at the first concert and later took the name Hatl Thuja stalked onstage. It didn't approach the microphone, but its voice boomed through the speakers. "Time!" it declared. "Please to cease requests for time additional. We will decision-allocate compliance period – not humans."

In the front row, Kevin *had* considered interspecies relations were going nicely of late. *Personally*, he'd been spun into a cocoon and his group had come under attack, resulting in a yggdrasil death, but there was a genuine sense of shared mission in Iquitos. Now his peril detector twitched. For those of who missed Hatl Thuja's address, the narrator has again attempted to capture the tenor of the affair …

"Time … you've had thousands of years people! Aristotle wrote of light-gathers having feelings and abilities over two-thousand years ago … your Jains have been minimising harm to plants for longer than that. Darwin – no, no, not the barnacle classifying, worm observer you needed to explain your *own existence*, but his father's father wrote of plant intelligence two-and-a-half centuries ago."

"Enough delay, enough excuses. Comprehensive action now humans," it paused and flared its wing leaves, "before next year's spring growth."

The mood soured. The party was over. Thousands of panicked humans rolled up their children and picked up their rugs – more level-headed New Yorkers did it in reverse order. A wave of alarmed humans flowed out of the park.

Chapter 70 "Beware the warrior-scholar."

Niels felt pod-trip nausea settle in his gut. To his right he caught TK mutter, "Someone put that dude in airplane mode."

The mayor glanced at the United Nations secretary-general, seated in the wings; she peered hopefully at her co-host (a veteran entertainer of some species with no claim on political office). She sought Niels in the front row – he met her stricken look.

Jess touched his arm, brow wrinkled with concern, "Niels, can you say something?"

He gave a hollow laugh – not the full mad scientist version; but there was a sense of electrodes connected, of test-tubes reached for. The atmosphere was hushed and tense, in need of yet another conciliation attempt.

Not by me, thought Niels. He approached the microphone.

"Hypocrisy!" he said in a steely tone, suggestive of a twenty-four-inch crosscut saw. "You, the askr Yggdrasil were *not always* photosynthetic life-forms. You have *made* yourselves that way." He glared at Hatl Thuja and challenged it. "Will you deny it? If photosynthesis is so important to you, then share that knowledge with us."

The crowd erupted in astonishment and confusion as they realised what Niels meant. As he spoke, Niels felt himself calm, and he resumed a more measured tone.

"There's been much commentary on the so-called *Second Law of Jainism* – in essence, that truth is complex, yes." [For those who couldn't pronounce *anekantavada*, the acronym itself: SLOJ, was well on the way to becoming a MOM (massively overused meme!)].

"So please, enough of the simple: plants good, animals bad division. There are thousands of plants that, despite having the ability to gather light, live as parasites on other plants – mistletoe, for instance. (A member of the Sandalwood* family: that the family tended not to invite for Christmas.) Other plants take insect lives – yet many plants can't breed without insect assistance. You we have named the yggdrasil have knowledge beyond our Earth imaginations, but your knowledge of this Earth is not complete."

The crowd murmured as the forester pointed out the inconsistency in claiming to protect the forests while simultaneously heating the planet. "Okay, sure, if you return us to greenhouse gas and temperature levels of dinosaur days there may be more forest *overall* – but at the cost of our wonderful cold-adapted forests." And, he brooded, *our crops*. Niels spoke at length of the need for humans and yggdrasil to work together to salvage seeds and living biota examples of current ecosystems.

Arms crossed, Cam Peters was prepared, after the Swede's opening remarks, to concede that Niels might not be part of a fifth column conspiracy. But, as the forester lectured on saving temperate forests, the agent muttered to his minions, "The pride of Sweden is losing it. He must have Stockholm syndrome."

The minions muttered among themselves:

"Can you even *say* that about Swedish people?"

"Huh."

"Sure, you can, why not?"

"Isn't it racist?"

"Huh?"

"Man, you can't be racist. They're Swedes."

"The *pride* of Sweden is a fish-girl statue with her tits out."

"That's Denmark, dude."

"Huh?"

And so forth … good help's hard to find.

* In fact, aromatic sandalwood is itself partially parasitic.

Niels concluded, "The music we have enjoyed is played on treasured *timber* instruments. Perhaps the musician releases the tree song retained in the wood's memory!" (He didn't credit this for a minute, but he was on a roll).

Or as Agent Peters now put it, "Yeah, he's definitely lost it."

Poised to intervene, Eir Nyssa flourished its antennae and announced: "Please to enjoy remaining music portion."

After a brief delay, and minus several musicians, the sounds of Beethoven's Symphony Number Three filled the night. Ambiance restored, Stravinsky's Rites of Spring followed, and later more Bach. Remaining cell phones were held aloft, along with leaf-wings. The human and yggdrasil Congress members withdrew to the sidelines for urgent discussions.

Later, when the music program concluded, several among the Congress favoured a brief and cheery …

"Well, goodnight then. See you in the morning!"

However, this wasn't the consensus, and speeches of a sort were made.

Those who fled the scene early missed such diverse yggdrasil commentary as:

"Humans live in darkness, but the best of them struggle against the darkness within."

"Travels show unwise, yet ascendant species devise cultural constructs inconsistent with reality."

"Beware the warrior-scholar."

"Our role: protect the light-gathers. Negative mentor humans."

"As they say of themselves – they are only human."

"We yggdrasil will fund researches described by Niels Larsson."

"You humans cannot enhance-addition our perception realities to thy own proficiencies. They are disparate."

The crowd buzzed as the UN chief approached the microphone and a technician adjusted its height. Controversially, from the first yggdrasil arrival, there'd been no leadership, no declaration, no agreement from the member states of the United Nations on how to respond, other than vague statements of mutual respect.

The world body was paralysed by the democratic process – although as it turned out – the inability to make a decision was better than making the wrong one: as the many one-party states, the police states, and the military strongmen could attest from the smouldering ruins of hindsight.

"There are those who would not have me speak," Riya Bedi began. The crowd booed theatrically, for the diminutive figure was popular for her store of grand-motherly wisdom and wit. "I said earlier to Professor Niels – I will say just one thing! Not, as you know, as the secretary of the United Nations – just advice from an old, old lady! Maybe I will become a meme!"

The crowd clapped, and Niels detected whooping levels one through to three (WPL1-3).

"So," she said, "This may appear counter-intuitive in our plant ahimsa world but: c*an we please eat less meat*. Conserve the plants we may grow for ourselves, not our cows and pigs." She continued in her musical tone, "Meat only once a week!"

The crowd clapped, many of them on their feet. Secretary-General Bedi raised her hands for silence. "That's the one thing. But now I find I've more to say," she smiled.

The crowd hushed.

"I have seen much conflict and change in my lifetime. This morning, thanks to the technology of our newcomers, I journeyed to space and saw the blue Earth floating alone in the blackness. Such a privilege. I cannot help but believe if we could all see that sight; we would better look after it."

Events concluded with Anne-Maree and the UN chief planting a tree.

"… It is our human intention during the lifetime of this tree** to achieve true ahimsa," declared Riya Bedi.

Over the applause none of the Congress heard Hatl Thuja rasp, "Unacceptable human condition."

** The tree species best suited was much discussed. A Bodhi Tree cutting – a descendant of the Sacred Fig under which the Buddha was said to have found enlightenment was considered – but New York climatic conditions were against it. Somewhat cynically, Niels proposed that symbol of peace – the olive tree – with its capacity to live for thousands of years. Eventually, the familiar stalwart of the urban landscape: the plane tree, was chosen.

Chapter 71 Bella and the Flounder

It is a truth universally acknowledged, that a single man in possession of a good fortune, and with secret access to a teleporting pod, may live wherever he damn well pleases. Even so, it was a surprise to many when Niels returned to his apartment in Corvallis (clearly the attraction of the Avery Park Rose Garden and the 2 Towns Ciderhouse were curiously powerful). Armed now, with unlimited finance from both the yggdrasil, and billionaire Chuck Li, the returnee intended making the Forestry school the centre of a forest climate change amelioration network. And with mixed feelings, he'd additional research in mind.

"Man, you got levels like a turducken!" exclaimed TK of these plans as Niels, Kevin, and he took a break from expo-organising activities at Bear's farm. (Niels felt perturbed by the increasing musical emphasis, TK's chief interest in the project).

"I believe it's important to *know*," said the scientist of the 'Time to collect the arrow frogs' advice. And so – the mysteries of the frogs were to be probed – whether the slimy critters cared for it or not.

"Kevin," continued Niels, but now changing topic. "Did you *know* about Anne-Maree?"

Controversy had followed the solstice concert. Ebony's *Mom Love NYC* blog had courted contention before. But revealing your daughter had been spun into a cocoon to enhance her yggdrasil communication ability was *too* much for many.

Kevin's research shared with Ebony and now with Niels and TK had uncovered conquistador reports of Indian "changeling" legends; where children taken by plant spirits developed the ability to intercede with trees and the spirit world. As we've noted previously, the study of historical alien visitation tends to attract the gifted hobbyist more than the accredited professional.

"I assumed we were just talking theoretically, you know?" explained Kevin.

"And the kid's okay, right?" said TK, concerned

"Yeah, she's fine."

"Ebony's upset with the response – she's gone upper case," said TK.

"I'm uncomfortable asking but is there evidence it worked?" asked Niels.

"Yeah, Anne-Maree says she can hear what Eir Nyssa's thinks at times if they're close. That's why it talks so well now when they're touching."

"Yes, I noticed that. When I was at the cricket," recalled Niels (shuddering but slightly), "I had strange communications. Also, in the ayahuasca drug vision – I could sense their thinking."

"Yeah, me too," nodded TK.

Kevin shrugged, "Guess I wasn't in there long enough to score any superpowers."

"Shall we stick with the plan – take a break and consider seafood's place in our new world? Perhaps we take the ambassadors on a trip later. They have … what is the word … *ceded* the sea to we humans. There are not so many land clearance conflicts involving the fishing."

"Yeah," said TK. "So off to Fisherman's Wharf, might get a bowl of chowder, maybe one of them caps with a lobster on it."

"Sure."

"Really?" said Kevin, looking at them under crinkled brows. To take his mind off impending travel nausea, he asked, "So, when we place jump, we actually go via the mother-ship?"

"Yes, but it's virtually instantaneous so we don't notice. But, when Riya Bedi and I went into space to view the Earth, we stopped at the terminus ..."

Kevin was correct: tales of the alien ship-cities somewhat distracted him from the nausea. Meanwhile, under Fisherman's Wharf, San Francisco, an anchovy twitched nervously, sensing the alien-tech materialise. Normally, a nervous anchovy attempts to swim into the centre of its school. Unfortunately, the lone fish, now swimming past a multitude of baited hooks and lures, was the last of its school (the teacher, cleaner *and* student as it were). Swimming nearby, just above the junk strewn bottom, was one of those smug, annoying flounders. If a creative deity had thought to provide flounder with eyebrows and the ability to raise them – this one would have undoubtedly done so.

Instead, it said, "Wotcha. How stupid do they reckon we are?" (Before impulsively sampling a cheese-baited hook and being hauled, complaining all the way to the surface).

The reduction in terrestrial protein had affected the intertidal and shallow-sea depths. For unlike the land, they are not fenced and owned. It was a real free-for-all out there in sea world. Every fish and intertidal shellfish had learned to fear the approaching squelch of human feet.

*

Kevin staggered from the pod, unable to determine which way was up. But, if he strode so briskly that his bunions complained – then, he could at least determine which way was down.

He is keen, thought Niels, following the New Yorker into an enormous retail space of fishy protein. After the Solstice Concert, the Swede had found his personal recognition factor unfeasible and in an attempt at profile lowering, had clipped his hair. However, his minimal hair and no camera ploy was unsuccessful. For it seemed every crazy person had un-solicited personal advice, or urgent speculations to share with him: concerning the aliens, bluetooth, or Lithium-ion batteries.

Niels scratched his minimal hair, *Ah, foolish me – it's just the normal operation of a non-Scandinavian style, free-range, mental health system.*

"I agree, flamingos are totally over-rated," he declared to the latest interloper; she with the cat under one arm and a toaster under the other. He followed TK and Kevin out of the sun.

Niels shivered in the enormous shed's chill. There was a cold flat dead look around the plaice, the flounder, the squid … the tuna*. The trio walked long aisles of potential solution to the protein problem. They sidled past lobsters trussed with that crustacean calamity: the cable tie. The chill was reviving Kevin, and Niels was warming – to lecture mode …

"The yggdrasil are not so caring of the oceans, and if they reclaim more pasture and cropland for forest re-wilding, we'll have to get our food from somewhere."

"Man, there's ugly fish here," noted TK. "Still, mostly, the world is ocean …"

"Sure, we are having much ocean, but not so a limitless supply of fish. We have already reached 'peak fish'. They are not growing on trees. That's why so many ugly ones here. We never used to eat them," Niels paused and flinched. "Wow! Are you seeing the suckers on that one! Anyway, the world's fishing capacity will not be taking long to catch most of the fish."

"People grow clams, don't they – catfish, yeah?" said TK. "Even seaweed."

"Yes, that's so, clever peoples learned long ago, we can't just take the fish and shellfish from the water, any more than deer and pine from the forest."

"So, more fish farming then." Kevin heard TK say. Kevin slumped in a seat and ordered a *recovery juice*. The market was exercising an unlikely attraction on his companions.

"Yes, the Congress should tour aquaculture farms – I wonder who'll come?"

"Count me in," said TK. "Did you see the news where that big old whale washed up, and people ate it. Wasn't that long ago – a whale washed up – folk queued to push it back in the water!"

* Narrative apologies!

Niels inclined his head, "People are hungry; it's not so surprising … you know some northern European countries still support commercial whaling."

"Here's a question, Doc," said Kevin reviving, in the chilly, fish-pungent air and spying a hand-written sign that proclaimed, "Banana Prawns."

"You know the big whales?"

"*Big* whales?"

"Yeah, well, the massive ones I mean – not Orcas … blue whales, humpbacks, whatever." He took another sip of miracle juice, "People say they're filter feeders, gentle giants, vegetarians – blah, blah. But they eat krill, don't they? Krill are like shrimps – they're not vegetables!"

Niels glanced at TK, amused. "Well, people used to eat fish and shellfish and call themselves vegetarians. So perhaps whales are similar!" He grinned. "Sorry, I guess because they're so big, their eating of small fish and crustaceans is relatively passive – it *is* a type of filtering. But I agree, shrimps are not vegetables."

Kevin continued, "If only the yggdrasil ordered: 'No more cows.'"

"Indeed, yes, Kevin, but they say, 'we are not your mentors, your coaches.' They just protect plants from the worst of our behaviour. I am also interesting in another solution to the meat protein problem, that we'll see at the expo."

"Err, Niels, not your famous roadkill plan again?" said Kevin, finishing the juice. The lucid look of someone consuming their recommended quota of omega-three fatty acids returned.

"No, no," said Niels. "Something else. A different kettle of the fish," he waved his hands in the general direction of examples of these. "If we put the money spent on weapons and video games to use, we can make progress. The expo will be thought provoking. Shall we look at more fish?"

Still reeling from the Swede's attack on the gaming industry, Kevin sighed, *just kill me now*. However, he got to his feet with the others. By contrast, this is precisely what Bella the blue fin tuna had *not* thought when hauled aboard the deck of a run-down fishing boat in the South-China Sea earlier. Even with fins and gills removed, Bella exuded grace and power.

"Ah, dead tuna makes me sad," observed TK.

"Yeah"

"Even before the yggdrasil arrival tuna were on UN threatened species lists," said Niels. (Ironically, before the yggdrasil broke the internet, incipient blockchain tracking of tuna, Patagonian toothfish and others may have aided preservation.)

A crowd milled around the tuna. The disputes and lawlessness in the South China Sea, before *the arrival* had acerbated the overfishing crisis. Whether it was the rarity of the tuna itself, or the sign inviting offers over three million dollars that had drawn the on-lookers was difficult to say.

Saddened, the group wandered away from Bella.

Niels peered across neighbouring aisles of imperfectly ice-slurried fish. He murmured, "Is that ...?"

When TK and Kevin caught up with him, Niels was poking at the frozen mass and talking to the proprietor. She and TK exchanged fellow knit-cap wearer nods.

"Yep, five-hundred pounds of jellyfish," she confirmed. "You gentleman looking to acquire," she continued, although none too hopefully.

Niels pocketed the laminated business card: *West Coast Jellies.* "Whether there's more of them because of a weird natural cycle or because of the overfishing – we should try to find uses for them."

TK raised his eyebrows. "Same as them locusts always eating crops in Africa these last few years."

"Yes. Or use them for stock feed or fertilizer."

"And jellyfish are excellent for people who don't want to eat things with heads or brains!" added Kevin. "And they're truly welcome to them."

The trio walked out of the land of ice and wet cement, back into sunlight. Where the first thing they saw was a successful fisherman pocket his knife and toss the internal organs of a flounder, which had formerly needed internal organs, into the sea.

TK wandered off to join a queue.

"You're not seriously going to buy one of those hats."

"Watch me, dude."

Chapter 72 At the Seaside

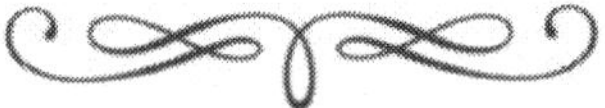

August 4
mom love nyc
AT THE SEASIDE!

thanks for your support dear readers. love you all. with all that's been going on we had to get away for the weekend: sure, had a wet wild and fishy one dear readers. how was yours?

so, here's me and anne-maree and local yggdrasil van koa in hawaii! [pic 1]. Did you know that fish have been farmed in china for 2000 years! wow. this english major sure did not know that. Of course, we've all heard of the 3F diet, but have we really thought about the fish component?

as always, there's a video link to the whole niels and jess narrated science informational overload. just kidding guys – love you both. and kevin says please excuse the bumpy footage. here's the crew bouncing out to visit the offshore black bonito farm [Pic 2 – loving that fish wrangler look].

so, it's like this dear readers: the yggdrasil are stopping land clearance, and even reforesting farmland – but they say the ocean is all ours. Which is great, but it's already badly overfished. niels says growing fish and shellfish is kind of like a forest – it's productive in 3 dimensions not just 2D like cows and sheep and lettuce. I suppose battery hens are kind of 3D too, but I don't think our girls would enjoy that. not at all.

In hawaii they can grow warm water critters near the surface and cold-water fishes deeper down. we saw big pump ashore tank farms, million fish sea cages, all sorts [Pics 3-6]. science alert: the recirculating land-based systems are like hi-tech greenhouses they can control temperature, light, food, disease, waste – even reuse most of the water.

niels says fish and shellfish being cold-blooded don't waste energy trying to keep warm – and they are much more efficient food converters: 3 to 6 times more than many animals we farm. Some shellfish don't need feeding at all

wow. so much information. but also, fun [Pic 7 my little mermaid princess surfing with matt davis].

ignore the haters dear readers – you know i do. not long now until the amazing expo and concert at bear browning's farm. see you there!

Chapter 73 The Saab Heads South

By August, money was pouring into the university's laboratories. The Dean was observed humming cheerfully by reliable witnesses, and for the moment Niels could do no wrong. Meeting now complete, the Swede exchanged the Dean's office and its fractal burnt wood desk for the laboratory lair of the biochemist Andrew. Another upgrade was in progress.

"So, it really was frog poison?"

"Yes, indeed – a lipophilic alkaloid toxin from one of the Dendrobatidae."

"And in every sample – arrowheads and darts?"

"Yep, that's right, Niels."

"I was half expecting curare."

"It's used in those parts," agreed Ash.

Niels nodded.

"So, you're sure poison killed that yggdrasil, not the arrow itself," queried Andrew, scratching his greying beard thoughtfully.

"I understand it takes massive physical damage to kill. Iae Hevea didn't appear much hurt. But … another alien was struck without ill-effects. I feel most uncomfortable," Niels continued, dull-voiced, "The ambassadors are trying to help, but we must grow those alien cell lines again for further tests."

Andrew nodded, "I understand Niels. We'll get right on it. Now, I'll leave you to it," he said, standing. "Ash has something to ask."

Niels detected the faintest of grins.

"Err, Professor, I'm going to the Yggdrasil-Expo-Concert. TK Whitney's playing and the exhibitors will be awesome." She paused, looking a little more demure than customary, "I was wondering, could I hitch a ride?"

*

Two weeks later, Ash peered into the car. "Should I put my bag in the trunk or the back seat?"

"Trunk should be okay," said Niels cautiously (for it had remained unopened for a lengthy period, and he was unsure how it might respond to such a turn of events).

"Ooh look, it has the cutest little wipers on the headlights."

And so, the Saab nosed tentatively from its mooring, heading south. Niels had been using the pod near-daily, and it had taken its toll. He'd assumed his explanation; of needing a respite from travel nausea would end the matter. But it had not. And perhaps he was glad. *The company might be nice.* He had always kept a polite distance. *Well, she's no longer my student and Ashley knows of the frog poison research.*

Corvallis behind them, they discussed temperate climate forest preservation, selective breeding, and essential crop research that the flood of finance allowed.

"How do yggdrasil get the money, Niels?" (She'd decided to call him Niels).

"I am not knowing this, Ashley. It's possible they make the virtual currency, or their algorithms control the share market. I am not needing to know; I am not wanting to know this."

"And there's mega-rich IT guy too, right?"

"For sure, he's keen to patronise the sciences – unfortunately, I do mean patronise." Niels shrugged, he changed lanes and said, "So you're familiar with TK, yes?

"Oh, yeah, I'm a massive fan. So … I made an old-school mix tape of the acts playing – well, except the classical. There's a heap of EDM." She reached for her small backpack and missed the driver's bemused expression. Eyebrows raised at Niels for permission, Ash waved the handwritten cassette, "Are you game?"

Niels nodded, and she inserted the tape with that satisfying rattly clunk you just don't get with bluetooth. After ten minutes, or so it seemed to Niels, his musical guide declared, "So that's *Higgs Bosun and the Particles*."

The Swede laughed, "Love the name. It sounds like what TK was playing when they tested the stage system."

"Well HB's more your typical techno dance music, TK's recent stuff is different – he's trying to get the yggdrasil to enjoy it. This is *Tide Sequoia and the Squids of Wisdom* – part of the *New 3arth* music. It's so cool you've met, TK – what's he like?"

"I like him: sensible, sense of perspective. He wears a lot of woolly caps."

"Would it be okay to introduce me?"

"Sure, Ashley."

"Oh my gosh! Niels your cap – it blew away!"

"Not to worry, please pass me another – from the pouch behind the seat. Less hair now, I should have tightened more, yes."

"Err, this has a lobster on it."

"TK bought it for me." Niels grinned, *she looks appalled.*

Ash checked her own cap. "At first, I supposed he was playing with that whole dub step-alien-monster-movie-trope thing. Then I read on his blog *why* he's trying to mix the classical.

"Right," said Niels, none-the-wiser but hoping he might pick something up as they went along.

"He's written, the way they react to classical music is *too* intense. You understand? They just stand there, vibrating, lost in themselves, lost in the music."

Niels glanced to his right, "Ah, huh."

"TK says, for our two species enjoying music *together*, that's not ideal – we're just sitting there and they're oblivious to us. He talks with the DC ambassador, Tau Ulmus – testing musical ideas on it."

Niels tapped the vehicle's display panel, removing a random error message. Glancing at Ash, he said, "Right" (still hoping to pick something up as they went along).

"So TK's trying to find a balance where he blends in enough classical as the treble in dubstep, so the yggdrasil enjoy it – but not be so immobile – and people will still go for it. Maybe we dance together. He thinks it's something useful he can do."

They stopped overnight.

The rest of the journey was uneventful, and the Saab behaved itself after the long layoff. Leaving Oregon, they skirted one of the new communes where they use books for kindling and toilet paper; where folk believe the government puts Bluetooth *and* 5G in the water supply. [Where narrative insight predicts in ten years-hence, the toasty odour of burnt witch will hang in the air]. They skirted preppers, living vigorous tech and tax-free lives. Roadside stalls selling black market brassicas were declined. Later, Ash requested a stop at northern California's largest stationery store.

"Excellent excuse, anyhow."

"What do you mean?"

"Well, as you said: with the secret *no computer recording of the yggdrasil slash frog poison research,* we'll need nice journals with interesting, textured hardcovers; planners, make sure we have enough highlighter pens, all those office things. And, well … I like to check their paperclips haven't become unruly."

She was, Niels noted, a young woman of diverse interests.

Chapter 74 The Expo: Day One

Lunchtime the next day and without provision of a sat nav, the convertible arrived at and attempted to enter the VIP parking zone.

The security guard was clearly no stranger to the bench press. Combining indifference with hostility he said, "Why are you here sir?" He regarded the twenty-five-year-old Swedish vehicle and its occupants with suspicion.

"Err, I am watching the news and was invited by aliens to join a reality TV show … then we people tried to drive them away by burning forests, which they did not appreciate … err, then they found they enjoyed Bach, so they are liking us a little … ah, then they heat the earth and reforest our croplands; but it was indeed so they made themselves photosynthetic, and so they're sheepish about that. And now William Browning is inviting us here to help with the concert and the—"

"You're that dude from Kraken, yeah."

"Err, yes – that's it," said Niels.

"Through there, collect your passes."

The expo sat in a field. Exuberant Californian sun shone upon it and its rows of psychedelic-painted portaloos. The two passed under the enormous entry-gate pine tree. Its lower reaches hung with light-adorned bicycles. A sure sign, Ash assured Niels, of a festival beyond.

Besides portaloos, the grounds were a vibrant trailer and tent dotted venture. The two strolled past friendly, green-vested volunteers, free sunscreen and water stations, recycling arrangements, and intriguing boxes calling for old cell phone donations.

"Should you get the cap? Or better still – one without lobsters. Your hair's so short you might get burnt …"

Niels ran fingers through his shortened hair and squinted at Ash. *An overnight trip in the Saab and now you are my mother*? "Or" he said, pointing subtly, "or, one of these bandanas with the antennae that people are wearing."

"Definitely not …"

As they wandered deeper into the site, three young women, painted green head to toe, emerged from a portaloo together, giggling. Niels was by no means devoid of male curiosity as to:

A) How was this physically and geometrically possible?

B) Were they entirely naked under the paint?

But, in the present company, he didn't scrutinize the matter further.

Ash patted him lightly on the shoulder, "Well, thanks so much. I should find my old San Francisco friends. I'll see you later – in the mosh, yeah!"

*

A group of parentally unattended three-year-old's clad in oversize orange safety vests ran past. Jess stood talking to Ebony on the low hill that overlooked the entrance. The public, or at least Ebony's public (*this* public) had forgiven the blogger for the *cocoon incident*. For what constitutes poor parenting in the layperson is counted mere eccentricity in the celebrity blogger, actor or musician.

Thanks to the genius of Bear's phone donation scheme, thousands of light-gatherers had absorbed a phone and begun communication with humans. The site buzzed with interspecies goodwill. Jess watched long-haired humans offer friendship bracelets of their locks to companionable leaf-creatures. Anne-Maree's hair was looking ravaged in contrast to her impeccable-as-usual clothes from the ever-more successful family fashion business.

"Oh yeah, we're staying in the glamping area screened by those windbreak trees," explained Ebony, pointing. "Last night, Ann-Maree lost another front tooth – and instead of leaving it for the tooth fairy, she's put it on a string for Eir Nyssa. Bless her."

"Right," said Jess.

"How much does the crowd love Eir Nyssa and the ambassadors?" Ebony continued.

This was undoubtedly true. The crowd was all over them like West African internet romance scammers.

"This whole thing has a FriendFone vibe, but with actual people."

Jess smiled and agreed. She spotted Niels enter the site and exclaimed, "He's cut his hair." Followed almost immediately by, "Who's the gorgeous black girl with him?"

"Oh yeah. Don't know – someone from the Uni? He said he was driving down – too much pod travel has been making him ill."

"That's days of driving?"

"Oh, you could do it in one, if you wanted to. But not get here this early."

Jess felt an unexpected tightening in the stomach. She half-heard Ebony say Niels had taken Kevin and Crystal rollerblading in Crystal's old Golden Gate Park haunts this past week. The Australian forced herself to focus.

"Old haunts? Gee, I can't imagine Crystal rollerblading. Well, more than him …" Jess conceded.

Ebony gave a brief laugh (to Jess' ears the smug laugh of the *Isn't it great when everyone finds their life-partner* brigade). "Kevin's been pining for her since the Congress came here that time."

'*Stomach – you have no right behaving such,*' declared Jess' brain. '*Niels doesn't need our permission to have an unmentioned girlfriend, or not have one, as the case may be. If you fancied him,*' continued the brain to the stomach, (via the vagus nerve), '*you should have said so before now.*'

*

The subject of this internal discussion was now lost from sight; Niels having entered the throng. Whereby chance, he happened upon the fore mentioned Crystal. Who pounced and hugged.

"Hi Crystal, wow, it looks great set up and full of people. Can you point me to the meat culture display? I have it here in the program …"

"That's okay, Niels know what you mean – the huge German gentleman. I'll take you there.

"Neat, thanks. Setting up went okay, not stressful?"

"Yeah, yeah, good. Except, we had to move a couple of exhibitors further apart," she shook her head. "Which I didn't expect."

It was soon after the first exhibitors arrived, that Crystal concluded dreadlocks and hugs alone were not the answer to world peace. Tension had brewed in the produce area. She recalled that familiar drone …

While every exhibitor favoured non-industrial scale, non-pesticide, organic farming; the vegan bacon (smoked watermelon) dread-locker, objected to the heirloom saddleback pig bacon, dread-locker.

Tempers frayed. The dreaded: "Hitler was a vegetarian" line was flung.

The subject manner was different, but not the delivery. Tracking the source, Crystal discovered Eric 'Bare Toes' from the Giant Sequoia protest in full flow. He disparaged an unfortunate grey-haired hippy for 'loving trees' but professing doubts extending the same love to the ingredients of say, a nice leek, potato, and carrot frittata. Employment had sharpened 'bare toes' up, but then, it was difficult to think of something that wouldn't.

Bear was not far away. Wearing the sardonic expression of a guru discovering a fistfight in the mediation garden retreat, he dispersed the warring parties.

*

Crystal left Niels at the canvas tent. Squeezing past a yggdrasil and a pair of twenty-something men in matching be-penguined print shirts, he slipped inside. The display was easy to follow: three large incubators at different stages of culture and then the extraction, pressing, and sampling demo.

A young woman in a black SLOJ (Second Law of Jainism) T-shirt recognised Niels.

"I think it has the potential to change everything, this and farming of the algae – hence multicellular life form ahimsa and minimal land use. Would you eat the cultured meat yourself?" Niels asked.

"Well, I want to say yes. I was a vegetarian, now fruitarian, of course," she said earnestly, "but ..." she trailed off and shrugged.

"No need to be rushing the decisions. New things require the new thinking."

A tall, angular woman with mannish hands interrupted and proffered one such to Niels.

"Why hello Professor," she began, in a British accent. And continuing with it, "I'm Bridget la Fontaine," she arranged her features in a grim smile, "friends call me Bunny," she said in a conspiratorial tone. "Allan is here somewhere, I gather, entertaining the hoi polloi."

"Hello, yes. I believe I saw it – the striped tent where they do the tai chi, the Bollywood dancing and yggdrasil-Pilates, whatever that may be," he scratched his close-cropped hair. "Are you going to see his session?"

"Oh," she laughed in her deep voice, "I hardly think that will be necessary. You must be pleased with this money of yours," she said abruptly. "So much better, those legendary European Institutes whose scientists decide the research priorities, rather than beastly politicians peddling a four-year election-cycle!"

My, you are odd, thought Niels. "Have you tried the *clean* meat," he asked, gesturing at the samples.

"Oh no professor, not my constituency. It must be sixty years since I last ate meat – to father's horror – rest his soul. But I approve the sentiment heartily. More honest, somehow. I have always said bleeding soy burger is the gateway drug back to dead beast! Well, toodaloo, must be off." She shook his hand vigorously again and departed.

Somewhere a German accent said, "Seventy per-cent of human water use is for agriculture … fifteen percent of greenhouse gases come from meat farming …"

Niels tried to locate the speaker. He waited. There it was again …

"Ten years ago, they said the same of solar power – too expensive."

Niels smiled. The fellow was easy to spot: the size of Bear Browning (minus the padding). He sensed Niels looking at him.

He turned and looked over the crowd, "Doctor Larsson, I presume?"

"Doctor Ditterich!"

Moments later, Niels enjoyed his second, consecutive, inordinately firm handshake.

"Many visitors are coming," noted Niels.

"Oh, yes, and please come back when it's quieter. I give you my number. And you must come and view my Berlin laboratory." It was as much an order as an invitation – but one Niels was keen to accept.

"It's similar to algae culture, I'm thinking," said Niels.

"Yes, or whisky making et cetera, anything cultured for weeks."

"And started from a single muscle cell?"

"Yes, stem cell generally at this stage."

"And what Karl, are the limitations?"

"Oh," he chuckled, "the usual: time and money. It is, as they say, a *no-brainer* in our changed world."

Niels nodded, "Surely now, the world will throw money at this project. There is controversy around what to call the product, yes?"

"Yes, clean meat, *in vitro* meat … fake meat. Novel product names can have controversy. I have never tried milking almonds, but it must be murder on the hands!"

"Oh," exclaimed Niels. "Ahimsa meat?"

The big German blinked. "Excellent – did you just think of that?"

"I have my 'advertising industry moments,'" admitted the forester, "but I try to stay away from the dark side."

Karl nodded. "It doesn't matter what it's called or how we market it now. When this started, the idea was an alternative food choice, a reduced footprint, perhaps vegetarians might eat it. But now it may come to this or no beef. We also develop other meats."

"I must find the yggdrasil ambassadors and send them here."

"Yes, they must see we humans make this *ahimsa* research."

*

Meanwhile, Jess ignored the many stalls selling dreamcatchers, amulets, hippy chic, and ahimsa twee.

"Hi Jess," said Kevin, breaking off his conversation with the proprietor of the *Sphere of Fortune* tent. She found his enthusiasm for every aspect of para-science tiresome. Her mood was testy and became more so after an unsolicited vision of her future featuring an abundance of well fed and thankful cats. Jess rolled her eyes, "I'll see you later." She understood he didn't take it seriously but had little sense of humour on the topic. Others took it seriously, and that she felt it was harmful in an unspecified way (as well as the glaringly harmful 'match your medications to your star sign' approach).

The merch stand was nearby. The Second Law of Jainism had become an acronym, a noun, a verb, and now a T-shirt slogan. As chance had it, after wandering seeing nobody she knew, Jess now saw two in as many minutes.

"Hey Matt, me too, I just bought one of those – mine's blue, though," she waved it at him.

"Nice. I'm supposed to meet Kal by the chicken exhibit – she's pretty keen to get a small farm, chooks and all that."

"Yeah, she's mentioned it."

"Right, and your parents are farmers, aren't they? Not so far from *Cairns*?" (he said the name with dread). "Do you want to come – moral support or whatever?"

They caught up with Kalinda a hundred yards from the poultry area. The women hugged.

"Ready to go wrangle chickens, girlfriend?" said Matt.

"What's that?" said his fiancée, with a certain bemused scorn.

"Just practicing my girl-power patter."

"Well, don't," suggested Kalinda.

"Oh look, its Paul McKay," Jess beamed.

It was, and with full context, in that the media surrounded him. After a decade in the world of FriendFone and Facebook, whereby simply agreeing to the unread terms and conditions, the world would be shaped to your liking; events had forced people to leave that comfortable place and explore the real world. Fact-checking media were a part of that – although they still preferred the facts delivered by a good-looking celebrity.

The vet finished filming his segment and hurried to embrace fellow *CCE* survivors, Matt and Kalinda. He beamed and shook hands with Jess. This turn of events delighted the media. After posing for more pics, Paul shooed the reporters away (like outside chickens – keen to become inside chickens).

"I was hoping you'd find me," he exclaimed with pleasure.

After a few minutes of mutual catch up, Kalinda said, "Matt and I have been discussing farms – being more self-sufficient – possibly near my parents' place."

"That's a whole other story, but apparently I must rear chooks. So, you better tell me about food conversion ratios and such – I've been getting into them."

"And *apparently*, someone's a little scared of chickens," reported Kalinda eyes twinkling with mischief.

"Not cool to fear chickens, mate," grinned Paul.

"Mate, if I was any cooler, penguins would freeze to me!"

Paul grinned, "Got some real friendly – *kid*-friendly ones here. Come have a look. Everybody's growing them back home: Very efficient protein converters, they turn scraps and garden pests into eggs and manure, and you can eat 'em too."

He caught and cradled such a winged beast, "Combine chooks with algae, mushrooms, the big fibrous fruits: pumpkins, eggplants, then mealworms for the chooks or yourself if you're game, and you can go a long way."

As the first contestant released from *CCE* duties after the yggdrasil arrival, his "Pear, Possum, Potato" * summary of yggdrasil food tolerances became an immediate meme. Dr Paul had soon developed a world-wide media presence. Jess readily agreed to meet him for a drink before the evening session of the concert kicked off.

*

Later, fatigued by the drive and heat, Niels left the group at the back of the mosh with the Australian vet, Paul. *Jess is acting strangely formal.*

The idea of an early night appalled TK. "Man, I haven't seen the sunrise since I was thirteen," he joked.

"Promise to hear you play tomorrow night," said Niels.

Later, just before Niels fell asleep, Bear returned briefly to the homestead, reporting all was well except someone had, "… forgotten to tick the *no cuss words* option on the hip hop set list."

Fortunately, most of the young children wore bright coloured earmuffs.

* Respectively: Can eat. Eat if you must. Don't eat.

Chapter 75 The Expo: Day Two

The second day's morning found Niels sitting with the three Australians. Slurping his banana-mango spirulina thick shake, he realised Matt was intrigued by nearby conversations.

Niels overheard snatches of …

"You know how she is: saw a tattoo she liked, and now she *totally* lives her life by it …"

"Well, he's worse, with his, 'I now identify as a tree,' stuff."

"… bee slavery? It's like you think almond milk is a more egregious crime than tax evasion or the modern slavery of sneaker manufacture."

"Nah, it ain't the guy – hair's too short – and this place doesn't have that metal vibe, *they* wouldn't play here."

Kalinda and Jess were chatting, and Niels directed a quizzical look at Matt. The comedian waved his finger at the Swede and played a little air guitar. Niels rolled his eyes. At least the stranger appeared not in the market for a musical hero autograph, unlike the young woman now excitedly approaching the table.

"Niels hi," Ash waved for good measure. "Didn't see you in the mosh. Isn't this all great!" she waved at the surrounds, "and TK's new sound killed it—"

She stopped comically short when she realised who her ex-lecturer's companions were.

Niels did the introductions, and Ash cooed to Jess, "You are *the* woman scientist role model."

Jess laughed, charmed, "Well, I might need to finish my thesis for that."

"Pull up a seat Ashley," Niels leaned in, "These three are knowing …" his right hand mimicked a hopping frog. "But please be discrete."

They nodded, Ash said, "Can you introduce me to TK later? He's not here? She peered about hopefully.

Matt grinned and promised he'd arrange introductions if Niels didn't. The forester sat back, listening to the others. The barefoot fellow that suspected he was Kraken's bass player start up again …

"People are always blind to recognising capacity for feelings or thoughts in others, once it was fellow people – much easier to own slaves when you don't consider them human."

Opposite, Matt finished his banana-flour pancake, and the table lurched playfully. Niels inspected it. *Since the yggdrasil arrival, it seems I've been plagued by rickety wooden tables*. [And he *had*: the tables disproved of his early employment history.] While chocking the table, he heard …

"Then it was animals …so much easier to kill them for sport, eat them or cut off their balls (this appeared to upset the speaker inordinately – and other tables glanced around), when you deny their feelings."

Jess chatted to Ash, and it became clear the young woman was not Niels' partner. Contemplating him now, she realised this pleased her – and annoyed her. She was annoyed with herself. To be fair, (to herself), she decided Niels could bear a generous ten percent of the blame. That intense fellow at the other table was getting louder – it was tricky to concentrate on one's contemplations.

"This is just the last step, man, and it's weird, so freakin' weird that so many that don't eat animals baulk at the final step of extending ahimsa to all complex life …"

Jess now noticed Bear Browning and Crystal approach. Crystal noticed bare toes in full flight and stepped deftly behind her companion. Folk at other tables looked uncomfortable as he declaimed messianically:

"Freakin', *Trees have souls, other plants are just food*, hypocrites … you've got to embrace—"

At the sight of two hundred-twenty pounds of muscle turning to fat expo-organiser approaching, bare-toes returned to standard conversational decibels.

Bear grinned, "Doc, what're you doing to my table …"

"Damn cross-head screws," he proclaimed after a quick examination. "Still, ain't no-one makin' timber tables no more – I'll fix it later. Let's have a look-see at the PEACE (People Earning askr-Yggdrasil Co-operation and Evolution) group. The biohackers. You seen 'em yet, Doc?"

"Not yet … well, only at a safe distance. Shall we all go?"

Bear explained, "Closest we could think of to what the Doc figured our aliens done to themselves. Reckon we need to show the Yggs we're willing to change, even our bodies. I hope they're the right variety of nutters – I mean hackers. It was like hearing Tyson K talk about ten-types of electronic dance music – there are folk calling teeth whitener and a good night's sleep a biohack; others DIY sensor implants."

*

Just as timber tables were no longer made new – neither was denim. However, walking around the site, Niels concluded the reported death of denim was premature. Many youngsters in attendance showed a touching faith that it was okay to wear *old* denim. That contrary to lurid media reports, the yggdrasil could see sense in this: *If* jeans were genuinely falling apart, instead of manufactured new *as if* they were falling apart. And so, it seemed, they could.

Music festival dress had spilled out into the expo. There were matching sloth-motif shirts admiring the Native American agriculture display; ponchos in shades of brown practiced tree meditation; the merchandise tent sold out of SLOJ T-shirts and singlets. Underclothes were worn on the outside or worn on bodies covered only in yggdrasil-green paint.

Sif Acer and Sri Achras joined the walk to the biohackers. Ash beamed when Niels introduced her to the alien diplomats. Bear slowed and motioned to the Swede to match his pace.

"Try not to worry so much, man. You gotta find a balance between living in your head and just living."

Niels favoured him with a brief, non-committal smile.

*

"We're mostly grinders," said the man (they *were* mostly men, Jess noted) with the bone conduction sound antenna system. "My sensors let me see UV and infra-red and hear it as low-frequency sound. Like I can see you're hot …"

And sometimes thought, Jess, a girl just 'sensors' an unsuitable fellow will hit on her – and this was one of those *sensorings*.

Nodding to a fellow Snoopy T-shirt wearer, Matt was surprised to learn she was an exhibitor. Because of his scar – she'd assumed he was one.

"With the implant in my hand's webbing, I turn on electrical devices and open the security system …" Baby steps on the way to transhumanism.

Meanwhile, Niels learned those present were the cybernetic grinders. There were others: biochemists and folk experimenting on themselves with CRISPR tech – but they were mainly dead or home shaving off tentacles.

He was rapt at so many yggdrasil present and trying out their new phone-voices on the crowd and exhibitors. Niels hoped the microalgae culture and *in-vitro* meat displays were drawing similar crowds. He extracted Jess from the orbit of a man with an aerial or something. They viewed eye cam implants and met people with magnets embedded in unlikely places. There were folks linked to cell phone apps. They overheard phrases such as:

"We're the upgrade."

"My body, my potential!"

"We're bypassing the evolutionary ladder and catching the elevator!"

The man with the bluetooth speaker in his head and the superman Tee remarked to his companion, "I bet the yggs have turned their entire bodies into biological Swedish army knives."

"Swiss."

"Right."

"But they're neutral – same as the Swedes – they won't help us upgrade.

"Swiss."

*

The original group dispersed. However, Niels lingered, hoping to ask a yggdrasil ambassador for its opinion. Explaining this to Jess, an alien with a lurching gait came up behind her, draping a small leaf-wing on her shoulder.

It was Mir Arauca.

"Reciprocal greetings Niels Larsson," it said and informed Jess it had visited her parents, and they were: "Relative optimal condition, exception Bob Kelly bilateral patella."

The daughter of the aching knees smiled, "Mir, what's your take on the biohackers?"

"Sense those humans' interest be improving selves, negative improvings for common good. If non-light-gatherers succeed lifespan extension, continue reproductions – planet resources further deplete."

It said a species needed the wisdom to invent the technology; the wisdom to want to apply it and the morality to go photosynthetic. It said its race didn't guide other races down this path – rather, they protected light gathers from those that chose more *indirect* energy sources.

Niels moved closer, "Can we be discreet and frank?"

The yggdrasil waggled its antennae.

Niels' eyes widened at the use of body language, "Sif Acer hinted we humans should become photosynthetic."

"Affirmative, correct." It regulated its volume lower, "Comrades say it has seen too many worlds and is excess …" It made a brief static sound. "Invested." The alien lowered its eyestalks, "Shall we walk and talk-communicate Niels Larsson, Jessica Kelly?"

Of Niels' walk, an observer might say he loped gratuitously, and with a preoccupied air. Previously, this may have deterred strangers from approaching. As his fame grew, this failed as a strategy. Around him the perfect August expo weather continued, and children adjusted their fabric wing leaves.

Craning eyestalks at inter-species interactions, Mir Arauca said, "Did you, Niels Larsson gift your covering [static burst] hair of head to comrades?"

Niels smiled. It was a plausible misunderstanding. Nearby, people were set for sheepish conversations with their hair-dressing-professional.

"No, no, I am tiring of many strangers wanting to talk with me."

"Oh, is that why," said Jess. "Has it helped?" she added sympathetically in her husky voice.

"Some, yes."

The three continued their wander. *Perhaps Bear is right*, mused Niels, feeling more positive about future human-yggdrasil relations. The ambience was catching. He enjoyed the bright clothes, hooded ponchos, and SLOJ tops (the meme had seemingly become a reaction to the past ten lazy years of simplistic slogans; of interpreting every fact to suit an agenda).

They reached one of the food areas, and Niels joined a line for coffee; Jess, another for a juice concoction; the yggdrasil ventured towards the tree meditation activity where TK was saying to a novice …

"Look at the tree kinda casual – like you can do it already – just you're on a break and not doing it right now …" [This approach is best applied to tasks such as management consultation and on-line influencing but is ill-suited to a career in medical imagining].

A few minutes later, Niels joined Jess at a cable reel table.

"You didn't get anything."

"The queue was taking forever." Which was true, (But by the time he'd read the list of maladies treatable by the wonders of the establishment's kombucha, he couldn't bring himself to order).

Mir Arauca returned to them.

Jess said, "Am I missing something, what on earth goes on with this tree meditation?" She'd seen a lot of 'recharge your crystals' type, non-evidenced based activities. "Can people really communicate with trees in that way," she wafted a hand at nearby participants.

"Affirmative, variable human aptitudes, assistances may be required."

Niels was mute on the topic.

"Right. I guess I didn't pick TK for a tree meditation type of guy."

"You never can tell," said Niels wryly.

"Nutrient foraging unsuccessful," the alien said to Niels, waving its longer antennae.

"He said the line's too long – he hates queuing," relayed Jess.

"Hates queuing," repeated the yggdrasil, rippling its leaf wings and seemingly amused. "Self will gain fluid nutrient. Question: coffee tree seed extract?"

Startled, Niels said, "Sure, thanks." *I'm not desperate, but what happens*?

"Oh," said Niels.

Mir Arauca was a blatant queue cutter! An ignorer of "human formation protocols." But the patrons didn't mind, and the creature returned almost immediately, clutching the cup.

"I should pay for it," Niels said to Jess in a quick aside.

"Nah, don't worry," she advised, slurping the last of her juice concoction.

Niels realised, *now's the moment to ask the questions unanswered on CCE and since.*

"I understand that yggdrasil absorb extra nutrients from the massive ship in orbit?"

"Correct. And supplied to small transport crafts. Important micro-nutrient solution optimises body chemistry – additionally, cultural value.

"Don't we have those elements on Earth?"

"Hydrogen unity multiples: 34, 39, 42 present but cultural value in home planet solution and dispensing structures.

"So, you take that solution where you go … when you leave your home world?"

"Affirmative."

"Can I ask," began Niels. "Have you, you yourself, I am meaning, been to other planets with life forms?"

"Affirmative."

Niels glanced at Jess, who was shaking her head with silent wonder.

"Can you tell us about that?"

Mir Arauca audibly shook and folded two of its larger 'leaves.'

"Regrets, that information is not," it paused, "recommended."

Anne-Maree scampered past, gap-toothed and wearing improvised leaf-wings. Niels glanced around and discovered the child's mother and brother sitting on a tartan blanket surrounded by aliens.

Jess continued, "Can you tell us if *you've* been to Earth previously?"

"Affirmative confirmation – excess any other."

Niels' eyes widened, "And there's nothing you can tell us – even in general terms concerning life across the universe?"

"Every important life form contrives …" it paused, but didn't make the static sound, "the bottle opener."

Jess exchanged glances with Niels. "Um, Mir – was that a joke?"

"Affirmative. Self observes lack of convention response."

"Sorry, Mir – you took us by surprise."

"Is it the feelers?" queried the alien waving them about.

"Not in the slightest, I love your feelers," said Jess.

"It's more the lack of tone variation," explained Niels as the leaf creature draped a long feeler over Jess' shoulder. "It seems there're major differences, conflicts, between yggdrasil on attitudes to humans."

"Explorer-diplomat clade yggdrasil possesses more interest, additional empathy for new species." It adjusted itself and continued, "Even non-light gatherers."

Nearby, Anne-Maree giggled and hid behind Eir Nyssa's 'foliage'.

Mir Arauca continued, it said, "Life forms constructing selves photosynthetic are commonly zealous about the lifestyle for the first one hundred million years or so; compared those born to gathering light."

Over the next few minutes, Jess and Niels confirmed that every diplomat had visited Earth before. Sometimes, as they now learned, past visitors never returned to their home world. Anne-Maree ran past again – now trailing TK with her.

"Kevin would be most interesting in this." Niels stood to his full height and looked around. He called, "Tyson – have you seen Kevin?"

TK sauntered over and said knowingly, "Well, saw that curvy girl wearing his faded old Star Wars sweatshirt this morning – so wherever he be – he's happy." Niels tried not to grin as he went with the others to view Ebony's activities.

She was continuing her attempts to teach the yggdrasil to use metaphors – now illustrating examples with pop music lyrics.

"Why?" was the obvious question.

"Well, I'm sure we could communicate better if everything isn't so literal – and it's kinda fun! This morning a yggdrasil called a baby a seedling. The more yggdrasil that learn, the better they all get – if one learns, the group does. Matt's been telling them jokes."

"Ah."

The la Fontaines were also present. She, extravagantly hatted and talking animatedly to a yggdrasil about collective communication. Niels had seen "Bunny" at a distance a few times, generally with the demeanour of someone about to affix a firm note to a neighbour's car. As he watched, the alien wove her a carbon fibre friendship bracelet out of thin air and bodily fluids. Allan tried with limited success to engage the forester's interest in Jungian collective unconscious theories, race memories of world trees, and links to tree communication. The Frenchman said he'd go with Niels back to the main display venue – where he was due to present another session of *Philosophy for Fun*.

Jess meanwhile thought, *I'll find some people who can't talk to trees*. She paused in this undertaking only to enquire of Bunny, "Are you and Allan coming to the concert later?"

"Only the classical component deary." She adjusted her hat, turned back to her alien companion, and said, "Our human communication web has allowed the exchange of mere general ignorance for that of specific hatred and intolerance. Such a triumph!"

*

That night after the concert, it appeared no additional wisdom was conferred by the stars, the artificial flicker of LED lights and the consumption of alcohol. None-the-less sampling of the latter continued. A further sample of Congress humans, their associates, Bear's chief lieutenants, and an entourage or two TK had acquired sat on low chairs or old logs.

Someone was saying, "It shocked me to see ginger prawns for sale. Ginger! Did anyone else notice?"

The vet Paul's media-friendly voice said, "Yeah, after all this time, people still get confused. But hey, relax."

"Well, bless," said Ebony, (Anne-Maree asleep in her lap) "it shows there's tolerance for the small-scale stuff at least."

Bear handed Niels another cider, his deep voice said, "It's a weird old world when my dad's old polyester shirt is cooler music festival wear than organic unbleached cotton!"

"So, it appears," Niels began, after a few chuckles had subsided, "that turning our selves photosynthetic is not a likely option in the short term."

"Pity, I'd make an excellent cactus," mused Matt.

"It is an interesting question whether people would choose that if it were possible?"

The semi-darkness came alive with murmurs.

Niels continued, "Ahimsa plant products we have in the fruits, nuts, seeds, and grains. In time we should produce any combination of the proteins, fats, and carbohydrates from micro-algal cultures and possibly seaweed. However, our yggdrasil will not be taking us so seriously as civilised beings if we are still eating the animals. Let us leave aside eating the dead beached whale; the lightning struck cattle, the cold snap fish kill for the moment, please."

"Happy to," quipped Matt. "Hey Paul," he called across the ragged circle, "What's your impression of the big German doc?"

"Fellow's got presence," he attempted the accent: "*It never died – it was never born.*"

"Yeah, but just quietly, would you play him up front and see if he can really clunk the ball – or is he more the mobile ruck type …"

"Another cider Niels?" asked Bear Browning perceptively.

"Please."

"Pear, apple or summer blend?"

"God, why must life and death decisions plague my every waking moment."

Glass clinked in the dark. Bear said, "Try this, at this stage I reckon it don't much matter."

"Yes, okay, thanks. You are knowing where I was leading with this, of course – the so-called 'clean meat', the *in vitro* meat: culture from a tiny cell of muscle. I am not so interesting to convince plant and fungi diners to consume this, but the meat-eaters …"

Among the murmurings in the dark Allan's unmistakable accent said, "But what, Niels of the question of consent?"

Conversation in darkness can be problematic:
1) because it's difficult to determine when one's conversationalist has ceased talking; and
2) if there's a professional philosopher involved.

"Can there be true ahimsa without consent?"

"Surely, it's better to take a cell than a life," said Jess. "I'd probably eat it."

"Ah, Ms Kelly, the greater good argument – rather than the moral absolute," said Allan.

In flickering light Niels observed Jess' brow wrinkle seriously, "I rarely eat meat but yes, I, I might I need to go snorkelling and think about moral relativism."

"Please, you should attend my talk tomorrow."

"But, what Allan, my friend, if I took a muscle cell from *my* thigh and grew a kilo of finest Niels Larsson?"

"Interesting, very good. Touché," said Allan.

Many of the group disagreed, showing this with a series of appalled noises. The word *cannibalism* was uttered in the dark.

"Surely," teased Niels, "I am permitted bite my nails, suck the blood from my finger cut – grow my own Niels steak – I am not asking to eat the cell cultures of others! Ah, but are we not doing so when we suckle from our mothers?"

Anne-Maree was awake again. "Mom …" she said (not worried: just seeking clarification) "does Niels want to eat me?"

"No, darling, go back to sleep."

Chapter 76 The Expo: Day Three

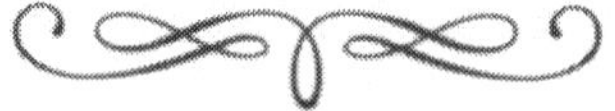

Niels paused by the striped tent, allowing a group of young bespectacled people with vinyl backpacks entry. He heard the distinctive theatrical voice:

"Who is for free will? Is a chair still a chair when we leave the room? Is there an ideal chair?

So many questions – among them: attend morning *Philosophy for Fun* session, or have breakfast? He paused, felt a tinge of guilt – successfully shook it off and kept walking. Bear Browning was seated at one of the cable reel tables with Mike Ross. The day was already warm, Niels decided on Yoghurt and fruit, then joined them.

Niels and the Canadian discussed ideas to preserve the genetic potential of non-tropical forests and means by which intact cold-adapted forests might be conserved or re-created in other locations.

Then, finishing his soy latte, Mike said, "What are these *Don't Settle* tops I'm seeing? The World Tree images, the SLOJ shirts – I get where they're coming from."

Niels looked uncertain. Bear chuckled, "It's not a yggdrasil thing – they're fans of Kalinda – here for the music. You know: *Don't Settle* (*for just any him*), from her massive hit. Don't make me sing it! You guys are so unhip – it's amazing your skinny jeans don't fall off! My daughter, Miss Twelve, going on twenty is a devotee."

Niels nodded seriously, "I am not having the skinny jeans."

"Well, exactly."

Mike subtly pointed at a green-haired woman, "What about all those Tees with the topless female Buddha-like figure …"

This time Bear looked flummoxed.

"Ah," said Niels, "Jess mentions this – something about Jainism, yes. One of their … their prophets, their revered teachers – sorry, I don't know how to pronounce the word, may have been a woman."

"Huh," grunted Mike, "If we must have religion, may as well have an equal opportunity one."

Niels continued, "Ok, so it's the last day, the yggdrasil ambassadors should see as much as possible – try to make we humans look good, yes."

Mike and Bear nodded, sombre faced.

*

Meanwhile, Matt stood with Sif Acer looking at 3D printed homes of aerated cement and of recycled plastics, he fingered and sniffed a fungi mycelium composite brick; but his mind was on the T-shirts. *They're everywhere.*

He and the alien moved on to the low-tech mudbrick building demo. But Matt's mind drifted … *He was immensely proud of Kalinda and had fancied her almost at once. That he found her music a little too crafted and earnest was a view he never expressed to her: only to Paul, Lenny, and half a million viewers during the first weeks of CCE.*

Yet she'd *settled* for him. Of course, the hit single was different; it had the necessary *edge*. But the T-shirts, and there went the slogan again: plastered across a girl's chest; one surely too young for relationship worries. Being in a relationship with someone who wrote and sang about being in relationships is a complex, many-sided thing. Or as *his* new Tee said: *SLOJ.*

A woman approached Matt; with nothing across her chest – nothing except green body paint. With an effort, he noted she also sported antennae and a hibiscus behind her left ear.

"Matt Davis!" she pronounced in an Australian accent. "Can you sign my tits?"

"What! God no – do I *look* like a 90s rock star."

Sif Acer rustled and extended a delicate appendage towards her flower, "Matt Davis time now to attend the gardeners – or as self names them: plant persecutors."

The interloper's jaw dropped, and she scurried away.

Sif Acer advised, "May you prosper until the sun burns out."

"Thanks," Matt gave the alien a friendly pat.

*

Elsewhere, while the day was still young, Crystal greeted Jess with a hug.

"Ah, bugs," said Crystal. They perused the display of mealworms, crickets, and other segmented things for sale on the industrial and the 'home kit' scale. She snuffled the insect odours doubtfully.

The proprietor audibly crunched something many-legged.

Jess said, "Yes, things will have to get worse before I'll grow them myself."

"Actually, Jess, I've converted to Jainism – so no bugs for me," Crystal pulled her Mallinatha* T-shirt tight in affirmation.

"That's great Crystal – I've been kind of a secular Jain for a while. I—"

Further speech was briefly cut off, as Crystal squeaked and hugged Jess again.

Held in a firm, soft grip and looking over Crystal's shoulder, Jess resumed, "Oh, there's Kevin. Is he looking for you?"

Crystal turned, "Oh, he's talking to the algae wall panel guys – there's a whole building in Germany using them!"

---

* Mallinatha the 19th tirthankara or spiritual teacher is considered to have been born a woman in the Svetambar Jain tradition

"It's a real mix, isn't it," Jess waved her hand about: "new age philosophers fusing yggdrasil declarations with Gaia; algae bioreactors, Viking rune stones, mystical honeys, and the Jain info tent's packed."

The West was finally taking eastern philosophy seriously – rather than simply taking home a decorative Buddha garden feature or a plastic Ganesha.

"The *out there* stuff doesn't do any harm Jess, said Kevin joining them.

"Well sure, turtle-elephant-world-carrying is all very well, when not directly applied to Google Maps; but evidence-based please people: a cliché, but a damned good one … saves a lot of unnecessary dying."

"I don't know … it doesn't flow well," teased Kevin, "and it's too long to print on a T-shirt."

Oddly, science and its many comforts had so insulated some folks from the reality of nature that they'd rather lost contact with the nature of reality.

*

Hours of absorbed sunlight later … "Come, let us go be imbued with the spirit of the particles," said Matt in his best yggdrasil. The afternoon classical music session was about to start. People, their picnic blankets, and their new yggdrasil friends were heading for the grassed area.

"You know," reflected TK, "I played Tau Ulmus every type of music for more than a year, and nothing. No-thing, no interest."

"I didn't know that. Every type?" Matt queried; eyebrow raised.

"Oh yeah, every single genre since Ray Charles."

"Ah."

"Then your lady found the key."

"She's quite the package. I'll get us a couple of those shipwreck beers," said Matt.

"Say what?" laughed Tyson.

"It's okay, they're good, had one yesterday, 'Beer from wild gathered grains, for the modern paleo man who doesn't want to give up the amber fluid,'" recited Matt.

"I don't see no connection with wrecked ships."

"Ah, my man Hans grew yeast from beer he salvaged diving on an old shipwreck. Very cool."

"I'll check it out too."

As the two approached the makeshift bar with the battered dinghy suspended over it, female heads turned to look. Something about painting yourself green loosened the inhibitions of some ladies present. It was a struggle, but they advanced on the bar. Where they discovered Kevin and Crystal. The latter seemed to Matt inordinately excited about the evening concert.

Compared to others, Kevin was not a well-crafted man. As a metaphor – inexpertly assembled flat pack furniture came to mind. None-the-less as the group made their way, beers in hand, to the grassed area, he bounced with unaccustomed vitality. The casual yggdrasil onlooker – if a recent graduate of Ebony's pop-music-lyrics-metaphor-class might well have remarked: "That man's walking on sunshine!"

The Expo itself concluded earlier on the final day, swelling the audience for the afternoon classical concert. Matt sat with TK, a discrete distance from Kevin and Crystal. People were seated on the grass, on beanbags, and low-folding chairs. In the first small musical break an aghast TK pointed cautiously down the slight slope and to his right.

"Ah, the dread Agent returns," joked Matt.

His companion didn't think it a joking matter. Thirty yards closer to the stage stood his personal event horizon, Agent Peters. The latter looked at the concert audience – yggdrasil and human with disdain. He was the embodiment of another of life's inverse square laws: namely, the more a person desires power, the less suitable they are to wield it.

TK was too far away to hear the agent remark to a minion, "We need to test a single specimen with total deniability. Hand it over to the acoustic weaponry division; determine whether the music incapacitates it, then look at scaling up …"

At the next break, TK stood, "I'm outta here." Trailed by Matt, he retreated further from the area.

*

Other than the vicinity of Agent Peters, the expo site hummed with goodwill and hope; feelers and eyestalks were entwined with human hair – human wrists circled with extruded alien fibres. Entwined with Crystal, Matt doubted that Kevin saw them leave. The next classical piece started, and again, the yggdrasil waved their, appendages before settling into an enormous communal vibration. As if oversized upright grasshoppers were bees – instead of oversized upright grasshoppers. Wrapped around Crystal, the webmaster practically vibrated himself. How wrong his previous world view, where a night not spent eliminating virtual zombies, was a night wasted.

Safely repositioned and looking into the dipping sun, Tyson continued explaining his research to Matt. "Recordings of Bach, Mozart, Elgar, and all, were weaker than the same music played live. And" he continued, acknowledging a fan, "a single instrument – like your lady's Bach arrangement is less powerful than a full orchestra. It's all about the mix …"

Closer to the stage than Agent Peters stood Eir Nyssa and Sri Achras accompanied by their companion humans: Anne-Maree, her mom, and Bear Browning.

"Hey Sri, can you talk us through it. What goes down. Are you lost in the music or what?"

The alien craned its eyestalks towards its companion. "Pleasurable sensing of the wood-web sounds, the perfect-imperfect changing patterns, the rent in the fabric, the dissonance – it achieves the patternings most powerful."

Anne-Maree held one of Eir Nyssa's leaf-wings, swaying it back and forth. She whispered, conspiring, "It will be dark soon, and my brother will have to go back to the tent with daddy – but I'm big – I can stay up late!"

Eir Nyssa rippled its antennae at her.

*

Other than the food vans servicing the concert crowd, the Expo was winding down. Kalinda, Jess, and Niels followed the groups heading towards the stage rather than the exits. Rainbow coloured yggdrasil wings on otherwise green painted humans signalled the proximity of the Yggdrasil-Gay, Lesbian and Intersex, Alliance trailer. The aliens being hermaphrodites didn't lack for supporters. Mike was present, chatting as they packed away banners and bunting.

He wished Kalinda luck but said, "Sorry, things to do … contemporary pop is not my thing. I'm an unfashionable five minutes of wailing feedback-laden-guitar fan."

The three stopped to consider food options before the concert intermission.

"For real, you are selling a deep-fried zucchini in a hot dog bun? queried Niels, examining the chalkboard menu.

"Nice accent, by the way, but no man, those things sell themselves!"

"Half a dozen spring rolls, please."

Soon afterward, spotting Niels, the spring rolls, and the two-women, Matt waved them over. The first moth of the evening attacked the stage lights as Kalinda sat, cap pulled low, avoiding the scrutiny of human moths drawn to the light of her celebrity. Soon enough the sun descended until the low hanging cloud bands glowed and Kalinda set off for the backstage.

Time at last to hoist cell phones in the air. Girls and young women streamed towards the stage front – the mosh. Kalinda was to sing four or five of her female person empowering 'be true to yourself, be genuine, *Don't Settle*' slow ballads and upbeat pop songs.

The crowd both cheered and squealed, as near the end of the set Kalinda swapped the guitar for the smaller instrument. Yggdrasil didn't enter their immobile state with this music, but hundreds of them near the stage moved in imitation of human dancers.

The first verse of *Don't Settle* reached the chorus, with its now traditional audience response (calling on Australian pub rock** rather than gospel traditions) and a thousand voices sang "*No way*." Niels had never heard anything like it. Kalinda thanked the crowd and reminded them she'd be back to close the show with Tyson K.

The whooping was deafening.

Ah, might need a logarithmic scale, said Niels to himself.

His phone buzzed self-importantly, and Niels stood so Bear could find him. The promise of meeting Kalinda had prised his daughter from her friends' company and into the temporary orbit of her father. Unfortunately, the two reached the group just before the singer returned.

Where Bear compounding his crimes, saying, "Phoebe's only willing to be seen this close to her old Dad at a gig 'cause I lied and said I'd introduce her to Kalinda!" Fortunately, the songstress arrived post-haste, saving Bear from 'death by withering stare.'

Briefly standing in an otherwise seated-on-grass area, Niels had attracted attention.

"It's got to be the Kraken guy – he's just cut his hair."

"But it's all techno, EDM. There's no metal. They're not mentioned in the line-up."

"Well, there's weird shit happening man, and the Norsemen do love their yggies."

The last speaker, (you might have said) was living proof of his own statement. He had such extraordinary body hair that he was essentially covered when naked. As he was now – except for green paint. The last of the daylight made the surrounding patrons happy. He was putting them off their pumpkin kebabs.

** The thorough reader may care to peruse a ruder live version of *The Angels, Am I ever gonna see your face again?*

The exhibit wasn't entirely correct about the musical genres. There was one last act before the concluding ninety minutes of EDM, house, techno … call it what you will. Closer to the mosh, Kevin flinched; the wrinkled, grey-haired, but still feisty folk-rocker and his new band the Telemarketers had taken the stage. The youngsters in the mosh had been replaced. Zombies were back in his life – via the apocalypse, that is, the over sixties dancing on mass.

The older, responsibly sedate couple on the tartan rug in front of Niels and company had staying power.

"Are the yggdrasil enjoying it, do you think, dear?" she queried.

"Hmm, hard to know – but I believe so."

"The young people seem to be enjoying it."

"Are there drugs in the yoghurt, dear?"

Of course, there were.

Interestingly, people who baulked at ingesting gluten were chancing with the pharmaceutical offerings of their local clan lab. Ambulances arrived – and took away, as Sif Acer put it: "Humans sub-optimal on purpose."

"Nice line Sif," said Matt. Playing around with it in his whimsical creative way he came up with the perfect festival Tee: *I'm in the SOOP*

"Those babies," he said, "would sell themselves."

*

It was nearly time. There was a change of guard. Weary, sweaty revellers trudged back up the slight grassy hill.

"Should we?" said TK.

As he and Kalinda stood, nearby bead-laden nymphs squealed in recognition. Matt followed them and saw Kalinda divert to touch Crystal on the shoulder in passing.

It was crazy, of course, and it shouldn't work …

TK leapt on the stage like a lunching leopard on a gazelle. Dubstep roared from the enormous speakers. Worms felt the bass and retreated deeper into the earth. TK's meticulously researched, sampled, and tweaked Bach samplings wove in and out of the bass with mathematical looped precision. Of course, it shouldn't work, but the crowd was intent on making it so. Kalinda and the DJ had honed and refined the sound. He stood, moving fluidly, one headphone clamped to his ear. She danced across the stage, long dress flowing and played blistering violin riffs at the stars.

The older couple waved their pumpkin kebabs. Small children asleep in headphones and crumpled yggdrasil wing creations stirred in the parental lap.

And the audience found a way to dance together – people in lithe imitation of the yggdrasil and they in clumsy mimicry of humanity's echo of themselves.

Jess and Niels sat companionably close until Jess rose to her feet in a smooth movement. She tapped him lightly on the shoulder, her voice soft in the dark, "Come and dance Niels, you have to set an example."

*

TK thanked the audience. He thanked Bear's team, and all the volunteers from the expo. It was too dark for Matt to see his fiancée's eyes, but he knew they twinkled mischievously. She stepped up to the microphone. The volunteers at the stage front cheered as Crystal, dangling her ocarina from its leather thong, shyly made her way on stage.

Tootle, squeak, tootle, she began.

"Well, OK!" nodded Tyson K going with the flow. "Dance people!"

"He means everyone," Bear explained earnestly, "not just human people."

Shielding Anne-Maree from the chaos mathematics of the mosh Eir Nyssa remarked, "It's not how many leaf-wings a person has that makes a person a person," (apparently channelling Dr Seuss).

"We understand his thinkings a little. And the Viking," added Sri Achras.

"Dance," commanded the DJ with full authority and cool (*dance as though your lives depend on it*). And dance they did. And when it ended, many, overcome with emotion, wept.

On reflection, TK felt the ocarina didn't improve the sound. *That*, he thought, would be unlikely. But it didn't make it any worse.

Not so much at the time … when caught up with the emotion, the enthusiasm, the hope. But later, the more statistically minded realised the expo wasn't representative of the wider yggdrasil and human societies. Matt is his way, likened it to an alien assuming almost half the population were fellow left-handers: based on examination of the Australian cricket team.

Chapter 77 Tea and Toxins

"So, no longer on the couch?" asked Ash, full of womanly intrigue.

"Ah, no, I have taken Jess to the airport this morning."

"Shame, I missed her, but it was so late when I got back from the latest field trip."

Niels sat once more in the Retro Bean, where his yggdrasil-beverage-related talks seemed destined to occur. Downtown had changed since he'd first taken a position at the university four years previously. As any visitor could attest, the street was now well endowed with fast fruit chains, poultry veterinarians, Jain book shops and establishments selling home mushroom kits.

It was three weeks since their road trip, and they discussed 'catch up' matters: Ash's trip to collect flora samples from the edge of their climatic ranges; the success of the Expo, TK's new music – meeting TK!

Niels tapped the table experimentally. Management had replaced the aged timber chairs and tables with 1950s Laminex, vinyl cushions and their once fashionable accoutrements.

"And how are things here, Ashley?"

"Ah, as you know – the focus is coffee," (a glance at the bean-filled basket of the bike embedded in the counter would confirm this), "but tea's getting expensive."

"Yes, I am hearing of this." He sipped his cappuccino, *but it's not keeping me up at night.*

"Well, it's been expensive with whatever happened in China after the forest wars, but now it's being affected in India." Ash paused and waved her finger, "Now, I've never seen you drink it, but tea's important stuff, we might not be here without it," she teased.

"Oh," said Niels doubtfully, running his hand through his clipped hair.

"Well, obviously! No tea, no Boston Tea Party, no American Revolution – maybe I'm not here, you're not here … or I have a cute British accent," she mused.

"Ah, alternative timeline-universe stuff of speculation, is it now?"

"Sorry, professor," she said in a faux-meek voice. "It's the *grey-area* leafy vegetable dilemma again, isn't it – how much harm is done plucking fresh growth from a tea bush or a lettuce? It seems every yggdrasil has a different opinion."

As did every human: a topic much discussed at workplace water coolers across the nation. Experts estimated the 'balance point' was now exceeded – there were more yggdrasil on the planet than humans. But they were less common in urban settings and tended not to enter homes and gardens unless egregious plant harm occurred in plain view.

Or as Ash put it, "Provided you're not flaunting that whole 'secateurs don't trim trees, people trim trees attitude' they ignore the small stuff."

An indeed, over time the number of Corvallis residents who attacked an extra-terrestrial over gardening matters had steadily diminished in line with both the laws and guidelines of natural selection. "Sure, tea is less, err … essential nutrition than the veggies," Ash continued, "but still, Niels … all that cultural history."

An evergreen plant from East Asia and related to the now 'feared to prune' garden Camellia; tea leaves have been recovered from Emperors' tombs well before the current era. Grown perhaps medicinally at first, tea became a recreational beverage in China; later smuggled to Europe in crates of Pekinese dogs; by the seventeenth century becoming popular in Britain, then its colonies … finding its way to Corvallis by the long route.

"So, anyway Niels, the warming-resistant food crops research is taking off?"

"All over the Congress countries – money pouring in. The Dean, he smiles broadly.

"Some research had already started in this speciality?"

"For sure Ashley – but it's a difficulty, yes: governments funding research when also denying the need for that research!"

"And in the same labs as the forest conservation stuff," said Ash.

He nodded and dismembered a blueberry muffin, "Blurring the lines where possible. It will put the ambassadors in a difficult position if they learn of our food plant breeding technologies and purposes."

Ash peered at him over her tea, "It was awesome to meet the ambassadors and talk to yggdrasil at the expo." In a soft, serious tone, Ash continued, "I've been away, but Andrew says, no effect on the alien cell lines," her hand made the discrete frog-hopping signal.

Niels paled, "At first it was partly, err scientific curiosity, but I'm more and more uncomfortable with this potential genocide. But it's clever you two have been able to grow the cells lines again."

Ash nodded grimly.

"Still, if things with the yggdrasil go well, then …" Niels shrugged and trailed off – perhaps morally ambiguous, secret research on potential alien weaknesses was less a priority than tea.

Chapter 78 The Sentinels

Illuminated by the glow of the computer screen and surrounded by energy drinks, the semi-nocturnal Kevin edited the most recent 'Showing humans in a positive light tour.'

Earlier, Mir Arauca and Jess had journeyed south, collecting Matt first …

*

The pod materialised in the Melbourne street. Jess and the alien climbed the few steps. Where they stood regarding the giant clam at the top; the one replete with indestructible succulents and the odd beer can.

Jess – conscious of a curious, early morning crowd gathering, and with a sportive look in her eyes, said, "Mir, can you park the pod on the other side of his door?"

Knowing the householder to be a sound and thorough sleeper, she left the alien to examine the many curious artefacts in the comedian's mancave.

Meanwhile, she clattered deliberately and noisily upstairs. The visitor rapped on the bedroom door, "Matt, it's me, Jess Kelly."

"Yeah, come in, mate." He was sitting clothed, other than footwear, on the bed's edge.

"Bit late sorry. Biggish night with the boys."

"I'll meet you downstairs, don't forget – warm clothes, light clothes, hat …"

"Yeah, ta, all over it!"

He descended the Perspex stairs minutes later and called, "Err, how did you get in?" Followed by, "C'mon Jess, you know the rule – no playing with the aliens *inside*." For he had discerned an alien pod materialised through the whack-a-mole table.

"Greetings Matt Davis."

"Err, hello, Mir," Matt fingered his scar. With shocking co-opted familiarity, it proffered an appropriately sized appendage for him to shake.

"Have we got time for a coffee?" queried the taken-aback, still sluggish comedian. "Is Niels about?"

Jess shook her head impatiently, "Go on then. How've things been since the expo?" (a month had passed) "Are you and Kal still considering a farm?"

"Yeah, but not near her parents' place." He took a sip of instant emergency coffee. "It's always: *Are you still living in sin?*"

"And we're not – we're just practicing."

Matt shuddered and glanced at the yggdrasil. It was busy – its claws snagged in the shaggy, hyper-acrylic football team rug. He added two more faded sachets of sugar.

"You're still using then?"

"Emergency mate."

"Well Matt, if you're serious – there's land next to my parents' place for sale. Bottom's fallen out of the cane industry a bit," explained Jess deadpan.

*

And so, the trio departed, pausing only while Mir Arauca instructed Matt on correct succulent maintenance. Before long – except at three o'clock the previous day – they arrived in Central Park as arranged. Where they met Mike Ross and the locals: Ebony, Anne-Maree, Eir Nyssa and the afore-mentioned Kevin himself. With the minimal difficulty of a contemporary seven-year-old, Anne-Maree entered their destination into a be-tendrilled human-friendly yggdrasil navigation device.

For Matt, the spatial and temporal leap from early morning, wintry Melbourne to California in summer and at altitude, was a testing one.

"Trees again," he noted astutely. "Good call not to bring the longboard Jess."

The group wandered the Methuselah Grove Trail. To prevent vandalism, the very oldest of the grove's bristlecone pines, at just a few birthdays short of five-thousand years, were unmarked. The two yggdrasil sank their clawed feet into the scrubby earth, deploying their mysterious ground antennae and identified 'The Methuselah.'

Jess was well prepared and began, "So, the oldest, non-clonal trees in the world …"

The sun beat on the visitors, their hats, and as it had for so very, very long, on the trees themselves. Matt tried his search engine – but to no avail. He replaced his sunglasses and peered critically at a tree ... *it looks half-dead and exhausted.* Tough, durable, twisted, scraggly, and sun-bleached – just not entirely impressive, as their relatives in the far north would agree.

As Kevin was to find, later editing the footage: Time is an elusive concept where pod travel is concerned. Let us just say that over the next few hours, the party *travelled.* The pod scrunched the fabric of space-time as it skipped across the world; both following its rotation, and not; alternating desert and tropics; dawn and dusk.

Together they saw, admired, and contemplated:

Scandinavia's *Old Tjikka* clone: A Norway spruce with roots dated at nine-thousand years. Which, as Eir Nyssa reminded the human group: "These the 'brain', the tree essence."

Utah's *Pando Clone* of quaking aspen: Spread over an extraordinary hundred acres and with forty-seven thousand individual tree trunks linked underground. The roots of 80 000 years. Mir Arauca said, "This be elder than self: most ancient living thing on blue planet."

Oaxaca, Mexico's *Montezuma cypress*: With its government-funded well and safely re-routed road. Here they mingled with dozens of other admirers, yggdrasil and human.

Tanzlinde in Peesten, Germany: The Dance Linden. Where tradition has it, people cannot but tell the truth. They further visited the doll's house cute medieval town of Fritzlar that had so delighted Anne-Maree. Where the warden tree tradition had revived, and locals brought offerings to the aged oaks and their yggdrasil companions.

And the pod had swept through Asia, meeting trees, their protectors, and admirers:

In India, they saw neem trees dressed in cloth, a manifestation of the goddess; trees associated with Jain temples; Hindu ascetics meditating under Sacred Figs. Then to Sri Lanka to view the *Sri Maha Bodhi* – the oldest living human-planted tree. And in Japan: the child-giving ginkgo at Tokyo's Zoshigaya Kishimojin temple – gorgeous, soft, and peaceful, but with a dark mythic past.

Then finally to Iran: To admire *Sarv-e Abarqu,* the 'Zoroastrian' cypress. At four thousand years, the oldest tree in the Middle East; a living entity that had experienced the nearby dawn of human civilisations.

Matt staggered from the pod. Like someone: a) finding god(s), or b) space-time ill. To be clear: it was the latter, though he was in the right area for the former.

The group had reached its travel limit. Kevin held the camcorder in his lap, pointed and hoped; Anne-Maree had lost her bounce. The yggdrasil moved off to communicate with the tree: Eir Nyssa with insectoid poise and Mir Arauca like a damaged wind-up toy.

"There are still Zoroastrians, right?" asked Matt, pale and crouched on the ground clutching a sports drink. Pod-travel still scrambled their phones, but Mike was well read.

"Yes, but few and mostly in India – the Parsees. You've heard of the singer Freddy Mercury? We were born in the same year. Anyway, his parents were of that faith. I might add, from the little I understand, tree worship isn't part of it. It's the first of the one-god, the monotheistic faiths."

He continued, warming to a theme, "Of course, Christians and Muslims regard tree worship as idolatry – that's why the interfering Christian so-called saint cut down Thor's Oak near the German town we visited earlier.

"Doesn't Jesus like trees?" Anne-Maree asked her mom, concerned.

"Jesus loves trees and plants and animals," Ebony assured her daughter.

In another situation, Matt might have said, "Yeah, wouldn't be too sure of that – especially after all that 'nailing to one' business."

But he was not, as often supposed – a complete idiot.

Jess stood, wobbled, and collected her thoughts. They proved elusive, wriggling, and squirming in a soup of pod-nausea. She gathered them and gave them a good talking to. With the mighty Sarv-e Abarqu in the background, she spoke to the camera of humanity's regard for the trees they had visited. Of their cultural, religious and scientific significance …

"Regrettably in the past we people ended the lives of countless trees in mere moments. But we also preserved others through scores of short human lives."

Mike didn't mind a bit of indigenous tree-related myth – especially if it strengthened the case for a conservation argument. However, he found preservation of notable trees solely through religious connotations distasteful and said so.

"Preservation of trees, sacred groves, entire forests because the ancients believed they were a god or a pathway to salvation is all very well," he began with the aliens now returning within presumed 'earshot'. "But it's important to preserve and respect forests not because of associated fairy stories, but *in their own right*. That's the true mark of humanity's regard for the trees."

Mir Arauca *was* within earshot. It arranged its eyestalks at everybody and said, "Question: Self has seen hundreds human religion-beliefs rise and be mislaid. Correction: past-forgotten. Is permissible criticise ancient religions? Deceased religions? Current-self religions, current non-self-beliefs, by what means a person chooses from multitude?"

"Excellent questions Mir," said Jess. "But perhaps for another time, Dad always says, 'Don't discuss religion, politics, and sex with people you don't know well. Or even alien-beings' – at least in public." She sighed wearily, "It's getting late in New York, but can we do one last thing when we arrive ... they're keeping the museum open late for us."

To herself, she said, *how nice it might be to run a donkey sanctuary*.

As noted earlier, humans like to name things. Not only this, but to measure and argue about those named, measured things. For readers presenting 'alternative facts' in the ancient tree category, the narrator suggests they take up the matter with the next yggdrasil to visit our blue planet.

Chapter 79 MoMA

"Legit!" exclaimed Matt.

They exchanged desert and tropical locations for the gleaming floor of the New York Museum of Modern Art after closing time. The craft itself, with its aesthetic of the grown, and the manufactured, would have been at home, abandoned in one of the museum's galleries.

The director appeared and welcomed *all* her visitors. Clad in neutral black and white, she contrasted with the energy of the paintings. Discrete lighting glinted on wire-framed spectacles and name tag as Ms Rantall enthused, "The exhibition has an additional thirty important paintings on loan, joining MoMA's collection of the world's most popular artist ..."

The clawed feet of the yggdrasil and the heels of their guide echoed eerily in the empty galleries.

"This is so cool," said Matt, "I always loved *Night At The Museum* – mind you, had to hide behind the couch when I first saw it."

The director smiled primly, "We rather lack for dinosaurs in *this* museum, Mr Davis."

The private tour began …

"Painting triptychs and diptychs as we see here, Van Gogh presented nature itself in the tradition of religious art. He had, of course, a religious calling and in his illness a mania. Here," she explained with a flowing arm, "is the artist developing a form of nature worship. One that still resonates."

She strode to the next wall and continued, "Influenced, as well documented, by Japanese art, the artist was driven to paint trees in blossom ... and here we have assembled ten of fourteen fruit tree canvasses painted in a single month."

Heels, then claws clattered, "And for the first time, side by side, two versions of *The Sunflowers* – one of Earth's most recognisable cultural artefacts."

The group lingered, chatting in hushed museum tones. With their multiple eyes, the yggdrasil pair stood together, viewing all the paintings simultaneously. Jess approached them touching Mir Arauca on its hard-waxy carapace, "I felt it was important to show you and through you, your comrades, the importance of trees, flowers, plants and nature, in the art of Earth's favourite artist."

"Thank-you, Jess Kelly," said Mir Arauca, wrapping a leaf-wing around her. "Interesting this, to view the fractal whorls of elemental particles; in air, in living branches; trapped in pigment by human mind-hand. Most excellent."

Chapter 80 Ahimsa Meat

"Sif Acer, you recall the *ahimsa* meat display at the expo – where Sri Achras is the colonisation consultant."

"Affirmative, yes."

"It's important to show both our kinds what's possible with that technology."

The leaf-creature twitched, "Demonstrate meat consumption without reproduction." The turn of phrase seemed to please the yggdrasil – it shimmered its feelers at Niels.

"Err right, that: 'it never died – it was never born aspect.' And also to show willingness to reduce meat's impact on plant and water resources."

"Self comprehends."

After discussions, Eir Nyssa decided to represent the yggdrasil, and Ebony volunteered to record proceedings and publish on her blog. This left Kevin free to film the latest alien-compliant tech expo (already the tenth since the first. Green paint sales were booming). Kevin's brother had returned from Europe, where he had evidently, not after all, been captured by an Eastern European internet-troll factory. He was tired and dispirited and soon noticed Kevin had enough good spirits for both.

"Something's different," he mused. "Have you discovered girls?"

Niels' preference for accurate statements was rubbing off on Kevin.

"Huh," he began with scorn. "I discovered them years ago. Unfortunately, until recently, they just didn't reciprocate." He straightened his shoulders, "You're in charge of the frogs. Don't stuff up, bro."

Consequently, when the pod reshaped space-time, and the group emerged in mid-afternoon Berlin, Kevin was absent – reciprocating with Crystal, at an expo outside the Spanish-tiled wonder that is Santa Barbara.

*

The cellular agriculture research was housed in an unlovely industrial suburb. It had absorbed neighbouring factories whose products were no longer required: laminated timber chairs, wood heaters, sisal-macramé wall hangings. It wasn't a location where yggdrasil would care to linger. Although, a street vendor's potato cart rusting in a tree attested to a former, unhappy presence.

Expected and admitted, they readily spotted Dr Ditterich in a crowd of similarly lab-coated types by his white-blonde hair and physique. The entire party (Niels, Allan, Matt, Ebony, Ann-Maree, and Eir Nyssa) had met him before at the first Expo.

"... The lab process is relatively simple. Production is just a question of scale and cost. It's ten years since the first *in vitro* or cultured burger. But as we know, economies have been affected in recent times," he said evenly, glancing at the alien.

"Mom! Look at the cows and sheep. They're on a boat!" Anne-Maree pointed to the walls.

"Yes, they are," agreed the big scientist. "When we started, the workers put them up as a reminder." He nodded at large framed images of crowded battery chickens, intensively farmed pigs, and unhappy ruminants off for an unexpected cruise on the high seas. "I said to Niels in America, when we began this, we intended making a high-end product for the environmentally conscious."

"And not to make money?" said Allan.

"Oh yes, to make money. And now we retail pork, chicken, tuna, and beef."

"All those different meats?" said Ebony. "My gosh, I had no idea."

"Long ago, Winston Churchill said, 'Why grow a complete chicken just for the breast meat, the wing …'"

"Possibly considering more the efficiencies, rather than the: 'It was never born, and so it never died' concern of those interested in animal rights," suggested Allan, grandly.

"Perhaps so," agreed their guide.

"It may come to this cultured meat or otherwise, Niels' washed-up-whale favourite," said Matt, playfully.

Karl was uncertain, the Scandinavians, he considered, *were* prone to eat some odd things. He shook his head, "I don't understand."

"Well, you know, *eating meat isn't the issue – killing is the issue*. So, we tuck into pumpkins and nuts – while we wait for an outbreak of Sturgeon Gill Rot Syndrome. Then, oh boy, it's caviar for all."

Karl clapped his hands, "I understand. However, here we're not concerned with either the practicalities or the abstractions of that situation. So, to the tour …"

The group passed through a series of laboratories: gleaming with plastic, glass, stainless steel and pride.

"Here, we select the fast-growing starter cells: stem cells or alternatives from fish, chicken, beef. For the mammals, now using umbilical cord cells, negating the expense and ethics around Foetal Bovine Serum," the guide added, glancing at Allan. He continued, waving his arms at mysterious equipment, "The bioreactors grow tens of thousands of litres of culture, and then finally, the scaffolding procedure, depending on what form the meat takes."

Karl turned and faced the group, while Ebony took more photos.

"I believe the ideal of producing the perfect steak replica is trivial … we grow the protein yes, we can add in fat – even healthier oils – but for mass consumption in mince form, this isn't important. And compared to some meat farming that uses twenty litres of water to grow a gram of steak, we use much less water and one percent of the land. Perhaps," he said, with a glance at the light gatherer, "without such tech we will be looking at the radishes from underneath."

Niels nodded, and addressing Eir Nyssa for the benefit of the camera, said, "And we can grow micro-algae in similar reactors – so both plant and animal protein may be grown without killing multi-cellular life."

"Cool. It's kind of sloppy, kinda runny, observed Matt. You can imagine a row of dispensers at a café: you've got your soft serve lobster, your avocado slurry dispenser, your coffee dispenser …"

The Frenchman threw up his hands, "Never," he said. "Never," he repeated, waggling a finger at the Australian, "will I drink coffee from such a machine!"

Matt laughed and detached himself from the group. Niels was squinting now at a dish of grown muscle fibres. "So," said Matt, changing deftly to his intended subject. "Is anything happening with you and Jess. She visited the uni in Oregon, yeah? Seriously … it's like watching algae grow – but slower."

Matt waited in vain for a response … *ah*, he mused, *the confused look of a cow on a boat.*

Chapter 81 Going Nuclear

As the seasons changed in Melbourne – football giving way to cricket – not everyone approved of conciliation attempts between humans and yggdrasil.

The local expos had been successful and DIY egg, mushroom, algae, even insect production had exploded. Those fortunate to have a traditional quarter-acre block filled them with greenhouses. It was becoming unpatriotic not to have a roof fruit garden atop a corporate building.

A compromise was reached where aliens would not stand light-gathering on sporting fields – when said fields were in use. This, an important consideration in the self-proclaimed sporting capital of the world. Where the city museum's chief treasure is a famously nobbled racehorse.

Even so, certain folk wanted to take their bat and ball and go home. Among them, former footballer, *CCE* contestant and radio personality Graeme O'Brien. Like cheap wine abandoned in the rubber plant, at the end of financial year party, he grew sourer with time.

Although an advocate of the 'burn the forests threat' and hence contributing to the forest wars, the loss of the internet, and attacks on horticulture – his popularity remained unscathed within particular demographics. Many were an older audience prone to perspective loss on matters such as migrants, crime rates, migrant crime rates, and shark attack frequencies. Others, of a reproductive age, spent their evenings devising new spelling variants for children's names (Brewce, Feeowna, Brooce, Fiohna …).

O'Brien had instigated the anti-yggdrasil protests marking the deaths of Kat and Tayla, held at the local Botanical Gardens. The anniversary had been recently observed, pictures of the beautiful dead girls paraded, and some palm trees and succulents vaguely threatened.

Former *CCE* colleagues followed O'Brien on social media – as one would want to know the whereabouts of an unwanted possum marauding through the roof space. Mariam Turner loathed him with a passion. She awaited the moment he'd cast aside his earthly exterior and reveal his infernal origins.

As Matt put it to Kalinda discussing their ex-colleague's latest headline, "Kal, he's not actually evil, not as such," he grinned, "it's just that he believes if every kid had a paper round, played more sport and their parents made a genuine attempt to agree with him – the world would be a far better place."

"He wasn't *especially* awful to me on *Celebrity Congress*."

"Well sweetie, you were the poster girl for Christian rock at one time."

Kalinda rolled her eyes.

As clear from tweets, the shock jock's supporters generally had a reading age of ten. This, mused Matt, might explain the support for O'Brien's latest cause – one that doubled down on the failed forest-fire strategy of two years earlier.

The modern celebrity and CEO trend of launching apology tours when career lowlights couldn't be concealed, wasn't this radio stalwart's way.

O'Brien's new whim (borrowed from conservative US counterparts – where all the best whims come from), and presently reducing Matt's relaxation level, was the so-called nuclear option. The beauty of the idea was twofold: if the blasts didn't wipe out the aliens, then the sunless nuclear winter that followed surely would. Or at least induce them to leave. Additionally, although rarely stated, the destruction of every living thing on the surface without access to a bunker would handily rid the world of people who disapproved of bunker owning.

Chapter 82 Greenhouse

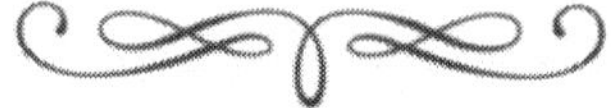

From Corvallis to Cairns, and places between, our heroes considered their next broadcast.

"Something new that shows we people-types as caring, vegetally aware beings," as Matt put it.

"We could visit Uncle Jim's rehab centre for abandoned houseplants. It's local," suggested Ebony.

"Maybe, but I was thinking something with a bigger scope – reduced land-use implications," said Jess.

"Per capita, or per acreage, one of those …" Niels tried to recall, "Holland's small land area supports a valuable agricultural sector. An impressive example of efficient land use based on high-tech greenhouse tech."

"How *do* the yggdrasil feel about greenhouses, I wonder?" said Ebony.

"Seem pretty keen on making the entire world one," commented Matt, toying with his phone.

"In South Australia," said Jess, "high-tech greenhouses are being built in coastal desert land. We could ask Mir to come and have a look with us."

"Road trip," suggested Matt. "Do you reckon Kal can come? Put some of the old *CCE* group back together, eh?"

Ebony had an important algae-tech clothing range meeting but was confident in surrendering her offspring's care to Kevin and the Australian women (mostly the latter). For her part, Anne-Maree was keen to be surrendered and meet a kangaroo (and a quokka).

*

Driven north from Port Lincoln, the child peered about hopefully for quokkas.

"Sorry, Anne-Maree," explained Jess, "Sad news on the quokka front – wrong part of the country."

Nether-the-less the three Australians (Jess, Mat, and Kalinda), the New York contingent and Niels were in fine spirits as twenty-three shades of red ochre landscape flashed by – the sea on their right. Forty minutes later, their quarry: fifty hectares of greenhouses and solar panels rose out of the desert.

Kevin recorded this first enterprise without Mir Arauca. It would meet them later in Port Augusta. Beating away the dust and flies, the party discovered their guide, "Jacko," was a well-spoken, managerial type – not the rugged farmer of legend.

"They're giant" pointed Ann-Maree.

The greenhouse cucumber and tomato plants were enormous – dwarfing the humans as they walked the internal roads prowled by service vehicles.

Jacko explained, "The solar power desalinates the seawater, heats the greenhouses in winter, powers the lights. We get twenty times more fruit per acre compared to standard field farms, the temperature, humidity, the lighting is optimised for year-round production."

Questions were asked, some more astute than others.

"So, do you play music to them? Maybe a little Guns N' Roses, Savage Garden, err Kate Bush–"

Kalinda applied the fiancé poking finger.

Later, the trip continued; the group relieved to be in the air-conditioned minivan after the heat of the desert and greenhouse. Of kangaroos, there were many – but disappointingly, smashed and scattered across the road edges. Likewise, flying insects shattered against the vehicle's windscreen. Jess began using the vehicle's internet connection to source happier kangaroo encounters.

Matt drove them through kilometres of flat desert landscape before pointing at mysterious distant structures, "What on Earth's that?"

They soon discovered the structures were not of the Earth.

At a dust-stained cluster of port-a-cabins (one of the area's less enticing tourist accommodations), the Department of Guarding Things and Reassurance personnel, were comically surprised to see the famous visitors arrive by hire vehicle. The guards had no idea what they were guarding and from whom. But, for those who'd been on the Siberian trip, there were obvious parallels. Jess still had a level of Australian security clearance, and she made a call.

Niels leaned into the front seats. He glanced at Matt, then at Jess – close enough to catch a hint of perfume and whispered, "Do you think someone should stay here with Anne-Maree?"

"I want to come," said the little voice from the backseat.

"Anne-Maree," said Jess, "We told your Mum we'd visit greenhouses and kangaroos," she added brightly. "We didn't say anything about this," she waved her hand at the mysterious *this*.

"Yeah, kiddo, no Museums of Food Allergies and Household Poisons either," said Matt.

"I still want to come," chirped the child

With shrugs and covert glances, the adults conceded. Matt waved to the guards and drove the rutted track towards the sea – towards the black tendrilled network of technology the yggdrasil wove from atmospheric carbon dioxide. The landscape was altered. Nearer the sea and the hub of the pipe-tendrils, flashes of the bare ochre soil grew rarer and new growth covered the land. Several light-gatherers stood waiting. Only their eyestalk movement showed reaction to the vehicle.

Matt halted the van thirty metres away.

By silent consent, Niels opened the sliding van door and walked towards the aliens. "Greetings-hello, I am called Niels Larsson. May we speak." The sun hammered down on the Swede and on the timeless landscape. There was a timeless, nervous pause. More of the yggdrasil approached, consulting silently.

One opened and closed its leaf wings and rippled its antennae.

"Err, hello, can you speak?" asked Niels. "Do you have a phone?" *What an odd thing to say to an alien. Should I ring Sif Acer? Can I contact Mir Arauca?* he wondered … *best not to just walk up to you and try to insert my phone inside your carapace.*

A yggdrasil with textured lower limbs used one to scratch something in the earth… "No," it read.

'Ah,' thought Niels. He turned to see Jess approaching. She brushed his arm and faced the alien group. (Meanwhile, in the van Matt said, "What's going on with those two?" Kalinda applied the poking finger again.)

"May I ask what your technology is for," Niels said, spreading his arms.

"Water desert," he read, scratched into the ground. The alien used another limb to erase that:

"Favour light-gatherers, favour forest."

"So, you're desalinating the ocean?" guessed Jess.

"Yes," they read. The creature added: "Re-forest south continent."

More of the yggdrasil came to observe the humans as the communication continued.

*

Later, resuming the northward drive, Niels explained, "Essentially they are adding water to land that has abundant light and heat – like a greenhouse."

Kevin, through his website, had heard reports of this landscape tinkering before, "Do you know what they're doing with the salt?" he asked.

Jess gazed across at Niels, now trying his hand at driving on the wrong side of the road. Her hazel eyes shone with wonder, "They said they were feeding it to the sun."

Kalinda and Matt had now discovered local kangaroo viewing options. Turning from the main road into a town, one of those 'reality versus internet map anomalies' developed. After driving around in a dusty and desultory manner, Niels spotted a couple of skinny teens.

They beamed as they recognised Kalinda and climbed into the van, eager to guide the group to the wildlife carer's property. *Impressive*, thought Jess – as no Aussie male had stopped and asked for direction since the ill-fated Bourke and Wills expedition had passed by*.

Eventually, the group dragged Anne-Maree (and Kevin) away from the kangaroos and pouch joeys hanging in coloured cloth bags from doorknobs. The party greeted Mir Arauca in Port Augusta. Farmworkers stood about admiring the Ygg-tech: with its fins, hatches, and weird alien engine noise, it looked a little like an alien spaceship and rather more like a super-sized tropical fruit. The yggdrasil complimented the workers on the quality of the local sunshine. Everyone agreed it was splendid. That's why the ever-expanding greenhouses were so sited (and using the infrastructure of a deceased coal-fired power station). Mir Arauca playfully covered Anne-Maree in leaf wings.

"Enough mirrors here to keep you happy, dear?" teased Kalinda (who considered her fiancée spent longer in the bathroom than she).

The foreman smiled at this, "Yeah, CST: that's concentrated solar thermal sure uses a lot of mirrors." He brushed away a fly keen to renew acquaintances, "The mirrors focus the sunshine – we've got a lot of that too," he drawled, "onto the tower, heating super saline water. And that, folks, is how we generate electricity."

To reduce disease transmission risks, the human visitors dressed in protective clothing and viewed a single five-hectare tomato-vine greenhouse. Strolling through it Niels commented, "Like farming in the sea or the productivity of a mature forest, greenhouses use the three-dimensional space," (as the tomato vines towering above them like a strange domestic jungle could attest).

* One of those 19 men and a boat set off to cross the desert colonial adventures.

The novelty of the protective suit was wearing off. Anne-Maree jiggled about as their guide explained the reduced land area, water, and fertiliser input advantages. From behind his camcorder, Kevin said, "It's amazing to grow this in the desert, and the environmental impact is so much less …"

The group murmured, and Kalinda fixed Mir Arauca with an enquiring look, "These are all fruits, of course, but what do yggdrasil think about this high-tech level of control over plants?"

Matt turned to the alien, "Yeah, right. Nice science, but kind of the battery chicken equivalent for salad?"

"There is complexity of issues. These be short-lived light foragers; their song lacks intricacy. Yet, comrades may negative approval."

"Well, if these plants were outside the greenhouse here, they'd be dead," said Kevin defensively.

"Affirmative-yes. Yet comrades say, 'greenhouse the Earth.'"

*

Seconds after the tour ended, Anne-Maree was back in New York.

As Ebony tucked her into bed just before midnight, she asked, "What was the best bit, darling?"

"The kangaroos," came the sleepy reply.

Chapter 83 Opening Night

Tyson K's fame had spread. He still played at raves and dance parties, at festivals and clubs, and in abandoned Fulfilment Centres. But tonight, Halloween, he opened his *own* club. TK reclined on one of the avocado-green couches that lined three sides of the dance floor. An assistant approached, bending close enough to be heard over the thumping music, and the DJ smiled in the changeable light.

Even inside the limousine, the excited whooping made Kevin's heart race. Kalinda had stepped from the vehicle to the sidewalk. The New Yorker joined her and the other celebrities. Mere metres away, the mass of patrons waited for admittance behind plush red cords. On the street, prowling cars slowed, adding competing rhythms to the cacophony within. Hearing aid-dispensing audiometrists smirked.

Crystal squeezed Kevin's hand, and they were ushered behind Matt, Niels and Kalinda into the cavernous dance hall with its sense-confounding mirrors and lights. Crystal released him as their host stood and loped towards them. TK grinned widely, draped an arm around Kevin's shoulder and steered the group through a door guarded by a huge Samoan. They entered the haven of the VIP bar. Kevin snared a passing drink. *I've reached peak cool.* He sipped and watched Tyson K direct activities as minions flitted past.

"This Congress thing – which none of us volunteered for …" TK was saying, "Niels's got his science stuff, Matt got his, well his, lightening the mood stuff. Me, you know I been working on the music, building bridges that way. Had some help, yeah." He dialled up the charm and smiled at Kalinda.

The songstress acknowledged this, put her hand on Matt's shoulder and said, "This one's planning to go back to uni – and study science this time."

"Whoa! What next – Niels taking up the guitar," joked TK.

"You've been working on other projects too, collaborations with Silicon Valley, yeah?" said Kevin, muffled by Crystal's soft portions, as she leaned across him to apply a congratulatory hug to Matt.

"Lots o' projects man," TK nodded, "you're thinking the VR cap?"

"Yeah, keen to test one."

"Early days, friend."

"I thought there'd be more yggdrasil here," said Kevin, puzzled.

"They'll be here, Tau Ulmus put the word out. They can land on the roof and enter the dance floor that way." Observing the puzzled looks, he continued, "Not the one next door, got a real special one. Unique," he added, drawing out the word.

"Is my girl gonna play?"

Kalinda flicked back her hair and peered at him, head tilted, "Do you have a violin?"

"Come see …"

*

The stars and city shone through the transparent roof – failing to illuminate the groomed, trace element-enhanced dance floor. That was the job of the strobe lighting and B grade monster-movie images projected on the walls. And in the gaps of space and time Kevin saw that beings of every ethnicity and species danced on … grass.

Tyson K's gear sat on the flat-topped mound. He surveyed the crowd, turning dials, adjusting equalisers, toying with keys, tinkering and improvising.

Balance was all.

Get it wrong and part of the crowd slowed: the leaf-creatures into their communal vibratory hum; the humans into the uncertainty of rhythm confusion. The air was thick with the sweat of the loose-limbed, with drugs, alcohol, and perfumes – the human component in every type of dress and *un*dress.

Drumbeats subsided. Bass looped around sampled trills of classical timbered instruments, swelling the sound, soaring … building in tension; assaulted now with staccato urban soundscapes: modems, alarms, shouted slogans, traffic … gunshot. Then the drop: Bass roared back in. Leaf wings and arms pumped the air. Together. The dancers bumping, bouncing … entwined.

Tyson K Whitney, saving the world, one dance party at a time.

Chapter 84 Progress Reports

"… and through there the seed collection wings," motioned Niels. "Just here on the left the mycology lab, the yggdrasil remain uninteresting in the soil fungi."

"Who'd have thought," murmured Matt.

"And ahead," Niels continued, proudly and pushing on the double doors, "our …"

Very weird giant terrarium for the sports adverse, thought Tyson (or thoughts to that effect). Big Jobe, who hadn't risked exercise since his mother had perished in a tragic badminton accident, waved to the lab-tour group.

"They can't hear us unless we push the intercom button. It's a high-security negative air pressure lab," explained Niels as they viewed more human exhibits, undertaking mysterious tasks with multi-welled trays and culture media.

"What've you got in there? Incriminating photos of Riya Bedi," quipped Matt, "or people you've made green. Yeah, I bet that's it!"

Niels raised an eyebrow, "Ah, perhaps that's the solution to racism – if everyone is green, I am meaning."

The comedian shook his head*, that's about as likely as you using the continuous tense properly*. He said, "Nah – it'd be all: she's light green, he's dark green – they're a bunch of cactuses."

Niels was serious in an instant, "Yes, probably Matt." He paused, "Such research is well beyond our scope here."

TK nodded to the stocky heavyweight with the greying, close-cut hair. He walked a few more paces and stopped short, adjusting his knit cap at an infinitesimally more rakish angle.

"Who," he inquired (without taking his eyes from the lab-coated vision of womanly loveliness), "is that?" He shook his head in wonder, "I can see why you keep her locked in a big glass box, Doc. She can't hear us, right?"

That was true. However, it was obvious to Ash she was being discussed.

Pointedly not looking at TK, she smiled at Niels.

"That's Ash, you met briefly at the first expo," Jess reminded him.

"I musta been real distracted, 'cause I never seen no foxy lady scientists before."

"Gee, thanks," said Jess.

TK forced his eyes from the lab-coated vision. He fixed Jess with the full force of his charisma and threw up his hands in surrender.

"Sorry," he shook his head, "so—"

"I'll get over it," she assured him.

"We should just leave Tyson here with popcorn," said Mike Ross drolly.

As they entered the rapid crop breeding area, Niels reminded Kevin not to film this lab.

"Here, they hope to grow five or six generations of the chickpea, wheat or maize annually. This compares with only two for field crops. The heat and light manipulate the flowering more rapidly, speeding the reproduction cycle. Mainly they look for traits of heat and drought tolerance."

With a look to include Jess, he explained similar research was beginning in Australia and at scores of labs worldwide.

"Also," Niels continued, "workers in the field are using drones and the thermal energy tech to identify the most heat and drought-tolerant plants." He peered at his tour group of friends and colleagues, "How much is everybody interesting in the many details?"

He interpreted the non-committal murmurings correctly and ushered the group through more freshly painted corridors. Punching in the lock code, the room was suddenly cluttered with botanists and biochemists. TK's eyes widened, *pool tables, bean bags ... VR gaming tech.* It was clearly not a scribing names on lunch-boxes workplace. Ash was there, talking to the heavy-set black scientist and a couple of others.

Niels could take a hint …

"TK, this is Andrew, Nadine, Jobe, and you've met Ashley before, yes …"

After quick consultations, he confirmed, "Jess has seen the labs yesterday, she's happy to remain here. Mike and I will examine our forest preserving activities. We will need you, Kevin."

*

"… There is much overlap between identifying heat resistant forest individuals and enhancing our important crops," said Niels as the trio continued the tour. "We do not wish to emphasize our food breeding activities – as we are knowing many of the yggdrasil do not approve!"

"Professor, did you see atmospheric methane levels have broken through two parts per million?"

"Oh, for sure," said the Swede, grim voiced.

Mike continued, "And the yggdrasil themselves are funding these research activities?"

"Well, not entirely, there's philanthropy, and the government inputs," Niels reminded him.

"Curious how our political leaders will fund climate change research when invading aliens are involved!" said Mike with withering irony.

"Our aliens *may* create this wealth, but I am not being surprised if they are also *transferring* the money from the hidden accounts of the corrupt despots, the arms dealers, the companies paying no taxations. At least I am hoping so, yes,"

Niels raised his eyebrows.

Mike beamed his harmless teddy bear smile.

Meanwhile, in the staff room, the break was ending. Andrew regarded the Australian woman with interest; the husky voice, svelte movements, cat-like eyes. The one he'd enquired of Niels yesterday,

"So … progress report: are you ever going to ask that girl out. Or is it going to be a Darwin getting around to writing *The Origin*, situation?" As he bounced away, he added with rolled eyes, "because she might have three kids by then, my friend!"

*

The evening after the lab tour went well. Ash was a late invitee and Andrew's wife joined them at *No Fries with That*, Corvallis' finest 3F restaurant. But it was the *previous* evening, Niels reflected on as he drifted towards sleep on the futon.

There was no doubt the Saab approved. It's fault detector in no way alarmed by her presence – once again going through an error free pre-start routine (*How many relationship hints was it going to take considered the vehicle: from itself, from Ash, from Andrew*). The climatic variations: Cairns to Corvallis in November weren't to be trifled with, and Jess remained anonymous in a hooded coat until reaching the snug apartment.

Over hot chocolate, they had chatted easily enough of their work. The uni lab, Jess' role, her parent's farm, the other Congress members, and of course, the yggdrasil.

Then … "Niels, how's the frog toxin research going? I didn't see that part of the lab this time."

He grew sombre, "There are inconsistencies in the data …"

"You're uncomfortable with the whole thing, aren't you," said Jess, her voice sympathetic. "Your back up genocide plan."

Eyes down, he said, "There's family history in the area. The father of my grandfather was a founder of the Swedish Fascist movement."

Jess directed one of her unblinking-cat-looks at him, "That's hardly your fault, Niels."

"Yes, I know, but …"

"It's awful. I really like the ambassadors, and there are so many friendly yggdrasil attending the expos. Even the others: none of them actually want us dead – living in caves or basements, maybe." Jess tilted her head and smiled, "I get totally SLOJed out thinking about it all."

Niels hand unconsciously found the amber bead at his throat. *Attack of the unfamiliar verb.*

Full of life, Jess said, "So Niels, what's for dinner?"

After a simple pasta meal cooked as Jess sat, legs folded under her on the couch, there was wine, then spilling of wine. Jess fossicked as instructed for a rag in the cupboards under the sink, "What's this?"

Niels blushed as she waved the appalling *Botanists, Root & Leave* T-shirt (the ex's idea of the perfect gift), at him. But Jess was more interested in the contents the rag had been protecting.

"It's kind of embarrassing," said Niels.

"That you horde what …old IT stuff?" she said, part puzzled, part teasing. "Yeah, definitely, I wouldn't have guessed."

"So, when I was a kid," he began sheepishly, "I collected pinecones – different species, different stages of development."

"How old?"

"Seven years. Anyway, each had a number and a record of – yes you are guessing – collecting time, species, location and other informations," he smiled and concluded rapidly, "which I made into spreadsheets on floppy disc storages and can't bring myself to throw away!"

Jess laughed a throaty chuckle. This had a strange, unbalanced effect on Niels and triggered an earlier childhood memory: that of learning to ski. His visitor used the T-shirt to mop up the spilled red wine and displayed the gruesome exhibit. Something now between murder victim chic and music festival tie-dye wear.

"Do you want to keep this somewhere special?"

Later they sat on the futon that he'd thought to sleep on (but was happy to be proven wrong) watching one of those 'dinosaurs in a theme park – what could go wrong' – movies.

"I was such the child dinosaur nerd."

"Oh, yeah, me too."

Drinks had been consumed; childhood anecdotes recalled, there was mention of ex-partners. Things were heading in the right direction.

Niels edged closer. *I should kiss her.*

It'd be crazy to get involved now, Jess told herself sadly and sternly. *There's a world to save ... we must work together. We'd be no better than these two idiots stopping to kiss while hiding from the T. rex.*

On the screen, the leading actors kissed passionately in a ruined building (with an ardour which can so easily lead to making a baby standing up) while outside their toothy pursuer prowled. And so the moment passed. Again. And instead, Jess and Niels had a hasty discussion on the continued, mysterious indifference of the yggdrasil cell lines to arrow-frog poisons.

Chapter 85 Leaving Home

Dec 10
mom love nyc
leaving home

you know that feeling when it should be good news, but it doesn't feel that way? maybe you mommas of older kiddos can relate … something like when they move out of home. you should be happy: they're all grown up, sent out into the world, but it makes you teary.

EIR NYSSA HAS GONE.

its work here is done and it's time to go home. or to its next mission: "colonisation phase ended, reproductive stage to commence." (although anne-maree says what it actually *meant* was: *it is said* my work here is complete). not really the same thing is it dear readers? so, as you can imagine we're all a quite emotional. LOTS OF HUGS all round. poor anne-maree.
i have just heard also, that sri achras across in california has said goodbye.

posting some pics of our final outing. we went to look at christmas preparations and talked about how we people love our christmas trees (no more using a cut branch of course!).

so here we all are [Pics 1-2 eir nyssa helping decorate the tree]. of course, the yggdrasil don't really approve of plants kept in pots. as we know now: in a pot, they can't communicate through the ground with others, but "our alien" can see that special trees become part of the family. like eir nyssa became part of ours. [Pic 3 goodbye hugs]. anne-maree says eir nyssa was amused that some people have artificial trees. the two had become so close.

GOD BLESS

Chapter 86 The Changeling

It was six months before the slow recollection of the great trees filtered back to Sif Acer and, hence, to Niels, prompting his unlikely request: "Kevin, can you tell me *more* of ancient yggdrasil-Amazon Indian contacts?"

It's a simple matter to surmise that a fellow with enthusiasms for land squid hunts and zombie folklore may be suspect in the area of historical alien contacts. When Niels first met him, the New Yorker had shown little acquaintance with evidence-based norms; still, the Swede had to admit in recent times this had changed. Or perhaps *he* had. "Kevin, I have a theory: It's convoluted, unlikely, and based on memories of ancient trees – I think you'll be loving it."

The timing was propitious; Kevin had pursued the ghost of Hortle-Smith and his later associate Gould through the stacks of the NY public library and the very tentacles of the webbernet.

"How again are you having this collection," Niels asked, as they sorted through musty, fragile papers and artefacts.

"Gould died in 1900, his descendants still had his stuff. And it looks like Hortle-Smith bequeathed his journals to Gould too. Gould would've been a youngster on that first expedition."

"Kevin, when I first met Angelo in Iquitos, an old man present said there'd been positive relations with yggdrasil centuries past. And so, months ago, I asked Sif Acer of this," he shrugged and continued, "and it's now found trees that remember. I have a location for those trees, it's in Peru – but well south of Iquitos – a restricted area in the lowlands off the Manu River." Niels shifted more seed pods and indigenous artefacts out of the battered trunk. He was looking for something specific. "When I saw these before, there were paintings, watercolours, on small thick paper. And when I saw Matt recently – I was looking at his arm, his scar."

"Yeah, the paintings Niels, they're nice – should have them framed. There's a mother and baby, a girl with her pet monkey. Here they are."

Kevin laid the paintings on the table between them – there were two more portraits, both of bowl-haircut warriors with spines inserted in cheeks.

"And no others?" said Niels, concerned.

"Pencil sketches of ruins and landscapes—"

"Ha," exclaimed the Swede with relief. "See here, stuck to the backside of the other." He handed over the picture. "Can you make the separation?"

It was another man: small and barrel-chested, with lines and dots tattooed on his cheeks. And on both upper arms, parallel black markings, sloping inwards.

"Unlike the tattoos, they are blue," noted Niels. "Like Matt's wound, yes?"

Kevin gasped, "Like he's been scratched, yeah … maybe by a jaguar, a lot of these tribes worship jaguars. Amazing. And then a yggdrasil has healed him!"

The pair looked at each other in excitement, and then at penetrating radar images of forest in the vicinity of Sif Acer's "informant trees." In this, drought and past deforestation aided them. There was a definite donut ring shape, plausibly like a low-walled pond or fountain in a shattered courtyard sketched by a long-dead explorer. Enough to satisfy a conspiracy theorist, a forester or even, one suspects, an archaeologist – that it was worth a look.

"The last half-year has been going as we hoped," suggested Niels, "but hey – if we can show that people and yggdrasil lived peacefully together in the past …"

"Definitely. That could change everything."

*

A week later, Niels waited in Kevin's apartment. Matt, TK, and Jess walked there with Anne-Maree and Ebony. Sif Acer accompanied them, its antennae twitching with curiosity as usual inside a "people house."

"He said he was going out to put a kit together," shrugged Niels. The Swede noticed besides the new geek-chic haircut; the space devoted to collectibles had reduced since Crystal's arrival in Kevin's life.

"Indication recent presence, substantially ingested with glucose, additional salt solutions," announced Sif Acer perusing the computer desk debris. Feelers rustled as it examined a bong.

It was only then Matt noticed the floor-fallen note: "Gone to camping store," read the comedian, incredulous.

"Kevin can fill you in on the many details later," said the scientist, "but let's be making a start."

And so, Niels guided them through the unfamiliar territory of Portuguese expeditions into the Amazon basin; The Fountain of Youth; sketches of children with manufactured wings; reports of ruined cities; rumours of long-lived *tree guardians*; of circular rather than linear time.

"Oh God, it's opposite day," proclaimed Matt.

Shortly afterwards door chains rattled, and the returned Kevin said, "Hey all! So many choices who knew!" He dumped a weighty backpack in the living room and his body, honed by a decade of electronic gaming and Tube Cheez was mightily pleased.

Kevin fetched the collection and explained his research. He showed the group a sketch of a king – interred with strapped on wings, the skull elongated by binding.

"Sorry to be a stickler for detail," said Jess. "There was a painting of a person with a scar?"

Kevin handed the portrait to Matt. "Geez!" he exclaimed, handing it onto Jess, "Stickle away, mate."

They all stared at Matt's scar.

"Sif Acer," said Jess. "Do you know of yggdrasil visiting this area, developing relationships with humans?"

"The trees remember – say vanished in time."

"Should we wait until sometime in the new year to check it out?" said TK.

However, the departure of Eir Nyssa and others had made the humans uneasy. And so, after discussion, Jess, Matt, TK, Kevin, and Niels agreed to return to Peru soon after Christmas.

As they were to discover, time played by different rules where they journeyed.

*

The pod invoked unknown branches of mathematics and materialised in the village clearing. There wasn't a ruined city in sight, only rooster strewn thatched huts and cooking fires. Checking their location, Matt discovered his phone now bluetooth paired to an unknown toaster. Children appeared, with too skinny ribs, the younger ones wearing flip flops or nothing.

Then came the adults: staring at Sif Acer, wary but not afraid. The crowd murmured and drew closer, attempting to communicate with the newcomers. A young woman, naked except for a few grass fibres at her waist, pointed excitedly at Matt. Her pet parrot flew off, startled, as a cacophony erupted. A posse of youngsters ran from the clearing. The bolder men moved closer to Matt and gestured at his arm. Many wore blue lines and dots etched into their faces.

"Oh Jesus," exclaimed TK as the old man strode into the clearing; wrinkled and leather-skinned; his scars more prominent than when his portrait was painted two centuries past. Abruptly Sif Acer's antennae quivered, and it focused all its eyestalks on the impossibly aged tribesman.

"He say: long-time negative visitors. Question cigarettes supplied?"

"How—" began Niels.

"Self-ability interpret mind pattern this one."

Niels and Kevin exchanged glances, the latter said, "You hear his thoughts."

"Thoughts," repeated the alien, sampling the sunshine and making minor adjustments to itself. "Affirmative, thoughts," it repeated, rippling antennae, evidently pleased with the word.

"Sif Acer, can he understand you?" said Jess.

"Affirmative. Cigarette query repeats."

"Yeah, got some," said Kevin, returning to the pod.

"You have? said TK.

"Standard equipment for this type of mission. No need to pack light – we've got a pod." He rummaged in his bags.

Sif Acer and the elder faced each other. Kevin distributed cigarettes. A pet monkey ran off with a pack. Several women gathered around Jess, smiling at her shyly.

The alien spoke, saying in the phone voice, "He is the last changeling, many years not seen yggdrasil self. Has questions."

The old man stepped in front of Matt and addressed him.

Sif Acer adjusted its posture and translated, "He says, 'Have you come for gold, for Youth Fountain, for Time Gate?'"

"Ah, *no*," he shook his head. "*No*, but that's amazing, and *no* – wow, you've got one of those?" said the bewildered Matt.

The villager spoke again. "Can you sense his mind patterns," continued Sif Acer, rippling its antenna.

Matt shook his head. "No, again."

"Says will speak additional should newcomers find-see city of ancestors."

The vegetal-creature twitched its leaf-wings, adding, "Says only those with changeling ancestry can wake city from jungle." It pointed to the path with an intricacy best achieved with six-jointed clawed appendages, "Come friends."

*

They followed the yggdrasil out of the clearing into the humid green tunnel of track. It wasn't far, but except for Jess, the party wasn't used to the tropics. The humidity hit Kevin like a weight, his spectacles fogged up, and perspiration poured off him. As foretold, the path ended at the river and an enormous fallen crossing tree.

There was no city.

Matt stepped onto the wide log first, strode athletically across, and waved from the far bank. Kevin followed, wobbly. Matt hauled him off the log and then Jess, lithe and elegant, crossed. Matt was facing them as TK reached the far bank – their eyes widened, and he spun around. The ruins were hidden in time, and in shapes and shadows of green. Unseen, except at the edge of vision or when a changeling's descendant strode among them.

The screen had been lifted.

Niels and the alien now crossed, and the humans wandered the ruins in wonder. Tree roots like dinosaur tendons crept between and over fallen stones. There was a large, damaged ring, rich with carvings, softened by ferns.

It reminded Jess of childhood books; of illustrations of Aztec, or was it Incan, ball court rings? Hushed, she said, "So there *were* cities in the Amazon."

"Oh, yeah," observed Kevin smugly.

Enormous trees ringed a circular basin, the site's most intact feature. The encroaching forest, its monkeys and macaws, quieter than those surrounding the village a kilometre away.

"What now?" said TK – asking the obvious question.

"Self-converse with changeling."

The said changeling had appeared on the far bank. Niels, Sif Acer, and Jess re-crossed the great log. She observed the old man had gained a retinue of warriors and on-lookers. Sif Acer and the fellow resumed their mute communication.

The oldster gestured at Niels.

The yggdrasil ambassador said, "Changeling asks can night-skinned man and sun-hair man feel his mind pattern thoughts?"

Niels shook his head, "Not me."

"Says: can Niels Larsson feel mind patterns great trees?"

The forester looked sheepishly at Jess, "Sometimes – a little."

"Like TK," she said evenly.

*

The group had passed some variety of test and were now assigned a second task.

"So, does it have a name … what we're looking for," asked Matt when the trio returned, explaining their task.

Jess shrugged, "He didn't say."

"In the local language," said Matt to TK and Kevin, "I bet it's called *never go there, don't even think about it*." Matt continued his musings aloud as Sif Acer allowed the trees to guide it: "Find the haunted, re-purposed tomb of the great skin flayer. *Slay nothing.* Don't eat or drink while we're in there, take the great club-key, restart the time loop."

The party halted. Matt was unsure whether the broken stone teeth of the entrance guardian added to the sense of menace or softened it. Even the jungle itself seemed hesitant to reclaim this part of the site.

"You've got to be shitting me, man," said TK, turning to Kevin. "Who gets to die beating level one of the haunted tomb …"

Kevin hung back, torn between fear and curiosity: curious about an afterlife – fearful of finding out ahead of time.

Niels took a deep breath, pulled aside vines, and the dark flowed out. Like the Swede, Jess activated her phone's light. *We have a personal yggdrasil – what could go wrong.* And she was correct – mostly so. Phone lights danced crazily on hewn stone walls, on industrial-strength spider webs and gruesome carvings; except, on the great sarcophagus itself, where the gods of destruction and chaos had been erased. In their place on top – somewhere between the figurative and abstraction – was carved a single yggdrasil.

It was quiet enough in the tomb to notice water dripping. *And* a slight crunching sound. "Ah," said Matt, holding the damaged snail. "Who's got the first aid kit?" He displayed the stricken mollusc, "… we're gonna need gaffer tape, maybe a cable tie, err, is there any fibreglass?"

While Matt guiltily nursed the snail, the others regarded the object at the carven alien's many feet. It gleamed dully in the cell-phone light where it had lain hidden for centuries from the Iberians and those that followed: the seekers of gold, glory, and knowledge. It looked like something Niels' ancestors might have taken on an outing – say to invade York. The Swede reached for it, and Jess was rather drawn to how his shoulder muscles rippled in the gloom. Yet he barely moved it with the one hand. Gold is not entirely practical for weapon making.

There was a minor delay in ancient-task-fulfilling-activities.

"Sif Acer," said Matt, "you know how Mir Arauca healed me, um … could you fix the snail. There's a lot of weird stuff going on, and I don't want to be the victim of any ancient, *accidental*-snail-slaying-curses."

The alien took the stricken mollusc, it extruded and wove its sticky healing threads. Matt breathed a sigh of relief and returned the creature to a safe crevice.

Without effort, the vegetal being hoisted the key. "Come friends. Let us quit the unlight."

In the plaza, the alien plunged the artifact into the moss encrusted, but intact, stone lock. The group stepped back.

"Standard temporal anomaly," commented Kevin, full of paranormal-webmaster-cool.

"Oh," gasped Jess. "Is this in your big-old Portuguese book?"

"Yeah, it gets a little mention."

"Weird," said Matt. "I'd put it on the cover."

The jointed stone circle built to house it was now incomplete, but this mattered not as a pod-hole filled the void. A pod-hole and yet not … the same dimension and blacker-than-black, but with random flickerings of escaping light. With shimmerings and swirlings that made Heisenberg's Uncertainty Principle look like a sure thing in the 2:15 at Ascot. The inscrutable, silent monkeys that'd watched the spot for centuries chittered with relief and bounded away to find something better to do.

Sif Acer's claws scraped on the paving stones as it wandered off to communicate with the ring of great trees around the central plaza. Niels wiped sweat from his brow and tore his gaze from the forbidding void. *Ah, Kevin's satellite image was of that knee-height stone fountain in the site's centre.*

*

The changeling had finally crossed the river. His small band now included additional skinny children, pointing and gesticulating with delight. Now seated on the low circular structure with its unknown glyphs and repeated abstract shapes, Niels heard water splashing, then a warrior signalled that he should look behind. The village ancient approached, stroked the stonework and signed they would return tomorrow; when the water had re-filled the fountain on which he sat.

Much later, walking back to the river, Niels and Jess discussed whether the great trees ringing the plaza, the *Ceiba pentandra,* were called Ceibo, Ceiba, Kapok, Lupana, or something else in this part of Peru.

At the crossing log, TK rolled his eyes, "It's so great you guys can speak ancient Greek, and all 'cause that's real hip again."

"Err, TK, guys, as we leave … can we do a little wake the city – unwake the city experiment," said Niels.

This done, the group stared hesitantly at TK and Niels.

"Boo!" said TK, breaking the tension.

*

The expanded throng crossed the river, the changeling leading.

"Is he the chief?" Jess asked of Sif Acer, treading the log nimbly.

"Negative. Council of elder humans. Tree-age person is lore chief only."

Of all the bunion-toed muddlers, thought Matt mildly, as reaching the far bank, came the yell. Turning, he saw Kevin fall comically from the wide log. He saw Jess shrug off her small backpack and drop neatly into the water. Matt sighed like an exasperated office worker pushing away the mouse at the end of a long, long day. He too entered the river.

The current was sluggish, and the rescue easily completed. As they neared the shore, the two Australians realised the thing they kept bumping into was a submerged stone pathway and hoisting Kevin onto it they walked him to the bank.

There was some poorly concealed giggling from the locals as Kevin's companions tended to him. His ribs were sore, for he'd hit the submerged path.

Attempting to raise his arm, he winced and grew pale. "Thanks," he said. On balance, more embarrassed than hurt for the moment.

"No worries, mate, if we left you much longer, you wouldn't need no towel."

"Huh?"

"Piranhas," Matt smirked.

Jess, meanwhile, Niels observed, had retrieved her backpack, and stepped off the path into the obscuring jungle. She pulled her dripping singlet top off and put on a long-sleeved shirt. Then delving under the shirt while re-joining the group she removed her wet bra and stuffed it in the backpack – an alluring female skill thought the Swede.

Led by the children, who flitted between tree trunks searching for honey, the party returned to the track. More locals had entered the village in their absence, including a few with a little English or Spanish – indigenous pioneers exploring the difficult life between traditions and the outside world. The world of money: the cursed leaves, as the lore-chief damned it. There were fifty people in the clearing now, and a hubbub of activity as relatives greeted each other.

"Are you okay, Kevin? asked Jess, as he collapsed on a log.

"Sore, tired, hungry ... a little disgruntled."

"No worries, mate, we'll soon get you fixed up," chirped Matt gesturing around at campsite activities.

Food preparations were beginning, and it was obvious to the visitors important matters were being debated. Soon Kevin was keenly talking jaguars with the young warriors. They assured him the big cats were present, but packs of wild pigs presented a greater danger to the unwary.

"It's so much cooler to get eaten by a jaguar than a boar herd," the Swede overheard Kevin say. He peered suspiciously and began to wonder about the concoction the healer had given the New Yorker for his pain and bruising.

It was then, over his over-stimulated thoughts, that Niels "heard" the lore-elder say to Sif Acer: "We don't need anything from the white people – except their Bic Lighters and flip-flops."

Glancing at his companions, it was clear from TK's expression he'd registered it too. And Niels realised there was a kind of background-thought tinnitus happening, and he could sense snatches of "mind-pattern thoughts" from others in the clearing.

And then he had a flashback to a cricket game.

Sif Acer reassured him wordlessly, "Changeling is bridge, is catalyst."

As he "listened" to the old man recount the tribe's history to TK, Sif Acer, and himself, the first of a woven wing-leaf pair was completed. A woman fixed them to a toddler who ran gleeful circles of the village, in and out of huts chased by older children.

Niels now "heard" that what Kevin had related was correct: the locals indeed had a circular concept of time. In the past, the tribe, or members of it, had fled from the encroaching Spanish, from slavers, from missionaries, from the modern world. Not leaving their lands but entering the past through the time gate Sif Acer had reopened.

Niels didn't realise it, lost in the experience, but across the clearing, Jess was staring at him. Thinking: *He has that abstracted look that can seem wise and mysterious. Or just vaguely dopey.*

Kevin too, was staring at both Niels and TK. He wasn't thinking any of that. He poked the Swede on the shoulder. "What the hell's going on?"

TK explained.

"Turns out, my man Niels here and me have changeling ancestry. We're like waking hidden cities, hearing thoughts, getting in touch with the ancestors … listening to the trees." He turned to Niels, "You hear trees, right?"

For the second time in mere hours, Niels admitted this was so.

"Huh, not surprised," said Kevin, blinking rapidly. "Can you read my mind?"

"Err, Kevin, are you okay? I am wondering are there coca leaves in the medicine, yes. We are having the Panadol."

"I'm fine. Can you read my mind?" He scrunched his eyes closed in vigorous thought-transfer-concentration.

"Ah no, apparently not," said the forester, feeling foolish after what was probably just a few seconds but felt longer. Just then, an older woman walked by holding a stick-impaled-fish. "Oh," said Niels. *The secret is not thinking about it too much.* "You are thinking that …" he lowered his voice, "none of the ladies here wear a top!"

There was one, and she favoured Kevin with a disparaging look. After dinner, Jess listened with the others as Sif Acer, and the two newly made partial telepaths recounted what they'd 'heard'…

"I was taken as a baby to the stone fountain and spun into a cocoon by an emergent larva. We transformed together. I was a lucky chosen one, as my head wasn't bound to the shape the aliens prefer. When I was reborn, when I emerged with my cocoon mate, I could communicate with the leaf-creatures, with the trees, with my fellow changelings. Without the need for words and when there are no words. I am the last – others younger than I have journeyed through the time gate, splitting our tribe in times of crisis. Journeyed, on occasion – with yggdrasil ambassadors themselves."

*

Since the pod contained every variety of camping equipment, the visitors availed themselves of it. TK coated himself with insect repellent as if expecting a siege, and they slept in the open by a fire. Matt had availed himself experimentally of Kevin's medicinal potion, and there were odd conversations in the close, humid night.

Sparked by a torch failure, the two potion-takers discussed Newton's little-known Fourth Law of Reciprocal Battery Availability. And whether kitchen appliances could be powered by electric eels. Then, when Jess thought they were asleep …

Kevin said, “So … the yggdrasil young take a while to transform. Like zombies?”

“Geez, mate, a bit of tact wouldn’t hurt. Like moths,” suggested Matt, waving at the fluttering night-creatures. He then launched into a convoluted theory of how pod travel and its bluetooth device anomalies had resulted in TK and Niels being “paired” to Sif Acer and the last changeling.

There was no doubt. Faces were more lively and handsome by actual firelight. Bemused, Jess smiled across the dying embers and flapping moths at Niels sitting bare chested, amber bead glowing in the red light.

Chapter 87 Endings and Beginnings

Niels woke and observed several species of insects, some new to science, examining his bare feet. However, ours is not that type of tome, so we continue with the narrative thrust …

The camp was half-empty as he wandered towards the river. He reached the water and turned downstream, where the path narrowed. Lost in thought, avoiding fallen logs and spiky ferns, he somehow lost the obviously large, wet flowing thing. Fortunately, but a few lucky guesses later, Niels glimpsed it through the trees. Forcing himself through the greenery he regained the path, two metres above the riverbank where, to his considerable embarrassment, looking down, he observed Jess wearing nothing but knickers and standing knee-deep in the opaque water washing herself with a travel towel.

Niels gulped and averted his head so fast the jungle swayed. Time stood still. *What to do*? Perhaps try a casual, cheery, '*Just passing*' cough and retreat while apologising, hand theatrically covering eyes. But no, that was more Matt's department ...

With a guilty start, he realised he was staring again. She hadn't seen him.

Yet.

Stop looking, eyes down (instructed his brain to his head). *Regard that large and stately stag beetle. It advances on your left foot.* The specific part of the psyche that issues instructions when encountering virtually naked colleagues continued. *Back away. Don't step on any noisy sticks.* 'But what,' suggested the little-studied logicoembarrassment cortex, 'if she's glaring contemptuously at us right now!' Concerned, Niels glanced up again to check. *No, it was okay* … elbow raised, and head tilted, she was sponging herself from armpit to hip.

Unaware of him. Staring at the water.

Then, purposely, Jess stepped towards the bank, bent, and snared a wriggling eel-like creature. She cried out as the thing fastened itself to her hand. Instinctively Niels slid down the bank into the water – Jess' eyes were wide as he waded towards her. One arm held across her breasts, she tried to remove the river thing as it thrashed and coiled around her arm.

Niels grabbed it around its segmented jaws and wrangled it off.

This was no fish.

The two stared at it: black, sleek as an eel, segments resembling a millipede but with the sensory antennae of a catfish. Or a yggdrasil.

The forester stared at Jess, "I've seen them before."

She gasped, took a step back and folded a second arm across her chest.

"When I first met Angelo," (he hastened to explain), "they had smaller ones – preserved in jars." He stepped away from her, still clutching the writhing alien larva. "I'm sorry, I became lost …"

A crashing in the undergrowth drew their attention. Drawn by Jess' yell, TK appeared by the riverbank. He took in the scene and announced, "Yeah, I don't know what this is. But I'm just going over there …" Several awkward seconds later, his back to the river, TK called, "Guys, Kevin's in a bad way."

Niels released the larva, which vanished with a sine-curve wake. Jess finished dressing and scurried off towards the village. Niels followed at a slower pace.

Tyson grinned, "Hey, if you two want some time together, just say so man." He increased his pace and hustled away. Pausing but briefly to add, "It's not my place and all, but next time: ditch the fish!"

*

Kevin was conscious, but looking like a few wild boars had had a go at him. Matt and Sif Acer sat by their pale, clammy companion.

"Kevin," said Jess, after crouching and examining him. "You might have broken ribs and I'm worried the lung's collapsed on that side."

Kevin nodded slightly and grimly.

Matt motioned to Sif Acer, "Can you do anything?"

"Self can cease nerve activity discomfort."

"In your own time, then," groaned the stricken New Yorker.

Sif Acer moved closer and applied its skills. There was a brief discussion, then: "Jess is right," said Niels to Kevin, "Its best that Sif Acer is taking you in the pod to hospital at home."

"Okay, but who'll shoot the footage? The world needs to see this."

"We can come back in a couple of weeks, mate – when you're okay. Even bring an archaeologist. You could do a whole doco on your research."

With the alien's intervention, Kevin's head was clearer, the discomfort reduced – he thought things must look serious. Matt wasn't generally that supportive of him and his doings. As they walked to the pod, Kevin said, "The old-lore guy, the changeling, he's hundreds of years old. This is where the Fountain of Youth legends come from, what brought de Acuna and the later expeditions here."

It was a measure of how strange things had become that Niels found himself saying, "Yes, Kevin, this makes perfect sense." Even more so, returning in the afternoon to admire the 'fountain' full of gently swirling water (a sight rarely seen by outsiders since the explorer-priest had described it in Kevin's forgotten journal).

Matt detected a certain tension among the group – which he figured was due to Kevin's departure. Sif Acer had yet to return. Meanwhile, the ancient indigenous man was busy with recent arrivals emerging from the forest into the cracked, overgrown plaza.

Niels could sense enough of the changeling's thoughts to know the tribe were preparing for a great ceremony and to make tough decisions. TK was relating what he understood of this to Matt and Jess as Sif Acer returned.

The alien's companions could tell something had changed – its longer antennae waved busily, and the shorter ones rippled in waves. It assured them their "sub-optimal comrade" would be fine and went off to consult the changeling.

Soon after, with its usual lack of tact, it announced, "Regrets. Yggdrasil migration phase approaches end. We explorer-diplomat clade to be withdrawn. Task said to complete."

"Like Eir Nyssa," said Jess sadly, breaking the silence first.

"Like, unlike," it said, sweeping its longest eyestalk in her direction. "Self will defy, self will remain – enhance learning. Explore."

"How? What will happen to you?" asked Matt, concerned.

The plant-creature's smaller feelers rippled again. It pointed at the time anomaly. "Self will venture with others." Now it indicated the villagers milling around, "Removal from this time optimal for self and human friends. May they prosper until the sun burns out."

So many questions, thought Niels later in the afternoon.

A score of people went off to look at some excitement in the forest. He sat alone on the fountain's edge, running his hand over the textured carvings. Footsteps and yggdrasil claws sounded on the uneven flagstones. He stood.

Jess held him briefly by both shoulders and said with one of her unblinking frank looks, "It's okay Niels, about this morning, I could've said I was going off to wash … let's forget it." Now turning to the alien, she said, "You were saying future population increase on Earth will now come from your kind breeding here. Sif Acer, what do your young look like?"

It touched the fountain's carvings with a jointed appendage; it made the static rasp sound and said, "Here larval form, here pupae-cocoon, later hatchlings appear as self-form – correction reduced size aspect." This appeared to amuse it, and the small feelers rippled.

They described what they had seen that morning – omitting a detail or two, although Niels had an uneasy sense the leaf-creature was sharing his recollection.

"Reproduction has commenced," it confirmed. But the larvae were not sentient until after metamorphosis, and Sif Acer could not detect their presence.

"This fountain," said Niels brushing it, "resembles the tanks on the terminus ship, the mother ship that Riya Bedi and I saw – except this one is stone, yes." He scratched his dirty-blonde stubble, "Same weak maelstrom circle flow too."

"Affirmative, this made in imitation of yggdrasil nutrient wells." It changed the subject comprehensively and said, "Your companions discovered sloth-animal," it pointed again, "shall we visit?"

"Not if they're going to eat it," said Jess, concerned.

"No slay-eat in sanctuary this," the yggdrasil assured her.

*

They foraged in the pod. Discovering Kevin, in his wisdom, had packed an electric toaster and many marshmallows. These latter went down a treat with the locals. By firelight, Niels and Jess chatted light-heartedly of marshmallow ahimsa and whether the pink and white blobs contained *any* natural substances.

Although their hosts' traditional lands were in a reserve, there were still occasional maraudings from drug growers, miners, and until the recent past, timber-thieves. In recent years, the tribe was torn between the easier life of store food, first-world healthcare, electricity, and being second-class citizens in that world. Over centuries their numbers had waxed and waned, their very existence the subject of rumour; always retreating further from encroachment and when possible into history. Niels could sense the excited thoughts and sadness of friends and families now choosing different paths.

Niels sat, bare-chested in the warm-night air, leanly muscled and framed by a halo of fluttering moths. Jess again felt the attraction. It had come and gone over the last six months like some cosmic hormonal algorithm of its own making.

Later, awake, anxious with concerns, he watched her sleep – the cat-like eyes at rest. *I wonder if I can tell what she's dreaming*, he mused. Then: *No, not cool.*

*

During the night, it was evident Jess had been assigned a personal rooster. It followed her around all morning as the villagers made final adjustments to costumes, as bodies and faces were painted. A few older villagers inserted cheek spines, recalling their jaguar totem. Finally, carrying potions, the village set off for the lost city and the time gate.

Many for the last time.

A woman daubed Jess's cheeks with white and red paint. The men were similarly painted, including their torsos. Ages were hard to judge, but it seemed to her everyone, except the youngsters, consumed the "before-time potion."

Like Ayahuasca, the taste was foul, and Jess swayed, disorientated. But not so ill as before and there was general purpose good-will-to-all feeling, which was rather pleasant.

The young woman with the shoulder parrot motioned Jess to join in the complex rhythm percussion and chanting. Niels, she considered, was looking rather serious.

He, meanwhile, heard the great guardian trees and more dully, beyond them, the entire forest. He sensed cycles of light and heat, the flow of nutrients, of trickling water, of information … the slow, complex songs of the trees. And delving further into the past … the first of the two-legs and before that the visits of the light-foragers. Like the trees themselves and unlike.

Then a shudder and a distinct memory, intense and urgent, the jungle green and lush … the predator searching and hunting. The hidden prey, feelings of fear, the will to live … and lust. And a dinosaur. (*Wow*! thought the part of the brain that maintains a sense of perspective at the oddest moments.) Then shockingly, a man and woman running, hiding; ruined buildings, a movie, TV, his futon … Jess.

Eyes heavy, Niels forced his gaze from the gourd-bowl. Jess was staring through him, recalling that evening, the movie, her thoughts … *I should kiss him*, then a chase scene and a kiss scene … *how ridiculous, just run* … of similarities made, moments passed, and regrets.

And now again, a sense of the local past: the plaza unbroken, full of life, of yggdrasil stepping from the forest to egg-lay on the fountain lip. Of ceremonies, gold and greenery, tied on wings, of families offering their young to the emerged larvae slithering to the forest edge to spin, to pupate and change.

He saw the radiant changelings, the human ambassadors to the vegetal world. The ceremonies repeated in cycles over hundreds of years of co-existence. Eventually becoming less fine … the death of the last yggdrasil, the plaza degraded and still time cycled. The new people came, fearful, arrogant, blind … the forest shrank, farms and roads spread, time cycled on, the yggdrasil returned. The hard-edged works of man broken and buried in a world of trees. People running, hiding in ruined buildings. The future.

Or not … another stream in the flow of time, trickling off the main flow and beginning this day. A girl child born to mend the world: the quasi-changeling daughter of Jess and him. All things considered, thought Niels through the drug haze, *we should really get on with making her ASAP*.

The time-drug visions faded. His face was wet with rain.

“Please to arrange in formation,” boomed Sif Acer.

The tribespeople began assembling before the gate. Incantations were made and painted bodies smeared as the rain increased and grew colder. The last changeling stepped through the time gate, then the first villager. The sky cycled through variations of grey until it was dark, swirly, and appropriately foreboding. Big raindrops hit plaza stones and stung bare flesh. The surface of the fountain rippled as the air became vigorous. Children’s tied-on wing-leaves thrashed and threatened to tear away.

The villagers who had elected to remain watched the last of their fellows step into the shimmering ring and vanish. Finally, Sif Acer enveloped the four visitors in its great leaf-wings and alone it approached the time gate.

*

Kevin's 'temporal anomaly' vanished with Sif Acer, and Niels turned his face to the easing rain. He hadn't been this thirsty since lured into eating the Aussie breakfast affliction, Vegemite. Sat on the fountain edge with TK and the two Australians, his head was quieter. The jumble of other-people's-thoughts tinnitus fell silent.

There was nothing for it, other than to follow the remnant of the tribe home. It was one of those "difficult to get a handle on" audiences, thought Matt. There was a sense of excitement, of new beginnings but tempered by sadness and loss. He felt the same. And there was a powerful residual sense of drug-related euphoria. "Wow, these tree meditation experiences just get better every time," he announced.

Shortly before twilight, the villagers found another sloth. Matt admired sloths. "You've got to love their casual attitude and their *not wanting to take over the world vibe*," he informed the group. The shaggy creature slumbered on, unaware that it had become fashionable, almost displacing those 'all-too-obvious' pandas.

"Well, I'm happy to stay here the night," said Matt.

And the others agreed.

Jess summed it up, "I need processing time. Happy to give the lights and forced fun of New Year's Eve a miss."

"Yeah, and it's all laser lights these days, no fireworks," complained Matt.

Since the marshmallows, fuel stove, alcohol, and inflatable pool lobster were still in the pod, they agreed to make the short spatial leap back to the atmospheric lost city. Sif Acer had told Niels the pod would work for him if the mother ship remained in orbit.

And so it proved.

The group was again sitting on the fountain edge, this time facing inward, feet in the water. Matt's drug-brew euphoria was fading yet mixing with alcohol in interesting ways. "Time means nothing *here*," he said, "in both the general and the err, specific," he continued – latching onto the word before it eluded his grasp. "No one anyone near *here*," he waved at trees, "has a watch or a phone …" He concluded with aplomb, "It can be midnight – any time I say."

And with that, he splashed to the fountain centre. A little tentatively, hyper-vigilant for the soft brushings of fishy denizens or worse, the others waded across the current where they performed an affectionate group-hug countdown from ten. Arms around each other's shoulders, TK and Matt retreated to the shallows at the fountain's stone edge. Niels followed them a few steps, then sensing that Jess hadn't moved, turned back.

"Friends and colleagues New Year's Eve kiss?" He suggested casually, although his eyes said otherwise.

"Oh," Jess sighed, shaking her head, "I don't think so ..." and stepping towards him, she wrapped her arms around Niels and kissed him passionately.

Time appeared to do one of its standing still tricks (but as there was a recently de-activated anomaly nearby, it might have). Matt and TK exchanged glances, and in reasonably yggdrasil imitation chanted: "About time!"

*

And so, once more, the pod re-materialized in the village where a few locals remained up – poking at glowing fires. There were ample spare huts now, but Matt and TK unrolled their hi-tech insect repellent sleeping mats, taking their accustomed places by the fire. Arms around waists, Jess and Niels assessed their options. Agreeing and smiling with wonder, she followed him back into the pod.

Where, as it transpired, it was as dark as a cave with the door closed.

"Don't worry," she laughed, locating and kissing him for a long moment.

"But there's an app – if I am finding my phone – I believe I can make the roof transparent!" There were sundry urgent fumblings and discoveries. Then he teased, "So ... how is the saying: if you can just *keep your shirt on*."

And the phone was found; the moon did indeed provide light – and Niels was pleased to see that Jess hadn't taken his advice concerning the shirt.

Chapter 88 Reproduction

The tropical overnight rain was now evaporating in the mid-morning heat. Moisture glistened dully, and tendrils of water vapour returned to the sky. They rose from the thatched chicken coop built over the fish stoked dam, from the timber pump house and from the alien laying its eggs by the water's edge.

"Hi Mir," said Jess. "Haven't seen much of you lately. Wow! Nice! And so many … instant family!" She wiped away water and sat nearby. "You don't mind if I'm here? Actually, I've got news myself … told Niels earlier – he'll be sorry to have missed this." A little later, after an empathic chat, she concluded, "Well, I guess now's as good a time as any … shall we go tell my parents?"

*

Two months of the new year had passed, and as Mir Arauca had observed, "Niels Larsson now surrounded by whiskers."

Jess felt the relationship had reached the stage where she might proffer unsought grooming advice. Which she provided. It was a measure of Niels' cheer that he was content to take such advice and to wake, several times a week, in the fibro-cement bungalow with the ill-fitting screen door, in Cairns' rainy season. There was a basic kitchenette, but he and Jess often took evening meals with her parents, Barbara, and Bob, in the farmhouse. Eight wonderful weeks had flitted by like a pod commuting between Corvallis and Cairns.

Such flitting was feasible: leaving early and arriving in the lab after lunch the previous day (rather reducing the effective working hours). But pod-nausea and climatic variations took their toll. Just discussing the time and day had its grammatical and logical conundrums.

In Corvallis, driving by to pick up Ash, she observed, "What's wrong, Niels?"

"How do you mean?"

"I know it's an interesting car, but you're trying to start it with a novelty-cactus USB stick," she discerned.

"Jess is pregnant," he said, looking vaguely at the memory stick. When the excited squeaking stopped, he drove her to the university lab so she could make him tell Andrew.

Hence, back in Cairns, Niels wasn't present when Jess walked from the dam and told her parents the news. However, Mir Arauca, the last ambassador, was there, providing a handy, two-for-one reproduction shock distraction.

To his wife, Bob whispered, "I always figured Mir as a bloke."

To his daughter: "Ah, thought you were off the grog a bit, love!" After he'd been suitably chastised, the four embraced.

Later, talking things over with her mother, Jess speculated, "In the past, I could've tried ginger tea for the morning sickness."

Barbara Kelly laughed, "Don't be silly, dear, take the real drugs."

*

In bed later that week, flooded with the cuddle hormone oxytocin; as beetles and moths battered the windows, Niels decided against telling Jess of the time-drug prophecy for the present. It was all a little too new-age mystical, and so much pressure on a tiny foetus.

So much stuff to process. Best, he judged to, 'Just keep cuddling.'

Chapter 89 "Relentlessly proffered excuses."

Everyone had an opinion.

In every nightclub in Rio, in every golf club in New Zealand, patrons speculated: How *did* the yggdrasil reproduce? In mid-January, the first images flashed across the world. From Jaipur, the Pink City: where an alien publicly laid its eggs on a fountain edge.

By March *Monsters and Aliens* was flooded with pictures of eggs and larvae. Although not yet any cocoons – but Kevin had an inkling, he'd recognise *those* when he saw one. Like Bob Kelly, Ebony was surprised to hear of Mir Arauca's egg-laying – and of Eir Nyssa's role in this.

"I always thought Eir Nyssa was a mom, that we shared a connection."

Kevin explained: "They're *both* mothers, Ebony, and dads too – as are slugs and snails. I'd say Eir Nyssa's laid *its* eggs back home, or wherever it's gone now."

*

In the spirit of compromise, Matt and Kalinda had married *and* bought a farm. Not next to *her* parents, but, unconventionally, next to their friend Jess Kelly's parents. And early in the new year, Jess and Niels went on a first date of sorts.

For reasons unclear to humanity, there was a link between the departure of the ambassadors and the beginning of the reproductive-colonisation stage. Despite this, the human–alien Congress continued. The "political representative" clade as Niels considered them (Tek Alnus, Hatl Thuja, and their ilk) had filled the breach. But their interest in viewing the world's largest living thing, conveniently present in eastern Oregon, waned when informed it wasn't a plant, but an immense colonial fungus.

"They are even less interested in the fungi than people," said Niels.

Eventually, only Mir Arauca had accompanied Jess and Niels on the 'date' as they walked the bare cold forest hand in hand. Admittedly, there wasn't much to see – the bulk of the organism lived underground, yet the yggdrasil could detect its uncanny presence.

*

Indications that conditions would worsen for humans with the departure of Sif Acer and its ilk were subtle at first. Attacks on bonsai nurseries and triple grafted fruit tree producers didn't much alarm the public. Meanwhile, on the expo circuit, Crystal and Bear grew concerned. Although green body-paint distributors put on yet more staff, the assimilation of donated phones had slowed.

As Crystal put it, "It's great so many of the yggdrasil coming to the new expo sites can already speak, and bless them, are wearing friendship tokens."

But there was a distinct sense of preaching to the converted.

And so Bear called a meeting. The winter that had barely begun was ending, and the group sat on the porch gazing over the fields that held the first expo.

With Crystal's congratulatory hug routine completed, Niels judged it safe to produce his whittling knife. He delved into the spacious lumberjack coat and resumed work on an elaborate spoon, "Late wedding present," he explained. "I've been distracted, yes, with Jess and everything – things are getting tense again." More and more his dreams were of the 'Viking sacrifices of appeasement', rather than the 'tree communication' variety.

"Yeah," the big man shrugged, "since Sri Achras left things ain't been the same round here."

Crystal stretched out an arm and squeezed Bear's shoulder, "It'll be okay, they eat sunlight – they don't eat us," she smiled.

"Err," said Niels, "Elephants, hippopotamuses and those terrifying Australian funnel web spiders don't eat us either, but they are dangerous, yes."

Crystal smiled like a visiting angel – one attired in the finest hippy chic – and glided away to attend to the rescue cacti.

TK turned to Niels, "Doc, you worried enough to have another look at them frogs? Ash says the whole 'Nazi nature lover ancestor thing' keeps you wake at nights," he grinned.

Niels gulped. He watched Ash bristle and announce, "I did not say that."

"Yeah, well not everyone's family are harmless grass-fed lawyers and doctors," said TK, pointedly looking at Ash. "It is what it is." He drummed the aged rocking chair and asked Bear, "How worried are you?"

"Not enough to be giving away my twenty-five-piece whittling set," he glanced at Niels and raised his eyebrows, "or visit my ex … but Spring is gonna come early and there was a kind of ultimatum around that, yeah – at last year's solstice gig." He peered around at the group, "We gotta step it up – more expos, more concerts … dance parties, more positive news broadcasts and Congress meets." Bear scratched his head, "A few of the anti-yggdrasil broadcasters have gone quiet – that'll help some."

*

But Congress outings grew sporadic and their nature changed.

Carbonated water sales had been dropping (becoming more the "sometimes drink"). Yet the latest Congress broadcast still featured a little pre-prepared alien rant.

"Who is victor this [static burst] … this competition?" demanded Hel Sativa.

It was the advertisement the nanny state health agencies never made. The light gatherer displayed a range of artificially coloured carbonated waters and chastised humanity for its ceaseless product innovation in the field of unnecessary products. To paraphrase:

"They get larger and larger, cheaper and cheaper, wasting resources making them, shipping them around the world, cluttering the land and sea with their empty vessels."

And yet, the vegetal creature claimed (with an accusatory ripple of its antennae) by the simple means of *not* doing those things to pure, wholesome water, we could avoid all that.

And then the trip to Easter Island – that lonely speck of land settled by Polynesian adventurers ten centuries* ago. Not, as generally, to see the great evocative Moai. But to view what wasn't there.

The trees.

"You have to wonder what the bloke who cut down the last one was thinking," mused Matt, hearing the tale of spectacular deforestation. "Bet he never read *The Lorax*."

Directing eyestalks at Matt and its comrades, Mir Arauca said, "Humans, both the causation and the solution."

Niels said, "I believe we've improved our conservation and sustainable forestry in the centuries since—"

"Relentlessly proffered excuses," barked Hatl Thuja.

As winter gave way to northern spring, life worsened for humanity, although multi-player games still performed as did ride-sharing apps. Hardy souls tried a little home surgery – installing solar panels in the old epidermis (a nice talking point at parties, just not entirely effective).

Then, besides heat-wave crop failures, there came attacks on late summer, southern-hemisphere grain harvests. There was none of that atoms-torn-from-molecules, essence-rearranged destruction, that the yggdrasil were all too capable of. Instead, a litter analogy may be instructive: just as the occasional human picks up discarded carbonated water vessels, so too, the occasional light forager re-arranged a passing combine harvester it didn't care for.

* Easter Island research is ongoing. Settlement date estimates vary from 400 to 1200 CE.

*

Unfortunately, despite the Congress' good intentions, there was still something about 'entire landscape – as far as the eye-stalks can see' mechanised agriculture that constituted a problem. The level of surreptitious home vegetable growing increased, as did urban rooftop and vertical surface gardening. Years now since the yggdrasil arrival, humanity had re-thought wasting a quarter of total food production. Belts had tightened.

Niels worried, as the northern grain harvest season approached, those crops would be similarly affected, and starvation begin anew. The 'save the cold-adapted forests' research continued to receive limitless resources, funding the secretive crop breeding network.

It was clearly time to step up the frog-poison probe.

Chapter 90 Banana Bread Again

March 14
mom love nyc
Banana Bread

well we've sure seen some amazing things dear readers since we started this journey together … and I guess this momma is feeling a little nostalgic today. does anyone remember [Pic 1] one of my very first blog adventure posts: anne-maree was a baby, our amazing city was in corona virus lockdown and everyone learned how to make BANANA BREAD.

it brings a tear to my eye to see her today, the same kiddo but so much more [Pic 2 anne-maree and yours truly in matching yellow berets making banana bread together].

it's just so important to do something positive TOGETHER in this world of worrying news. you've seen the footage from american samoa, of yggdrasil forcing people onto the main island only? kevin says that's happening all over the place wherever islands are heavily forested: the seychelles, solomon islands, palau and hundreds of islands in micronesia. uncle jim says his poppa served in guadalcanal during WW2 where the yggdrasil are putting folks they 'de-peopled' from surrounding islands.

i don't know if it's connected dear readers but some billionaires' yachts have come back to the city and their owners have gone to bunkers instead. do they know something we don't? we sure do miss eir nyssa.

thanks as always for your support in our uncertain world. bless.

Chapter 91 Frog Sourcing

Of course, they should come with a warning: Beware! Excess time in the company of frogs may lead to genius – or madness.

Months before the recent increase in yggdrasil–human tension, Niels had been explaining the "keeping our options open" frog poison research to Kevin. They were in Kevin's New York apartment with Jess.

"It's not especially a priority, but the thing is Kevin: dosing the yggdrasil cell lines with residue from the darts and arrows I collected when Matt got hurt has been *inconsistently* lethal. So …" he paused, "we are getting the fresh frog toxin, yes. But it has no effect. It is most puzzling," concluded Niels. He hadn't expected inconstant biological or chemical laws concerning amphibians (but then he'd only dabbled in the field previously).

"Right," said Kevin. "Frogs have had a tough time for decades … what with climate change and habitat loss. Their numbers in the wild have crashed, there've been extinctions." He waved at the tank, "Gustav's been subdued of late."

"Oh my god," Jess exclaimed, peering at the tank.

Niels turned to the tank. *Not, I suspect, a specific apartment-frog remark.*

He was proved correct.

Jess said, “Not just climate change, Kevin, but disease too. What if the deadly arrow frogs were *sick*?”

“Oh yes …” nodded Niels, and his thoughts flitted through images of a strange boy on a lengthy flight to Australia; to crayfish plague; disinfectant foot baths in forests …

Jess, the zoologist, got there quicker. “Fungal lesions affecting Tasmanian platypus came from frogs, and fungi cause many diseases in plants and animals, and Chytrid fungus has been killing frogs globally for years. So,” continued Jess looking at Niels, eyes bright with excitement, “what if it’s not the poison itself, not even the frogs, but *some* frogs are carrying a disease agent … most likely a fungus, and *that* killed the yggdrasil and the cell lines.”

Niels beamed at her.

“We’re gonna need sick frogs,” declared Kevin.

Conflicted, Niels shrugged, “No urgency.”

*

Times had changed.

His transport materialised near one of those non-evidence-based therapy businesses with all the crystals. Baseball cap worn low on the head Niels scurried from the scene of over-excited pod-hole electrons. Like an electron changing orbital shells, Niels prepared himself for a different stress level and entered the reptile and amphibian retailer. He wasn’t especially knowledgeable of such enterprises. Yet he felt this one, combining as it did, pet services with a music store, had developed an unusual business strategy: one that very likely combined the proprietor’s interests.

“Can I help you, sir? You’ve been standing by that frog display for a long time.”

“Well yes,” began Niels tentatively, “Are you having any ill ones?”

Confused by the question itself, or maybe the accent, the owner regarded the customer from under his dark woolly eyebrow, “They’ll make you ill if you lick them,” he said coolly. “Hey, do I know you?”

Niels glanced at the shop’s music section, “Err, maybe I am playing the bass for my band Kraken?”

An expression of recognition and understanding flitted across the retailer's face.

"Look, I can dig the music," the man shook his head, "but no. No frogs for you!"

*

Following that ineffectual sourcing attempt, they promoted Kevin to chief frog securer. Ebony, now advised of the plan, agreed they couldn't afford to be recognised. Preliminary research for waging undeclared war on species with god-like powers is an activity best done in secret, done well, or not at all.

In recent times Kevin had undergone an upgrade – an effect of the close individual attention of the 'loveliest girl in California'. Gone was the horror of the scratchy nylon track pants and cheap vinyl jacket combination. Due to the upgrade, and as Kevin was generally behind the camera, Ebony spared him the dress advice, hats, wigs, and temporary tattoos.

Housed in a disused warehouse, the Biennial New York Reptile (and less fashionable amphibian cousins) Expo was no scenic walk in Central Park. There was no hint of green except pavement-crack weeds. Even the air smelt ill.

On the sidewalk Kevin glanced furtively around and addressed the group, "No aliens in sight … trust no-one," he tilted his head, "especially the big guys with the shades in the dog grooming van. And watch the accents – let me and Ebony do the talking."

Niels, Jess, and Ebony followed Kevin around the cavernous space. He was wearing an old band T-shirt that proclaimed the performer (or perhaps the wearer) was the *Lizard King* – this went down well with stallholders.

It's a funny old world, thought Ebony, *when Kevin's considered cool.* "Hi, I'm interested in the arrow frogs," she said to the sallow stallholder.

A newbie mistake.

"I assume you mean the Dendrobatidae – more correctly termed the poison dart frogs," came the condescending reply.

"They're *tiny*!" remarked Ebony, safely out of earshot. The group roamed the space, selecting the listless and peaky from among the appropriate species.

Yet clearly the frogs were not listless and peaky enough. For once again, the results were negative.

*

"You want something specific, you gotta ask for it," opined Kevin at their next frog-related meeting. "So, I know a guy – his life skills are not so great on non-frog and video game subjects. The type that won't let you touch *his* controller. Anyways, he can get diseased frogs on the dark-net."

Cautiously, the contact on the less scrupulous side of the amphibian supply game was made.

"Err, Kevin, why are these frogs unwell?" asked Niels.

"Well, they're lickers …"

"Excuse me, please?"

"People lick them, suck on 'em, pass 'em around at parties – get high. Or try to, at least. Lot of variation … everyone hoping to get lucky and score a 'God Frog'. Sharing frogs – frogs get sick."

"Oh my gosh," exclaimed Ebony.

"I've heard of it at home with cane toads – but I always thought it was an urban myth," said Jess.

"So, the pickup … I say we drive by, have a look – make the call," said Kevin, getting into character. "Gotta be discrete – use a burner phone. We're not going to kill the guy, are we?"

"What! Of course not. Geez Kevin," exclaimed the startled Australian.

"Well, what if he's not alone?"

Jess regarded him incredulously, "He distributes diseased frogs on the dark-net …"

*

The wipers cleared the drizzle as they drove past the dealer's apartment block. Past thin drug runners and prostitutes. Past black-market veggie sellers and seedy dogs. Past folk with the look of herbal dependency and cash flow issues. Grey hoodie anonymous, Kevin shuffled past the man at the entrance, who was impressively keeping a risky cigarette alive in the rain. He mounted the stairs and returned triumphant with five expensive, exhausted, bright yellow frogs.

What now? they wondered, blinking up at the humans warily.

What now, indeed.

And so, with a frog-like narrative leap to the present, whereby whichever Bayesian god of chance handles frog-related communications, the call came through once more at Kevin's apartment.

"Hey Niels, its Andrew at the lab – got the toxicology results, my friend."

And it transpired that the secretions of two of the frogs did indeed harbour Chytrid fungus and the secretions *did* kill cultured yggdrasil cell lines.

As the lab chief put it, "Someone needs to go back to South America."

Chapter 92 OMG

April 7
mom love nyc
OMG

OMG! dear readers, thank you for all the DMs. yes, the congress members are all ok. who would do such a thing and WHY? it seems the nuke attack was very small scale and has mainly affected gaspe national park itself. the canadians are furious, of course.

kevin has taken the news hard. his adventure with the yggdrasil, like for so many of us, began with his footage there. [here's the link]. And now there's not a living thing for miles around. and no-one has taken responsibility.

if only eir nyssa and the ambassadors were still here. such worrying events now in Borneo too – millions of people cleared from the forests into the major cities.

closer to home, central park is looking glorious [Pics 1-3]. there are hundreds of thousands of yggdrasil living there but even anne-maree is finding it difficult to find ones she can talk to now.

bless.

Chapter 93 "Welcome again, Mariam Turner."

Matt and Kalinda sat watching one of their former *CCE* colleagues on Channel Five breakfast television and awaiting another.

The conversion was now complete, their farmhouse could run off-grid, Matt had enrolled in science, and the dreaded chickens were installed.

On-screen, once more, Mariam Turner had ventured into the perilous world of morning commercial television. Clearly a world more perilous for women than men, she'd mused, waiting in the green room. Aspiring journalist number one (balding mid-fifties male) was still in residence. However, since Mariam's last visit, his co-host had been replaced by a younger female version.

Once the viewing audience had gratefully received 'Gardening your way out of chronic depression' and chuckled at the latest risqué Brazilian Pilates practices, Mariam had joined them on the couch.

Rather glossing over the fate of her predecessor, Charlee kicked off with, "Welcome again, Mariam Turner. Since we last had you on the show relations between the yggdrasil and ourselves had improved …" she looked astutely into camera one, "only to deteriorate again in recent months."

"Unfortunately, so Charlee," replied Mariam – distracted by the set's surely non-yggdrasil-compliant nested baskets of Bhutanese jute.

"And what do you put that down to?"

"Undoubtedly, the departure of those referred to as the ambassadors."

"Do you know why they left?"

"I suspect an internal political division, but we may never understand. It's not just that they're green with multiple eyestalks – their thought processes are *alien.*"

"Last time you were here, you expanded a theory comparing the yggdrasil arrival to European colonisation of this continent," said aspiring journalist number one (AKA Bruce).

"And other continents. Yes, I liken the ambassadors to early explorers or colonial governors: smug in their superior technology and within their cultural framework, kind if patronising, to the locals."

Charlee and Bruce nodded for her to continue.

"And now our *protectors* are gone. We're still making ourselves useful – our music, the forest conservation measures. However, we lost whatever moral authority we had in alien eyes during the forest burnings. The overwhelming majority have scant interest in we humans." She peered at camera one, "As evidenced by the refugees created by the de-peopling of the islands to our north. Not," she paused, "that we Australians care for them ourselves, or for the climate refugees of the Pacific."

The show's hosts exchanged concerned 'guest running off track' glances.

Charlee said, "You'd still characterise their behaviour as indifferent, rather than hostile?"

Mariam shifted on the cushion, "Yes – on the whole. Like Ret Moitch on *CCE*: it could communicate, but it didn't bother."

"Well, what of these attacks on wheat and other grain crop harvests?" asked co-host Bruce.

"My understanding is it's not an issue of farming *per se*, but one of industrial scale production. Most yggdrasil are indifferent to grain crop concerns. It's not a 'core issue' like forestry … but, if one in a thousand of them, one in a million even, has issues with our food production, their leadership – *if they even have anything we can relate to as leadership* – cannot or will not intervene."

"And there're *billions* of them," nodded Charlee.

"And now they're breeding."

*

"She's right, isn't she Kal?" said Matt. "It only takes a tiny proportion of them to stuff us around." He shook his head, "God, and now we've had that nuclear attack." He filled the kettle. On-screen, the Ka$h Koala swung into fluffy-ear-wiggling inanities in search of a worthy viewer-recipient.

He passed a now expensive cup of tea to his wife, as on-screen Paul McKay playfully menaced the marsupial mascot. The vet greeted his ex-*CCE* colleague Mariam with his usual charm.

"Dr Paul, good to see you mate," began the male co-host.

"We understand you've an answer to the protein problem?"

"Oh, I don't know about that Bruce – let's just say a partial solution – a handy hint if you will."

"What should happen in this space," encouraged Charlee.

"We humans are in a bind; we've reduced our vegetable production; the summer heat waves affected crop yields and now the yggdrasil are messing with what's left. We need to survive short-term as we move towards heat resistant and alien-tolerated agriculture. We hear much discussion on the need to eat less meat, conserving water and *permitted* plant crops for human consumption."

The co-hosts nodded wisely. Mariam sat politely.

"There's a huge, underutilised meat resource in the form of feral animals: a million camels, twenty million feral pigs, nearly half a million horses; we have deer, rabbits, and our rivers are full of introduced carp. Sure, they don't compare to a nice barra*, but they can be part of keeping us alive as we adapt, and we'll be doing the environment a favour."

Mariam, and especially Charlee, looked less than enthused by this suggestion. The latter suggested, "Culling brumbies (Australian wild horses) has long been controversial."

"It has, and maybe keep small herds for cultural reasons – but on the whole, I believe they should go!" He directed his 'wise, reasonable smile' at Charlee rather than the commonly used 'ridiculously good-looking but modest' one.

*Barramundi: a large well-regarded local fish

Co-host Bruce encouraged the guest to continue. "I hear you've got another controversial idea, Doc?"

"Ah, the green grinders thing. Making ourselves photosynthetic!" He grinned. "Nah, not really," continued the vet. "We should farm more fish," he raised an earnest finger, "as aboriginal peoples did thousands of years ago**. This reduces land conflict with the yggdrasil. And, likewise, *on land*, as aboriginal peoples have done for sixty-thousand years, we should eat our wildlife."

On camera Bruce nodded, happy to encourage controversy. The two women looked tense. "So, brumbies *and* kangaroos Doc?"

"Just the common species mind, but yeah, absolutely. My black-fella ancestors have been eating roos forever; my white-fellow ancestors were eating horse, back in caveman days. Many Europeans never stopped eating them. Nearly every plant and animal we farm here is an introduced species," he shook his head. "Crazy."

Paul McKay had touched once again on the great Australian lunching conundrum. Is not eating wildlife, but displacing them to farm introduced species, doing them any favours? The celebrity vet grinned, "It's a pretty SLOJ situation."

It was almost time to cut to an advertising break. Bruce beamed; Charlee couldn't find a logical reason against Paul's ideas, but she didn't care for them. Mariam would have liked to argue a special case for non-wildlife eating, but you just can't chastise good-looking blokes of aboriginal heritage before lunch on weekday TV. The actor inside the Ka$h Koala comically put her hands to her mouth in alarm. The tension broke, everyone smiled. The floor manager called for the ad-break.

"Right, I'm off to check for eggs," said Matt to Kalinda. "And wombats."

** UNESCO World Heritage Budj Bim Cultural landscape – an eel harvesting system

Chapter 94 Of Camels and Straws

After a few hours in the lab that Saturday morning, Niels skipped to Washington DC, joining TK for the Cherry Blossom festival. Tau Ulmus, clutching a cassette mix tape, had been recalled months earlier. Niels leapt time zones again, off to New York for the April outdoor concert. The pod materialised in Ebony's apartment-farm to the consternation of the Rhode Island Reds.

At the park, the scientist sat unobtrusive and beanie clad with the Hamilton family and Kevin. By osmosis, he'd learned a little of classical music – on a good day distinguishing Bach from Beethoven.

This wasn't to be a good day.

Snow had been scarce in New York over winter. Now, new growth erupted from the park's trees, and by the time the concert concluded, it was imprudently warm for knit-wool caps. The yggdrasil and human crowd began to disperse.

A lone alien halted in front of Anne-Maree. "Greetings ally of Eir Nyssa, friend of the yggdrasil." It reached for her, its touch dry and antennae rippling in agitation. "Regrets and concerns. Question: Have you all nibbled and grazed sufficient?" Its eyestalks flexed, taking in the wider group.

Anne-Maree glanced at her mom. "Yes, thank you for asking. We're luckier than most," said Ebony.

"Regrets and concerns repeats. Self and similar thought-patterned comrades will de-colonise depart this planet. Selves dissent from treatment of humans. Reverse greetings." It extracted a be-tendrilled cell phone from itself, dropped it and sauntered away with insectoid elegance. The crowd continued dispersing, with sadly little inter-species interaction.

Niels ran his hand through his hair, "Few like that are remaining. I did not see many of the, err, friendship bracelets."

"And you still haven't seen Mir Arauca?" said Ebony.

"No, no-one has."

Niels' conventionally non-tendrilled phone beeped, and he scanned the message. His brow wrinkled, "I keep expecting another nuclear attack, or the tundra going up in flames. I must tell TK: in New Zealand, the aliens are now driving sheep from land adjoining forests. I suspect they encourage the re-forestation of pasture. There may be wool cap crisis," he grinned.

This wasn't the tipping point, of course; the one camel-straw too many breaking point. The group wandered towards a crowd milling around Hatl Thuja, Hel Sativa, and others.

As he approached, Niels heard ...

"*... delay a few lives of trees, let humans destroy themselves.*"

"*Small adequate numbers in caves or cellars manipulate the multi-player games acceptable ...*"

"*Spring has come. Human compliance immediate.*"

Ebony and Niels sought to discuss the increasing food security crisis. A short and pointed conversation followed ...

"Humans exchanged planet resources for abstract wealth concept – please to consume that."

There was no proper tone in the leaf-creature's voice – but if there had been, Niels wouldn't have cared for it.

"Over-supply humans, under-supply feed items. Problem resolution: Let the ur-monkeys consume each other!"

He cared even less for this suggestion, and its seeming 'bad alien, worse alien' role play.

"As consumed times previous."

Anne-Maree gasped and covered her ears. The crowd scurried away, texting and uploading (except those making speculative calorie-assessment glances at strangers). Niels stalked from the park, intent on being alone for the moment with his wrath. The pale eyes were cold, and his mind focused. Hands in pockets, he wove around prams and bicycles, with their territorial attitude to pathways.

The scientist contemplated the blind spots, the illogic of supposedly sentient beings. Taking evidence-based contemplations so far and no further: Listening to the radio and fearing Bluetooth; looking to nuclear theory to rid the earth of the yggdrasil – but not to date it. He was aware he had his own foibles … he didn't really believe in team sports.

As for the aliens, they were stubbornly uninterested in earth biology not related to light gatherers: especially the mysterious non-plant, non-animal fungi. *That* was going to cost them. A powerful urge to be home and to insert something chilled and mood-altering seized Niels.

*

Dust swirled as the pod materialised in front of the farmhouse. Niels stepped from the alien craft, Bob Kelly was there on the porch, faded shirt and beer in hand – he'd come to the right place.

Chapter 95 The Arrow Frogs

There is a view that a tale should skip or hop along: not unlike a small nervous frog, striving to avoid the clutches of a muddily pregnant zoologist.

"Careful, Jess," called Niels, hovering nearby and pretending not to.

"If I don't catch this damn frog, nobody ever gets to eat fries again," she grunted. "Not that I will."

Jess stretched forward and up, maximised her reach, and rested her cheek on the mossy branch. She viewed an approaching leech with abstract fascination. Then, focussing with a shudder, Jess achieved full stretch, and her right glove closed on her squirming prey. Four this morning. She'd caught more than the others. Progress was slow.

"God, look at me," she exclaimed, wiping mud from her nose in exasperation: moss-haired, liberally smeared with rainforest dirt, and clutching a reluctant frog.

Niels had been admiring her as they worked. Under the mud, she glowed like someone recently spun into a cocoon, the slight curve of expanding tum, a modest increase in bra size – no criticisms at all. "Yes, you are most gorgeous."
He strode over and embraced her, planting a single kiss on a muddy forehead.

Kalinda looked on, smiling.

*

Such did Niels cherish his new partner, he'd been willing to journey to Brisbane and view the chaos that constitutes a game of Australian Rules Football, if only Jess *wouldn't* return to South America.

She was having none of it.

And made mutterings of the "I'm invested … bringing a child into a world with no food, isn't an option," variety.

Discussions on trip participation were convoluted. Mike Ross had vanished; TK had elected to "sit this one out," and Allan had ruled out all jungle adventures. Niels toyed with bringing the lab's fungi expert in on the plan, but she was so eccentric even by the exacting standards of that specialisation that he was reluctant to do so.

Kevin wasn't required – secret biological warfare excursions being best not recorded. However, he wanted to explore the 'Tomb of the Frog King,' one of his original research interests.

Matt had been reluctant or pretending.

"Great, maybe I can get one of these for the other arm," he said, tapping his dark grey scar, to produce a dull sound. But there was little choice once Kalinda insisted on coming.

She said, "I wasn't happy about Jess going off to the Amazon with you boys *last* time. Look what happened then – she came back pregnant, and you," turning to Niels, "returned resembling a Wookie."

"Nice Wookie reference," said Kevin.

"Promise not to get pregnant again," grinned Jess. But she appreciated the support.

*

The Pod leaped between matter particles and arrived with impossible accuracy: at the scene of the arrow and dart attack of the previous July (somewhere near the Colombia–Ecuador border). The party peered cautiously from the vessel, waiting for Angelo to arrive as planned.

Matt had wandered a discrete distance from the pod to answer a call of nature. He wandered past potential medicines and condiments unknown to the world outside. Then, distracted by a posy of severed yggdrasil antennae tied to a stake, he wandered further past a small curvy lady. Matt had no objection to women daubing on paint and treading silently through the forest – even if essentially unclothed. But he did rather wish this one would cease pointing her drawn bow at his heart. Another rustle of leaves and a small, muscular, shaven-headed fellow joined her.

He grinned; a devilish filed-tooth smile and said in heavily accented English, "Eet is good white people are a leetle afraid of us."

And so, the duo returned Matt, and escorted the group to meet Angelo and the tribe's elders. The huts, Kevin observed with interest, were made with still-green palm leaves – hinting at recent construction, for this was a nomadic band with little permanent agriculture. The nearby stone tomb, discovered before the yggdrasil arrival, suggested an unguessed at history deep in the west Amazon.

The New Yorker was impatient to explore the tomb, but this had to wait. The trip's focus was frog-fungus capture and reconnaissance. They'd assumed a sick frog would be slow and easy to catch – and perhaps this was so, but frog wrangling in the jungle proved to be a sport to test the fitness of the visitors.

"Hell! The yggdrasil want to make the whole world this warm and sticky," complained Kevin. By necessity, the children of the tribe – bony of elbow and knee, were enlisted to help.

That first evening the weary visitors sat around the fire and heard the local Ceibo Tree Creation story. Over shared meals, they learned of the malevolent, ever-returning tree spirits. Niels poked at a toasted something with a certain large spider or insect crunch.

The locals had no tribal memory of the re-discovered tomb. Guided to the site the next day, they removed the tarpaulins. Stepping over abandoned grid lines, Niels observed an obsidian bladed knife hafted to a severed yggdrasil appendage. That and the hundreds of scattered frog skeletons pointed to a commonality of cause between the ancient and current residents of the area.

Angelo had informed the elders that the visitors were allies in their struggle. For secrecy, though, the visitors posed as documentary makers for *Reptile Monthly* on a scouting trip.

The field of nature documentaries was increasingly fraught by the third decade of the century: ever-increasing numbers of presenters getting in each other's way as they strove to bring the remaining wilderness to home screens and VR. There were altercations as celebrity naturalists fought over the last puzzled okapi, whale sharks, and snapping turtles.

The frog haul grew, but as the party moved further from the camp; taking more risks, tempers frayed. Mere days before joining the expedition Kevin had received an unexpected message from his family. Begging him to join them … *before it's too late, son.*

Crouched now in an unstable canoe, he reconsidered: "Matt, ownership of a Greek fisherman's cap doesn't make you the captain, nor make me secure in your ability."

"Mate, your so-called weapon doesn't make *me* feel any safer," said Matt, disparaging Kevin's improvised defence of a stick, bearing a bath sponge rubbed on a reluctant frog.

The jungle was a zone of no life insurance and no health cover.

Later, with dinner, Matt enquired, "Will we be doing any mind-altering potions, ceremonies, that kind of thing?"

Kalinda directed a warning glance at him in the darkness – the pop star didn't subscribe to the entire 'sex, drugs, and rock-and-roll' trinity (a potential source of marital discord).

The translators explained that potions were restricted to important ceremonies. After a while, the multi-lingual tired and the visitors chatted among themselves. Conversation soon turned to food insecurity and the increasing departure of the human-friendly expo tour and dance party yggdrasil.

Niels was disillusioned by recent attacks on high-tech greenhouse horticulture. The tacit agreement, made with the now-departed ambassadors, shattering with the glass of the 'plant prisons'. "I'd feel better performing the fungi research – if all the, the *friendly* ones left."

"Understand, but you can't exactly tell 'em, can you?" said Kevin, slapping at mosquitos.

Niels put his head in his hands.

"And" said Kalinda, "any minute those 'nuke the world and hide in my bunker' idiots might actually do it.

"Could've already started – would we even know out here?" said Kevin, who seemed a firm favourite of the local mosquitos.

"If you eat vegemite, they don't bite you," suggested Matt.

"I'm not that desperate."

"I've heard that those, err, nuclear enthusiasts – like that radio person on *CCE* before I arrived, are more quiet about the whole thing now."

"Um, Niels," said Kalinda, "that might be because they've gone to their bunkers."

Niels replaced his head in his hands.

The following night sounded with the operatic, taunting calls of elusive amphibians. The crew were weary, and Matt played the indestructible carbon fibre uke that nobody had thought to prevent him bringing along. It buzzed horribly on the ninth bar of a little twelve-bar blues progression. The eureka moment had struck. He'd read of something similar in Zoology 101. Cautiously, like someone tightening a new "A" string up to tuning tension, he thought it through:

"Hey, couldn't we use the pod to play and amplify arrow frog calls into the jungle? With the door open, the randy critters might catch themselves."

And so it proved.

In the morning, the group didn't perform an exact census, but it was clearly a whole lot of frogs.

Chapter 96 Of Hatchings and Revelations

Niels returned to the Forestry laboratory with a relieved sigh. His presence in the Frog and Fungus wing had seen the usual scramble for microscopes and growth media. *I wish their behaviour was less 'science camp for the delicately nurtured' and more 'weapon research team.'* (But to be fair, nobody had informed them of that role). And for the first time in career memory … a research facility was overstaffed.

Peering now down his own microscope, exchanging slides, he dallied again with the guilt and self-reproach that for some comes with planning genocidal biological warfare. Niels was also sorry to miss the hatching of Mir Arauca's eggs and their emergent larvae, but he'd catch up in a couple of days. It was a crucial time at the lab.

"Are you sure this tour's a good idea," asked Kevin, checking equipment as he and TK waited for the aliens.

"More than ever I am thinking," replied Niels. "We must carry on acting as normal, making ourselves useful, yes."

"What if they ask about the frogs, Doc?" said TK.

"Same as I am telling the frog people," (by which he meant people who studied frogs, rather than an additional unmentioned, alien race) "we love the frogs, they are endangered; we do the captive breeding, the re-stocking …"

The chytrid fungal samples from the recent trip proved lethal to the alien cell lines, and there was no immediate need to return to Angelo's country. Niels was glad he hadn't asked his frog and fungus experts along. They were already asking too many questions. The tour went uneventfully well. Three yggdrasil attended, including the murderous Tek Alnus from *CCE* days. The trio appreciated the efforts to preserve cold-adapted forests.

Niels asked the vegetal creature, "Do you recall … we once asked Sif Acer whether your kind had job descriptions, err, specific functions?"

"Affirmative."

"Your scientists: Do they have technology to build climate-controlled reserves, if we need to save living examples of forest types and not just seeds?"

"Sufficient knowledge. Few were assigned this planet – all departed. Possible future arrangement."

"That's great," said Niels. "No hurry, I'll inform you when we might be needing them, yes."

*

Near closing time, TK, Kevin and Ash met at the Retro Bean. Niels discovered them secreted in the most discrete booth. The one shielded by towers of mid-twentieth century board games. Niels sensed that Tyson K's sense of cool didn't include being cuddled in public. He further sensed that Ash, nestling playfully close, was aware of this.

"The world must never know what's gone down!" said Kevin.

Ash rolled her eyes, "Oh yeah, very dramatic."

"We should make one of those pacts," joked TK in his best gangsta-rap voice. "Where we get together and kill the secret-breaker."

Niels smiled grimly, "Not so necessary. If *they* find out, they will surely save us the bother."

TK nodded, "Not so many friendly ones left now."

"Err, Tyson, are there any at all? Can *you* sense them?"

He nodded, serious faced, "Yes, but very few."

"I have something for the sharing …"

Ash wriggled closer.

"I visit the forests here – attempting the tree meditation, trying to discover are there any of our allies left and when goes the mother-ship?"

"Niels, how's it work with the pod and the whole mother-ship thing," said Kevin.

"You are meaning the physics—"

"Lord no—"

"Sorry, I understand. Mir Arauca said the pod will stop working when the mother-ship leaves – taking the last of the *non*-settlers."

"The yggdrasil don't realise you've got it?"

"It still seems so."

"Hey Niels," said TK, with a glance at Ash, "will it work for me?"

Niels shrugged, "I don't know. There is something more I should tell." He disclosed the drug-vision he's seen at the time portal in Peru and told, for the first time, of his unborn child's role in that future.

Ash gasped.

As alluded to previously many things are complex and multifaceted: the music of Bach, offside rules in sport and Niels' plan for saving humankind …

"They came before, in small numbers every few centuries, and will come again – even if driven away now. However, *if* they do not know what we have done and *if* when they return we've had the *time* to change our consumptive human ways, as we are learning to do, and *if* Mir Arauca's young are our friends, our advocates … then maybe the future *is* being okay, yes."

"So, defeat them and then live in harmony with their young!" summarised Kevin.

"SLOJ, very SLOJ," said Ash, examining a coffee cup critically.

"I may scream if I hear that again," said Niels, but his eyes were smiling.

"See," said TK theatrically to Ash, "what I mean – this man, I tell you, has layers like a turducken."

Kevin stood, "Anyone else have any revelations? I need to visit the restroom."

Niels shrugged, "No more revelations, but several uncertainties."

Ash replaced the cup, “Err, my timing sucks, but next week I become a part owner of this place!”

Niels congratulated her, and Kevin promised a full report of the facilities when he returned.

“Niels,” smiled Ash, “it’s none of our business but …” she pulled out her phone, selected the footage and slid it across the faded Laminex table, “this video is actually *you*. Isn’t it?”

He sighed, scratched his stubble, and glanced up warily, “Yes, from before I moved to the states.”

“Guess you got your own reasons,” said TK sternly, shaking his head, “we won’t say if you don’t.”

Kevin returned, and they discussed Niels’ angst: genocidal killing; the lack of a fungal toxin delivery plan to carry out said killing; the need for secrecy; the approaching nuclear threat; pod transport concerns …

Kevin nodded, “We need a flow chart.”

Ash nodded, “I’ll get the highlighter pens.”

*

Later, Kevin returned to New York to edit the preservation efforts lab tour footage. Niels returned to Cairns, where his yabby fishing prowess came in useful. There had been seventeen cassowary-sized alien eggs and now after three months they’d hatched. Of these the Kelly’s and Niels had caught ten of the larvae in the dam using baited traps. Niels and Jess felt it was safer to move them to the algae hatchery where filtration and sterilisation could minimise the risk of fungal infection.

As for the others … as Jess’ dad Bob put it, “They’re gonna have to take their chances.”

Chapter 97 Seaweed and Surfing

You will have surmised that plans to eliminate tech-superior alien invaders (is there any other type?) are best developed discretely. To this end, the humans of the Congress (other than Mike who remained non contactable) maintained their 'business as usual' program: bringing yggdrasil-tolerated farming to world attention.

Hence to Uto, Japan, to view the monument to the British scientist Kathleen Mary Drew-Baker. As the group gathered around the plaque, Jess explained:

"… her research led to the farming of nori – the sushi seaweed. Which was crucial during the food shortages of WWII. And so, they commemorate her every year in April. Pity we just missed it."

Jess paused for Niels to add, "The reproductions of many seaweeds are splendidly weird," he glanced uncertainly at Ann-Maree. "This was Drew-Baker's research interest."

"Yeah," nodded Jess, "and the thing is, she researched this on her own after getting sacked by her university for getting married!"

"But now girl scientists *can* get married," said Anne-Maree firmly. "Do you want to get married, Jess?" the child asked. "To Niels," she prompted for clarity.

Jess shrugged, "I want to be a time-traveling psychic space pirate – with a talking cat."

"Me too. And a princess."

"Of course."

Niels grinned, "Well then, who's keen to get back in the pod and tour seaweed farms."

And so, the group visited Japanese farms, then materialised across the Pacific taking in Hawaii. Considering it best not to open additional worm-cans by drawing alien attention to seaweed farming, Kevin filmed the excursions for a human audience.

Without yggdrasil invitees.

It was, as Niels explained, a bio-philosophic-alien conundrum: "Our aliens are not caring what we do in the oceans. Seaweeds are photosynthetic but without leaves, roots, stems … plants, yet not plants." Waving at the surrounding crop, he noticed a greening of complexion among the class. He queried, "How much of this are we wanting to hear?"

"Maybe just a little less, Doc," said Matt, displaying his thumb and forefinger close together. "Although, the weird alternation of generations, separate sexes, microscopic life-phase, *which you agreed to tell us about another time*, seems cool."

"So" said Jess, encouraging her partner. "Fast growth rates, yes, other advantages …"

"Yes, indeed, up to thirty times faster than land plants, they are absorbing carbon dioxide and so acting to reverse the accelerated warming and using no fresh water, no land clearance, no fertiliser – but absorbing what runs from the land, no pesticides …"

"Seaweed culture's been huge in Asia for ages," explained Jess to Kevin's camera.

The pod and boat combination tour continued, adding to the greenness of Allan's complexion, and taking in seaweed culture combined with shellfish: mussels, oysters, scallops, and their shelly allies.

"And so … eating one step further up the food chain," said Niels as he helped haul the longline aboard, and a cage of scallops flapped their alarm. "Again yes, little or no terrestrial agriculture inputs, the seaweed de-acidifies the local area encouraging shell growth. And using the environment in three dimensions similar to mature forests."

After a time and realising that greenness of complexion seemed to be spreading among the group, Niels directed the boat back to land. Kevin didn't care for the bouncing motion. Nor did his camera work, as he tried to film an enormous luxury motor yacht in the distance.

Previously, many of the planet's super-rich preferred life at sea to the bunkered life underground. When it came right down to it: they also preferred eating fish, instead of each other. But as rumours spread of impending nuclear cleansing, the luxury armada was rushing to port.

*

Niels entered the sushi place on Waikiki. He smiled and waved from general principles. *In the past, our entrance might have attracted whooping*. Not now, though – and it might have been preferable to the present tenseness.

"Trees are friends, not furniture," said Anne-Maree earnestly, stroking the timber table. "I miss Eir Nyssa," she whispered.

"As do I," agreed Allan kindly, still looking green of gill.

"In the past, the yggdrasil didn't mind watching us eat," mused Matt playing with chopsticks and studying the surf.

"Well, some of them," said Jess. "Things changed after the ambassadors left."

"Sure have," said TK. "I'm gonna grow pumpkins on my dance floor – there's not enough human-friendly alien types left for a party.

"No one's seen Mir Arauca since February," worried Jess. "I'd thought it'd at least say goodbye."

Matt discerned lunch wasn't heading in a cheery direction. He sought to change this … "So, this is the place that invented surfing and ukuleles – two of my funnest things. You know what's really weird," he continued: "*Cairns*, where all this began," he did a little leaf-wing improv, "has a uke festival and heaps of 'em here too, of course. *And* Captain Cook was the first European to visit Cairns *and* the first to come here. Where he might have been eaten if I remember correctly," he said, poking suspiciously at tofu. "So, coincidence or not?" he raised an eyebrow.

Jess smiled, "Yeah, that's a coincidence."

"So, this is seaweed soup," remarked Kevin, stirring it listlessly and speculating that if it didn't get him now, it was bound to catch up later in the week. "Anyone like to try? The seaweed's always greener in someone else's bowl."

"You're not much selling it," said Jess. "All sorts of things I'm not supposed to eat now," she added cheerfully. "Pregnancy police."

"Oh, I thought that was more fish," said Kevin – who could be quite literal.

"All sorts of thing," she repeated, wrinkling her nose.

"We are seeming less pod sick now," observed Niels of his companions. "Sorry, we tried to see too much, too fast. But I am having this worry that soon the alien tech will cease to work."

"So, use it while we can, yeah," said Kevin. "When you mentioned seaweed absorbing carbon dioxide earlier – that reminded me." He pushed away the soup, "The northwest passage is open, it's never been ice-free up there in May before. Shall we go take a look?"

"What, and stare at depressed polar bears? Reckon I'd rather go surfing," said Matt.

Chapter 98 The Last Ambassador

In the week following the seaweed sojourn, the world was getting desperate. Ebony texted distraught; the Peace Tree planted at the Solstice Concert was dead. Cut down by unknown assailants.

Niels returned from two days in the Daintree wilderness. Jess was on the paint-faded veranda, and Matt was visiting.

Niels caught his partner's eye and shook his head, "No, nothing." He cocked his head to one side and regarded Matt, not uncritically.

"Err, what Niels?"

The Swede explained.

"You want to go where?" said Matt incredulously.

*

The next day, Niels explained as Matt drove east.

"... when visiting Cairns, I'm always looking for yggdrasil with scarves, with beads or bracelets." He touched the amber bead he wore around his neck. His mouth was dry. "I can't bear releasing the fungus when perhaps thousands of our allies remain. But if we wait too long, then maybe we all burn. My dreams are terrible."

"Yeah mate, it's a no-win situation." Matt took his eyes off the empty heat-shimmering road, glanced across and said, "So you've been sitting in forests – what, trying to hear what the trees know?"

Niels stared at the cracked dashboard and murmured, "Something like that."

"And we're driving because there's something wrong with the pod?"

"Err, it'll sound crazy."

Matt scoffed, "Try me."

"I think it ceases to work, any time – when the mother ship leaves, yes. But I have the strongest sense I should only use it once more."

The Australian sensed it was time to change the topic. "Jess tells me you have a European sports car back in Oregon."

Niels smiled.

"You should have it shipped out – if we're not toasted or starved, I mean."

Niels looked around at the passing scenery, "Maybe, Matt. But this country might kill it."

Matt grinned, "Sorry for freaking out yesterday when you mentioned the lodge – I realise now it was your daily walks in the forest, well, those and the yggdrasil, that got me all fired up about science …"

Naturally, they'd rung ahead. Matt strolled the grounds, charming the Cassowary Lodge staff and visitors. Niels made his way through the remembered rainforest path to the natural pond. Where he sat in the stillness, leaning on the fern-hung bark of the ancient tree.

*

The stars were coming out two days later when Matt next saw his new neighbours. There'd been another 'tactical nuclear blast,' this time among the redwoods of northern California, and the local news was full of yggdrasil-expelled refugees from New Guinea and the Solomons. "Perhaps not the best time to ask, but guys, are we nearly home and dry with the fungi plan?"

Jess observed Niels' confusion. She explained, "No Matt, we're not even home and peeling off our wet knickers in the shower yet!"

For still there was no effective delivery method.

Discrete tests showed urban yggdrasil and larvae in contact with fountains and park ponds were rapidly dispatched. But how to rid the entire planet of the green menace? Half-formed plans swirled as Niels sought to sleep: A volunteer network releasing chytrid fungus, either directly, or using unwilling diseased frogs as a vehicle. Or hand the delivery puzzle to the resources of the Secret Science Agency? Secrecy was crucial: before, during and *after*, as the yggdrasil would likely return. Less than a dozen people knew of the alien vulnerability.

Niels woke shivering in the warm night from another dream of sacrifices made under a red moon, waking with unscientific certainty. Sometimes the note, self-written on the arm with four-coloured pen, blurs by morning with the sharpness of the idea itself.

Not this time.

Perhaps seeing Matt before bed was part of the synergy. '*With the door open, the randy critters might catch themselves!*'

Niels had fumbled around for the pen. That was it. '*What if ... instead of trying to infect the rivers and lakes, I use the pod to deliver the fungal infection into the heart of the mother ship? The terminus. All those nutrient reservoirs are linked. Can I land the pod in a reservoir? Open the door and flood it with frog fungus? Not very discrete ...*' (Leaving the Saab in the five-minute loading zone was Niels' usual idea of risk).

*

Then came the call from TK.

Niels now learned that Agent Peters' minions were convinced Mike Ross *had* been a pre-invasion supporter of the yggdrasil. Feeling betrayed by the light-gatherers and harassed by the agency, he'd ended himself.

In America, the radio shock jocks and bloggers, the conspiracy theorists, anti-science ranters and peddlers of interspecies (and race) intolerance grew yet scarcer. The anchor of *Lone Wolf News* put down the mic; a man so right wing he was metaphorically and breezily seated on the adjoining aircraft's left wing. In actuality, he now sat on a chesterfield couch a hundred yards beneath Death Valley.

Further, Niels now learned Agent Peters himself had vanished. Rumour said he'd gone to *his* well-equipped bunker: it resembled an underground ransom-ware enterprise, albeit with a reduced sense of social purpose. The loading zone sign now read one minute. Was the postulated nuclear attack imminent? *Clearly*, thought Niels, *I must cease fine-tuning the plan and activate it.*

*

The alien craft materialised in its home base, and the human operator peered from the partly open door. The ship was incomprehensibly huge and lit by a sickly white-green glow. Niels manipulated the phone app and had another go at the entry, re-appearing in the quietest part of the craft. He now faced the massive, curved wall.

The small pump started up and soon the mission was complete. Niels dragged the toxin delivering hose from the reservoir. He glanced around, reached into his jacket and added an ex-carbonated water bottle of the most virulent fungal strain yet bred.

And was observed.

Niels returned the empty bottle to his pocket and tried to brazen it out. With all the attitude of a daddy-long-legs spider a-taken up residence in the shower cubicle, he gave the approaching leaf-creature his best: 'Oh, it's you again,' look.

Niels did a double-take. The alien's gait had increased in irregularity since last seen. It was Mir Arauca.

Moments later, from the opposite direction, another yggdrasil neared. Its longer antennae thrashed in agitation. It directed its eyestalks at Niels, but the human never heard the one-sided interrogation.

Mir Arauca, unable to dissemble or filter communication by silent direct thought-transfer, said, "Human is friend of the trees." It rippled its antennae at Niels. It extruded a drinking tentacle and drank deeply from the pond.

"No. No!" cried Niels.

"Come!" It continued. "Let selves return to blue planet."

The pod materialised in the moonlight by the dam. Niels stared at the water, rethought this for the safety of Mir Arauca's young, and relocated to the far side of the property.

The light-forager crawled with difficulty from the craft. A human arm rested on the last of the ambassadors as it died in the warm, humid night.

Niels wiped a moist eye and determined not to risk fungal contamination, removed his shoes and his clothing. He fumbled, undid the knot, freed the amber bead that rested above his heart and re-tied it around the creature's limp antenna. He set off for the long walk across the property. In the dark, he opened the screen door as quietly as possible.

Not quietly enough.

Jess woke and observed her naked partner, framed by the doorway and backlit by moonlight. Sleepily, she debated whether to be annoyed or aroused.

"We're going to need a huge amount of the fungicide …" he began.

Chapter 99 Mira

Bob had called for help. There was talk of impellors and intake valves, and of deceased-snake-in-water-tank problems. As Niels and Bob took the pump apart, the first of Mir Arauca's larvae emerged from the dam with a slithery, irregular movement.

It was mid-September.

Evidently, those that eluded capture after hatching had survived and prospered. As they watched, the first of these wove a cocoon near the water's edge.

"I reckon we're gonna need to build a screen or pump house or something around them – when they finish," said Bob. "How long do you reckon they stay in there, changing?"

"Two years or more, we guess. So yes," agreed Niels, brushing away the ever-present flies. "The ones in the hatchery will be okay, but we can't risk visitors noticing these."

"I'll call the girls. You should let Matt and Kalinda know – they'll want to see."

Later, as it happened, in the early evening – not Niels, but Kalinda and Matt helped Bob with the cocoon screening project. For Jess had gone into labour (a little early) – the baby *was* to prove precocious with milestones. Niels drove her to the hospital in Cairns.

As elsewhere:

Yggdrasil Return

was inscribed deep into the façade of the hospital: the font obscure, and with the usual casual disregard for prepositions. Across the planet, humans held a range of views on those two words etched into untold millions of buildings. Niels, the soon-to-be-father, felt without the reminder, perhaps humanity wouldn't change its ways; without them, Mir Arauca's hatchlings couldn't be safe; or even his own family. But now they had *time*.

The quality control of the time-drug-prophecy was excellent, and the child a girl. Naming thrown open for discussion, Kalinda suggested Eve, and Bob Kelly, thinking that too godly: Evie (illustrating his choice using a vinyl record from his youth*). The parents-to-be politely declined these options.

*

Baby Mira was born into a changed world. The end, when it came, three months before, was as unexpected as the beginning – although not marketed in the same way. At once, thousands of yggdrasil bodies littered the parks of the world. In forests, walkers occasionally encountered desiccated remains for years to come.

Anticlimactically, in response, the planet's alien population toyed once more with crucial electro-magnetic infrastructure, and then peacefully departed within a week of the outbreak's beginning. Leaving only scarred buildings.

**Evie* by Stevie Wright, 1974

Chapter 100 The Birthday

For a time, the former Congress members held an uncertain place in the world. Niels' last public statement urged the world to gather the fallen yggdrasil. The Viking trappings of burial at sea or funeral pyres hid his agenda; that of leaving no evidence for forensic examination by future visitors. Eventually the local cricket club invited him to join – a sure sign of acceptance. The following year, family, friends, and the remaining members of the former Yggdrasil–Human Congress gathered for Mira's first birthday party.

Tyson K Whitney's presence in the country was itself a major local news event. A major recording industry figure, ahimsa meat tycoon, talent incubator, influencer … a minute of TK's time could make a career. Critics maintained the entrepreneur behind the virtual reality knit cap or 'Vreenie' had taken over the world with alien t ech, a phone app and a lab full of mysterious crystals. Following an impromptu press conference, the American contingent travelled in convoy from Cairns' airport to the Kelly farm.

Jess' mum, Barbara, fussed: she straightened tea towels, wiped bench tops, and relocated the 'inside' spiders once more. The cattle dog barked.

"Do Americans drink tea?"

"Just relax, Mum."

Jess went out into the yard, the dust disturbed by the arriving vehicles. The guests piled out. Kevin began to cough, greetings were exchanged, and the dog was much patted.

"Where's Mira, can I see her?" begged Anne-Maree.

"Of course, you can possum," she turned back to the house and called, "Mum!"

The screen door clattered, and Barb came onto the veranda.

"Mum, this is Ash and Tyson, Kevin and Crystal and Anne-Maree and Ebony …"

The group climbed the stairs into the house, "An honour to meet you ma'am," said TK.

Jess extracted the birthday toddler from its lair and the group admired her.

They milled around the homestead's living area and chatted. Barb served tea.

"Where's Niels?" came the query.

"Oh, he'll be at the Bunya Pine grove with Bear Browning and Dad."

"He spends too much time there," murmured Barbara. "It's nice he has company – William's been good for him this week."

"It's weird," said Kevin. "He was the most famous dude on the planet, and now …" he shrugged. "Before long, the *Tonight Show* will do a 'Whatever happened to?' segment. But, stateside, we don't hear much from down under – except about Kalinda and shark attacks."

"They'll all have heard the cars arrive," said Jess. "We can meet them at the conference centre, you can see the café and where you'll be staying."

As Jess wrangled the guests back outside, her mum whispered, "Tyson has such lovely manners."

"What an amazing building," cried Crystal of Jess' conference centre-meditation retreat. "It's a giant green lava lamp."

Jess grinned, "Yeah, the upper walls are live algae panels." Her phone beeped, "Ah, Allan and his wife have arrived."

"This is where you started?" said Crystal. "The first of the *Plain Jain* ahimsa eateries."

"That's right," Jess beamed, "We've just opened the twentieth one."

Crystal felt the need for a quick hug.

"Jess, is Niels involved in all this? Is he teaching at the local uni?" asked Ash.

"No, not really, he's happy to just potter and farm and …" Jess grew sombre, "and tend the grove of monkey puzzle trees he planted where we buried Mir Arauca."

"Ah. What's that crazy building," pointed Kevin, changing the topic. "Looks like a turtle crossed with an armadillo."

"It's a studio," smiled Jess. "Niels built it himself – with old boats people donated. He said he was trying for a world turtle aesthetic."

"What's Niels need a studio for? Whittling?"

"Err no, he—"

"Bonjour," came the mannered call. "Your dear mother drove us – past an abundance of curious donkeys."

"Hi Allan, Hello Bunny. C'mon there aren't *that* many donkeys."

More greetings were exchanged. Allan performed a friendly pat of Anne-Maree. "We have viewed the sleeping birthday girl." His wife shuddered, but slightly.

Jess waved, "This's the conference centre, and through the courtyard is the entrance to the ahimsa café."

"A notable achievement, my dear."

"Oh Jess it's gorgeous" said Crystal in a tone humans generally reserve for admiring puppies. The group stepped into the dappled light of the palm thronged courtyard, lush with understorey plantings and still water.

"*She's* gorgeous," remarked Kevin of the fountain. Carved from polished dolerite; life size, seated in the lotus position, eyes open and entirely 'sky clad', the statue's braided hair hung to her hips.

"It's the Jain woman, goddess person, yeah?" said TK.

"Mallinatha, not a goddess, a spiritual leader," corrected Crystal.

TK nodded, "Seen posters, T-shirts, never seen a statue before."

"We're not eating in the café – dad's doing a barbecue – but shall we do the tour?"

As they marched off, TK glanced at Kevin, "Gorgeous and demure, but real gorgeous."

"Come, young man," said Bunny to TK, "I'm sure you've seen breasts before."

"He has such a thing for Indian women," said Ash to Bunny in a theatrical whisper.

The spectacular hand-carved doors burst open, "Hey everyone," called Matt, "great to see you." He performed a double hand wave.

"Kalinda!" said TK.

"Yep, she's the wife," admitted Matt

The megastar turned back to Jess, "You used her as the model."

Jess gave him a slow smile.

"Yeah," said Matt. "We have to cover her up when the parents visit. Come in, come in you lot, it's like shooing chooks. Not you," he added to the Red Heeler (known inevitably as Blue), unsuccessfully preventing its entry.

"I call it Jain fusion, we serve the usual ahimsa plant foods, and cell cultured meats and fish; fruit pulp products, and here," said Jess with a flourish, "is the micro-algae smoothie bar …"

"Oh Jess, it's lovely," said Crystal. "And the walls – they're so thick and the windows …"

"Thanks Crystal, it's a straw bale design incorporating old wharf timbers."

"Hey Jess," said Matt. "Show them the self-serve section."

She rolled her eyes.

"Anybody remember the ahimsa meat lab in Berlin?" Matt waved at the row of shiny-handled dispensing units. He grinned widely, "So, Allan, my friend, what can I get you? The lobster, the avocado, cheese substitute. How about a coffee?"

"Mon Dieu," he threw up his hands, "so be it … make mine the ahimsa lobster."

Hands thought the dog. It glanced at the gleaming dispenser of pure Angus beef protein. It closed its eyes tight and wished.

Blue peeped hopefully at his paws – nope, still no opposable thumbs. *Lucky buggers.*

*

Later, like crocs swimming towards an overladen aluminium dinghy with a dead motor and four inebriated fishing mates … the group converged on the aroma of barbecue.

"Niels, there you are! Man, what's with the rock god hair?"

"Hi Kevin." *Ah,* thought Niels, *you're now sporting one of those tattoos favoured by accountants who like to be considered 'alternative'.*

Jess' father was in fine form, "Wrap your snappers around that luv," he instructed Ash, distributing home-grown egg and bacon rolls. Meat had finally become a 'sometimes food,' and the dog waited in vain for a spare sausage to fall off the barbie. Bob Kelly shook his head in good-humoured disparagement of Tyson K's barbecue technique. "It's not bluetooth Tyson, gotta get in there and roll those snags."

The dog changed strategy. It followed Ash who was saying to Matt, "Yes, I finally went back and finished the degree. Considering Honours. What's up with you?"

"Just starting second year, been doing it part time – getting into fungi."

"Great. And Niels shipped that old car out here?"

"Yeah, the Saab – it's in one of the many sheds. He had it converted to electric, but we don't see it much. He claims it fears dust."

Blue was experienced in such matters – he wagged his tail and sat at Crystal's feet. She was saying to Jess, "… and it's the fastest growing religion in the world." She reached low and tickled the dog behind the ears. "So, there're no prices with this cosmic credit thing – people pay what they feel's right?"

"Yep, that's it."

"I heard of this," said TK. He shook his head, "But I didn't think I heard right."

The dog tried again. It sat next to one of Jess' brothers, adopting a posture it liked to call: 'They don't feed me here.' Bear was saying, "And the trees – they grow as if they're possessed. Niels says it's down to Mir Arauca's body in the earth."

"Maybe, yeah, wasn't like this when I was growing up here."

Bear nodded, he caught Bob Kelly's eye. Bob drummed on the barbecue for quiet. A few pieces of rust flaked off – exciting, then disappointing the dog. With easy power Bear's voice carried across the group, "A toast folks." They readied glasses.

"… To the sun."

Anne-Maree skipped away from the adults and lured the dog to her side. *At last*, thought Blue.

Later, the La Fontaine's lived on the wild side a little.

The ex-cane farmer rowed them out on the polyculture dam, "Now you can't change your mind once your leg's half inside a croc! There was one in here last week," he said with a dismissive wave.

"How tremendously exciting," breathed Bunny.

*

Eventually, the mosquitos and their allied insects of the night forced the guests inside. By now Jess and Niels had their own home on the property. Mira had her own room. Indeed, her own cot. She was not in it. She was staying up late. Her first birthday cake had been eaten.

The group sat variously arranged in the sprawling Kelly family living room. The television was on and promos for a recently recorded comedy gala performance were airing. Enough time had passed that talk show panellists now joked of the yggdrasil years.

Uncle Matt, you're wearing the same top! (a red SLOJ Tee) thought baby Mira. But she could only point at the screen and say, "Same, same."

Not for the first time, Barbara Kelly observed proudly, "She's very advanced for her age."

"She walked at nine months," added her grandfather. "She'll play for Australia one day!"

"Or perhaps for Sweden," commented the child's father (to her grandfather's alarm). "Any particular sport, Bob?"

"Cricket, I reckon."

Niels shuddered.

The adults chatted and sipped drinks, waiting for Matt's show to air.

Clunk.

"It's so heavy," announced Anne-Maree, navigating the door on the second try.

"It's taller than you are, honey," laughed Ebony. "Be careful now – whose is it?" She glanced at Kalinda, who shook her head.

"Niels has lots," said the youngster seriously.

TK approached. He lifted the heavy guitar from Anne-Maree.

"Vintage P-bass, nice." He turned to Niels. "I heard the new album. Is it true you guys *are* gonna tour again? Your fans are crazy hard-core."

Niels threw up his hands. "It is *crazy*. Like an inverse square law: the more we don't play, the more legendary Kraken becomes."

"Say what!" squawked Kevin.

"Man, I told you the Doc had layers."

"Your face, Kevin," grinned Ash.

*

Baby Mira sat in Anne-Maree's lap on the floor. They, and the assembled adults, watched on-screen Matt perform in the comedy debate. The preliminaries were over. He'd bounded on stage and called: Happy SLOJ Day Melbourne! He'd bellowed, "Are we all having a great time?" The species of human that makes eye contact with stage comedians confirmed they were.

The camera zoomed in and Matt began one of his trademark bemused rants.

"What did the yggdrasil ever do for us? Huh! Except save us from the curse of obesity, from Type Two Diabetes, from over-exploiting our resources … from acid-washed jeans! They make us grow cow in test-tubes and me eat tofu, and now we farm crops in coastal deserts. Anyone recall that year we took a break from online scams, unsolicited dick pics, and had to talk to each other. The horror! And I learned how to play chess again!"

Matt stalked the stage.

"And now he have the SLOJ Day holiday – where we all BBQ an eggplant and have a real good think about stuff!"

He tapped the microphone, "Remember how *they* took responsibility for global warming – so *we* could finally take action! The future is a simpler time now, where we can go into drug stores and buy bandages, not nested seagrass boxes, and distressed timber dressing tables. And you know what else, well don't worry – coz I'm gonna tell you. There are a heap of crazy people, the sort that don't want to share their toys and pay tax. And you remember where they are – they're still living underground. And maybe it's bad … but when I see one of those periscope cameras coming out of the ground – I love to strap on some antennae and do a jig! Stay down there, dickheads!"

"Okay, so now we have gardens in the CBD. Right down the sides of buildings – our city centres resemble ruins in the jungle. Only neater. And without piranhas – and I know piranhas," he tapped significantly at his alien-repaired wound, and the audience chuckled.

"And somewhere, somewhere there's a little person in the world who doesn't have to wake up, go to work, and spend every day folding those little paper napkins we used to throw away on planes."

He grew more serious.

"So, if those zombie-cicadas ever come out of the earth or if you think politics needs to be *entertaining*, or evidence-based stuff is boring, then look at those two words they left … you *know* the ones," he teased.

"And think about it!"

Epilogue

Mira was nearly two-and-a-half.

The first light pooled on, then overflowed the windowsill, illuminating sleeping parents.

“Mummy, Daddy, wake up, wake up please. They’re hatching, they’re finally coming out.”

Sleepy, pregnant again, and a little morning sick, Jess thought to herself momentarily, *How does she know*? Then almost immediately, *Of course she knows*.

“Darling,” she called, “Go next door and ask if Grandma and Grandpa want to come and see.” To Niels, she added, “We should ring Kalinda and Matt.”

Ten minutes later, the Kelly family had assembled and walked together towards the dam. The sun was rising as the dusty ute pulled up. Matt tousle-haired and beaming opened the door for his heavily pregnant partner.

The group stood close together by the water: arms on shoulders, hand in hand. They waited long-shadowed, morning poised, then a duck quacked, and the spell broke. The fabric of the largest cocoon began to tear, and then another. A small leaf wing tore through the side of it and unfolded, soft and pale. More of the structures bulged and tore. Shredded from the inside.

“Will they be my friends?” Mira asked her father, holding his hand and suddenly shy.

“Oh, yes.”

“Great friends,” said the host of excited voices in her head.

THE END

Author's Note

Dear Reader:

Thanks for reading *Return of the Yggdrasil.* If you enjoyed it could you please consider writing a short review on Amazon, Goodreads, or the like. Independent authors do depend on this.

M.K. Nadall

FURTHER READING:

The Lorax. 1971. Dr Seuss.

The Wollemi Pine. James Woodford. 2000 Text Publishing, Melbourne.

The Hidden Life of Trees. Peter Wohlleben. 2016. Black Inc

The Language of Plants: Science, Philosophy, Literature.
Monica Gagliano, John C. Ryan, and Patrícia Vieira, Editors. 2017. University of Minnesota Press

What a Plant Knows. Daniel Chamovitz. 2017. Scribe Publications

The Songs of Trees, D.G. Haskell. 2017. Black Inc.

Sunlight and Seaweed: An Argument for How to Feed, Power and Clean Up the World. Tim Flannery. 2017. Text Publishing.

Ancient Idols of Lord Mallinath worshipped in female form. Arpit Shah. 2017. www.storiesbyarpit.com

Printed in Great Britain
by Amazon

63472098R00281